I0590562

DEMENTED

SILENCE OF SHADOWS

TATUM DIRE

TATUM DIRE

© 2025 Tatum Dire

All rights reserved. No part of this book may be reproduced in any form, except in the case of brief quotations in critical articles or reviews, without permission in writing by the author or publisher.

The characters and events portrayed in this book are fictitious or are used fictitiously. Any similarities to real persons, living or dead, is purely coincidental and not intended by the author.

Edited by Morgan Waddle

Cover Design by Artista Gráfico

Published by Crimson Pages, LLC

Printed in the United States of America

ISBN: 979-8-9997026-1-6

For the girls who like their men a little crazy...
and for those who like to show men *we are crazier*.

TATUM DIRE

AUTHOR'S NOTE:

This book and these characters were written out of pure fun and creative freedom. Please remember that this is a work of fiction and is created for your enjoyment. If you aren't into things that make you question your sanity or morals... this is probably not the book for you.

This work is meant to be dark with unredeemable characters. This is not a warm and fuzzy, bad for the right reason, story. These characters are traumatized and have serious issues. There is content that may be triggering or unsettling to some, and it is advised that you read all warnings and consider your mental health before continuing.

This is an adult dark romance that contains the following tropes:

Secret Society/Shadow organization
Stalker
Touch her and die
Best friend's brother
Found family
Pitch black MMC

Secret identity
Bikers
Masked men
Hit men
Obsessed with each other
Unreliable narrator

Content warnings include but are not limited to:

Explicit Sexual Scenes
Explicit language
PTSD
Mental Disorders
Murder
Mutilation
Stalking
Drugging
Abduction
Torture
Gore

Sex Trafficking (off-page)
Somnophilia
Knife Play
Sexual Assault
Sexual Harassment
Child Abuse/CSA (off-page)
Non-Con/Rape
Dub-Con
Dog Eating People
Cannibalism

If any of these themes are uncomfortable for you, now would be the time to close the book. However, if you're still here... hold on to your panties. Reaper might steal them.

TATUM DIRE

CHAPTER 1

DAITH

My bloody blade hangs at my side, not a single ounce of remorse coursing through me as I stand idly, music playing in my ears. My victim's blood drips down my nose, into my open mouth, as I mouth the words to "Pocketful of Sunshine" by Natasha Bedingfield.

A delicious feeling of what I have labeled as joy blooms low in my chest as I look at the lifeless man, his head now three feet from his body, his blood splattered across my face.

I was only meeting with him to get info on the frequent flyers, only threatening the use of safety pins to hold his eyes open while I slaughtered his family. But the little prick had balls, and my temper got the best of me. The only thing I hate more than disobedient rats are disrespectful larvae.

Maybe I am as fucked in the head as everyone says.

I discovered at a young age I didn't feel things society deemed normal, but I never thought it made me that different. Everyone has their own flaws that make them less likeable. I figured I'm just not the kind of man you bring home to mama. I was born this way. The ability to feel emotions, guilt, was stolen from me as a child. One tends to lose their ties to such damning things when they are abused and tormented by their supposed protector. So, what makes me any different from the men that have a weird fetish like sniffing women's socks before they jerk off into them? Or the guys who like getting pissed on?

I guess killing people might be seen as an unacceptable fetish, but I enjoy my occupation. There is just something about slitting a throat that calms that lost little boy inside me who couldn't understand why everyone looked at him differently—looked at him with caution. The boy they said was clinically insane, incapable of feelings. But I'm not, it's just selective, and for those few I do care about, the limitations of what I allow are defined and have a hair trigger.

1

And this lifestyle gave me a home, gave me a place for my black soul to grow. It taught me that no matter what, eventually, everyone figures out how fucked the world is. Each in their own way, a completely different story from the next, but they all lead to the same dead-end—me, standing in the darkness, waiting to take them to whatever destination their little lives have led to.

Like the poor fucker I'm cutting up.

I am who I am.

An unforgiving killer, staining my hands for money and self-solidification. I take what I want. Apologize for nothing and answer to no one. Part of a careful collective, never stupid enough to get caught, never slow enough to be identified. And at fifteen I was one of the youngest.

Three years later Redwater task force believed they caught an arsonist when I burned my house to the ground, killing my foster parents in the process. They found me covered in soot, holding a gas can, and that was enough to convict me.... or so everyone believed.

I spent that time making needed connections and building who we are, preparing for today. The day I finally get to take what has always been mine—this city.

Sighing as my high crashes, I grab the man's scalp, shove it into my backpack, mount my bike, and shove my earbuds into my pocket. My head snaps to the side as a *click* has my ears perking. It's faint, but loud enough when you've spent years training yourself to pick up things most would miss. I scan my surroundings, only relaxing once I feel content that whatever I heard is no threat to me.

I grab my phone and call Felix for clean-up. I don't bother myself with such tedious work, usually. And Felix has always had a knack for covering tracks, the weirdo truly enjoys it, taking his time, leaving not so much as a fiber to tie any of us to the missing people. I bought him a maid's outfit as a birthday gift one year; he didn't find it as amusing as I did. But how could I not, the white ruffles complemented his eyes, and it was fitting attire for his job within the ranks.

Personally, mental warfare, games of the psyche, picking people apart until I can see so deep into their brain — that's where I find joy. Inflicting pain is the only thing that brings me something other than the constant

2

numbness and annoyance I feel for simply breathing. The terror in their eyes gets me hard.

I am a Reaper of Redwater.

Death's right-hand man.

I pull the heavy church doors open, blood smudging the old wood my shoulder brushes. My boots echo the same rhythm they always do as I make my way to the sanctuary. I'm late, though only expecting one voice to filter through the cracks of the decaying fortress we turned into our home. So when I hear two, my interest peaks, wondering who is in my house without me knowing. But when I hear a female voice, I stop, hand on the door, muscles taut, irritation rising.

"We don't let women join," Ezra's voice echoes in my memories from one of my first years with him. *"That's not their role."*

I peek through the gapped wooden doors, getting a glimpse of Ezra's face. Stern, though his usually cold features hold an unusual softness to them as he speaks to the woman in front of him. They speak low, but they aren't arguing. She steps closer—too close. And Ezra's back stiffens.

I can't see her face and her hoodie blocks her hair, but I'm sure I know that frame, the way she stands with one leg cocked out and her hand braced on her hip.

My stomach tightens, instinct flaring. What the hell is she doing here without me? What do they have to talk about that doesn't involve me? She reports to me.

"You know how this turns out?" she asks, the first sentence loud enough for my trained ears to pick up.

"Yeah," I see him mouth with a single nod. "We will figure it out as it comes."

She shakes her head, clearly uneasy with his response and lack of shared concern. Her head tilts lower. "And this?"

"I'm not sure what you mean." Louder, clearer, and with purpose as his demeanor shifts back into the familiar dickwad I know and somewhat give a shit about.

"Understood."

As she turns on her heel, I pull the doors open, and her familiar face meets mine. "Hi'ya Skid," I chime. "Did we have a meeting I forgot?" I ask playfully but full of sarcasm.

"Oh, no. I just—" she motions over her shoulder at nothing specific. "Forgot my computer here from last night's planning."

I nod. Yeah fucking right. I watched her pick it up and place it in the largest zippered compartment of her backpack, that has a quarter-sized hole next to the right strap. "No, worries. Better get out of here though, he's a real dick for rules."

She gives a half-smile. "So I'm learning."

Now, I'm wondering what he's done that pissed her off so much, but instead of asking, I'll keep it to myself until I have enough to use to get something I want, as I usually do.

"Later Rick," she throws over her shoulder, tossing her nickname back at me as she pushes through the church doors. She rarely uses it as often as I use hers these days, so I can't help the smile that brushes over my lips just before the weight pulling on my shoulder brings me back to my earlier task.

My smile shifts into a wide grin, that small sense of joy tingling in my fingers once again as I reach into my backpack.

"Daddy's home!" I chime, singing my self-praise. Blood drips from the severed head in my hands, and I smile wildly at Ezra, staring absently back at me from across the room.

"You're late." His eyes fall to the floor. "And staining my new rug."

I toss the severed head back and forth playfully like a ball, taunting him yet again. The brute has a stick up his ass, and I find enjoyment in shoving it just a little further. Thick blood coats my fingers, causing me to drop the head. The bastard's skull cracks with a thud against the floor, splattering, rolling a few paces across the white rug, and Ezra groans.

"Oops," I grimace, stepping over the bloody mess, wiping my hands on my thighs. Who decorates a house of criminals with a white rug, anyway? I

4

move to stand next to my best friend on the old church stage we converted into the meeting room of our home. He begins rambling under his breath about business while I make use of the cloth in my back pocket, attempting to clean the rest of my crimson-stained hands. It's verbal lectures like these that remind me of our age difference, Ezra being old enough to be my dad.

"Who picked that out?"

"What?" Ezra asks, seeming to barely hear me over his own thoughts.

I pinch my brow, staring at the pooling red stain. "Red, or even black. You're too calculated to pick white."

"That's seriously what you're worried about right now?" He moves in front of me, blocking my view, and I raise a brow waiting for my answer, which comes with a defeated sigh. "It was a gift."

I hum a sound of acknowledgment, but my mind wanders further away as I get lost in the rust color settling in the creases of my hands. Such a contrast to the white of my skin. It had pooled under him, like a blanket comforting him into death. I need to change my shirt and clean under my nails. I hate the smell once it's not fresh anymore. It lingers.

"Call them in," I finally say, pouring myself a drink, then fall into my chair facing the pews filling the room.

In my home, I'm king, only sharing that power with Ezra and Felix. My family. The three Reapers of Redwater—a name given to us for our occupation as killers for hire, and occasionally for fun. The general population doesn't know for sure how many of us there are, and that's the beauty behind us having the same appearance. Black hoodie, blacked-out clothes, skull mask, no identifying marks to be seen.

Ezra taps his foot, his tell that he's worried, impatiently wanting to know every detail to go over repeatedly until he's confident we will make it out successfully.

I don't have that little voice in my head telling me to worry about everything or, for that matter, that something is morally wrong. I have a voice... He's just more of a fun little nuisance, always getting me into trouble, daring me to do the most deliciously heinous acts.

The sanctuary doors creak open, and our little rats fill the large room, taking their seats. Ezra begins by commending the CHAOS hired crew for our most recent job. A successful hit and a payout of two hundred thousand dollars. I sit lazily at his side, leg hanging over one arm of the large velvet chair, my head over the other. Swirling the amber contents of my glass above my face.

"Please extend our gratitude to headquarters. Having you available when we need the extra hands has been such an added pleasure in our lifts and kills," Felix says, formally ass-kissing as always.

"Now," Ezra snaps, looking at me, causing my head to tilt to an upright position. "Care to step in and inform us of your plans moving forward?"

I nod a few times, groaning as I sit right in the chair. With the non-stop planning, I haven't gotten more than six hours of sleep in the past couple of days. We all play our roles, and here recently, the planning has all been shifted to me.

"The Fuzzy Peach." I clear my throat, set my drink down, and straighten my black leather jacket.

A whistle comes from one of the crew and I nod, agreeing this particular target comes with a few visual perks.

I stand, eyeing the severed head that had been cautiously stepped over. "Dorian Vic, known gambler, dealer, and head of Victorian Co. has recently bought out the strip club." I shove my hands in my pockets, rocking back on my heels, needing an outlet for the growing anticipation in my chest. "His pockets run deep, and his connections are a trench." I smile wide. "So, we're gonna take him for everything he has now that we have the approval from CHAOS."

I've had my eyes on him for years, something about him makes the hairs on my neck stand on end. CHAOS has to approve kills that will draw attention, and despite our ability to make moves by our own accord, this would be messy. That's when they want to step up to make sure we get out clean, protecting everything they stand for. If we bust, they clean it up and take everything for themselves, eliminating us before there is a possibility of ratting them out.

Not all criminals are part of CHAOS, but those that are, have an extra level of protection, move smarter, and have soldiers at their ready. Vic is nothing but a low-life scumlord, and I want his connections. His power.

Whatever shit he's stepped in, I want to get a good whiff, and to do that, I've got to get close and personal.

Ezra speaks up behind me. "He has gun power and security. If he sees our angle before we're in, it's game over."

We never bother the crew when it's a simple kill. They are only needed when we need more than six hands and five eyes. Felix clears his throat, moving to stand beside me. "Your job is to be invisible on the inside. Report anything useful. As soon as the job is over, you're gone. No extra kills. Keep this clean."

That brings me to the setback Ezra so kindly pointed out. Killing the bastard wasn't in the original plan.

"As we can see." I nod toward the discarded head lying near the doors. "I've disposed of their new bouncer. Ezra, having the closest resemblance to a hipster with his groomed beard and man bun, will be taking this position and name."

I glance at Ezra, his foot now resting on the floor. He nods, content with my backup plan of using dead guy's ID. He definitely looks like a Jeff.

Dalton, a younger hire, speaks up. "Are our girls gonna be working the pole?"

"Yes, a few of our hired boys have chosen to bring their girls in on this job. If you are interested in adding to this, we can always use them as tools," Ezra answers. "Of course, you must be able to put the job before your reactions."

Meaning if someone gropes their girls, he will have to postpone cutting off the fucker's fingers until the money is in the bag. The Criminal Housing and Order System, CHAOS, provides the extra bodies needed to complete an order, with the simple request of staying within their approved kill orders and protection guidelines. But we are not responsible for protecting anyone outside of our individual organizations.

Ezra follows their rules without question. Me? They can get fucked and put me down like a dog with rabies when they've had enough. I don't have the patience to deal with fancy fuckers telling me when I can get my rocks off. The Reapers have been on their shit list before—me especially for my less than approved kills—but for the past few years, I've been a good boy, saving up my gold stars for this one move that will set us up for life. Not that I would stop my personal pleasures afterward, but we wouldn't have to take jobs that seem so... mundane.

A few heads nod around the room, and I retake my seat.

Byron, a stocky man in the front row, smirks. "So we get to be customers?"

A few chuckles sound around the room as the voice in my head laughs manically, darkness swarming my thoughts once more.

"Precisely." I tilt my head.

The blood river this is going to make is going to be orgasmic, and I can't wait.

CHAPTER 2

Dismounting my bike a block away from the club, I hook my helmet on the handlebar, avoiding any security cameras. My black leather jacket, hoodie, and gloves conceal the tattoos covering my skin. Running my hands through my shaggy brown hair, I slick it back before pulling my chrome skeleton mask on and my hood into place, securing it firmly.

Gravel crunches under my boots, wind blowing around me, cooling the sweat coating my skin. I'm anxious for the next step, but I need to get this recon done and over with so I can track her down. My sweet girl.

I cross the street to the brick building with a bright neon sign reading "The Fuzzy Peach" the new bouncer greeting me at the door. I give Ezra a nod as he pulls the large door open for me, allowing me to skip the line, making a point to show his immediate respect and fear. Anyone that values their life moves out of our way, but having Ezra here ensures there won't be any issues, giving us another pair of eyes on me and the club.

The perk of being a Reaper is no one knows what we look like, so we have two usable faces at all times. We could be anyone, and that is the power in who we are and what we do.

Music and smoke fill the large room, fog falling off the stage onto the front row of customers. The club looks better than the shitshow it was when I was a teenager, desperate to see a woman's body.

I move through the crowd with no effort, each person a fleeting detail in my mind's eye. I memorize the shade of pink lipstick and the way a guy's hip juts out when he leans against the bar. My brain stores it all, whether I want it to or not—every detail—like it's supposed to be there. I don't need to look twice. Every detail of every person secured in a vault I couldn't empty if I tried. And I have. Repeatedly. But there's not enough voltage on this earth to burn

9

out Ezra jerking off without killing me. I've tried, but I think it only contributed to twisting my mind into something even darker than it was before.

A dimly lit booth in the back corner catches my eye, the perfect place to watch and take notes.

"Hey sugar, can I get you anything?" a woman purrs in a sweet voice.

I take my eyes from the stage, trailing them down her legs then back up to her face, taking in her pink ruffle lingerie, over the top makeup, hair extensions, and splotchy spray-tanned hands.

She's not one of ours. Too bold. The girls working undercover for us are trained to blend in and not provoke. Ezra hand-selected the girls and made sure they were trained well enough to be unnoticeable to someone oblivious to the picks.

"What's good?" I ask behind the voice modifier in my mask. No one here would likely recognize me by my voice, but we take no chances; each mask has built-in technology that keeps our voices disguised.

She shifts her weight, propping her tray on her hip, her too-sweet perfume wafting my direction. "Food, cheese sticks. Drinks, whiskey. Girls, Jewel. Or, if you are looking to raise the stakes, poker upstairs."

I hum a sound in thought, then pull my Platinum Amex card from my wallet and hold it out between two fingers. She reaches for it, but I pull it back teasingly, making her lean further into my space. "I'll have a whiskey on the rocks. Keep it open."

I let her take the card, and she sets it on her tray with a nod. "Yes, sir. If you need anything else, my name is Jewel." She throws a wink over her shoulder heading to the bar.

I chuckle to myself. *A for effort Jewel*. But tacky and blonde isn't my type.

My focus trails to a man across the room being taken upstairs to where I assume the VIP rooms are—that special place you can get a private dance, and sometimes, something more satisfying.

Jewel breaks my focus, setting my drink on a napkin in front of me. "Can I ask you a question?"

A nearby pen tapping grates on my nerves like sandpaper, and I have to rein it in. There are a few things that will instantly piss me off, and that is one of them. Looking around her, I find the culprit, and grit my teeth. My jaw tight, nerves on edge.

I give her a hum of agreement. Anything to soothe my rage before I have to cut tonight's plans short and get a lecture from Ezra—again.

"Why the mask? Are you ugly?" she teases, and I find a small amount of enjoyment in her bravery. I like a woman with some fight in her, but this one just seems unintelligent. Everyone in this city knows what these masks mean, and the deadly consequences for wearing one.

"Actually, I'm quite attractive to those that like the mangled bad boy look." I grab my drink, swirling it slightly, giving my hand something to do as the tapping continues.

Jewel chews on the side of her lip, her nervousness shadowed by the curiosity that is sure to get her killed one day. "Mangled?"

"Comes with the occupation." I shrug, and she quirks a brow in question. *Is she stupid?* Were the various glances, whispered panic, and mask not enough? *Maybe she's new to town...* A smile she can't see tilts the corner of my mouth.

"Reaper," I say, lowering my voice and hardening my stare.

Her posture stiffens and discomfort flashes across her face, fear rolling off her like the sweet smell of death I love so much. Suddenly she doesn't seem so eager to talk, and I find much more amusement in that than her attempt to seduce me. "I didn't realize. En-enjoy your night," she stammers before scampering off like a scared mouse.

I roll my eyes with a scoff. No woman ever wants to play with me.

Begging my time to pass quickly, I spend it watching, committing everything to my steel memory. Every employee, their jobs and shift changes. Every customer, the big spenders and where they go when they are ready for some extra fun.

With each passing hour, more eyes turn my way, careful not to linger. I pull my mask up carefully, staying hidden in the shadows as I toss my drink back before putting it back in place.

"Don't stare," a whispered panic comes from the dressing room entrance as the music dies down just enough to let a woman's voice travel.

I turn my head, waving my fingers at a shorter woman with blonde hair, a pink robe wrapped around her loosely. Her eyes widen before she pulls the curtain shut.

I snort a laugh. God, I fucking love how easy it is to scare the wits out of someone with a simple look. Women are easier than men, and so much more fun to kill.

We make it a point to switch up with each kill, never giving a pattern to follow. This time, I'm thinking a bullet to the head and his heart in a jar on my nightstand.

"Not tonight, buddy," I hear Ezra say from the front door.

I send him a quick message.

Daith: Who was that?

Ez: Cop. Smells like courtrooms and depression.

I nod as dim lights and a voice replace the low music, announcing the next dancer. "Ladies and gentlemen. Please make some noise for one of our favorite girls, Scarlette!" He draws her name out dramatically, and a woman hidden in darkness makes her way to center stage.

There's something alluring and electric about the way the atmosphere shifts.

Intrigued, I sit back and make myself comfortable. The music begins, and the white spotlights merge into one, turning pink right above her, accenting the neon blue lingerie. My eyes focus on her perfectly round ass, appreciating the thong cutting high on her hips. She hooks her arm around the pole, walking around it, keeping her head low, revealing two lacy strips of fabric covering each breast, meeting low at the bottom to cover her pussy.

She jumps, wrapping around the pole, flipping upside down. Her toned stomach flexes, holding herself in place as she spreads her legs and lowers them. The pole helps to cover what her thin scrap of fabric struggles to do as she twirls, tying herself intricately around the pole, bending in ways that would make any man in here hand her his wallet.

She flips back upright, dropping to the floor in front of the pole, spreading her legs, whipping her hair around, grinding her hips on the floor. Leaning back onto the pole, she runs her hands down her body, and the lights shift, giving a clear view of her face.

I stop breathing, and the lump of rock in my chest where a heart should be aches. For a second, I think I'm hallucinating, staring at a woman I have dreamt about since the day I left. But as she pushes her hair back, smiling wide at the crowd, driving them wild, I can't deny it.

My Little Laurel, my sister's best friend, my lingering obsession. The girl I swore I would marry or kill. The woman that is *mine*. Anger and jealousy merge to form a deadly urge. They're looking at what's mine. Touching what's mine. Going home and jerking off to what is fucking *mine*!

No. No. *NO*.

I had a plan. I was going to come home and she—She was supposed to be waiting for me, perfect and pure, mine for the ruining. Not on some stage, stripping, showing everything she has to offer to every Tom, Dick, and Harry that look her way waving a twenty-dollar bill.

My sister said she was home, but she failed to mention this small fucking detail. Though I'm not sure I would have believed her. Back then, Laurel couldn't say the word "dick" without blushing. I pushed her, seeing how far she would go, how far she would follow me into the darkness she craved so much. She wasn't ready. She needed time to grow into herself and her confidence.

She moved to New York, and it might as well have been across the world. But I knew she would come back to me. She loves me. She said she loved me, over and over, begging me to be who she wanted. Time and time again, she begged for me to love her back. But I couldn't, not in the way she wanted.

Fuck.

She's grown into herself perfectly. Ripe for my picking. I just need a brief adjustment period to mourn the loss of the girl she was before I left her.

But I'll make her remember who owns her. Who haunts her dreams. I'll break her. She'll be so fucked up when I'm done with her, she won't know whether to beg me to stop or beg for more.

Leaning forward, I focus on every inch of her skin. Her smile, the slight tilt of her eyes, her thighs. That perfect ass.

Destroying her is going to be so fucking fun.

My obsession is home, working for my next target. Fire lights in my veins as everything I've ever wanted lies right in front of me. A laugh bursts out of me, a few heads glancing my way, but I barely notice. I have tunnel vision and she's at the end, covered in blood, kneeling at my feet.

She's ready now, I know it. But I need to see it.

I stand, wanting to make my exit before she spots me. Not that she would recognize me as anything other than a Reaper, but I can't chance her seeing me before I want her to. I have to get my thoughts together. I have to get close to her to know this new version of her.

A broad man steps in my path before I make it to the bar to close my tab, and I recognize him instantly. His gray suit, about a size too small, screams "I'm power hungry but have masculinity issues."

"Dorian Vic," he says, extending his hand, and I shove mine in my pockets. He clears his throat. "Owner," he continues, doing his best to exude his power over me.

Cute. I give him a respectful nod. I can't piss him off if I want on the inside of his games. "Pleasure. Reaper."

"Well." He shoves his hands in his pockets, mimicking my stance. "I'm honored you chose our establishment for your entertainment. I hope everything was satisfactory, Mr.—"

"Reaper is enough."

We don't choose our outing sites carelessly. He's smart enough to know that, and the small amount of fear in his eyes has me all but kicking my feet like a schoolgirl. Fucker knows he has enough enemies to have a hit out on him.

He nods, his jaw clenching, hands returning to his sides, seemingly annoyed at not getting the information he wanted. "So, I take it we will be seeing more of you?"

I glance around. "Yes. I suppose so."

Chapter 3

U nable to help myself, I follow her after waiting all night for her shift to end. Is it smart? No, but I need to gauge her reaction. Did she grow into a woman that shoots first and asks questions later? Or is she the kind to be as intrigued by sex and power as she led on at the club. It's not like I can walk up to her, tap her on the shoulder, and say, "Hey, Laurel. I enjoy killing people and I was wondering if that freaks you out too much to be with me." I mean, I could, but I doubt it would go the way I want.

She glances over her shoulder, feeling me close, and a rush of excitement courses through me. I've always loved the chase. I want my prey to feel me near, sense me coming. The buildup is almost orgasmic.

I step out of the shadows, but she doesn't move. The streetlight cascades over her face, shadowing her like abstract art. Her long coat blows in the light wind, tossing her hair around her shoulders. She's so beautiful. Just as perfect as the day I left her.

She flinches as I take a step but doesn't move. Not yet. She lets me get close, toe-to-toe. My chest heaves with the anticipation of touching her, feeling her skin. My gloved hand reaches out, but she turns her head, denying me.

Irritation and possessiveness rush through me, lighting a fire, brutal and unforgiving.

I slam her against the wall, protecting her head with my hand, and lean in, inhaling her scent deep into my soul. Fuck, she smells better than I remember. Of course she would. She would have traded her sweet perfumes for something more mature, more alluring. Changed her shampoo and lotions for a scent that is seductive and addicting.

I groan, letting my head fall on her shoulder, pressing my body into hers, needing to feel her against me. Her chest rises and falls with her heavy breaths. The fear rolling off her is edible.

"What do you want from me?" she whispers, shuttering as her skin collides with my clothing.

I remember the first day I met her, perched on Celeste's porch, waiting hours just to see my baby sister. She came home with Laurel, hand in hand and caked in sand. Fuck, her laugh—loud and contagious, a smile showing all her teeth. I didn't realize I was smiling back at them until my cheeks started to hurt. It was one of the first times I remember smiling, truly, without bloodlust attached to it.

I take her in now, brushing the side of her face gently, sweeping her long brown hair behind her ear, ignoring the small grimace of her denial. Her skin looks soft, pupils dilated, hands flat against the wall behind her. The same chipped nail polish, right middle fingernail shorter than the rest, just as they were the week I left.

She's not scared, not really. Frightened, but not fearing her life ending. She never feared death, just the idea of not living a fulfilled life.

Testing her limits, I grip her hips firmly, and she sucks in a breath so beautiful, it's like a symphony. Slowly, I drag my hand down her thigh, and my mind quiets, only hearing the overwhelming need to have her on my lips. I kick her feet to a wider stance, moving my hand to the inside of her thigh, inching up slowly, watching where my gloved fingertips tease her skin. Her head falls against the wall as she gives in to me, wanting me to take all of her, offering herself to me.

Naughty girl.

My finger hooks into her thong, and her head snaps up as she grips my shoulders, jerking her knee up in a swift motion, slamming into my groin. I stagger back, groaning, hunched over, gripping my damaged goods.

She takes off running, kicking off her heels before breaking into a full sprint, and I can't help but chuckle, growling through the pain as I snatch her heels and chase after her.

Run, baby. I love the chase.

She dodges down an alley, and I laugh maniacally, thinking of all the ways I'm gonna play with her when I catch her. Not tonight, no. Tonight I get her worked up, give her a little taste of me. Let her know I'm going to be everywhere. In every shadow, in every dream. Never leaving again.

Chapter 4

LAUREL

I slam my apartment door behind me, panting like I've just outrun a monster. That's what a normal person would do, right? Run from the man in the mask. The chrome face promising death.

I press my back to the door and close my eyes. Count to ten. Pretend I'm shaking. Pretend I'm scared. Pretend I didn't recognize him as my wet dream the moment I saw him.

I run my fingers through my hair, mussing it up for effect. If I look disheveled enough, maybe I can convince myself this isn't what I wanted. That I didn't walk down that alley hoping he'd be waiting in the dark.

I should call someone for help. Instead, I smile. Just a flicker. Just for me. Then it fades. Because he's good at playing games, but I'm better.

I've never seen one that close before. Opting for stolen glances from across a street or the click of my camera in the shadows, obsessing over the life Reapers get to live. Biding my time. Waiting for him to find me.

It's fascinating, the way they live in their own world, uncaring for anything in the real one parallel to it. I've dreamt about holding the power they do, wondering what I could do with their money and the authority they invoke with a single word.

His fingers were inches from being inside me, and I wanted it. Fuck, I wanted it even more, knowing I shouldn't. But there I was, pussy wet, knees weak, and half a second away from asking him if now was too soon to promise forever. In that moment, I may have just done anything he asked of me.

I might be a little messed up in the head, but I'm not suicidal. Just altered. And it's because of Daith that I chase the high I do. Maybe that's what brought me back in that alley. This Reaper reminded me so much of the kid I grew up with and fell hopelessly in love with. The kind of kid that set fires, experimented with drugs, and taunted the police. He terrified me, yet I was completely and irrationally obsessed with him. And there was something about the Reaper that screamed of the same reckless and untamed energy that Daith does, taunting me with the hope of filling the void Daith created, promising Death if I got too close.

I move to the window on autopilot, parting the sheer curtain with two fingers. My eyes sweep the parking lot like I'm expecting to see a stranger. But I know better. The skeleton mask leans against the tree like it's posing for me, wiggling his gloved fingers in a wave. My hand trembles as I close the curtain. Another performance. Another lie.

I tell myself it's fear. That I'm afraid of him. That I should be. But the truth is, my stomach is fluttering. Before he disappears, I grab my camera off the shelf and push the curtain open again to snap a picture through the glass — the chrome mask caught perfectly in the streetlight, framed by leaves like a predator in the wild, surrounded by darkness.

It's beautiful. Horrifying.

Careful and measured, holding secrets in a vice, *like me*.

I lock the front door, not because I think it'll keep him out, but because it's what I'm supposed to do. I quickly shut the curtain and double-check the door locks before running to my bedroom with a sick thrill squeezing my stomach in a tight fist. I lock the door and slide to the floor, the cool hardwood grounding me. I dial the first name that comes to mind, muscle memory and poor decisions assisting the expected need to call for help.

Bryce picks up on the first ring. "Laurel? What's wrong?" His voice is soft. Safe. Forgettable.

"Hey, uh... Can you come over?" The words are out before I've decided whether I mean them.

"You just left. Already missing me?"

I close my eyes. Picture him showing up. Picture the Reaper watching from the shadows, amused or maybe murderous. Maybe both.

Bryce would die, brutal and at my hands, indirectly of course. That thought makes me sick, blood coating my hands, his dead body at my feet with my name on the bullet.

"Laurel? You there?"

My fingers curl tighter around the phone as I try to decide what to do. Then I hang up. Why did I ever think fucking the bartender would be a good idea? We see each other every day and cutting it off is impossible without making work super uncomfortable for everyone. No fucking way I'm giving Vic another opportunity to be a prick if he was to lose his only bartender.

With shaking hands, I open my bedroom door and slowly walk to the front window. Carefully, I pull the curtain back again, prepared to see him and confront him by sticking a note to the window or something, to let him know I'm not interested, though that may be a half-lie. But he's gone. I look around the parking lot and into the trees lining the side of the complex, seeing nothing.

For a moment, I think about the night again. His hand on my thigh, the gravel in his voice, the way I didn't say no until the very last second. I could've stopped him sooner. I didn't want to.

That's the part I can't say out loud. Not yet. I grin to myself once again. Now that I have his attention, this is going to be so much fun.

Chapter 5

I toss back drink after drink in a shitty dive bar, trying to focus on a single stream of thought. Why wasn't I told she was back? I roll over every possibility before I pick my phone up and dial the person that was supposed to have eyes on her.

My teeth nearly crack with every ring. Her sweet voice sings from the other side. "Hey Ricky Bobby," she says, sounding unbothered and completely unaware I'm about to rip her a new one.

"You want to tell me why I just found out Laurel is working at The Peach?" I growl, barely able to speak through the red-hot fire blazing in my blurred vision.

"Uh," she says, and I nearly crack the shot glass in my hand.

"How long?" It's the only question I can get out of the jumble happening in my head.

She sighs. "A few months."

I slam the glass down on the counter. She's been so close to me for months and I've been clueless. Dropping meaningless bodies. Sleeping with woman after woman when the only one I could ever love like that was only miles away from me?

"Be at the church tomorrow."

I end the call, not at all bothered by the fact I have to punish one of the people that mean something to me.

It took everything in me not to break into Laurel's apartment tonight and fuck her until she couldn't breathe. But I knew I needed to fight that impulse. I need to know just how much either of us can take and how far I would go. I haven't been this close to her since we were kids and so much has changed since then.

When I picture fucking her, my mind goes straight to choking her until her lips turn blue and she's fighting for air. I don't think I'd be able to stop. The connection we have, the thrill of spilling her blood would be too consuming. The need to have her is so strong, it crosses with the thrill I get from dropping a body... and that is clearly a problem.

Kill her. Fuck her. Play with her. She knows you. She'll figure it out.

Stay away from her.

Eat her fucking heart.

Shut the fuck up!

I slam my glass on the table, shattering it. *Fuck.*

Excellent, Daith. Draw attention to yourself in the middle of an episode. Pure genius. Why not just stand up and tell everyone you're a psychopath. Go ahead, tell them all your secrets. Bring them to your dumping ground and hand them the cuffs.

"Hey, sugar. You look like you could use another drink," the bartender says sweetly, swiping the broken glass into her rag with a soft smile. I eye the name tag sitting high above her recently done boob job. *Lizzie.*

I give her the best smile I can manage, though by how awkward my face contorts, I know my efforts fall more than short. Hanging my head, I fish out my wallet and grab my cash, handing it to her. "That's alright. I better get out of here before I end up on the floor."

She grins softly and nods, taking the cash.

I glance around the bar before tossing my hood up over my head and slinging my backpack over my shoulder. Liquor isn't going to cut this shit. I need to slit a throat and fuck something other than my hand before I slip up and kill Laurel like I almost did tonight. I could feel the urge crawling over my skin the moment she thought a locked door was going to stop me. But, instead of showing her just how wrong she was, I left before I broke my favorite toy.

Slinking into the shadows outside of the bar, I light a cigarette, biding my time, waiting for just the right girl to grab Little Reaper's attention. Women pass down the dim sidewalk, stammering and stumbling over themselves, giggling with their companions as they attempt to make it back to a bedroom and fuck themselves into a coma. Though I imagine some of them may wind up puking or passing out before they make it that far.

22

No one grabs my attention, and it's been almost an hour, my temper thinning with every passing second.

I pull out my phone, needing to look at the cameras I set up outside Laurel's place, glad she hasn't closed the blinds in her room. Then scroll through the screenshots of her, none the wiser, prepared to rub one out in the alley as a stream of cusses comes from the bar exit.

Kneeling, she collects the scattered contents of her purse. Dark brown hair flows around her in a tangled mess, shoes tucked under her arm, leather jacket wrapped around her waist. Intrigue pulses through me, settling in my cock. She looks so much like Laurel.

I grin, putting out my cigarette, rushing out of the alley, kneeling beside her.

She looks up at me, only a small hesitation before resuming scrambling, and an amused chuckle leaves her plump, pink-painted lips. "Thank you. I was in such a hurry to get away from a fucking creep I didn't see that damn step."

"I'm more than happy to help. I'm all too aware of dates going bad," I say, scanning over the items laying between us. Notepad. Cigarettes. Lipstick. A multitude of pens. Hair gel. Tablet. Earrings. What looks like a beat-up book with a vampire choking a half-naked woman. And I certainly don't miss the bullet vibrator she quickly slips back into her bag.

My guess is an office woman. Very successful, looking for a good time in the small amount of spare time she gets. Her freshly shaven legs and new set of eyelash extensions say she had high hopes for tonight.

Just my luck.

The wind blows through her hair, and she tucks it behind her ear, taking the compact mirror from my hand. Cherry, vanilla, and lilac collide together, drawing me closer.

"Couldn't have been as bad as mine," she says, taking my hand and getting to her feet.

"Wanna bet?" I smirk, raising a brow.

"Ten bucks," she says, with a damn good poker face.

I tuck my hands in my pockets. "Girlfriend dumped me." Easiest card in the book. "Said my face made it hard for her to..." I add a little extra for flair, hinting down for the sexual notion. I grin, easing the awkwardness that can

23

come from drawing attention to my scars. I love them. Though losing my depth perception has been a real dick in my ass.

She smiles softly, raising her hand to her mouth, hiding her chuckle to be polite. "My date was a co-worker," she says, straightening her shoulders, and I make a face of dismissal. "He asked me if I would get him off using my feet while he recorded it."

"Ha!" An uncontrollable laugh bursts from my chest, unrestrained and a bit too psychotic. I quickly press my lips together and she shakes her head, holding out her hand. Reaching back into my wallet, I hand her the ten-dollar bill. I was not expecting something as odd as that. I am not one to kink shame, but that's wildly bold for someone that plans on having a second date.

"He should have kept that one in his pocket 'til marriage," I say, pulling out a cigarette to buy more of her time, hoping she is someone who can't resist the urge to socially smoke.

"Better to get the 'no's' out of the way sooner than later," she says, reaching in her purse, visually relaxing. She inhales deep, looking me over, and if I was a self-conscious man, I would concern myself with fixing my hair for her appeal. "For what it's worth, your face is one I would be happy to ride and wake up to the next morning."

Well, shit. This is going to be easier than I thought. "Mind if I take you up on that?"

She takes a long drag before dropping it and I follow, stomping them both out. "You got any weird kinks I should know about?" she asks, teasing.

Oh, honey, more than you know.

"I'm pretty vanilla, believe it or not." I wash my gaze over her.

"Not," she says, taking the arm I hold out for her.

"Help! Help!"

She screams beautifully. Music to my fucking ears. If I ever had a soul to feed, this would do it. I close my eyes, smirking. My Little Reaper is damn good at sniffing out the ones that die beautifully, and that feels pretty fucking good.

Sighing, I open my eyes, staring at the little thing that's got me hard as stone. I didn't pick this girl for her eyes or for her curves, or her laugh. Not even for the way she screamed like a mountain lion when I hauled her down my stairs to this very room.

I picked her because she looks like Laurel. Not perfectly, but just enough. Same strong jaw. Same brown hair, if you squint. Same little mark on her cheek that could be mistaken for a dimple when she smiles just right.

I can't kill Laurell... so this is the closest I can get to scratching that itch.

She sobs, her body finally stilling, free of the adrenaline shakes. I stand from where I knelt in front of her for the past hour, silently watching her squirm and scream in our basement from the moment she woke up.

"I need to ask you a question or two," I say, pulling a chair in front of her. I make myself comfortable, now so close to being satiated, I could wait all night. I had the full intention of fucking her before flipping the switch and bringing her down here, but the questions burning holes into my skull are like fucking cancer, and more pressing than my need to fuck apparently.

"Anything you want! I'll tell you anything!"

I close my eyes, letting the streams of thought cloud my mind, letting Laurel win the internal fight of her taking over every inch of my consciousness.

She's going to leave. She doesn't love you anymore. Murderer. Sick in the fucking head. How could you make her stay? Why would you want to? She'll turn you in the second she gets free. You could make her one of you. No, they would never accept a woman in the ranks. You'll kill her before you get the chance.

"Please don't kill me!" the woman in front of me whimpers, crying like a fucking child, and my cock's stone structure waivers.

"Shut the fuck up!" My echoes bounce off the bare walls as I glare at her, grabbing the closest thing to me, throwing it at her head. The tray clatters to the floor, barely missing her and my cock falls a bit. Fuck I hate the pathetic begging shit. I should have worked my way into her bed before I introduced her to... all of this.

No, instead, I listened to the impatient fucker in my head that told me I had to know the answers to this now or my entire world was going to implode. Not likely, I know that now, but you couldn't have told me different in that moment.

I inhale deep. "Now, I need you to answer honestly and from the heart. This is a real fucking problem for me."

She swallows, nodding slowly, her chest heaving again.

"There's this girl that I... I can't stay away from. I need to touch her as badly as I need to breathe, but I'm worried I'll kill her," I say, furrowing my brows.

Another tear slips down her cheek.

"Maybe I want to kill her. I have a hard time separating those feelings when I want something. She's too perceptive, and oh, the fucking rush I'd get," I say, throwing my head back. "But afterwards, it would hurt too much, so I need to win her over." I lean closer. "Do I continue to stalk her? I think she liked it. Maybe send her a gift?"

She's silent for a moment, and I give her the chance to choose her words carefully and honestly.

"All girls like flowers," she chokes out between panicked breaths and tears. I scrunch my nose as snot runs down her face. *Gross*. She really isn't a pretty crier. Not like Laurel. "Or keep stalking her and when you attack her, maybe she'll kill you."

The fuck did this bitch just say to me?

I lurch forward, gripping her face firmly between my fingers. "I asked for relationship advice, not snide remarks, you little cunt," I say before running my tongue up the side of her bloody face.

"What kind of flowers?" I grip her tighter, glaring into her glassy eyes as if they hold the answer I'm looking for.

"Lillies. Roses are too basic," she says in a struggled voice.

I cut my eyes into her, rolling that over in my mind, and she jerks her head from me as I release her, chuckling to myself. This could work. I pace the floor, mulling it over, but sounds of her sniffling and the begging whimpers send me over the edge.

26

Rushing back, I grip her throat tightly and she squeaks.

"Please! Let me go! Please!"

"Please! Let me go! Please!" I mock her, the voice in my head matching the shrilling tone. "Sorry." I jut out a lip. "That was never part of the game." I tilt my head, irritation igniting my skin as my dick falls flat. My appetite just isn't in its usual place and the face staring back at me isn't the one I want. *Fucking Laurel.*

My cock doesn't even twitch at the idea of cutting her eyelids off so she would have to watch me cut her open.

"Please!"

Pulling my knife from its sheath, I flip it in my hand and hold it to her chin.

"Say please again, and you'll wish you didn't."

She tilts her head up, trying to avoid the sharp edge, and I grin. I love these little games, watching them squirm. doing everything to fight me off until the last minute when we both know it's useless.

Hovering above her, I dig the tip into her skin, focusing on the crimson bead it draws, only to be ruined by her plea again. I snarl and press my weight into the blade, eyes widening in sick fascination as it sinks into her skin, piercing her jugular. She gurgles on her blood, still begging me to stop, though now her words are just muddled gagging.

Shut. The. Fuck. Up!

I yank it out, and blood gushes, coating her body and splashing onto my jeans and boots. I move to stand over her body, and a wave of disgust washes over me, completely dissatisfied. You have to be fucking kidding me. Nothing?

Pure anger rushes through me realizing nothing will satisfy the hole Laurel dug and left gaping in my chest. Not even as a place-holder so I can figure out how to fuck her without killing her.

I groan. I'm going to have to move this along faster than I originally wanted and roll the dice, but I'm going to lose my fucking mind if I don't.

Grabbing a longer blade from the scattered tools on the ground, I hold it up and thrust it down into her head. A small sense of satisfaction surges to my limp cock, making it slightly jump, but it's gone just as fast as it came.

I whistle, calling in Dom before stepping over her and storming out of my basement like a child throwing a temper tantrum. All that fucking work for so little reward.

Fucking damn it, Laurel!

My sister comes like I knew she would. She's silent, deliberate, and already bracing for whatever this is going to be. The door creaks open and shuts behind her with an echoing slam. Her steps echo across the cracked stone floor, a slow rhythm that fills the hollow bones of the church. She doesn't say anything as she walks straight down the center aisle and stops under the ruined stained-glass window, directly in front of my chair where I sit.

"I'm here," she says. "So go ahead."

I stay still for a moment longer, just watching her. She doesn't fidget. Doesn't pace. She stands like someone already sentenced, just waiting for the blade to fall. When I finally stand, she meets my gaze without flinching.

"You didn't tell me she was back." My words come flat, clipped.

Cee's mouth tenses. "What difference would it have made?"

"It would've made every goddamn difference. I could have had her sooner."

She exhales through her nose, slow and even. "She's not something to own. It's her decision."

I take a few steps closer, the floor grumbling beneath my boots. She doesn't move. "I could've *known*," I snap. "Instead, I was left in the dark. That wasn't your call to make. You held me back."

"You don't get to call that betrayal," she says, but it's softer now. "She asked me not to say anything. I honored it, as her best friend."

I step closer, lowering my voice as I enter her space. "You and I both know you weren't honoring her. You were protecting her. From me. Your brother."

Cee looks away for the first time.

"She didn't need protecting," I say. "She needed me."

"She needed peace," Cee replies, almost a whisper. "And you weren't going to give her that. You never do."

"You don't know what she needs. You try to mother her, but in reality, she doesn't need you as much as you think she does. You can't protect her." I let that sit. Let it burn. The silence stretches out, long and uncomfortable.

"Someone had to," she says, and now her tone shifts into something more defensive. "She needed more time before you came back in and wrecked all the progress she made. She came back to see if the ghost of you still existed here. To heal herself and start over before you came back into her life," Cee says. Her voice is quiet now, but steady.

I stare at her. At the woman who's always known more than she lets on. Always played both sides like it was a game she couldn't lose.

"She has always wanted the world I have," I murmur.

Cee nods once. "And what if you go to far to have her in it?"

I straighten my spine, pulling my gun from my waistband. Laurel has always been the one thing that causes a rift between us. To Cee, Laurel is just as much her family as I am. Sometimes, maybe more. "I, am death. And she will always be mine." I load the gun and hold it to her head. "If you think you are an exception to my wrath, you are very wrong, sister." She holds my eyes, refusing to cower. I rear back and slam the butt of the gun into the side of her head, knocking her sideways. I catch her by the collar before she falls and slam her back against the stone column behind her. The crack of impact echoes through the church like a shot. She gasps but doesn't scream. Doesn't fight. She just glares at me through the pain.

I press a forearm against her throat, just enough to cut off ninety percent of her air.

"Next time you decide what I get to know," I murmur, "make sure you're ready to lose more than your breath."

She chokes out a bitter laugh, blood at the corner of her lip. "You done?"

I hold her there a beat longer, just until I feel her legs start to give out, then I let go.

She slides down the column, coughs once, then straightens slowly as she gets back to her feet.

"This is your only warning," I say again, quieter now.

Cee wipes the blood from her mouth with the back of her hand and looks up at me. Then she turns and walks away, slow and steady, like she's already made peace with whatever happens next. I let her go. But not because I've forgiven her.

Because the next time she lies to me, I'll be standing over her unmarked grave.

CHAPTER 6

LAUREL

I sit on Cee's barstool, swirling my coffee like it holds answers. I didn't sleep. Not really. Every time I closed my eyes, I saw the chrome mask. Felt the leather glove on my thigh. Heard his breath in my ear. It was so vivid and exciting. But I don't dwell on it.

That's what sane people do. They don't dwell.

Instead, I switch my brain to the fact that it was an excruciatingly late night of training new dancers. I know we need them, but Vic posted *one* hiring poster, and we got six new girls, and only two existing girls experienced enough to train.

"By all means, make yourself at home," Cee says, coming out of her bedroom, not at all surprised I'm here. My key makes it easy to come over and frequently come raid her pantry and closet. She takes another look at me and her smile fades. "What's wrong?"

"Oh, dear God, Cee! What happened?" I ask, eyes wide as I take in the angry purple bruise on the side of her face.

"Oh, girl, nothing," she dismisses. "I was cleaning and whacked my head on the side of the table like a moron. Stop avoiding my question."

With relief in my chest, I open my mouth, but the words get caught somewhere between my chest and tongue. How do I even explain last night?

So, an infamous Reaper of Redwater nearly fingered me in an alley and I liked it. Also, it made me think of your brother who was also released from prison last night. Weird, huh?

Yeah. That's a no.

"Didn't sleep," I say instead. "Argued with Bryce. Work's a mess."

She narrows her eyes. She knows that's a deflection. But Cee doesn't push unless she has to. "Want some cheesy eggs?"

I nod. I don't eat breakfast, she knows that, but she still offers and every time, I accept.

Telling her about the Reaper would only make her worry, and she's busy enough with work lately as it is. Working from home hasn't seemed to make her any less stressed, not that doing whatever she does with coding is any less stressful than what I do. The last thing she needs is to worry about me getting murdered... or me fucking a murderer.

Who knows how it will play out.

Once she's got the food done and she's a few bites in, I let myself speak again.

"I just feel lost in myself. You're my best friend. Give it to me straight," I say, knowing she has something to say.

Cee licks the remnants of her cheesy eggs off her fingers with an audible smack. "Your outfits are cute, but if you did more lap dances, you'd get better tips."

I narrow my eyes at her, and she draws a loud breath, catching on that I'm not in the mood for jokes.

"Fine." She sighs. "You gave up when photography didn't work out in New York and now you're settling. You're better than dancing for unshaved dicks, wearing butt floss, and fucking a man who thinks missionary is edgy if he fondles your tits too."

I choke on my coffee, laughing in spite of myself.

She shrugs. "You're better than this.

Maybe. Maybe I'm exactly this.

"So what do I do? Start over? Again?" I ask, my humor fading into a depressing reality.

"Start with something that actually excites you," she says, like she can't believe how far I've fallen.

The word *excite* tastes like last night. Like fear and arousal and leather and danger. I sip my coffee to hide the way my lips part just thinking about it.

I needed to leave the rot of Redwater and I had a lot to learn about the real world. Then when Daith's release date was close, I practically self-sabotaged my life there so I would have an excuse to move back.

"Dancing does excite me," I protest. I enjoy the actual dances, and hell, the money isn't bad.

Celeste clutches her chest, mocking me as she moves back around the island. "Oh my God! STD-riddled pervs, handsy bosses, and bitches for co-workers. I see it now!" She doesn't let me counter, so I raise my coffee to my lips, hiding my smirk. "However, if you want my help shopping for butt floss and nipple tassels, I wouldn't hate a girl's day." She winks, and I laugh into my mug. "I thought you liked Bryce," she adds.

"I do," I say. "He's safe."

"Is that what you want? Safe?"

I want knives and strength and someone who knows how to say my name like a curse. "I don't know," I lie. Again.

Her face shifts, something unreadable tightening behind her eyes. "Speaking of men who aren't safe..." she says, slowly. "There's something I need to tell you."

My stomach knots — part dread, part thrill.

"Daith's out."

"Oh," I say, taking another sip of my drink. "I wasn't keeping track." Another lie as I turn away from her.

I knew the date down to the hour. I knew it before he did.

"Just... like I said. Don't tell him where I work, yet."

"He's actually—"

A door shutting has my head jerking to the side and nearly choking on my lukewarm coffee as I see the face that has haunted my dreams coming around the corner in nothing but a towel. Half-naked. Wet. Tattooed. Standing in front of me, seeing me back, for the first time in five years. My mouth dries and my heart plummets into my stomach.

His presence is striking, his features sharp and defined. He's always been a beautiful boy, rugged, with a strong jawline. He's pure chaos, always tempting fate and coming out the other side. The kind of man who catches your attention with the energy he carries. It's intoxicating. My fingers twitch toward my phone on the counter. Old habit. But no lens could capture the perfectly destructive scene here.

His remaining eye gleams with confidence and arrogance, as though it holds thousands of secrets. The strip of fabric covering his other eye only adds to his allure, as if that was possible, giving him an increased appeal of resilience.

His dark, wet, tousled hair has my skin begging to be touched, and the tattoos covering his skin scream to be licked.

I groan at the sight of him and my eyes nearly bulge out of my head as my brain realizes I just made that sound out loud. I snap my head back to Celeste, widening my eyes in panic.

What in the fuck is he doing here?

Still in the process of tucking the corner of his towel in, he heads straight to the stove, snatching the last of the bacon.

Celeste protests, smacking him on the back of the head with the plastic spatula. "Have some respect, Jail Bird."

He just grins and chews. My nipples harden as I stare at his muscular tanned back, now fully covered in ink, inwardly—hopefully—groaning. The skeleton face across his back ripples with his muscles and has me wondering how it would look in a mirror as he fucked me senseless.

Suddenly I'm overly aware of just how thin my shirt is and the fact that I didn't wear a bra. I subtly cross my arms to cover my chest.

Celeste winces, obviously realizing she should have led with the fact her brother was here.

He turns and his brown eye stares back at me.

The sight of him has my stomach in my throat and my heart leaping onto the counter in front of me. I might as well put it on a plate and serve it to him. It's his anyway.

Daith moves towards me, heading out of the room, one hand holding his coffee, a strip of bacon hanging out of his mouth, his other hand firmly gripping his towel where it has come loose, threatening to fall. My eyes lock onto the V pointing straight down.

"No hi? Just straight to eye fucking me again like old times, Little Laurel?" he says, chewing the piece of bacon he ripped off.

I swallow hard, hating that fucking nickname, not because it hurts, but because I like how the memories taste. I attempt to hide the blush I feel rushing to my cheeks as he stops in front of me. He grins knowingly, leaning down to whisper in my ear. "Still *such* a good girl."

Oh, God.

Good girls don't fantasize about flipping the lights and riding their best friend's brother over the kitchen counter.

For years, he picked on me, toyed with me, knowing I was in love with him, but wasn't as courageous or daunting as him. He used it against me, claiming it was the reason I would never be right for him. Little Laurel, the good girl. As if I could never change.

He was wrong about that, though the way I'm blushing, it's like nothing has changed.

I slaughtered Little Laurel when he left. He killed that version of me, and something far more fucked up took its place.

For as long as I can remember, all I wanted was for him to see me. For me to be the one thing he looked at and couldn't deny. That he'd let me see the soft heart he kept hidden, one that perhaps beats a little differently. But I'd convinced myself I was the only one who knew how to love him correctly. Convinced myself I would be the one to show him love wasn't conditional.

It's no secret prison changes a man, I just didn't think it would change me too.

My jaw tightens as my sights set on him. *I'm gonna make you eat your fucking words.*

I watch every step he takes leaving the room, noticing the fresh scrape down his left side.

The second he's gone, Celeste turns back to face me, having tucked herself in the corner of the kitchen trying to escape the burning tension between her brother and me. I give an exasperated look, and she removes the hand stifling her grin.

She raises her hands in defense. "He stopped by early this morning after laying his bike down in the storm." I roll my eyes, trying to avoid the tingling in my stomach and hide my true emotions. "Come on. He walked like five miles in the rain, and he'll probably be MIA soon, just like old times," she adds, begging me for mercy.

Once Daith was old enough to work, he took every chance he had to leave town. Disappearing for months at a time, child services eventually bringing him back every time they got their hands on him. I would have run too. I just wish he would have taken me with him.

I put my mug and plate in the sink and start clearing the counter. "You could have given me more of a heads up," I almost whisper. "I could have worn something more... edible," I tease, wagging my eyebrows.

She scrunches her nose. "My God, you two need to fuck already. I know that's gross because he's my brother and all, but I'm suffocating in the heat between you. It stinks." Her lip curls dramatically, bringing her point home.

If I ever work up the nerve to fuck him, it will probably kill me...

A smirk pulls at my lips as I hide behind my mug.

But I'm sure as hell going to try.

Chapter 7

LAUREL

Daith stands at the edge of the pool, like the water offends him, arms crossed, boots still on, dressed in all black as usual. I inhale the chlorine, loving the way it smells—like memories that my soul clings to, as if they faded away, I too would stop existing.

"You don't like to swim anymore?" I ask, raising an eyebrow, remembering all the nights we spent in Cee's parents' pool.

"I don't see the point now," he replies flatly, as if my question is childish.

Cee's already gone inside, claiming she "forgot laundry," which is code for "leaving you two to fuck like rabbits." The night is warm and quiet. The pool is still, aside from the ripples my legs create where they hang off the side and sway idly in the water. The moment feels weirdly normal, like time is standing still.

"You don't see the point of a lot of things," I say.

Daith's gaze flicks toward the surface of the water, then back to me. "That's because most things are distractions."

I shrug. "Some distractions are worth it."

He takes a step closer, and for a second, I think he might sit beside me, but instead, he shifts to stand near the end, eyes narrowed, calculating something. Analyzing the water's depth the same way he does everything else.

And then...

He steps toward me. His foot hits the edge wrong, and the next moment, one foot slides, the other jerks upward, and his arms instinctively flail out as he tries to stop himself. There's a splash, a curse muffled by water, and I'm already laughing before he resurfaces. He emerges soaked, furious, whipping water from his face and scowling at the betrayal of his own body. His black shirt clings to him, his hair slicked back against his head.

I cover my mouth to stifle a laugh, but it doesn't help. "Are you...okay?"

He glares at me. "The edge was slippery."

"Wow," I manage between giggles. "Daith, defeated by... gravity."

"I have limited depth perception now," he mutters.

"You're making excuses," I grin, as he pulls himself out of the water in one smooth motion, his soaked clothes clinging like a second skin and spilling water onto the concrete. I'm still smiling when I meet his eyes, and I realize he's staring at me with a look that betrays his annoyance. It's something darker now. Something softer. Happier. Then the corner of his mouth lifts, just a little.

Daith comes out to the back porch again, now in new dry clothes, his features somehow even hotter in the moonlight.

Celeste grabs her purse and keys from the table, cutting our talk short. "I gotta go to this stupid staff meeting at the office, but y'all are welcome to hang out." She casts me a knowing look that Daith doesn't miss, and I can't help but grin. "I'll be home late. Lock up if y'all leave."

She shuts the door, and I grab the shot of tequila to quiet the silence filling the back porch. The tequila burns, but not enough to distract me from the butterflies in my stomach or the way Daith looks, poking at the small fire burning in the pit. He shakes his head as he props the poker up against the wall.

My eyes find Daith's, and my grin turns into a wide smile, mirroring the one spreading across his face.

"What?" I ask, taking another sip.

"You gotta stop smiling like that," he says, taking the seat across from me. The weight of his stare that follows me is intense, and I drop my eyes, suddenly grateful for the space between us, giving me the room to breathe under the weight.

"Why?" I ask, unable to look up at him.

There was a time when I couldn't help but stare at him every time he walked in a room.

But he never looked at me like he is now, that same desperate, hungry expression looks back at me every time my eyes find his.

"You already have me on my knees with those eyes, and with that smile, you might just kill me."

Breath gone, I look up at him and that boyish smirk. He knows what he does to me, my poker face seriously lacking tonight. My heart thumps wildly, my head reeling with the image of Daith on his knees in front of me. Oh, the way I'd ride his face into oblivion.

"My eyes?" I ask curiously. He's never been so open. Whispered passing comments and occasional glances I'm sure I misread are what I'm used to.

His head tilts as he seems to dive into my eyes, finding his words. "They've always had so much to say, and even more beautiful now than I remember."

I drop his stare, choosing a spot on the ground to occupy my view. Daith's boots appear in front of me, and he squats low, forcing me to look at him.

"Why are you fighting me so hard baby? Do you not want me anymore?" he asks, tilting his head toward mine. "Tell me you don't want me anymore, and I'll leave you alone."

My throat tightens with the words I want to spill, begging me to tell him he's all I've ever wanted. My legs ache with the urge to wrap them around his waist and demand he carry me to the first solid surface and show me all the ways I could never forget him.

"You might break my heart," he says, grabbing my calves, rubbing them gently.

I look up, holding onto a moment of bravery, and I hold his face in my hands. "You know there's not a single day that would even be remotely true," I say, taking a moment to calm my tightening throat. "You aren't good for me."

I know I deserve better. But I want you.

The words burn, sour and wrong, but they hold truth. If I give in to him, he'll consume me, and I'll die letting it happen. But his words are not enough to convince me I'm more than just a fuck to him.

Not that the swirling storm inside me is listening. It's screaming to give in. To give him everything, to chance everything.

"Do you remember when I used to take you riding?" he asks, his hand idly playing with the ends of my hair.

Those memories flash through my mind. The comfort in the silence as I held onto him, letting him take me anywhere. The ringing in my ears as he touched me, the taste of his skin in my mouth. The heat flaming in his eyes as he told me it was our little secret. It was just a little fun, secrets in the dark that disappeared as if they never happened.

"Yeah," I say softly, terrified those memories will vanish if I speak too loudly.

"Those were the days, huh? Nights that held nothing but the promise of the future being anything we wanted it to be." He pulls his hand away, intertwining them between his knees, and my skin grows cold.

I crave his touch like a drug, always scared to ask for more. Knowing I would want too much—more than he has to offer.

I pull my knees up and rest my head on them. "Yeah." The three margaritas burning their way through my inhibitions have me thinking about the way he tastes.

"We were so free," I say, closing my eyes, imagining the wind whipping around us, me clinging tightly to his back, safe, heart soaring. I'd give anything to go back to those days, push just a little harder for him.

"You still ride?" he asks, nudging me, and I sway heavily to the side.

"Not since you left."

There's more resentment in my voice than I intended. I don't hate him for leaving. He did something stupid, but it wasn't the act of freeing himself from the hell he was forced to grow up in. I hate him for being careless and getting caught, forced to leave me when something could have bloomed.

"Come on, let's go for a ride."

I open my eyes to find him standing, hand outstretched in front of my face, and I smile wide. "Really?"

"I'll wait for you," he says, nodding toward the house. He always was a stickler for "dress for the slide, not the ride."

CHAPTER 8

I stand outside, leaning against my freshly painted bike, waiting for her. She comes toward me, practically skipping with joy, her camera hanging from her hand. She's so carefree, so happy, like nothing has changed.

I wanted her, even back then, though I made sure she never knew for sure. I used her, taking what little I could steal to curve the craving, leaving her wanting more when I pushed her away.

Her soul was promising and bright, and I was becoming the thing that goes bump in the night. My soul turning blacker than the pits of hell. Waiting for the time I would bleed my black soul into hers, and now that the time is here. I'm foaming at the mouth to test her limits, and my Little Laurel seems like she's planning to do the same.

"What the fuck are you wearing?" My eyes trail down the length of her body and back up for good measure. She's dressed in all black down to the boots, but the bralette under her leather jacket leaves nothing to the imagination. My hands twitch at my sides to touch her—to run my hands down the soft curves of her sides.

"You don't like it?" she asks, pulling her jacket open to give me a better view.

"Are you trying to learn what road rash feels like?" I raise a brow, only to be met with a challenging grin.

"You sound confident that wrecking is a high possibility with you. Maybe you need a little more practice."

I stalk toward her, and lean in, looking back and forth between her hazel eyes and dilated pupils. "Keep it up, I'm begging you."

She chuckles.

Fucking brat.

"Turn around."

Without question, she obeys, letting me braid her hair, just as I did many times before, years ago. Grabbing her helmet, I slide it on her, fastening her chin strap. "This one is yours to keep."

She climbs behind me. "You just had this with you by chance?"

"I was hoping you'd let me take you for a ride." I shrug and shift the bike into gear. It jumps, causing her to lurch forward into my back, her hands instinctively wrapping around me, holding me tight.

CHAPTER 9

LAUREL

I fight my instincts to lean away from the pavement as we take a curve and lean with Daith as the muscle memory comes back. The bike slants, the ground close enough to touch, and that old feeling comes rushing back.

My smile widens as we right, and I retract my clawing grip from his hoodie. I sag into him, not realizing what I'm doing until his hand reaches back and rubs my upper thigh in comfort. Knowing he can't hear me, I let out the moaned confession dying to rip itself from my chest.

"God, I love when you touch me like that." It feels liberating—voicing it out loud.

He gives my leg a gentle squeeze, then his touch is gone, bringing his hand back to the handlebars.

We come to a stop a few miles down the road and I immediately recognize the cliff we visited many times as kids. I reach for the clip under my chin, so glad that I brought my camera, but I stall as Daith's voice comes from inside my helmet.

"You did so good."

He dismounts and hooks a finger under the rim of the helmet, forcing my head back to look at him.

"There's a mic in these?" I choke out, embarrassment rushing to my face as he unfastens the strap for me and pulls the helmet from my head.

"Mhm."

Shit.

He heard me. I know he heard me. And the grin passing over his lips as he hangs our helmets on the bike tells me he enjoys that I know.

"I'll touch you any way you want, all you have to do is ask Little Laurel."

My face warms and I look down, unable to hold his stare yet again.

44

"You'll never stop shying away from me, will you?" he says, gently turning my face back to him.

Finding some strength somewhere deep inside me, I hold his gaze. "I'm not shying away. I just don't believe you." I swing my leg over the bike to face him fully and he spreads my legs, stepping between them.

"Is that so?" A fire ignites in his eyes. Something wild and dangerous. He moves closer, leans down, pressing a gentle kiss to the bare skin above my breast.

Electricity ignites every nerve in my body, pulling a soft whimper from my lips. He straightens, caging me in, his gaze dark, lips parted slightly. Slowly, he pushes my jacket off my shoulder, and I turn my head, giving him more access as he plants another kiss just below my ear.

"Then tell me what you want, and I'll do it," he whispers, and I ache, needing him more than ever.

"Touch me."

His hand finds my thigh, hiking it up on his hip. My chest heaves with each struggled breath growing heavier as he inches his fingertips further up my leg. I move my hips, grinding on his thigh with need for the friction he's teasing me with, and his fingers dig into my ass with a firm grasp.

"Do you want me to keep going?" he says on a labored breath, the heat between us growing stronger, starving us.

"Yes," I rasp, shutting my eyes, anticipating his moves.

A light brush over the middle seam of my pants has my legs shaking. He moves to the top of my pants, and I bite my lip, preparing for his fingers on my skin. His lips drag down my neck as I push into him, groaning at how good the contact feels. My heart pounds in my chest and I dig my nails into his shoulders, needing more. So. Much. More. He groans, deeper and quieter, filled with the same desperate need.

I grit my teeth, needing him to move faster before I rip his clothes off.

Finally, he pushes his hand into my jeans, cupping me between the legs, sliding a single finger between my lips, feeling how wet I am. His tongue caresses my neck, licking up to my ear before his heavy desperate breaths cloud my mind.

The cold air brushes over my wet skin, sending another jolt through me, and my pussy clenches. Daith groans, moving his hands and leaving me hungry. In a haze, I let him take my camera and hook it on the bike's handlebar. Then his hands slide under my thighs, lifting me up. My legs wrap around him, and I bury my face into his neck as he carries me further from the road. He sets me down gently, protecting my head as we collide with the ground, our bodies never parting. I raise my hands above my head as he pulls my pants down. My heart stops as my fingers wrap around the edge of the rocks. We're so close to the edge, the rocky ocean daring us to jump.

He grins before he lifts my knees up, throwing them over his shoulders. My back arches as he dives in, sinking between my legs, licking up my pussy. I clench and exhale, giving my body to him.

He moans against me, and my praise kink soars, knowing he's enjoying himself just as much as I am. His tongue pushes between my lips, dragging up to my clit, flicking it furiously. He looks up at me, and the sight of him on his knees, devouring me with the same desperation, causes my pussy to throb. As if reading my mind, he shoves two fingers in me and I gasp, clenching around him greedily, digging my fingers into the edge of the cliff.

His fingers curl perfectly, fucking me hard and fast. I cry out, moaning and whimpering, loving the way he makes me feel. My whimpers turn aggressive as I reach for his shirt, wanting to pull him into me. To kiss him, bite him, taste him. Whisper everything I want him to do to me.

He swats my hand away and pulls his pants down just enough to free his dick before flipping me to my stomach. He jerks me up to my knees and shoves me forward, my face hanging over the edge. I reach back for him, and snags my hand then, pulls my other arm back, pinning them behind my back, shoving my chest into the ground. One slip or wrong move, and all possibilities of our future fade to black, only death's cold grip holding us together.

I tighten every muscle in my body on instinct and Daith thrusts into me, driving to the hilt. I scream out, a dull ache accompanying the overwhelming pleasure. He fills me perfectly, hitting all the right spots. His other hand wraps around my throat, leaving me completely at his mercy, dancing on the edge of oblivion.

"Don't let me fall," I pant between desperate breaths, and he hooks his pointer finger into my mouth. I close my lips around the tips, sucking it greedily.

"If you die, we die together, baby," he moans, pumping into me with punishing and desperate thrusts.

Fuck that shouldn't be so hot.

His grip on my body tightens, and I find comfort in his words and hold. If I were to die tonight, this would be an okay way to go. Getting everything I ever wanted, ending this life with him, spending eternity with our souls bound.

I struggle to breathe, but don't tap out. I let him have me. Let him have anything he wants. My body rocks back and forth, and he uses the motion to fuck me harder. There is nothing soft and loving about it. We are hungry and feral, desperate for a connection we have deprived ourselves of for far too long.

"You feel so fucking good," he groans, and that sound will scar my memory forever.

Hunching over me, he buries his face in my neck, his thrusts turning slow and punishing. He releases my hands, and I push one between my legs, helping my orgasm that is already close.

"Come for me, baby. Say my name."

I groan at his request, eager to please him, furiously rubbing my throbbing clit.

His fingers intertwine with mine in the rocks, the other wrapped around my throat squeezing. My eyes grow heavy, and I clench around him, giving into the explosion shooting through my body. I see stars, his desperate groan in my ear amplifying my orgasm, drawing it out as my body hangs on to every possible second he's inside me.

Daith releases my neck as he thrusts into me one last time and I suck in air greedily, my vision returning. He comes hard, his body giving me everything, and worlds collide. Nothing else matters but this moment with him. Our moment of perfection.

He pulls me up, staying inside me as we sit back. His hands run up the sides of my body before he pulls my jacket and bralette off, baring my chest to the ocean. Muscled arms drag me back against his bare chest moving to my shoulders, and the contact of skin on skin is electric. I close my eyes, clenching around his dick, hands trailing my body. Cum leaks out of me and I fight the urge to push it back inside. A baby locking me to this man wouldn't be so bad. He cups my breasts, squeezing firmly, dropping his face to my shoulder, softly kissing my skin.

I exhale heavy breaths, soaking in the moment that is quickly getting me ready to go again.

"You're so beautiful," he whispers, his words almost lost in the sound of the waves crashing below.

I tilt my head against his. "I missed you."

His arms wrap around me, secure and claiming, anchoring more than my body to his.

We sit like that for what feels like eternity before I dare to move, scared I'll wake up in my bed. But on a sigh, I stand, struggling to keep my feet under me as I get dressed. Daith slips his shirt on and pulls up his pants before sitting on the edge, dangling his feet over.

"So, you dating someone?" he asks, catching me off guard.

"Not officially, no," I say, moving to sit beside him.

"We should go on a double date. I'd like to meet him."

My brain takes a second to buffer, not wanting to register what it just heard. "You're dating someone?"

"I can be," he says with a hint of amusement.

I clench my teeth, but don't react the way he expects me to. It's just like him to try to get a rise out of me. Instead, I open up, hoping it will get him to do the same.

"You know I have loved you with my entire heart my whole life." I reach for his hand, something in my chest cracking when he pulls away. "But all I'll ever be to you is something to play with when you're bored." I fight to keep the tears at bay after letting him have every part of me—again.

Silence falls around us, the water crashing on the bank filling the long minutes stretching between us.

He finally turns to me, his brows pinched. "I wish I was capable of only playing with you when I'm bored. God knows I've done it enough times to know how to make it work."

I narrow my eyes. He did not just fucking say that to me.

"But there's something about you."

I swallow, softening my glare as his words cut deep. "Am I not good enough?"

48

He reaches out to hold my face, a tear sliding down my cheek to meet his finger. A soft smile crosses his lips. "You are... everything."

My heart leaps, flipping in my chest, hope reigniting. "And that's a problem?"

He pulls his hand back, turning to the water again. "Yes"

I say nothing, unable to find the words. I watch the water crash over the rocks, molding around the space they take, becoming what it needs to be to exist in the same space. The waves wear at the rocks, demanding its presence be felt. The rock unmoving, embracing the water, accepting the possibility of its damage or demise.

I look at Daith, taking in the way he sits so still, as if he's not breathing and move my hand to rest on top of his, grabbing him firmly, demanding to be felt.

"I will always be the thing missing from your life. I pray you don't realize that too late." I lean in, pressing a kiss to his cheek. "I admire many things about you, Daith. But your fear of love is not one of them. I grieved you twice. Once for who you were and again for who you will never be."

CHAPTER 10

Thinking of the way she looked at me last night, the way she let herself fall into me as though time stood still has me hard. The warmth of her skin, the softness of her voice, yet she was so firm in what she wanted. It took me by surprise, knocked me on my ass. But fuck, she felt so good. The faint smell of her clings to my skin, like a mark I can't wash off. Last night was... easy once she let go. I can feel her desire for me even now, like it's echoing in the air between us. Like nothing else mattered but her skin on mine.

She's beautiful—God, I can't deny that. There's a certain power in the way she looks at me, the way she believes in me, trusts me. It's a weakness to love someone that much, but I couldn't rip it from her chest even if she let me try. I am rooted in her being, forever changing the way she grows and stands with purpose.

But I can't let myself get too tangled up in her. I'm so close to running the city, and it would be too easy to lose myself in her the way I did last night. She could ruin everything I've worked for.

I glance at the phone vibrating on the table, the screen lighting up with a name I know too well. A name I'd rather avoid right now. I hesitate, fingers hovering over the screen. I already know what's waiting for me on the other side of that call, and it won't be good. It never is when she calls this early.

Sighing, my thumb presses down, accepting the call.

"Yeah?" I answer, the word coming out rough, like I've been holding it in too long.

"Don't sound so tense," she says, as calm as ever. But I can hear the undertone—the urgency, the weight of something bad about to unfold. I clench my jaw, waiting for her to drop whatever bomb she has.

"What is it?"

"A flag just came up in the system. You dropped two bodies this week," Skid says, not holding back the scrutinizing tone.

"No, I didn't." Slurping my coffee, I put it on speakerphone, needing both hands to make my breakfast. I can't think on an empty stomach, much less decipher whatever's happening.

"You didn't kill someone yesterday?" she asks, her tone perking up in confusion.

Felix comes in, pushing me out of the way to make his coffee, with a shot of whiskey. He wags a finger at me, taunting me, and I return the gesture with my middle finger.

"No, I did, but only one," I say, squishing my egg sandwich together.

A hum sounds, followed by the clicks of her computer as she types. "A woman that works with Laurel."

"That's not mine," I say, idly, defending myself. "I did kill a woman last night, but I handled clean-up." I cast Felix a wink, and he gives me a sarcastic thumbs up at me taking his credit.

"That wasn't an approved kill, Daith," she berates, irritation clear in her stern voice.

"I know, mother. But did it raise a flag?" I ask, taking another sip of my coffee, not bothering myself with the possibility. We are too good, too cautious.

"Not yet," she says, but there is a clear hint of relief.

I let her doubt and accusing tone slide because this is literally her job, but it doesn't stop the irritation that grates at me.

Felix taps his spoon against the rim of his mug repeatedly, and I snap my head to the side, instantly feeling my blood pressure rise to a dangerous level. He avoids eye contact, but a slight grin appears on his lips.

Prick.

"Who was the woman last night?" I ask, realization hitting me.

Someone is targeting women where Laurel works. I grind my teeth, my mind racing as I wrap my head around the fact that it could've been her. That it *almost* was her.

"Jewel."

I stay silent, working that over in my head. I'm not just angry. I'm terrified. For all the control I think I have over her, for all the plans I've made, I couldn't control this. If she hadn't been with me... It's something I can't stomach. The thought of her life being in anyone's hand but my own.

I lose my appetite, shoving my plate toward Felix who takes it greedily, dumping the rest of my bacon onto his plate.

"If not you, you have someone pissing on your tree," she says, groaning, and I can hear the exhaustion in her tone. "She was estimated to have died around 3am this morning. Any ideas?"

"No," I mumble, going over last night in my head. I left Laurel at Cee's house around 2 o'clock and I went straight home to drink myself blind after her verbal knife to my heart. I look to Felix who helps monitor things like this more than I do. He shakes his head with a shrug as she begins talking again.

"What are the chances someone is trying to get you in trouble with CHAOS again?"

"We're not particularly liked in these parts, Skid, so yeah, I would say it's feasible to have made some enemies that would like to see me go down." We've created plenty of enemies over the years. Some were created by Ez before I joined the ranks. "It's just narrowing down who is capable of pulling it off."

"Her eyes were cut out and shoved down her throat. Someone is trying to replicate your previous work. Sloppy work, but clean execution with nothing to go off of. So they have done some research without throwing a red flag."

"Not bad." I slump on the couch, kicking my feet up on the table. "Check the club out for me. Send me a list of everyone that went in or out in the past week and anyone around with so much as a parking ticket. Tail us. Find out who is watching us."

"Keep an eye on her, Daith," Skid says, preparing to follow orders without question. I trust her completely, and she'll have that list to me within the day.

She doesn't need to watch over the people I care about. I'm going to find this bastard. And I'm going to make sure he knows just how much of a mistake it was to come anywhere near Laurel.

The line ends and I groan. "Happy fucking Monday."

My phone chimes again and Laurel's name pops up with a text. I toss my phone across the room, nearly hitting Felix in the forehead.

"Why are you so on edge," he asks, seeing through my tantrum.

"Laurel is working at The Peach and it was targeted last night. Our job just got messy."

"And what part of that pisses you off more?" Felix asks, bracing his arms on the table.

"The part where I care more about her safety than I do about CHAOS trying to get up my ass without lube. Having her around me has been more compromising than I remember it being." I lean forward, scrubbing the back of my neck, running my hands through my dirty hair. "I feel like the hourglass is glued to the table with a hole in the side."

"You wanted her." Felix chuckles, setting his plate in the sink before picking up my phone and bring it to the coffee table. "She's already in love with you man. She'll be putty in your hands, ready to be whatever you need her to be. You just have to be smart about these big boy feelings you have for her."

"Putty," I repeat, nodding slowly, my mind working over my plans, ignoring his insinuation that I feel anything but mild affection for her. "Love turns messy. It's tears and whining and wanting things I can't give her." She'll want the fairytale, white picket fence future. She'll want me to open up, show her more of who I really am, and I can't do that yet without risking everything. It has to be at the right time, after I have given her time with The Reapers, let her see the way things work. Explain the way we live. Show her the possibilities. I tap my finger to my forehead. "You think it's possible to remove those pesky things about her?" Emotions. Such crippling aspects of being human.

"Like a lobotomy?" he asks, and I raise a curious brow. *There's a thought.* "Jesus, man. No."

I roll my eyes, trusting him as my moral compass.

"Have you ever thought, maybe you would be okay with her loving you?"

Sticking my tongue out, I mime gagging. "Love is a weakness. She would be a liability if I let her in any deeper."

"Love and loyalty go hand in hand, brother." He shrugs before tapping his finger to his temple. "Think about it. You can't avoid what you want. Either it will ruin your life when it inevitably takes over or you will die miserable, watching someone else have what you were too scared to reach for. Ez's word isn't law."

The thought of her ever belonging to someone else has my teeth clenching. That would never happen. I need her. I need her *here*, next to me, beside me—where I can control her, shape her. Sooner than I planned, but I'll make sure she stays in line.

I'll make her believe that being with me means she's part of something bigger, something important. She has always dreamed of her life being more than a 9 to 5 with the promise of 10 years of retirement waiting for her once she is old and grey. With me, she'll have that golden dream staring her back in the face now. The possibility of her imagination being the limit for where her life goes.

She'll come to see that the rules are different for us. She'll accept it. She has no choice. She chooses me and my life, or she dies at my hand.

Fuck, I'm horny again just thinking about Laurel, and I really haven't straightened out the connection between killing and my hard-on for her. This could prove to be a problem.

They say humans can't watch themselves die. That our brains reject the image in order to protect itself. I heard that somewhere, but right now the haze is keeping me from placing it. That's why most people shut their eyes, look away, pretend it's not happening. Self-preservation, down to the last second.

I want to test that. So I brought mirrors. Four of them. Floor to ceiling. One on each wall of this basement room. They're tilted just right so she can see every part of herself. The sweat, the shaking, the tears running into the bruises blooming on her throat.

She keeps trying to look away. That's what the zip ties are for. I sit cross-legged in the middle of the floor, sipping from a convenience store energy drink and swaying to the music that plays through one of my earbuds. It's calming—grounding, allowing me to quiet the voices that try to overthrow my own.

"You ever really *looked* at yourself?" I ask.

She doesn't answer. She can't. I cut her tongue out. I really didn't want to hear all that mumbo crap. She's naked, except for the duct tape across her mouth, holding her pantyhose as gauze in her mouth, and she looks so much like Laurel, but totally different at the same time. The same hair and face shape, but her lips are thinner and her eyes are smaller, tilted at the sides, and more green than brown. But she doesn't carry herself like Laurel. She doesn't smell like Laurel. But I do my best to imagine it.

The blood on her shoulder has mostly dried, caked like rust, but fresh blood still drips from her chin, down her chest, and to her stomach. She's shaking like a leaf, but she's still alive.

The mirrors force her to see it all. Everything she is, inside and out, when it comes down to her final moments.

"You know," I continue, "they say your pupils dilate when you're scared or turned on. That your heartbeat pulses in your eyes if the lighting and angle is just right." I lean closer, studying her reflection instead of her face. "Do you see it? That panic? That shame? You wear it so well."

She makes a muffled sound, half plea and half panic.

"See, most people lie to themselves. They think they're kind. Good. Innocent." I take another sip, then set the can down beside me. "But strip them down, and they are all the same shade of ugly." I tap her reflection. "Human. Doing anything to pull the shades over their eyes and say they don't see anything wrong with who they are."

I reach into my jacket and pull out a disposable camera. Like Laurel. To capture moments in time, just like she does.

Snap.

I take a photo of her in the mirror.

Snap.

Another. Different angle. Her eyes glisten, filling with tears that she doesn't hold back.

55

"This isn't for blackmail, sweetheart," I say softly, though my modifier keeps it rough and distorted. "This is for me. For later. For when I need to remember that under the surface, we are all the same. Weak. Cracked."

I rise to my feet, slow and deliberate. She jerks back, but the ties hold her tight.

"So I can show Laurel. Hopefully, she thinks my work is beautiful too." I smile to myself, looking at my reflection, welcoming the acknowledged broken and filthy parts of myself.

"This is the part where I kill you," I whisper, bringing my eyes back to her, "but not because I'm angry. I'm not. I just want to see what your face looks like when the light goes out in your eyes. See if that's the same as everyone else too."

I press the knife to her chest and watch the reflection. Not hers. Behind her. My own.

Calm. Cold. Delighted.

Snap.

One more photo.

Then I sink the knife into her chest, watching erotically as the light fades from her eyes and the panic on her face fades to solace. But as I imagine Laurel lying beneath my blade, washed from this earth, something deep in my gut twists.

I turn my phone over, now cleaned up and relaxed, thankful my tantrum earlier today only resulted in a crack across the glass screen. I check Laurel's message after letting it go hours without a response. She hates that, and I need to give her a little push, something to grate on her nerves to remind her of just how much she wants me.

Peach: Last night was great

I grin, glad she didn't completely shut down after my emotional vulnerability with her last night. I was honest and opened up just enough give her that connection she's craving.

My finger hovers over the send button, finally replying with a smile on my face and an evolving plan in place.

Me: Still on for the double date tonight?

I sit back and wait, the excitement building inside me. Bryce is a distraction for her, a place-holder, something to pass the time and dull the ache left as residual pain from me ripping myself from her life.

Tonight, I'm going to make her realize it, make her feel it so deep she won't be able to tolerate the excruciating truth that Bryce is a bore and an utter waste of her time.

The reply comes fast, and I can almost hear the anxiety in the tone she would have.

Laurel: This is stupid. Just... don't antagonize Bryce too much, okay? He doesn't know about our past.

I almost laugh at that. Oh, it's too easy. Not only is Bryce as boring as a cinderblock, but he is just as blind to the fact that I have his girl wrapped around my finger, and last night, my cock. He's in my way, but not even worth considering a hurdle. Not when I know she's practically aching to admit how little she cares for him. She needs something more. And I'm the one that gives her that. I'm the only one that can.

I type back casually.

Me: Don't worry. Just here to have a good time. Remind me, has he tasted the way you taste when you're begging to come? It really is such a memorable experience. I'd be happy to give him some pointers. I can't stop the grin spreading across my face. I have no intention of taking it easy on him tonight, and I plan to watch her squirm as she tries to hide how much I make her feel. Then, watch her reactions as I give all my attention to my date, the one who isn't her.

Because I know she's already jealous, the need to know who I'll bring is killing her. She's just not brave enough to admit it. The only reason we are playing this game is because some part of her enjoys the back and forth just as much as I do.

And by the end of tonight, she'll know that I'm the one she wants without a doubt in her mind. Not Bryce and certainly not this version of life she's pretending to want. Then behind the scenes, Felix will go and set up cameras in her apartment, giving me access to everything I need to see beyond the surface.

I told her this wasn't a game for me anymore, and though I was honest about the way she makes me feel, this absolutely is a game. She just doesn't know just how much I have already won, and she won't realize that she's lost until she's in too deep to back out.

CHAPTER 11

LAUREL

My stomach churns, a mix of butterflies and sickening anxiety threatening to have me vomiting before we ever make it to the table. I run my thumb nail under my index nail, picking at the dried blood... or maybe it's dirt, focusing on anything other than the man beside me. A tug on my arm has me looking up. Looping my arm in Bryce's, I smooth my dress down and follow the waiter. When Daith proposed a double date, I figured he would go for cheeseburgers and hanging out, but no. He managed to get into one of the most exclusive, high-class restaurants we have. *Note to self, ask him how he managed to swing that.*

"This place is nice," Bryce says, sitting next to me resting his hand on my thigh under the table, gently rubbing his thumb against the expensive satin black material. I smile politely, trying to calm my nerves. "I'm glad we're finally going on a real date, even if it includes two other people I've never met." He laughs half-heartedly, but I can see the unease under his false confidence. He's intimated and slightly emasculated that the first time I agree to a date, it involves another man, even if he stupidly believes Daith is just a good friend. "I guess I can't complain if you are giving me more than after hours behind the bar." His voice is lower, as if he didn't entirely want me to hear his words that have a hint of snide within them.

The soft hum of polite chatter drowns out the rest of his small talk, blurring him to the background as the front doors swing open and Daith steps in, my breath lodging in my chest.

He's cleaned up nice, hair lightly gelled and swooped back in perfection with a classy, but not overdone suit. He's traded his usual tattered black cloth covering his missing eye with what appears to be a prosthetic eye. It's the first time I've seen it uncovered.

The woman on his arm is beautiful. Her long dark hair falls in soft curls, a likeness to mine. As they move closer, I take in the soft curves of her face, so similar to my own, it feels cruel. She smiles softly, looking up at Daith with adoration and he's smiling back at her, looking completely at ease with her on his arm, unlike the tense and firm holds he has when it's me.

They make their way through the restaurant, and it's like watching a scene from a movie—perfectly effortless. He's the perfect gentleman, guiding her to our table, pulling the chair out for her with smooth grace. He glances over her head, his eyes meeting mine as he slides into his chair next to her.

He smiles at me, his eyes gleaming, shining with perfectly executed charm. "You look great," he says, and words get lodged in my throat, focused on the way his false eye makes him appear as a ghost from my past, haunting me. I feel it deep in my chest—a slow burn of hurt that threatens to burst into flames, waiting for the smallest encouragement to create devastation.

Bryce nudges me, jolting me back into the moment and I inhale, smiling softly as I firmly place my mask back in place.

"Thank you. You both look amazing," I say, reaching to my leg and grabbing Bryce's hand. "Bryce, this is Daith. My good friend."

Bryce lets go of my hand, reaching out to shake Daith's, extended across the small table. "It's a pleasure, man."

Daith nods, scooting closer to his date and placing his hand on her back, leaving Bryce's hand stranded. "This is Malia," he says, purposefully leaving out who she is.

I reach out to shake her hand as Bryce pulls his back, and I take in her freshly manicured nails. A French tip, classy, and the first thing that is unlike me.

The table is silent for an uncomfortable minute, and I clench my jaw as my eyes draw back to Daith, the hurt in my chest growing, my eyes stinging with the tears I fight to hold back. Sitting in front of him like this, after having him again, it's torture.

My hurt shifts towards the woman sitting at his side, and I release the tension in my jaw, forcing a smile in its place.

"How did y'all meet?" I ask, eyes flicking from her to Daith.

"Oh, we actually met a few years ago at a music festival but just started getting serious a few months ago." She bats her eyes innocently, and I want to claw them from her skull.

I force a smile, because as far as I have been told, he's been firmly behind bars. "That's wonderful. Who was playing?" I ask, keeping a polite smile plastered on my face, hiding the ugly green monster hiding beneath the surface.

"What?" Daith asks, seeming unprepared for the question.

"I've never known you to like events like that, so I was just wondering who you went to see and how you connected?

He chuckles, taking her hand, resting them on top of the table for a public display of affection. "Honestly, I can't remember. We didn't stay long."

She giggles, as if they have a meet cute that is coming back to her as if it was yesterday. It's very possible they did meet yesterday, and he's holding this poor girl hostage. Some pathetic attempt to make me jealous like he used to. And I hate that it still works.

Bryce laughs, feeding into the conversation. "Sounds like us, huh," he says, looking at me with an insinuating expression.

I force out an agreeing laugh, but as I look up from the table, I feel the tension shift, something in Daith's eyes darkening into something that looks a lot like murder.

"So, when are you two going to take things to the next level?" Daith says, looking between the two of us. "From what she's told me, it seems like it's getting pretty serious." He smiles too wide and Bryce's face lights up with false hope. *Damn you Daith, you meddling manipulative fucking shit wipe.*

I keep the glare inside, instantly getting a new read on what this is. I was stupid to think that was anything other than a chance for Daith to stroke his own ego and make me look stupid.

Bryce stiffens, turning to me. "Well, we haven't talked that far ahead, but I could definitely see us moving in that direction." He leans in, pressing a kiss to my cheek. "I didn't know you spoke so highly of us."

He looks at me as if Daith did him a favor, spilling my true feelings for me and giving him hope for a future that will never exist. Irritation floods me as Daith backs me into a corner, but instead of becoming a flight risk, I straighten my back, cutting my eyes at him. *Game on motherfucker.*

"You know me. I can't help but brag that I snagged such a great man." I lean in, pressing my lips to Bryce's, taking a moment to draw it out, slipping my tongue between his lips, moaning softly. "You take such good care of me. No one could ever compare."

Bryce's eyes ignite with a fire that I know will be hell to extinguish, but that's a battle for another moment. I hate myself for feeding into this, knowing I'm stringing him along when I was just handed the perfect opportunity to come clean, as awkward and painful as that would have been to do in public.

"Y'all are absolutely adorable," Malia says, followed by a small squeak of what sounds like pain.

Jealousy briefly flickers in Daith's eyes as he clears his throat, leaning back in his chair. "Speaking of taking care of you, I'm so glad he took *such good* care of you last night on the edge of that cliff. You really had me worried. Those screams were so loud." The way his gaze lingers on me for just a second too long, waiting for my reaction, makes the tension almost unbearable.

I swallow hard. Okay, so that's how we're going to play this?

Bryce turns to me, concerned as he looks me over. "What happened last night? Are you okay?"

Yes, you dunce. I was more than okay at that moment. I was... liberated. Right now, I'm feeling a bit like a rabid dog about to rip someone's face off, and Bryce's inability to catch social cues is going to push me over the edge.

"Were you there?" Bryce asks, turning to Daith who is smiling like a fool.

"No, he wasn't Bryce," I say, glaring at Daith while trying to keep my face impassive. "I slipped and was close to falling over the edge. Luckily a man I barely know came."

Daith's smile widens. "Yes, he did. Hard."

"Pardon?" Bryce says, pinching his brows.

"Hard and fast. Wasting no time or effort saving her from the fate that was so close to consuming her," Daith says, attempting to save himself, still leaving it wide open for obvious interpretation. "I apologize. I must have gotten the story mixed up."

62

"Truly traumatizing. Never want to experience that again," I say, turning to Bryce. "Sorry I didn't tell you sooner. I'm fine."

The worrisome crease on his forehead disappears as the waitress comes to take our order. I order first and excuse myself to the restroom, desperate for some air.

I shut the door behind me and walk to the sink, gripping the edge, staring at my flushed cheeks in the mirror. I can't breathe, the air is too thick, the lies and tension palpable. My walls are crumbling. He's walking right through them, as if they never existed. I laugh to myself. Of course, there was nothing I could ever do to convince myself not to let him in. Not to cave the moment he told me he wanted me. The words I've waited to hear for years.

Before I can finish gathering myself, the door opens. I don't turn, knowing it's him, his familiar presence filling the small room instantly. He locks the door with a click, the sound echoing through the space.

I tense, my breath catching as he moves to stand behind me. His hands brush my thighs, and I watch in the mirror as he watches his controlled movements lightly dragging up to my hips. My body reacts before I can stop it, the intensity of his hands on me too much to ignore, bringing me right back to last night.

It's as though my entire being is drawn to him, pulled by something deeper, something beyond logic or reason.

"You're playing games you can't win, baby," he whispers, his warm breath brushing my neck, sending heat rushing over my skin, settling between my thighs. A soft kiss touches the base of my neck, and I suck in a breath. "Stop pretending you don't want this." Hands grip my waist, spinning me to face him. "Stop running."

They pull my body flush against his, his breath brushing against my skin as he lowers his voice. "If you don't end it with him, I'll end it for you. He doesn't get to have what is mine."

Reaching up, he brushes a lock of hair behind my ear, his fingers lingering too long, and my chest aches hearing his claim on me.

My heart pounds in my chest and my ears ring as I stare back at him, putty in his hands. I nod.

There's no escape. Not from him. Not from this.

"I will. Tonight."

He steps into me, pressing my back against the sink, pushing a leg between mine, feeling so fucking good, heightening the need to have him.

"That's my good girl."

I groan inwardly. No matter how many times he says that it will never stop making me want to suck his soul out of him through his dick.

You know, why the fuck not?

I place my hands on his cheek, looking up at him with doe eyes as I force him back a step. He gives me that inch and I hike my dress up, sinking to my knees in front of him. Reaching up, I flick his belt open, dragging his pants down to his thighs. His dick stands at attention for me, staring me right in the face. My jaw clenches and I salivate at the anticipation of having him in my mouth. His lips part as he peers down at me, letting a small gasp slip softly into the air between us as I wrap my hand around his shaft.

"Say my name," I say before licking up his length and taking him deep. I wrap my lips around him, sucking as I pull up and use my hand to work him.

"Fuck," he whispers, groaning low, full of hunger, gently placing his hand on the back of my head, digging his fingers into my curled hair.

I work him at a steady pace, keeping my eyes on him as I suck him deep, gagging on his length as he hits the back of my throat. I bob my head, keeping him deep, his grip on my hair tightening, but he doesn't force me, letting me stay in control.

His eyes roll, and his head falls back feeling the same pleasure I am. Pussy aching, I proudly show him how much I want him.

"Laurel," he groans, looking back down at me. "You take me so fucking good."

You're damn right I fucking do. My eyes water as I grin, holding him down my throat until I can't take it anymore, then I suck him fast, working my hand at the same pace. I wrap my other hand around his balls, squeezing them gently, and they tighten, letting me know he's close. I keep that pace until his breath comes fast and short and he spills into my mouth.

His eyes gleam, watching as his cum paints my open mouth, my hand slowly working it out of him. I close my mouth, swallowing him down, going in for another taste. He jolts at the contact, and I pull him from my mouth with an audible pop, pulling another spasm from him.

He tucks himself back in his pants and sinks to his knees, mirroring me. "The things I would do to you if they weren't waiting for us right now," he says, wiping my chin.

"Since when has someone else's needs kept you from doing what you want?" I ask, silently begging him to do every filthy thing he can think of to me.

He grins. "Never. But I want to leave you wondering."

I take his hand, pulling it between my legs, running his finger over my soaked panties, pushing them to the side, and sinking his finger deep inside me.

He watches in awe as I pull it out and direct it to his mouth, running it over his tongue that he holds out for me.

"Then get a taste of me, wonder how I'll be satisfying myself tonight. I want to see you kiss her with me on your tongue."

He sucks my finger and I stand in front of him, straightening my dress. "Get out. This is the lady's room, you perv."

I turn away from him to fix my makeup, focusing on that so I don't have to watch him leave. Otherwise I'd likely pull him back the second he turned the lock and fuck him right here on the bathroom floor, not caring who heard. What is self-control? I want to have his fucking babies.

I wait a few minutes, finishing the final touches to hide the fact that I just did something very naughty in the bathroom. As I walk back to the table with slow and steady steps, the weight of my decision settles inside me.

Bryce sits there, completely unaware, and though we have only ever been something to pass the time, for him, I know it's been more. He's made that clear, and after tonight's earlier conversation, I've given him false hope. I'm going to look like a real bitch but doing it later doesn't end in a win for anyone. It's time for me to be selfish and do something for me, consequences be damned.

I can feel the shift inside me—the undeniable truth that despite our past and the many ways this can end in a broke heart, I am going to give Daith everything.

Bryce looks up as I sit down, his smile easy, his hand reaching out to mine. I give him a half-smile, before preparing to start eating to avoid conversation. But my eyes quickly shift to Daith who appears to be completely lost in Malia, adoring eyes, laughing easily as she talks low, only for him to hear. Despite knowing his game, I can't fight the jealousy roaring inside of me. Every minute spent here, doing this, and not being in his arms—in his bed, feels like wasted time.

"Are you okay?" Bryce asks, his voice soft, eyes scanning my face with concern that makes my chest tighten. He's such a sweet man, but my thoughts are more clear than ever. I look at him, and for a moment, I think about ending this here and now to give Daith the satisfaction. But I tuck the words away, deciding Bryce deserves more than the humiliation ending this now would cause him.

"Yeah," I say, brushing my dress down, sliding back into my chair.

"You look like you've been crying," Bryce whispers as he leans closer. Daith and Malia talk softly, giving us a false sense of privacy. Bryce's question fades to the back of my mind as Daith takes Malia's face in his hands and leans in, kissing her deep, appearing full of passion. The green monster inside me grows another head and I want so badly to ask her how my pussy tastes. I clench my thighs as he releases her, casting me a quick knowing glance.

I quickly turn back to Bryce and the concern on his face. He's utterly clueless and an unexpected pain comes to the surface, threatening to pool in my eyes. I hate this, so much.

"Actually, I'm not feeling well," I say, needing to get the hell out of here.

Bryce pinches his brows, glancing at my untouched meal.

"I'm so sorry. I must be coming down with something," I say, gently pushing my plate away from me, despite the raging apatite I have.

"Okay, I'll take you home," Bryce says, standing from the table.

"Sorry to cut this short, everyone," I say, gathering my purse and standing. I place a hand on my stomach to sell it, for no one's benefit but Bryce's.

"Oh, not problem. I'll cover this," Daith says, standing from the table to shake Bryce's hand.

"It was a pleasure meeting you. Let's do this again when she's feeling better," Bryce says politely, holding Daith's hand for longer than necessary. He grimaces slightly, Daith no doubt squeezing his hand.

Daith speaks directly to me, eyes gleaming with filthy promises. "See you soon, Laurel."

I stay silent the entire ride back to my apartment, trying to get my words in order. I stare at Bryce's hand resting on my thigh, rubbing soothing lines with his thumb. Closing my eyes to pass the time, I pray to God I don't have to quit my job after this. The car stops and my eyes pop open to the driver door shutting. Bryce rounds the car, opening the door for me, helping me out before walking me to the door like the gentleman he is.

He shifts awkwardly, hands shoved in his pockets, trying to mask the tension that has settled in the space between us as we stand by my front door.

"Thanks for tonight," I say softly. As the words leave my lips, my heart begins pounding, a strange mixture of relief and guilt filling my chest.

He shifts on his feet, a hesitant smile tugging as his lips, though his eyes seem to search mine for something. "I had a great time," he says. "You're looking better."

I inhale deeply, steadying myself as I rip off the band aid. "We need stop seeing each other."

His smile drops and his blank stare is haunting. "I don't understand. Tonight, you said—"

"I was trying to be polite," I admit. "Daith knew that. He was just." I stop, deciding not to get into his twisted sense of humor.

I shake my head slightly, keeping my gaze low. "I'm into someone else, and you know that me and you, we're just fun."

The words hang in the air, almost too heavy to bear as I watch his confused expression turn to hurt. "I wanted more with you."

I nod, not wanting to say the words.

His posture shifts as he begins to understand. "But I'm not what you want."

"You are a great guy, Bryce. I care about you, I really do. I just—" I fight back tears as his face turns impassive, shutting me out. "I can't string you along, knowing I'll never be on the same page."

He steps back, running a hand through his hair as he processes the blow to the chest.

"I want us to stay friends, but I understand if you can't," I say, filling the uncomfortable silence.

"What was tonight?" he says quietly, his voice more vulnerable now. "If you knew you didn't feel the same, why let me take you on a date?"

My chest tightens, guilt overtaking everything inside me again. "Daith wanted to meet you." My voice is barely above a whisper, realizing how shitty that sounds.

Bryce doesn't say anything at first, just looks at me in disappointment and disbelief. Then after a long beat, he nods. "That's who you want. A man who is already taken?"

I swallow, not wanting to explain any more. I'll take that hit if that's the way he needs to see it. Paint me in a bad light to hate me. I can accept that.

He gives another small nod, as if he's accepted it. "Classy, Laurel."

My chest stings, but I deserve it, even if not for the right reason.

With a final, quiet sigh, he steps back. "I'll see you around, I guess," his tone flat, before he turns and walks away.

I watch him go for a moment before slipping inside my apartment, pressing my back to the closed door. I take a deep breath. Now, I get to face whatever is waiting for me.

CHAPTER 12

LAUREL

I sit on my bed in sweatpants, wearing the same soaked panties, staring at my phone. I've waited for a call or text from him for two hours, and now not knowing what he's doing has my insecurities rising. I hate this feeling. It's old and familiar. He knows I'm waiting. Questioning everything. That's the kind of game we play.

I try to talk myself down, try to force myself to believe things are different now that we are older. He's not going to disappear after being inside me, after digging his scythe into my heart. The same way he used to, pretending it didn't mean anything, like I didn't see the way his breath caught when I bit his lip, or how he looked at me in those moments. But I know what I saw. I felt it. It's different this time.

So much is different this time.

Fuck this!

I tap my phone nervously, my thumb hovering over the screen as I try to figure out what to say, hoping I can trust his words he so beautifully spilled to my needy heart.

I need him tonight—to feel the pull between us again. To feel the security and finality of being in his arms. He doesn't realize how deep beneath his skin I already am, but I'll let him think he's got the upper hand. For now.

Without warning, my mind wanders, and it's Reaper's masked face that fills my thoughts. The night in the alley replays. His hands on my body, his weight pressing into me, the smell of whiskey. Though it wasn't the first time I had been close to one of them. I have pictures of them, dozens, maybe more. I've been feet away, but nothing as exhilarating that night.

My thoughts pause. What am I saying?

Daith.

I type the words quickly, pressing send before my mind loses sight of the game at hand.

Laurel: Any guesses on how I got myself off?

I stare at the screen, watching the little dots blink as he begins typing, a small amount of victory exploding in my chest.

Daith: Something that isn't nearly as satisfying as what I could've given you

I grin, quickly typing my reply.

Laurel: Trick question. I haven't yet... Come over?

His next response takes longer than the first, and when it comes through, my chest caves.

Daith: As much as I'd love to be buried between your legs, I have something I need to take care of. Soon though.

The words hit me harder than I want to admit. And I read them again, hoping I'm missing something, but it's clear. He's not coming, after all that happened tonight. *Are you fucking kidding me?*

I begin typing. "What's so important that you can't make time for me?"

The question feels sharp, like I'm putting my vulnerability on display in a way I don't always do. I erase it, not giving him the satisfaction. Less than 48 hours and he has me right back where I was five years ago.

My chest hardens as I grit my teeth. I refuse to let him make me feel like that again.

I feel more satisfied with our standing now as I sit in my car, my radio playing low as I clean the gunk from under my nails. Sitting in a dimly lit parking lot a mile from Celeste's house, I wait for Daith to leave. I followed him here from his location he started sharing with me, to my convenience.

A memory of him when we were teens replays in my mind as I grin to myself.

I pull my warm clean clothes from the dryer, my mind replaying the painful events from earlier today. Sitting across from Daith, spilling juice down the front of my shirt, and it seeping down my shorts and into my panties. I waited until everyone was asleep to wash, not wanting to overstep by ruining their normal routine.

"Little Laurel"

I turn to Daith looming in the doorway, bottle of Crown hanging at his side. Intimidating me—even scaring me a little, but that doesn't stop the butterflies. It only excites them more. Something about danger excites me, gives me a thrill that I chase.

He steps into my space and my feet freeze to the floor. His eyes lock on mine, the inch of space between us is electric. My body begs for him to touch me, even just brush my skin to give me something to fuel my fantasies.

"Can I help you finish?"

My mouth parts, his words sinking low in my stomach, feeding into the daydream.

He nods toward the remaining clothes on the dryer next to me before he leans in to grab them. "Bringing these to your room?" I exhale a shaky breath, too scared to move a muscle.

I blink, trying to come back to reality. Of course, the fucking clothes.

I search for a coherent thought anywhere in my brain, but the only thing in there at that moment is his dick. I nod instead.

He tilts his head curiously, looping a thong over his index finger, holding it up between us. "You gonna wear these for me one day?"

The folded laundry I was holding slips through my shaking hands, a few pieces falling to the floor. As I bend to scoop them back up, he stoops with me, tilting my chin up to look at him with a single finger. His cold thumb brushes over the burning skin of my cheek, a smile tilting his lips. Enjoying how easily he flusters me.

"So good." His smile turns to a pout "Shame," he says reminding me once again that I am inexperienced and shy, unlike his adventurous and well sexually educated self.

That's what I feel. Shame. Shame that I'm not everything he wants, shame that I want it so desperately.

*I stand, and he sets my panties on top of the clothes in my arms.
"Little Laurel, wanting things she can't have."*

My best friend's brother looked at me like I was a stray puppy, and I
looked at him like I would worship at the altar of his being. Given the chance
now, I still would.

I am. Every day.

I groan, sinking lower in my seat. Even with the power I have now. He
created me, so in a way he still won and that really grinds my fucking gears.

Just as I'm about to change my mind on that alone, I see him speed
by, tucked low on his bike and I quickly revert

I start the car and follow. My fingers gripping the steering wheel a
little too tight as I trail him, keeping a gap between us. The streetlights cast
long shadows on the pavement, but I can see him clearly, his form cutting
through the night.

I get onto the highway, tracking him with my eyes as he guns it,
weaving in and out of traffic before taking an exit and heading down a back
road. I kill my lights to avoid drawing attention as he turns again. I round the
same corner a minute later, and he's off his bike and walking toward the back
door of a sketchy bar. I've never been on this side of town, and for good
reason.

Curiosity gets the best of me as I pull my camera from my purse and
snap a picture of the bar, catching him just as he enters.

The cool night air washes over me as I step out of my car cautiously,
suddenly wishing I had worn something warmer than sweats and a T-shirt. I
tuck my keys into my pocket and hold my hand in my purse, wrapped around
my gun. Knowing I won't get in the back door, I go through the front, flashing
my ID and a smile. I head to the bar, taking an empty stool, spinning around to
look into the crowd.

"What'll it be, sugar?" an older woman says from behind the bar.

"Nothing. I won't be here long. Just looking for someone," I say,
glancing over my shoulder at her. Her bright red lips and over exaggerated
blush compliment her bright eyes and blonde hair done up in a curly bun.

Turning back, I search the ocean of people, not seeing him and my
eyes wander up the stairs to a door that looks to be off limits to general
admission, betting my money he's in there.

"Who you looking for?" the bartender asks, and I spin around, giving her my attention as she cleans a glass.

"He's my..." I search for words to describe our relationship that doesn't make me sound like an obsessed girlfriend.

What I think about saying is... I'm here looking for a man that I'm totally in love with, only he doesn't know I followed him here. He's been recently released from prison, so I'm slightly concerned with what he does in his free time. Who he talks to. What he is getting himself into that he doesn't want me to know.

But that would be a lie.

I blink.

Oh my God. I'm an obsessed stalker.

"He's just a friend but actually." I swallow, suddenly feeling gross and embarrassed. "This was a mistake." I move to stand but her eyes are no longer on me, looking past me, and something in her eyes has my gut churning.

"Is he about six-foot, sexy jawline, eye patch?"

I swallow hard, my heart nearly falling out of my ass before a warm hand lands on my waist, and he leans into my neck.

"Thought so," the woman mumbles with a grin, walking away as she continues to clean glass.

"You think I can't sense the moment you walk into a room?" he asks, sending chills down my spine.

I spin on the stool, tilting my head up to look at him. "I, uh—"

He grins, grabbing the bar behind me, leaning further into my space. His gelled hair is disheveled. I instantly flood with jealousy, wondering if it was Malia that caused it.

"Get lost on your way to bed?" He pauses, drawing out my torture, letting his gaze shift down to my lips. "Or did you come to chase down that satisfaction?"

I get lost in the heavy energy surrounding him for only a minute, then I push past him and rush back toward the doors. What was I thinking? Needy and obsessed is not the look I want to have these days. I need to prove to him I am not the same Little Laurel he left behind, and right now, I look just like her.

I rush through the front doors, the cool night air stinging my skin as I try to shake off the frustration simmering inside me. The sounds of laughter and chatter fade behind me, but the tension in my chest doesn't disappear.

I keep walking, faster now, hoping the distance between us will give me some space to breathe, to think and get my emotions in check. I can feel the heat of the emotions building up inside, the way they threaten to spill over and turn ugly, and I hate it.

"Laurel, wait up," he calls, his voice softer than I expected, but there's an edge to it, a sense of urgency that catches me off guard.

I stop, one hand on my car door, and my chest tightens as I feel him draw closer.

"Why are you running off after coming all this way?" he asks, his voice low but direct. He's close, the wind blowing his scent around me, but I keep my back to him, knowing I'll fall apart if I turn around before I can breathe. There's concern in his tone, but I can hear the frustration under it, like he's trying to figure out what's going on inside my head.

I take a shaky breath, finally turning to face him. "I'm embarrassed," I say, my voice sharper than I intend. I didn't have a plan, but him spotting me instantly leaves me empty-handed and looking like a child throwing a tantrum.

There's a pause, his expression unreadable for a moment before he steps forward, his eyes searching mine.

"I like that you are the way you are, baby." He moves in closer. "Obsessive. Needy." He inhales, and his face softens ever so slightly. "I'm not avoiding you, and the only reason we aren't fucking until the sun comes up right now, is because I have some loose ends to tie up and you don't need to be anywhere near it." Ease settles over me and I let out a breath, visibly relaxing, though I still wonder what kind of trouble he has himself in. "I'm keeping you safe. Can you let me do that, hard head?"

"Yes," I whisper, relenting with a soft smile. I sharpen my eyes at him. "Could you just say that next time? You come back and drop a bomb on my life. You can't leave room for doubt," I say, irritated at the insecurities he brings out in me. I slam my hands into his chest, but his tall frame doesn't budge. "You make me crazy! Fuck!"

He grins, eye glimmering. "I like crazy," he says, his hand going to my waist, fingertips digging into my back just enough to make my heart skip a beat and something darker in me is tempted to step out of the shadows.

"Are you in trouble?" I ask, letting my curiosity climb out of its box a little more.

He leans in, his mouth a breath away from mine. His tongue darts out, flicking my lip and my stomach flips. "I am trouble."

I want to offer to help, but I stay silent, letting him have his way. Deciding I'll never leave if I don't move now, I open my car door and toss my purse in, breaking the bubble surrounding us.

"Oh, and keep your gun loaded if you're gonna chase trouble. Having an empty chamber defeats its purpose."

I narrow my eyes at his accurate assumption. I don't carry it loaded. I've always been scared it will go off by mistake.

"Goodnight, Daith," I say, dismissing his comment playfully.

He leans in, grabbing my cheek, pressing his lips to it, kissing me gently. "I missed you too."

My lips turn up in a grin as I slide into my car, the door shutting softly, a single tap of his hand against the glass before he's gone. Just like that, he sends me on my way, smoothing things over while quietly whispering for me to mind my own business...

And I obey whatever he wants, blindly.

DAITH

As soon as she's gone, I head back inside to the upper level of the dive bar to resume my meeting. I watch Skid closely, noticing the way she tenses, but it's only for a second before her mask falls back into place.

She's good at hiding her emotions, but the mention of CHAOS obviously has her on edge.

"She followed you?" Skid finally asks, her voice steady, but there's a sharpness to it that I don't miss. She doesn't entirely approve of my antics.

I take a long sip from the drink in front of me, savoring the strong burn as it goes down. "As I predicted. She's in deep. She even shared my location with herself when she thought I wasn't paying attention." I find amusement in that, partially because she should know better, and partially because she is trying so hard to be non-cholent about her need to be in my business. It's adorable really, and I think I prefer it. "Oh , and Felix broke into her apartment to set up while we were on our first date. How romantic of me, huh?"

"Are you sure you want to do this with her?" she asks, looking up from her laptop, concern clear on her face. "You are going to get her killed, Daith. If this is CHAOS, they aren't going to approve of you bringing someone else in when you give them enough shit to deal with. Not to mention the Reaper's standing on women."

I set the glass down with a soft clink but my gaze hardens. "I'm not here for your approval."

Skid holds my eyes for a long moment before she relents, tucking her empathy back in where it belongs.

"What do you have?" I ask, pulling out a cigarette.

She doesn't speak right away, as if she's weighing her words, choosing them wisely now. "No one I can find has a connection with CHAOS. I ran everything you asked, and nothing." She turns her computer to face me, the privacy screen blocking anyone else from seeing the blueprints staring back at me. "But moving on to you asking about his imports and exports, I found this. He's got an entire room dedicated to storing something he doesn't want found. Heavy security and surveillance. Retinal scanners and steel doors that lock from the outside. He had this added during the renovations and there is no trace of it in the city's building records. I can't even tell where it's at."

My curiosity peaks. Whatever he's moving is big, and it's something I want my hands on. I don't like other kids having better toys than me.

"I'm still digging on the kills. Something isn't sitting right with me. What I think, is that you pissed off CHAOS with your unapproved kills and now they are out for blood. I think they are trying to frame you for more than are rightfully yours to justify a sweep."

Someone is killing with my name on it so they can take me out without repercussions. Plausible, but not probable. CHAOS likes to keep me tucked away for those jobs they need a wild card. Someone who won't gag at the thought of shitting in someone's mouth and then ripping their guts out to see how it looks on the inside. They look the other way as long as I clean up my messes. And I always do.

"How are the scenes?" I ask, idly running my finger along the rim of my glass as I think.

"Spotless. You would think this was ours. Your style, Felix's clean-up job. It's nearly perfect." My brows pinch. If CHAOS was wanting to have a reason for a sweep, they would make me look messy, not just add more unapproved kills. It doesn't make sense.

"You need to be more careful," she says, giving me a pointed look. She's been my adviser and sounding board for years, for good reason, though she lets the lines of our relationship blur occasionally.

"You dumped a body in a factory meat grinder and shut down an entire corporation one time." I roll my eyes sarcastically, but she doesn't find the same amusement.

"You're not understanding." She glances around the room, making sure we're not overheard. When she speaks again, it's quieter, more deliberate. "This isn't about human meat found in the city's weenies."

Her computer chimes, drawing me out of my thoughts. Her eyes widen and she leans in closer, reading whatever it is that has her entire body language changing. "There was a CHAOS member killed tonight." Her eyes shift up to mine. "Malia."

What the fuck?

"They wouldn't kill their own to..." I think out loud. They are trying to make me look rogue. Disobedience within an organization that attempts to organize and profit off of recruited criminals is one thing, but for one of us to kill a higher up. That's a death sentence.

"I'm going to look into Malia, but if you are on the hot seat, you need to be very careful with the bodies you drop. Even if we kill whoever they sent out here, they will just send another until they have enough to execute you."

I inhale a long drag of my cigarette, blowing the smoke above my head. She's right. CHOAS has a disposable army and if they have decided to end me, there is nothing I can do to stop that. Criminals working for criminals. An injustice is bound to happen.

I exhale slowly. "So what do you suggest?"

She shrugs, a nonchalant expression crossing her face, but I can see the flicker of uncertainty in her eyes. "You keep moving, keep playing the game. But remember, you're not the only one on the field. They will show themselves eventually and you better be ready. Either you bring in their man and spin it on them, or you run."

Either I beg a corrupt government of criminals to have mercy on me with a trial, or I spend the rest of my life as a ghost.

I don't particularly care for either of those options.

"I have a date. I need to go. Stay safe."

CHAPTER 13

I watch as she enters the apartment after finally having her landlord come unlock her door. A quick sleight of hand allowed me to change out her house key and a signal jammer kept her stranded outside her front door until I was ready for her.

The moment the door clicks shut behind her, I lean in, feeling that familiar rush of anticipation. She doesn't see me, not yet. But she will. She's a smart girl and watching her, unaware, is only half the fun. I want her to know.

Her tired eyes droop as she goes through her normal routine. Keys on the hook, lock the door, drop her purse on the counter. "Today is not my fucking day," she grumbles. Then she stops, scanning the space. I grin as her eyes wander to the thermostat.

The heater is off. She's already starting to sense something is wrong. She moves to check it, her brows pinching in confusion.

Slowly, she makes her way further into her home. Her steps a little slower now, cautious, as if she's already beginning to doubt the safety of her surroundings. Her fingers twitch, eyes flicking to the hallway as the discomfort creeps up her spine, gripping around her chest.

The anticipation inside me tightens as she moves into her bedroom. It's like watching someone open a gift you bought them. Except instead of happy tears and smiling faces, you're hoping to terrorize them.

When her foot crosses her bedroom door threshold, she freezes. I can feel the sharp intake of her breath, the way her body tightens as she takes in the wall that has my poetic work scrawled across the eggshell white paint in her favorite red lipstick. An hourglass sitting at the end of my words written just for her. Our calling card—the mark of a Reaper.

"IM ALWAYS WATCHING."

Her pulse spikes, her unease visible from this distance. She's scared. I can see it in the way her body stiffens, the way she backs up a step like she's expecting something to jump out at her.

But then, her eyes flicker, and I see something else as her gaze falls to the picture I had Felix leave on the bed. A photo of us, clothes missing, lost in a moment as she let me fuck her close to death. Her back is pressed against mine, my arms wrapped around her chest, covering her from Felix's camera. From the angle, her camera is visible, hanging from my bike, and I appreciate that sense of irony.

She looks at the photo, holding it between her fingers with the tiniest tremor. She's scared, but there's a strange fascination. A curiosity.

Her breath catches in her throat, and I can almost hear her thoughts—*He's been in here. A Reaper was in my room. What does he want? Why hasn't he killed me?*

Her body tenses like she wants to bolt, but her feet don't move. She's trapped between fear and... something else. She doesn't want to admit it, but I know she's aware of the rush she gets from the hunt.

She glances around the room again, her eyes slowly moving to the windows, the door, the closet, wondering if someone is still here with her. But she's alone. Except for me, of course. I'm right here, hidden behind the lens, watching every second.

She takes a few unsteady steps forward, her eyes never leaving the photo, chest rising and falling a little quicker now. She stands frozen, her fingers still resting on the edge of the photo, staring at it like it might reveal a secret. Then she flips it over.

"STAY AWAY FROM HIM."

The realization settles deeper into her, her hand flying to her mouth. Fear. Not for herself, but for the man she loves.

Her fingers begin typing on her phone and she pulls up my contact.

DAITH. With a tiny pink heart next to it.

Her thumb hovers over the green call button, but as her eyes flick back to the writing on the wall she hesitates. I pull out my phone, finally ready to play, sending her text from my burner.

Restricted: Good. You're learning.

Her eyes widen as the restricted number crosses her screen and she slowly lifts her head. I can feel the suffocating tension through the screen as her eyes scan the room before focusing on the small camera above her bedroom door. She looks right at me.

Hi'ya, baby.

"Hello?" she calls out, like every horror movie ever, as if the man hunting her is going to pop out and say "hey."

Restricted: Hi, baby.

Her eyes drop to the phone then back up to the camera.

"Oh, my God," she gasps, running into her bathroom.

She comes back a moment later with a step ladder and what looks like a nipple pasty. She climbs up putting her face inches from the camera and I prop my head on my hand, adoring her for the last minutes before this camera gets covered. She didn't take it down, leaving the audio intact for me, along with the microscopic camera I hid on her TV and the access I get through her computer monitor facing her bed.

But I play along, letting her think she's protected part of her privacy and successfully cut off my eyes.

"Why are you watching me?" she asks, voice shaking but laced with anger.

I switch to the feed from the camera on the TV, watching her pace back and forth in front of her queen bed.

Restricted: I like you. I don't like people often.

Sure if "like" means completely obsessed to an unhealthy level that leads to completely going off the rails if I can't have you. Yeah, I like you, Laurel.

"What do you want from me?" she asks, falling to sit on her bed, chewing on the side of her lips anxiously.

Restricted: You're guts as a necklace and your wet cunt on my face. Not necessarily in that order, but I wouldn't mind.

I send it before I register that she may not find the humor in that. I quickly type again.

Restricted: Kidding. I want to take you on a date. Isn't that what sane people do?

Her eyes widen in disbelief, but she chuckles quietly, so low the camera audio almost misses it, but her laugh is a distinct sound I could recognize in a crowd full of people.

"You're not sane. You kill people." I let that sit in the air, echoing in her ears. "Do you plan on killing me?"

The thought has crossed my mind, but knowing that's not the most effective way to have her fall in love with a Reaper... again... I lie.

Restricted: No. Sociopaths are capable of having relationships. I'm trying something new.

A knock sounds on her door and she jolts. Slowly, she gets up, hands trembling as she walks to her front door. She moves out of view as she leaves her room and I listen intently as another sharp knock sounds on the door. She curses under her breath, letting the anticipation get the best of her, making her see ghosts in the shadows. I move to the feed in her living room, another camera she'll never find.

"Please don't kill me," she says lowly, talking to herself, whipping her hands on her pants before she grips the doorknob.

The door creaks as she slowly opens it before a man's voice comes through my speaker. "Are you Laurel Wittington?" a male voice asks and I confirm it's a delivery man.

"I am," she says, worry lacing her voice.

"Sign here."

She carefully reaches through the door to scribble her name with a shaky hand, her eyes glancing around cautiously. I chuckle to myself, thoroughly enjoying the jitters coursing through her.

The delivery man, light brown hair, stout build, and left-handed, passes her a large vase of flowers I ordered and quickly disappears.

She locks her arms, holding them as far away from her as possible as she walks quickly to her living room. She sets them down, the glass vase clanging against the metal table. Pulling her shirt up over her nose, she carefully flips the card attached to the lilies.

FROM YOUR FUTURE LOVE. I GET A PHYSICAL REACTION WHEN I'M AROUND YOU.

"What the fuck?" she mumbles, stomping back to her room and grabbing her phone. She types furiously and a moment later, my phone chimes.

"I'm deathly allergic to lilies, prick!" she yells into the camera as I watch the GIF of a middle finger play on my screen.

I lose it, laughing hysterically as I watch her rush to her bathroom to wash her hands three times, then even harder as she begins to wipe her entire body and home with sanitizing wipes, doing everything she can to prevent the hives that would coat her entire body.

Restricted: I know

I type back through the tears. The best part about this is that despite the fact she will turn into a balloon around them, she thinks lilies are one of the prettiest flowers to exist, second to Indian Blankets.

Restricted: Get the joke?

She stops wiping her phone then promptly throws it down on her bed and I lose it again.

Restricted: Is this a bad time to ask if I can see you for real?
In a consensual way.

Reluctantly, she picks it back up, clearly enjoying this as much as I am, even if she doesn't want to admit it. She hasn't called the cops. She hasn't blocked my number, not that it would do any good. She is playing hard to get, but it's so clear, that Laurel, for all my intents and purposes, is just as fucked up as I hoped she was.

She scoffs, typing out another text, as if anything she said would truly stop me, though I am more than half convinced that she would enjoy that too.

"Are you insane? Stay away from me, you fucking freak! Whatever you think this is, is over."

But the way she looks back at her wall and decides to leave the camera intact, I know she doesn't want that. Not really.

Oh, I'm so excited. She does want to play with me!

What a great ending to a bad day.

CHAPTER 14

LAUREL

The neon lights of the club pulse as I walk to the dressing room, the low hum of the music vibrating against my skin. It's another long night, leaving my feet aching and the longing for my bed outrageous. The familiar sound of heels clacking on the polished floor echoes as I pass the stage, catching a glimpse of the usual crowd—half-drunk businessmen, lower bracket men blowing their entire paycheck, and groups of boys that still get giddy from seeing a pair of titties.

But pushing through the dressing room curtains, my mind isn't on my job or anything around me. It's on the man that was in my home. The one threatening to do the unimaginable to Daith, just because he placed some claim on me in some criminal and obsessive way.

The text keeps replaying in my head. He was in my home, possibly days before I realized it. I can imagine him watching, listening to me while I touched myself.

Oh my God.

And not to mention, he ruined my favorite lipstick. I had to buy a new tube before work, because I refuse to use any other brand or color. My deep red lip is my signature look. It's what makes me Scarlette.

But that aside, the worse thing is... I think I like it. More than a little.

I slide into my vanity chair and stare at the picture I took of his note on my wall and slide it into the corner of my vanity mirror, adding it to the other random images I've taken.

I stare at my reflection in the mirror, the dim lighting casting shadows on my face, though the faint rash on my throat and cheeks is still visible. Not only can those stupid flowers kill me, but they are ugly as hell.

I groan, doing my best to cover the pink skin. My fingers move with practiced ease, applying the makeup with precision, each stroke intentional. I roll my lips, smearing the deep red lipstick in perfectly before looking back at myself. I tilt my head, watching my eyes, staring deep into the window of my own soul, finding swirls of black smoke wrapping around the small bright ball in the center.

My bright green eyes do little to portray the darkest parts of myself. To the onlooker, I am nothing but a sweet girl playing dress up. The perfect honey trap.

My eyes slide down my body. I adjust the straps of my costume and run a thumb over the soft fabric—a soft purple lace number that clings to my curves and accentuates my green eyes. It's just another outfit, just another part of the job, but tonight, it feels different. Has the Reaper watched me dance? Watched me undress? Touched me while I was sleeping the way Daith used to? Suddenly, every flaw is under a microscope and my every second observed and evaluated in a test I don't know the answers to.

Some sick and fucked up part of me finds that... intoxicating. I like the attention, the way it makes me feel worth more. I want to be perfect for him, and that feels like a drug in itself.

The thought of him, one of the most powerful men in this city, watching over me. Toying with me, fantasizing over me. Of all the women he could have chosen in this club, or in this entire state... he chose me.

He was careful and attentive. He could have broken the door or window, stayed and waited for me to get home, even followed me to Celeste's house. But instead, he taunted me, wanting me to know he's there, forcing me to wait for the next moment he acts. Like some twisted foreplay.

I should be terrified and repulsed. I should have called the cops. But... I don't want him to stop. I don't have to change who I am or work harder to prove myself to Reaper. For once, someone worthwhile has chosen me.

I stare into my own eyes, deep into my soul, or rather to that dark mirrored face in my head screaming to take over, demanding me to let go and act on the curiosity that is lingering just below the layer of caution. I smile darkly back at myself, realizing that if I lean into Reaper and whatever he has planned for me, Daith will feel the sting of me not choosing him, for the first time. And if I ever get to tell him who, it may just kill him that someone in his playing field snatched me up before him.

"You're no longer in control here, baby. *Welcome to my games,*" I whisper lowly, so many ideas rolling my head around the vision of Daith on his knees begging for me to choose him, the same way I wanted to so many times before.

A loud clatter comes from outside the curtain and I shake my head, trying to focus on my job, touching up my makeup, running my red gloss over my lips. I go over my dark eyeliner, making my eyes vibrant, more intense. Inhaling, I steady myself, listening to the music as it shifts to a slower, more seductive song. The beat low and heavy, rattling the wall that connects to the stage. *It's time.*

The curtains pull back and my stage manager pops his head in. "You're on in five.

I nod, already aware.

My body moves to the stage almost on autopilot, but my mind is reeling, shifting from Reaper to Daith, that same dangerous pull tugging at me. As enticing as it is to give him a taste of his own medicine, the pit in my chest is telling me that won't be as easy as I am wishing. Am I stupid for thinking I could ever willingly choose something over him? Daith's danger is branded with something safe and familiar. I know his kind of unpredictable and he would never hurt me. I couldn't promise myself that with this Reaper. But now, one thing that is promised, is Daith's interest in me is going to get him killed if I don't remove the option.

As the lights go down and the music starts, I step into the spotlight, the crowd's eyes falling on me immediately. The beat of the music pulses through my body, my hips swaying with practiced ease. The rhythm pulling me deeper into the performance.

But underneath, in the back of my mind, a war begins, trying to decide what to do. Do I tell Daith the truth and report my stalker to the police, which has proven to have no effect in the past? Or maybe we could outrun death once we piss the Reaper off, and for the first time ever, deny a one what they want.

Or do I obey the Reaper? Leave my love for Daith in the past, and survive by becoming whatever Reaper wants me to be, even if that is a corpse for him to play pretend with. Follow the pull in my chest and dive into the unreasonable intrigue that has lured me to them for years, and keep Daith safe from them.

I turn, my body arching in fluid motions as I move to the ground, the heat of the stage lights warming my skin. The music wraps around me, drawing me deeper into the performance. I tease, glide, and turn, using every inch of the stage, my body flowing as if the music is an extension of me. Every slow roll is deliberate and powerful. The room shifts, the heat building, the energy growing. The stage becomes my world, and I surrender to it, riding the high of the beat, drawing the crowd in deeper. When the music fades, I pause, catching my breath, eyes scanning the crowd with a wide smile before I exit the stage with my hips swaying.

"Scarlette!" I hear my name yelled from the back of the dressing room and my attention sharpens as I try to find the source.

"Scarlette!" someone yells again, sounding more panicked. My walk turns into a sprint once I see Lilly lying on the ground, and my stomach sinks, every previous thought leaving my mind. "She's not waking up!" Crysta pleads while making room for me in the small hallway.

I put my ear near Lilly's mouth, listening for even the smallest of breath sounds, just as I was taught when I started. Relieved at her shallow breath, I stand and scoop her up. "She's barely breathing. We need to get her to throw up." My blood boils knowing exactly what happened. Vic forced her to start working the VIP and gave her something to help her relax, as he has done for all the girls that work up there.

I sit her on her knees in front of the toilet and hold her hair back into a ponytail with one hand while doing my best to hold her upright with my other arm around her chest. "Stick your fingers down her throat," I say, doing by best not to be loud. Vic doesn't like seeing or hearing the consequences of his actions.

"What, no. I can't do that." Crysta's eyes nearly fall out of her head at my order, her face twisting in disgust.

"Scarlette, get on the floor! We're short tonight," Danny, yells.

"Do you want her to die?" I grind out with growing irritation. "Put your fucking fingers down her goddamn throat."

Crysta grimaces but obeys, pulling her best friend's slack jaw open more before diving her fingers deep until Lilly starts gagging. Vomit spews out, coating her hand. Lilly gasps, coughing and sucking in air, giving me the indication of survival that I needed before I take the stage.

I check that my hands are clean before fixing my fishnets and turning back to Crysta stroking her friend's back. "What do I do now?" she asks, tears streaking her makeup.

"Get her home. Keep her out of the VIP room," I say, giving her the best general advice I can. I tend to look out for everyone, but this job is every woman for herself. Between the drugs passed around between the sketchy businessmen that practically live here and Vic's ownership, it's easy to get yourself killed.

"Scarlette!" Danny yells in a hushed tone and I cut him a glare.

Not many people here care about anything more than their paycheck and not pissing off Vic. Vic can eat a dick.

"Keep your fucking panties on!" I bark, moving to Danny's side, giving myself another once over.

"Daisy's late. If she doesn't show, you're on again."

I roll my eyes, though the extra pay for those dances are nothing to whine about. Pushing through the curtains, I walk out into the club, lights low, a layer of fog on the floor.

The tables are packed, and more are pouring in by the hour. My face hurts from the plastered smile as I take drink order after drink order. Weaving through the tables, headed for the bar a man to my right whistles to get my attention, waiving his hand for a dance. Despite my better judgement or respect for my job, I jerk my head to side and my mouth opens, frustration pouring out.

"I'm not a fucking dog. Okay, prick?" I snap, glaring at him. His eyes bulge at me and I grimace as I keep walking, realizing it's one of Vic's poker guys.

"Where the fuck is Daisy?" I ask, slamming my tray down on the bar, looking around the club desperately.

"Haven't seen her," Bryce says filling my order, keeping eyes level with the bar. "She didn't show up for her last shift either."

Fuck. With everything going on, I forgot about Bryce. At least he showed up for work. That at least means he doesn't hate me enough to quit. His eyes lift then linger on me long enough to disturb my irritation of having to pick up Daisy's slack. I narrow my eyes playfully, knowing his look all too well, and he gives it back. A weight lifts off my shoulders, knowing we are okay.

"Did she quit?" I ask, trying to ease the tension between us as Dolly steps next to me.

"Not that I've heard. Last weekend everything seemed fine. She was working the VIP room," Dolly says, her eyes dropping low. She's the youngest of us here, only here to save up for college. "She's been making good money. Maybe it's just a night off." And by far the most timid and naïve.

I groan, accepting that Daisy's just blowing off her shift with no warning. Grabbing my tray, I scan over my section, mentally preparing myself for what is left of my shift that's turning into a double.

"Scarlette," Bryce says, and I look over my shoulder. "Drinks tonight?"

My eyes soften. *Don't make me do this again.* "I'm making a rule not to date co-workers anymore. Makes things awkward," I say, taking my tray with a playful smile.

He leans over the bar to whisper in my ear. "No, you just let them eat you out after closing then dump them at your front door."

The amused grin that was forming quickly falls and I pull back to find him smiling mischievously.

"No hard feelings, babe. Just friends work for me. I'm sure one of the other girls would love to take me for a ride. I'm sure my undying love for you will fade eventually," He smirks and I suck my lips between my teeth in a grin and flip him the bird, getting an amused laugh in return.

Plastering my cheeky grin into place and poking my chest out, I step back into the chaos propping my tray on my hip as I make it to one of my usuals.

"Here you go, sugar," I purr sweetly, exchanging his empty glass. He slips an extra five into the waistband of my panties, eyes plastered to my tits as usual.

One of the new girls brushes my shoulder, leaning in to whisper above the music. "There is a very intimidating man staring a hole into your ass." She lifts her brows and smiles. "He just requested you."

I spin around and my heart lurches at Daith standing against the wall with a hungry gaze. Despite my heart beating out of control, I stalk toward him, putting myself in his space. The hair on the back of my neck stands on end, fear conjuring the feeling of someone watching me. Standing in front of him nearly naked feels exhilarating, and the way his eyes stay on my face sends electricity over my skin.

"What are you doing here?" I ask, eyes flicking to his mouth then back to his face. His gaze darkens to something more challenging.

"I told you *soon*. Here I am," he says, and everything in me rattles and shakes, like he unearths everything holding me to the ground. He reaches out, caressing the length of my hair. "You look... edible."

His hand shoots out, landing on my waist, pulling me into him firmly. His cold hand contrasts with my warm skin, and a sigh leaves my lips in ecstasy. I peer up at him, my chest brushing against his jacket.

"We have rules about touching," I say, the enjoyment in my tone completely betraying my words. "You have to pay extra for that."

His lips tilt in a half grin, dangerous and promising. His hand slides down an inch, his fingertips teasing the waistband of my panties.

The lights dim, queuing the next dancer and our stage manager pops out again, whistling at me with his hand in the air. I roll my eyes at his five-minute cue. "I'm covering someone's shift tonight." I run my hands down the front of Daith's jacket, righting it for him as I push out of his hold. "Why don't you stay and watch?"

There's a knot in my stomach that tells me this will inevitably get back to Reaper, even if I don't see him here, however, I can't miss the opportunity to dance for Daith, and just maybe, Reaper will enjoy the little game of resistance.

Turning, I sway my ass as I head backstage and prepare to go on next. I quickly change costumes, thankful Daisy and I are about the same size, and quickly fluff my hair before moving to the stage stairs. The lights go off and I take my place, resting my hand on the pole. My eyes fall shut and my spine straightens. Someone moves in front of me, taking the seat directly in front of my pole, and his voice travels up to me in a whisper. "Dance for me, baby."

My stomach swirls with excitement, my pussy throbbing, his words soaking me. The spotlight comes on and "Diamonds Are A Girls Best Friend" begins pouring from the speakers. In my all-black lingerie with sheer cut outs,

I prance around the pole in my 6-inch heels, swinging a strand of pearls in my hand, living out every burlesque girls' fantasy.

It takes a moment for me to find the strength, but when my eyes finally hold his, everything else disappears. For the next few minutes, it's only me and him. His focus solely on me as I present myself to him in a way I've only dreamed about. He tracks my every move, silent and still, and I dance for only him.

Needing to be closer, I go off routine and move to the edge of the stage. My hands roam my body, and as I drop to my knees in front of him, spreading my thighs wide, mouthing an exaggerated moan.

Then the lights shut off and I'm lost in darkness. My chest heaves as I catch my breath, on such a high I wonder why people do drugs.

He says nothing, and the silence between us is lost in the claps and chatter resuming. He only reaches up, holding a 10 dollar bill out in front of me, but as I reach for it, he snatches it back and wraps his hand around the back of my neck, nearly pulling me off the stage.

"I don't pay for things that are already owed to me."

I swallow hard. Excuse me?

I want to be slightly offended, but if we're going off my math, I'll be naked and shaking my ass in his face for the next decade, and I don't see a problem with that.

But as the very large and intimidating bouncer comes striding over from the front door with a look of death across his face, I'm reminded that Daith has a target on the back of his head.

Right. I don't know how literal Reaper wanted me to take his warning, but my guess is private dances and naked wrestling is probably off the table.

My eyes widen over Daith's shoulder and just as he releases me to turn, the bouncer has one hand around his throat and the other holding a gun to Daith's head.

"No touching, douchebag," he growls, pulling Daith to his feet.

Daith groans with a challenging smile and I silently beg him not to pull his tough guy maniac shit here. "Fuck you, Andre," Daith spits.

Fucking hell.

The mountain of a man pulls the hammer back with his thumb I panic.

"Oh, my God!" I scream, trying to be heard over the music. "He's a friend! He didn't hurt me!" I scramble off the edge of the stage and try to force myself between Daith and this man that looks like his father was half giant. My eyes search for a name tag but I can't find one. Quickly searching my mind, I think I remember someone calling him Josh. Fuck it.

"Josh! Let him go!"

"Yeah, Josh," Daith snorts. "Let me go," he says sweetly, full of sarcasm that only makes the man snarl. Then, he drops him, putting his gun away with a finger in Daith's face. "Watch yourself. Keep your hands off her."

Daith raises his hands in surrender that I know he doesn't honestly mean for a moment. "Yes, dad."

I roll my eyes, narrowing them at the man I adore for some idiotic reason. "You are a pain in my fucking ass." Without another word to him, I rush backstage and wrap my robe around myself, dodging the girls preparing to take the stage next. I look around for Lisa, wanting to ask her if someone else can fill Daisy's slot so I can leave with Daith, despite the guilt looming in my gut. *I have to tell him.* He's got to have some kind of shady connection that could fix this. He's not going to let go of me easily, not now.

Not seeing her at her usual post, I race up the unguarded stairs and check down both ends of the hallway. Groaning, I turn back around. Where the fuck is she?

Just as I'm about to head back down to ask Bryce, glass shatters, coming from inside Vic's office. Unable to resist, I step closer, carefully pressing my ear against the crack. Are they fucking? That might be the most disgusting thing I've seen in the club, but I wouldn't put it past her. Lisa does whatever she's told, no exceptions.

"I don't give a fuck what you want. I have to keep my business running. You get one," Vic says in a hushed and angry tone.

I listen closely, more than interested in his dealings. Vic never takes a call in front of us and is sure as hell secretive about the things he does in his office. The one time I went in, looking for him to get my paycheck, he nearly choked me to death before throwing me out on my ass with a lecture to never open his door again.

"Yes," he says, confirming something I can't hear. "You think if I knew, we would be having this conversation right now?"

A long silence follows, and I begin to worry that he ended the call, sweat forming on my lower back, but the adrenaline of spying on him is exhilarating.

"Yes," he says, more reserved. "I'll have another to you by the end of the week."

Another moment of silence follows before he slams something on his desk, cursing vigorously. Whatever just happened, he's pissed, and apparently, about to be short on whatever stock he's dealing. There's something unsettling about Vic, and the churning feeling in my stomach tells me it's more than drugs.

Rushing back down the stairs blindly as I check over my shoulder, I run straight into Lisa as I hit the bottom step. Her eyes widen.

"What were you doing up there?" she asks, holding a shot glass in her hand.

I snatch it from her, throwing it back. "Uh, looking for you." I look down at the empty glass of tequila. "And this." I inhale deep, trying to catch my breath lodged somewhere deep in my lungs.

"You know the rules. You can't be up there unless it's cleared with me or Vic."

I nod, smiling softly.

"Another one, kid. Thanks," Lisa calls out to the bar. Bryce rolls his eyes at her usual comment, though with Lisa being 50 years old, everyone is a kid to her.

"Anytime, mama," he quips, throwing me a wink before he begins refilling her glass.

"Cutie," Lisa says to no one in particular with more than intrigue shining in her eyes.

"He likes you," I say, teasing. "He likes to be dominated, just so you know. Come on strong, smack his ass or really grip his balls." I make a squeezing motion with my hand and her mouth falls open before her eyes flick to Bryce in shock, though not disinterest.

Bryce, although excellent at what he does, is only a step above vanilla. She's going to scare the shit out of that poor boy, and I can't wait to laugh my ass off. My eyes trail down the bar, landing on Daith sitting next to Serenity.

My amusement fades and I quickly decide to postpone my plan to leave early with him. Then my feet are moving.

I stand to the side, staring at Daith with fire in my veins. I say nothing, letting the uncomfortable silence eat away at the chemistry that was forming.

"You know, Scarlette," he says, putting emphasis on my stage name as he motions toward me.

"Oh, I didn't know you guys knew each other. How do y'all—"

"Walk away."

A crease forms between her brows. Serenity is sweet, naïve, and certainly not Daith's type. I know the game he's playing all too well.

"Rather I ask again nicely or with my hand around your neck, you heard what the fuck I said," I reiterate, sliding into her seat as she moves, doing as she's told.

I quirk a brow at Daith in question and Bryce sets another drink in front of me that I grab greedily, needing more than a single shot to deal with tonight.

"Don't like when people play with your toys?" He smirks. "Me either."

I hesitate, wondering if he knows about Reaper watching me. If he has been stalking me, he probably saw the way my apartment looked, or maybe even saw Reaper there. In my frozen state, he takes the newly filled drink out of my hand and tosses it back before setting it on the bar with a loud clink.

"I needed that," I say defensively, scowling at him, still wondering if he knows about Reaper already. Though my anger, it's almost entirely fabricated and forced.

"I like you feisty," he says, holding the lime out for me. I lean forward, bracing my hands on his thighs, taking it in my mouth, licking his finger as he lets go. His jaw clenches as he watches tentatively as I suck the lime and drop it in the empty cup. I take a page out of his book, getting to my feet and leaning into him.

"You keep pushing my buttons, and I'll rip your other eye out," I whisper. "You owe me a drink," I add, patting him on the chest as I return to the floor, ignoring him the rest of my shift to think.

CHAPTER 15

LAUREL

I grab my bags, done for the night now that we are closing. As I make it to the front, the bouncer doesn't turn to hold the door for me.

"How long are you going to keep this up?" he asks.

"Excuse me?" I snap.

"Be careful what house you play dress up in. Reapers don't write love stories. They write obituaries."

A moment of uncomfortable silence passes between us, and when he has nothing else to say, I shove past him and open the door myself. Annoyance fills me that yet another person is in my business, and I wouldn't put it past Bryce to have said something to him in an effort to keep me safe. My sour face turns to a smile as my eyes meet Daith's the moment I'm outside.

"You're still here?" I ask, adoration clear in my tired voice, though I can't shake the weight in my chest.

Daith looks down at his own body, then back at me. "I am," he says dryly, seeming annoyed at that fact.

"Holy shit, are you going to be a gentleman and walk me to my car?" I ask, clutching my chest.

"Why would I do something like that?" he asks, scrunching his nose. But we both know, that's his normal for me. Even when he had no interest in me, he looked after me, in ways that could easily be seen, not as brotherly, but as genuine love.

He reaches for me as we start walking, fingers brushing mine in that casual, deliberate way he does. It still makes my stomach tighten. "Of course. You're here to put me out of my misery," I say, walking toward my car with him at my side. "Where is your weapon of choice?"

"If I have to endure the hell of humanity, you do too. When I get to leave, I'll take you with me."

I giggle, a tad delusional from sleep deprivation. "How chivalrous."

As we get closer to my car, a shadowed figure steps out from behind it, light shining across his face, revealing his chrome skeleton mask. My steps falter.

Fuck, fuck, fuck.

Daith grips my hand, pulling me with him as we race toward my car. The Reaper sprints into the dark, then his bike revs and is flying down the street in a blur.

Red letters are sprawled across my car window, jagged and dripping. My heart pounds as I read it. "You'll pay for that."

Daith intertwines my fingers in his, and I stare down, focusing on the way his hand feels holding mine so tightly, completely ignoring the way he pulls me with him as he searches around my car.

He bends, letting go of me, picking up a knife left on the ground behind my car. "Isn't this the girl that missed her shift?" he asks, flipping the knife for me to read. *Daisy* is written in marker down the blade, the edge tinged with blood.

I nod, silently moving to the window, running my finger through the words, bringing it to my nose and inhaling, confirming what I already knew.

Daith pulls me into him aggressively. My knees feel weak, but tears don't come. Maybe it's shock, or maybe I didn't know her enough for it to sting. I look up at him, his beautiful eye so round and full of fire.

"What the fuck did you do to get a Reaper's attention?" he asks, his demeanor blazing with anger. Maybe a hint of jealousy mixed with possessiveness.

"You knew?" I ask, needing clarification.

"Of course I knew. Why did you think I showed up here tonight?"

My head is spinning too much to process that right now, much less be offended that he didn't come for *me*. I shake my head, not knowing how to answer. I didn't do anything. *He picked me.*

"Laurel," Daith says sternly.

"I-Nothing. He just... likes me, I think."

"Likes you?" he asks in disbelief.

96

"He wants me to himself. That's all I know."

Daith nearly bursts a blood vessel and my head reels as his rant becomes distant and muffled. Part of me always wondered if Daith had gotten himself into something darker once he went to prison. Him becoming a Reaper had been a lingering thought. Though his reaction tells me, that's not the case and my heart sinks a little bit.

I think part of me had hoped he was playing a prank on me. It seemed like something he would do. But now, sorrow crashes into my chest as I realize it's not him, and certainly not a joke.

Reaper will kill him without a second thought, and I just signed his death warrant.

I say nothing. Nothing to explain that a Reaper has stepped outside of their usual behavior, obsessed with me, because some part of me enjoys it. He sees something in me. Something intriguing. Something Daith never wanted to see until now.

"I'm following you home," he says, pulling my car door open, my mind in a fog and not at all focused on the same urgency that Daith feels.

I watch as he grabs a pink shirt from my car and uses it to wipe the blood from my window, which only smears it. He wraps the knife in my shirt, tucking it in the back of his pants before turning to me.

"Get in the car, Laurel."

"Go home, Daith." I scowl, sliding into my front seat, just wanting to go home.

His jaw tightens, a crease forming between his brows. "You're fucking joking. You-"

"Go. Home."

I turn the engine and leave him standing in the gravel. I don't look back, not because I don't trust him, but because I don't trust myself.

CHAPTER 16

A girl is dead. I slit her throat and used her blood to leave Laurel a message, letting her know I'm coming for her.

One, two, daddy's coming for you.

I can't help but laugh as the words sing themselves in my mind. Luckily, with her relevance to our current job, we were able to get approval for this kill. Considering we are half sure they are trying to kill me, I can only imagine how that phone call went. Two-faced dirty cunts.

Despite my entire empire being at risk, I have to admit, toying with Laurel, putting on this show to test her loyalty to me and self-preservation, is far more fun than I expected it to be. Killing that girl wasn't on tonight's bingo card but through watching the way Laurel acted around her, I could tell she cared for her.

Vic planned on selling Tulip, or whatever the fuck her name was, and I know if Laurel ever figured that out, she would hate me for not doing something about it. Though honestly, I'm half thinking I should have left things alone because the thought of Laurel charging at me with a weapon and tears in her eyes has me leaking pre-cum into my Ralph Lauren underwear.

Come to think of it, this is my first mercy kill. The first that wasn't done for my own pleasure or vendetta. I didn't even keep her eyeballs or shove one of her own body parts down her throat. I bet her thin little lips would have looked so cute with her own foot severed and shove between them. I can almost see the way her throat would bulge awkwardly, like a snake eating something half its size.

Sigh. Laurel may be bad for business. She's making me soft.

I pull my hoodie up further, sticking to the shadows as I follow her on the walk she takes to clear her head. *Such a stupid move, little one.* Taunting me, testing my restraint. She thinks I won't kill her because I haven't, but she doesn't know how much self-control it's taken to leave her breathing each time I have been close enough to satiate that hunger inside of me.

Part of me wants to let her in; force her in. Make her part of my life forever. The other part wants to know what it would feel like to taste her screams. See how thick her blood is and savor it as looks of horror paint her face. I've done it before. Seducing women before I kill them. Fucking them just before I end their life. It's so fucking good, watching their life drain out of them as I cum.

Fear me. It gets me hard.

But with Laurel, I'm conflicted for the first time in my life. Killing her would be cosmic, I can almost taste the pleasure on my lips, but the thought of her no longer being here with me makes my skin crawl. Like the entire world would just stop existing if her and I were not on it together. It's like scratching an impossibly persistent itch but forcing yourself to stop when the pleasure starts mixing with pain as layers of your skin peel off.

She stops, glancing over her shoulder as she pushes her earbuds into her ears, effectively killing one of her senses. Just for me? How sweet of you, Peach.

She takes her time inspecting the shadows, searching for the thing that goes bump in the night. She feels me. She's baiting me.

I'm everywhere, invading her senses, her dreams, every moment of her life.

This is my city. My world. My fucking girl.

Resuming, her head bobs as she walks down the dimly lit sidewalk, her coat wrapped tightly around her. But no gun—no protection. She's doing everything she can to make herself look like the perfect unsuspecting target, but I know her better than that.

I stay behind her, protecting her from anything that's not me, watching her the entire three miles she walks before she stops, a frustrated look on her face. She pulls her phone out of her pocket and disappointedly shoves it back in with a heavy exhale.

Her shoulders are tense as she begins walking back home. I follow in silence, keeping just out of sight until I think she's had enough. Purposely, I create a clattering sound with the drop of my lighter, still sunken deep in the shadows of an alley.

She stops beneath the broken streetlamp that flickers and flashes, illuminating her striking features showing just a dash of fear in the determined pinch of her brows. Her breath hangs in the air, sharp and quick as she looks around.

"I know you're there," she calls out flatly.

There's a challenge in her voice, but it still conveys a question as she doubts the very statement.

Using my personal phone, I call her, wanting to make sure I seem a healthy level of concerned for her safety. She jumps out of her skin, gasping and then cussing low as she fumbles with her phone, denying the call to focus on the Reaper she's baiting.

I step out of the alley and move behind her. Close enough to touch. Close enough to inhale the scent of her and see the relief as she feels me.

"Careful," I murmur near her ear, my voice disguised. "If you keep yelling, someone dangerous might hear you."

She doesn't turn, but she doesn't move away.

"You're the only thing out here that's dangerous and I'm not scared of you," she replies. Her voice is low, controlled. But the edge in it is too fine. She's rattled.

"Clearly. You wanted me to follow you."

Now she turns. Slowly. Eyes searching my mask like she's trying to picture the human behind it. The face of a monster.

"You killed her," she says.

"And that's on you," I reply sternly, hands in my pockets.

"Because of Daith?" she asks as she tries to hide the hurt in her voice.

"He touched you, and you let him stay," I snap, stepping closer. The words burn in my throat. "I warned you. Stay away from him."

"She didn't deserve that. Why not punish me?" she asks with tears forming in her eyes.

I inhale, jaw clenching as I brush the tear away just as it falls. "Are you not hurt?"

She looks away as the realization dawns on her. The thought of physically hurting her makes me sick, so it's others that will receive the punishments that call for such measures.

"So what? I'm just your pet? Expected to push away everything that hurts your fragile little ego and come when called?" she asks sharply.

"Exactly." I purr, loving the sound of that. *Pet.*

My dick jumps as I see it—the flicker in her eyes, the slight parting of her lips. She's angry, but it's not real. She's trying to bury it, but I see the truth.

The thought of being owned by someone like me, being safe with me, it excites her.

"And when will you call?" she asks. "You *ran* when I saw you tonight. You want to control me, you like me, but you won't take me?"

I step in until there's barely a breath between us, ready to tell her a partial lie. "I ran because I didn't trust myself to stay."

Her breath catches, and for a second, we just stare at each other. "Trust yourself to do what?"

"Not kill you. You really pissed me off Peach."

Her heart is pounding. I can hear it, steady and loud.

"I should turn you in. You are sick."

I smile with a tilt of my head. "Then why are we standing here? Why lure me out if I repulse you?"

She swallows, standing a little straighter.

"Do you want to hear the truth?" I ask, voice dropping low. "Or should I lie and say I know you don't want me just as badly as I want you?"

She doesn't move. Her mouth opens, but no sound comes out. Then, finally—"I don't want to want you if that means people I care about keep dying."

I lean in, brushing my finger against her lips, barely a touch. Her breath hitches. Her eyes close.

"They don't deserve you," I whisper. "But I do. I chose you, and I will have you, willingly or not."

When she opens her eyes again, I'm gone, back in the shadows and as silent as death, leaving her with her own convictions.

Still, I follow her home and watch as she pushes through the front door of her apartment and shuts the door softly behind her, locking it. I hear her system arm, and I grin, making myself comfortable as I pull up the live feed from my camera that she hasn't found yet. Though, this one has a less satisfying angle.

I watch her, waiting to play as she disappears into the bathroom. Suddenly I wish I had replaced her bathroom mirror with double-sided glass for a camera, but the anticipation may be even better.

Only ten minutes later, she moves next to her bed, a white towel wrapped around her, and a bun on top of her head. The quality allows me to count the water drops on her shoulder blade. My cock throbs at the thought and I firmly rub it, trying to ease the tension.

She drops her towel, her ass the center of my view, and she takes her time, fishing through her dresser, thinking I can't see her. I sink into the darkness, letting it cover me as I make myself comfortable against a tree. She climbs into bed, forgoing pajamas, letting her hair down before sliding between her sheets.

She inhales and turns her head sharply before inhaling again, deeper this time, trying to get a stronger hit of my cologne I spritzed lightly on the edge of her bed days ago. I've had to be careful not to wear it when Reaper me is near. It would be too easy for her to figure it out. Her brows pinch before she releases the question of Daith being there and lets the scent of me take her back, her eyes closing, a soft smile brushing over her perfect lips before her hands fly to her face and she sobs softly with the grief of losing someone still alive.

I know she hasn't stopped thinking about the me she knows. I'm invading her mind just as much as she does mine. Wiggling my way through those cracks in the wall she desperately put between us while I was gone.

She stares up at the ceiling, her hands resting on top of the covers across her chest as it heaves heavily and I wonder if she thought about me in the shower, getting herself worked up over the thought of me. Imagining my hands brushing across her skin as she soaped herself up. Daydreaming of my hand pushing between her legs as she leaned against the shower wall, the scratchy mesh of her loofah teasing her clit.

But which me did she think about? Did we take turns, fucking her brains until it was mush and she was bracing herself on the shower wall, hating herself for her depraved fantasies of a Reaper?

I test my theory, playing with her like a mouse as I send her a message from my burner.

Restricted: Did you think of me?

She picks her phone up from her nightstand, staring at the restricted number for a long minute. Her eyes widen, then her brows pinch together in question. She tucks her bottom lip between her teeth as she types her response.

Peach: When?

I grin, loving that she doesn't deny the general idea of thinking about me. We both know better than that.

Restricted: In your shower. Did you touch yourself wishing it was me?

She pales nervously, looking directly at the covered camera before she relaxes, clearly believing it's just a strange coincidence. Then she drops her face into her pillow and a muffled groan comes through the audio. Fuck, I'm so glad I spent the extra time to ensure I got that hooked up. The sounds she makes tells me I'm right on the mark.

She blows out a breath and begins typing, trying to regain her composure.

Peach: Why would I do that? You killed my friend and are treating me like nothing more than another whore you can manipulate however you want. You're disgusting.

But her truth betrays her words has she slips her left hand under the covers, squeezing her breast before slowly moving it between her thighs.

I give her a moment, enjoying the view of her with her eyes closed, working herself to the thought of me.

Restricted: I want you and only you, but I have to make sure you can be willing to give everything to me and understand that following orders is not a suggestion.

Her eyes open with the chime of her phone and she snatches it off her chest, eagerly reading. She curses under her breath.

Restricted: I know you want me too. Because since the first night I touched you, you can't help but wonder about all the ways I would make your body ache for me. Even when your heart wants someone else.

Restricted: Am I wrong?

She curses under her breath.

Peach: Reaper

A single word. My name to her. My title. A plea for me to stop, but so many questions lay just beneath the surface.

She chews on her lips, staring at the screen.

Restricted: Laurel

I don't give her an inch. I need her to tell me what she wants. I can't have her too scared to ask for something so simple. Sure, I enjoy playing with her, but she's got to know that I would do anything for her if she only demanded.

She drops the phone face down on the bed for a moment, running her hands through her hair, emotions swirling through her mind so clearly I can almost taste the panic. Minutes pass and I grow impatient, my cock throbbing, begging for her to say the words.

Her hands slam into the bed and my cock jumps excitedly as she picks the phone up and types furiously. The anticipation nearly kills me, wondering if she's going to tell me to fuck off or take the leap and beg me to keep going.

Peach: Do you think about all the ways you would make me ache for you? Or do you just enjoy making me squirm?

I grin, responding quickly.

Restricted: Yes

She smiles and I want to climb through her window and fuck her pretty mouth, watching those perfect teeth slide down the length of my shaft. I groan low and feral, barely restraining the voice in my head that wants to see the way her mouth would look held open with a ratchet mouth gag and hear the pretty cries she would scream as her jaw shatters for me.

Restricted: You didn't answer my question.

She sits up, the blankets falling to her waist, baring her perfect breasts to me as she moves to reach for something under her bed, then stops.

Peach: You know I did, so are you going to do something with that or are you going to continue to be a tease and play stupid games for attention?

Holy fuck. I had expected many different answers, but that wasn't one. I stare at her; completely taken back at the balls she has. The Reaper in me wants to show her who the fuck she's talking to but all in good time. Not yet. I need this to continue just a little further without her challenging me to come fuck her senseless.

She rolls her hips slowly, her right hand moving in back-and-forth motions as she fucks herself with her fingers beneath the blanket. My balls ache and I know I'm going to be a goner in less than five minutes.

>Restricted: Fuck yourself, Laurel. Show me how bad you want me and then send me a picture of your pussy, dripping for me.

Her breathing turns heavy, and she pulls her fingers from herself, holding them in front of her face to inspect the way they drip with her arousal. She spreads her fingers, watching the sticky strands stretch before she pushes them in her mouth, sucking them clean.

Holy fucking shit.

She reaches under her bed again, pulling out a large box, setting it on the foot of her bed. My curiosity peaks, eager to see what kind of shit she uses to get herself off. She fishes through the box before grabbing a few things and pushes the box to the side. I narrow my eyes, trying to see what she has.

Rope, a dildo, and some kind of metal box. I watch intently as she binds her feet to the metal rods at the end of her bed before propping her phone up and pressing record. Then she grabs the metal box and connects the dildo to it and my mouth waters as the realization hits me. She binds her hands, using a knot that allows her to tighten it as she pulls harder and slips the final loop around her neck.

She's fucking perfect. I blink, making sure this isn't another one of my hallucinations, delighted when I look up at her window and her shadow confirms the truth that the small, twisted part of her I sensed all those years ago has bloomed into this beautiful art.

Excited, I slide my zipper down and free my cock, letting it bounce free before I wrap my hand firmly around my shaft and stroke it. My left hand grips tightly around my phone as she lifts her hips and slides herself onto the silicone dick with a groan.

Using the remote in her hand she starts the machine and her rhythmic gasps match the slow pace of the machine fucking her. I clench my teeth, stroking myself harder, matching the pace, as if it's me that's got her at my mercy. My eyes burn, refusing to blink, not wanting to miss a second of this masterpiece that so closely matches the things I've done to her in my dreams.

She pulls on the ropes and her wrists are cinched in tighter, gasping as the rope around her neck follows. I imagine it's my hand around her neck, my fingertips living angry marks on her skin. Her head tilts up and her breathing hitches as she fights herself for air. She clicks the remote again, turning up the speed. I match the pace, a moan falling from my lips, something inside me cracking.

I fight for breaths as I furiously fuck my hand as the machine pounds into her, her body jolting and shaking with its power, her ropes tightening in response. She pinches her lips shut, desperately trying to hide her moans as she nears her peak. A squeak leaves her as she fights for the small amount of air she can get, then her orgasm crashes into her and it's Reaper that she cries out as her body convulses. I can't wait to hear her scream my real name again, but there is something in her using the name a part of her fears.

I curse, spilling into my hand, finally allowing my eyes to shut, sweat pouring down my face in relief, the sound of her screaming my name echoes in my mind.

I look at the screen again, watching her fall limp wondering if she can get out of her restraints. I shake my hand off, slinging my cum unto the grass and wiping the rest on the side of my jeans before tucking myself back in. She pushes her right fist against the metal bar, and it gives, separating from the frame where she had cut it just an inch or so, and she slips her wrist free before freeing her neck.

I give her points for creativity, but fuck, that could easily go wrong. Stupid girl.

I love it.

After cleaning up her toys, she grabs her phone and stops the video. She plays with it, and the shutter of her screen-shotting a frame fills my ears.

Excitement floods me again as I eagerly watch our messages, waiting for a close up.

> Peach: I have the picture. Now prove to me that you deserve to see what I look like when I cum. Leave Daith alone or I turn in your knife you left behind.

Notifications will be sent silently.

I switch back to the live feed, my brows pinched as she slides her box back under her bed, climbs back into bed, and turns her light off.

What the fuck?

It's not the fact that she's blackmailing me that bothers me. Honestly, it's a turn on, but her threat falls flat considering I have the knife, cleaned and back in its rightful place.

No. It's the fact that this little shit just edged me... hard.

I wait hours until she is sound asleep. Until I'm confident she won't wake up fully. Just enough to give me what I want.

I disable the complex's cameras with Felix's help of a small blackout, only spanning a few miles radius. I pull my hood up, my mask concealing my face that I keep low, quietly walking up to her door. Slowly, I turn the doorknob, bypassing her personal security system that is down for the time being. The red light on the modem flashes in warning and I shut the door softly, locking it behind me before moving to the edge of her bed.

Her hair is a mess, curled in every direction around her head, her hands are tucked under her face. Carefully, I peel back her heavy comforter, revealing her perfect body, positioned like a work of art created just for my pleasure. Her leg is hiked up, thrown over a pillow, forcing her hip off the bed, adding accentuation to her perfectly round ass.

I groan low, begging myself to stay calm enough to keep the pace my plans need. I can't rush into this. I have to savor it—every last second I can get before I draw out the fear. Essentially edging myself before I make her scream, and it forces me to come all over her chest. I have a couple hours at most.

Reaching for her, I brush my fingers across her hair spilling over the edge of her pillow. I didn't wear my gloves, needing to touch her skin. The risk of her recognizing my tattoos in the black of her room is one I am willing to take. The soft moonlight falling through her window illuminates her profile, accenting the perfect lines of her face. She breathes soft and even, completely unaware of my presence. I lean over the bed, slipping my hand beneath her blanket, feeling the warmth from her skin. I don't touch her yet as I close my eyes, letting that warmth crawl up my hand.

Inhaling, I open my eyes, my gaze trailing down to her neck, imagining the gentle pulse of her blood just below the skin. I move carefully, using my free hand to softly run my finger along the length of her neck, tracing a line slowly to her collarbone. She stirs, and the dazed hum she makes in response to my touch sends a thrill through me, stronger than anything before.

I crouch beside the bed, leaning close to her face, breathing her air hungerly. Leaning in, I lift my mask enough to free my mouth, and I dart my tongue out, flicking her lips, tasting the sweet addictiveness of her skin. She doesn't move.

I free my cock, wrapping my hand around it and stroking down the length as my eyes focus on her perfect mouth. I picture her lips wrapped around me, her siren eyes peering up at me, the depth in them threatening to swallow me whole. I step closer, lightly pushing the head of my dick across her lips as I continue to stroke it, strong and slow, the same way she would take me. I suppress the groan in the back of my throat as my mind conjures another image of her, leaning over me, spitting on my cock before the takes me as deep as she can. Faster and needy, desperate to taste every inch of me.

Fuck, I know she would be such a good girl. She's always done exactly what I wanted her to, and now, some part of me wants to see her take what I have deprived her of.

Testing her again, I move my hand under the sheets further toward her, caressing her thigh, moving up the hill of her ass. Not even her eyes flutter, so I move, climbing further onto her bed. It tilts with my weight, and I hover over her, slipping my hand between her spread legs, gently brushing my finger over her bare pussy. My heart hammers as I push them down and through her lips, feeling how wet she is.

My cock twitches, screaming for the release that only she can give. Slowly, I push two fingers inside her, twisting them to feel her walls before I curl them, teasing the spot that makes her toes curl.

The smallest gasp comes from her parted lips as I push further inside her, leaning in closer, wanting to eat every sound she gives me like a starving man. She shifts under me, rolling more to her back, throwing her hands above her head in surrender, just the way I like.

I dip down, taking one of her breasts into my mouth, and her eyes flit softly as she stirs, being pulled further away from sleep. Satisfied with the progression, I pull my fingers from her sweet cunt, licking them clean before I pull my mask back into place. Baring my weight on my knees, I fist my cock. I roll my thumb over the head of my cock, smearing the bead of pre-cum that has formed, then I wrap my hand around my length, stroking a couple times before lining myself up at her entrance. Gripping her thigh firmly, I hold it up to give me room as I slowly push into her, inch by inch. My head falls back and a groan I don't try to conceal rips from my chest.

Fuck, she feels so fucking good. Just like I remember when we used to play our little games as kids. I would fuck her while she slept, and if she woke up, she would still pretend, just for me. And in the morning, when I noticed the small limp in her step, she would say nothing, pretending it never happened. Our little secret.

She groans low, then again, louder as I draw out and push back into her. I keep the slow pace, drawing her to me as her eyes begin to flutter and blink.

There is a subtle shift in the tension between us as her eyes widen and her hands flatten against the sheets. The air between us thickens, charged with fear as her body stiffens and she tightens around my cock.

"Shh," I whisper, the modifier disguising my voice. "I'm gonna take such good care of this pretty pussy, baby."

The stunned and terrified expression of her face is firm for a long minute, but I don't stop. She's gripping me so fucking tight.

"If you don't relax, this is gonna end a lot sooner than either of us want," I bite out, fighting against the orgasm that is building too fast.

Her eyes soften, the tension leaving her face and her pussy relaxes. I grab her calf, tossing it over my shoulder to open her up more, and I grip her hips, slamming myself into her.

"Good girl," I grunt and her head tilts back, hands fisting the sheets.

She lets me work her for long minutes, responding to every touch of my hand and motion of my body. She gives into me, giving herself to me completely, mine for the taking, but she says nothing. Her body tenses and she reaches up, slipping her hand into my hood.

My heart stalls and I snap a hand up, gripping her wrist, but she digs her nails into the back of my neck, pulling my face to her as she screams, crying out as her orgasm wrecks her, and I relax. She arches her back, grinding back against me, and I snake a hand under her, pulling her tighter to me, forcing her to fall apart in my hands.

She comes down, relaxing into the bed once again. Her eyes gleam and hold mine with an intensity that courses through me, stronger than any drug. If I could have her look at me like that every day, nothing else in this life would matter.

She slowly draws her leg back, pulling it off my shoulder. Then, in a swift motion, she thrusts it out and in the center of my chest, surprising me with a force that sends me flying backward and off the end of her bed.

"You're stronger than I expected," I say strained as I get to my feet.

She reaches for something on the side of her bed, cursing as something clicks. As she yanks it from the wall and the moonlight shines on the marbled ceramic base, I realize she was trying to turn her lamp on.

"It's just you, me, and the silence of shadows, baby," I say, low, taunting as I brace my hands on the end of her bed, struggling to catch the wind she knocked out of my lungs.

She scrambles to the edge of the bed, holding the lamp above her head. Just as I think she's bluffing, she swings, releasing the lamp, sending it crashing against my temple. I waver but stand firm until my eyes open and she is flying toward me, lurching off the end of her bed, teeth bared like a wild animal, hands wrapping around my neck as we crash to the ground.

I groan, breaking her fall, landing on the shards of broken ceramic. Blood rushes to my head and cock, the thrill of it, the way she's fighting back like a caged animal. She shouts a guttural scream in my face that only makes me smile more. "Get the fuck out of my life! You're ruining everything."

I raise a hand in the air, requesting permission to speak and her brows pinch together.

"What?" She scowls.

110

"I believe you told me to prove to you that I deserve to see what you look like when you cum. Is giving you an earth-shattering orgasm not enough?"

Her face softens just a tiny bit. "A woman's orgasm is more mental than anything. I was pretending you were someone else."

I grin again. She's trying to make me jealous of *me*. But as my smile fades, I wonder why it's working. I reach out, wrapping my hand around her throat, pulling her closer.

"You belong to *me*. You do what *I* want." She wraps her hand around my wrist, digging her nails into my skin again as she tries to pry my hand away. "And let's get something straight. Your actions caused this. Turn me in and I'll make sure you go down with me." I pull my phone from my pocket and turn the picture of Daisy bloody and breathless with her entrails lying on the ground beside her. "Don't forget how easily I can make things disappear. Your little boyfriend is next."

Laurel turns her head sharply, clenching her eyes shut, a tear streaking down her cheek. As she struggles, wiggling in an attempt to break free, she rubs over my cock, and I see the moment she realizes that I still have a raging hard-on, and this is only making it significantly worse.

A look of pure defiance takes over her face as she lifts herself before slamming down, making me jolt. A desperate and pitiful sound of pleasure rips from my chest, and it surprises me, just as much as her, but she doesn't stop despite the tears rapidly streaming down her face now. I loosen my grip on her neck, but she uses both hands to hold it into place. Using my arm as leverage as she rocks her hips back and forth, fucking me fast and hard.

"This what you want?" she spits, angry and spiteful but full of lust. She moans, feeding off the power. "You want to claim me? Fuck me? Keep me to play with when you're bored?" Pure rage pours from the depths of her eyes. Defiance. "Kill me?"

My balls tighten, loving the way she talks dirty to me.

Her breathing becomes more ragged and rushed. "You leave Daith alone forever and I'm yours."

My cock jumps at hearing my name and her need to protect me. I say nothing, focusing on the way she bores her eyes into mine with aggression and passion that could destroy the world. She's ruthless, fucking me to get her way, unforgiving and determined.

"Say it!" she screams.

"Deal," I growl, giving her whatever she needs so she'll keep fucking me so damn good. "Say his name again."
I need to hear it. Again. On repeat. For the rest of my life.

She hesitates for only a second before she screams it, anger and lust raging war in her tone.

It's pleading and laced in sex, effectively sending me over the edge. I spill into her, jerking and tensing, tightening my hand around her throat punishingly. She comes hard, right after me, squeezing, pulling every last drop from my cock as she mentally replaces my mask with the face of her lover.

But maybe, that's not a fact, and it's possible she hates herself for screaming another man's name, lusting after him while she gets off on fucking me for who I am. A deadly murderer.

Does that get you off, Laurel?

She collapses on my chest, and I wrap my arms around her.

"Don't kill him," she whispers between heavy breaths, bargaining his life for hers.

I stroke her back softly, comforting her.

She would live a life with me, or die at my hands, if it spared Daith's life. Even with the uncertainty of finality, she lies on me, bearing herself to me in the rawest form of the word.

She would sacrifice anything she could give to save me?

CHAPTER 17

LAUREL

I finish scrubbing the lipstick from my wall, brushing my loose hair from my face with an exhale. I step back, making sure my landlord won't notice, before nodding to myself and moving to the shattered glass scattered across my floor.

He was right last night. I knew, with the right moves and incentives, he would come to me. I needed to know how willing he was to negotiate. He's killing the people in my life he feels threatened by and I knew I had to do something before it is someone I can't live without.

Something in my stomach tells me not to trust the word of a psycho, but Reapers are known for their code of loyalty. So, I'll take my chances.

I bend to sweep up the broken pieces of a vase I didn't ask for. A gift I never wanted, but didn't throw away either. I tell myself it's because I needed proof if he comes after me. But maybe it's because some small part of me wanted to keep a piece of him close. He knew me enough to know what could kill me... and that's kind of cute. Right?

There was a time, not long ago, when I wondered if Daith might be A Reaper. The way he moved. The way he wanted me suddenly. Everything was too much of a coincidence but that can't be right.

Daith's rage is more in check now. Reaper's is obsessive and wild. Reapers are more calculated and Daith is reckless. And last night, Daith looked too furious, too confused, to be behind the mask. I know him too well to believe he could fake that kind of reaction. He's as honest as I am.

I'm confident in that.

I slide into my chair and connect my camera to my computer, excited to see everything I managed to capture over the past few weeks, and in desperate need to calm my mind. Beautiful images appear in rows. Dark and mischievous, unaware and draped in freedom. My subjects change to anything that catches my eye, but this is subject is constant, one that I follow wherever it lurks in the darkness, waiting for me to seek it out. Not many people appreciate its beauty, but I see what lies beneath. Beauty born of things most people run from.

My phone chimes and my stomach drops, fear causing a wave of panic to scorch through me.

Restricted: Make your final moves. I have plans tonight. If I get bored, he's next on my list.

I don't need to ask who *he* is. I stare at the screen, not reacting. It's what he wants. For me to panic or beg. But I've learned how to play this game years ago.

I roll my eyes, breathing easier and continuing to look at my gallery. Selecting the pictures I love, I submit them to be printed and delivered to me, adding to a growing collection I've built over the years. These would be groundbreaking if I was to include these in an art show, though I find something exhilarating in having these stolen moments belong only to me. My little secret. Some things need to stay in the dark, only being shared with those who crave the forbidden and depraved.

I spin around in my chair, eyeing my phone on my bed as I think of my next move. It's like a game of chess or a juggling act. I have to do this right in order to make sure I come out on top and with my head still attached to my shoulders.

I haven't talked to Daith since I turned him away last night, partially from the growing guilt of what I let Reaper do to me, and partially due to the fear of Reaper's word meaning fuck all. Picking it up, my thumb hovers over Daith's name before I press call and hold it to my ear. My stomach churns as the dial tone plays, the anticipation more sickening with every passing second with how close my two worlds are to colliding. His voicemail picks up and I swallow, secretly thankful I don't have to speak to him yet.

"Hey, uh. Can we talk?"

I do my best to make it seem as if I'm preparing to break things off, listening to that tingle inside me that tells me my favorite stalker is still lurking close.

Flopping back on my bed, I cover my face with my hands, half to sell my motive and half-real emotions as I try to figure out what the fuck I'm going to tell him to sell this.

I need someone to talk to. Everything in me wants to tell Celeste what's happened, but part of me is concerned she might have me committed. What sane person gets off on a serial killer stalking and toying with her then lets him into her house in the middle of the night to fuck?

Though, Daith being her brother, she's no stranger to those who live a less than moral lifestyle. He confided in us both when he killed his foster father, whom we had never had the displeasure of meeting. And though she is just as aware as I am to his petty crimes and twisted ways of thinking, she chooses to keep herself separate from his world. And I wouldn't want to let her down with my choice of pursuing a trained assassin.

But if I am completely off the rails here, there is a chance that I end up dead before my darkest desires are fulfilled, and I would need someone to know where to start looking for me. The Reapers' reputations are ones of anonymity and secrecy. They never leave evidence, no one has ever seen their face or an identifying mark on their body and lived to tell anyone. He would make my disappearance believable, and when Celeste got suspicious, she would be next.

Reapers are smart. Calculating. Not careless thugs.

I pause at that thought and a revelation rings in my mind.

He wouldn't be stupid enough to hang around my car last night with everyone leaving the club, much less leave his knife behind. He wanted me to see him and to have it, then Daith took it home with him.

Fuck. Daith has his murder weapon and I know he isn't smart enough to do *nothing* with it. I sit up, chewing on my lip nervously. An idea sparks and I grab my phone, sending Celeste a voice message, trusting that Reaper will get the message.

"I'm headed to The Peach. Wanna grab a drink and hangout tonight?"

I get dressed, making sure to show a little skin, and paint my lips red, just for him.

"What are you doing here?" Bryce asks, sliding my usual drink to me.

"Meeting Cee," I say, tucking my phone into my purse.

I tip the glass at him before tossing it back. Then blow out a breath with the burn, sliding the glass back across the wooden bar top.

His eyes sparkle and I can't fight my smile. "You just couldn't stay away, huh?" he says, teasing, though it misses the mark. The last thing I need is another risk on my hands on top of backtracking with Daith.

Damn it. This is a shit fest.

"Grow up." My eyes trail around the room before connecting with the back corner booth. Or rather the man sitting at it. His skeleton mask concealing his entire face shines eerily in the low light. My eyes hold his and a wildfire settles low in my stomach as last night comes rushing back.

My chest suddenly feels like a ton of bricks are sitting on it. I can't tear my eyes away, my mind wandering to all the different ways he could make me come again. He knows his way around a woman's body, I'll give him that. I don't think I've come that hard in my entire life. I was halfway there before I fully woke up.

Something green and ugly forms in my chest as one of the other newer dancers walks past him, slipping him what looks like a napkin with her number on it. Oh hell no.

"What's he drinking?" I ask Bryce without taking my eyes off the corner booth, too scared that a split second is all he needs to find something else to focus on.

The masked man tilts his head to the side, almost in question, and my chest heaves with the thrill.

"Scarlette," Bryce says, though I barely hear him over the blood pounding in my ears.

The reaper motions with one finger, beckoning me, and I smirk playfully.

"Don't be stupid, Laurel," Bryce warns, reaching for my arm.

I peer over my shoulder, breaking eye contact with the masked man and clutching my chest. Bryce's eyes scream a warning at me, though I don't miss the hint of jealously in them. "Me?" I gasp, acting as if his warning is completely uncalled for, though we both know I am absolutely stupid enough to do something so careless.

He narrows his eyes at me, using his towel to dry a glass before he fills it and slides it to me.

"Don't worry about me. I'm a big girl who can take care of herself." I toss him a wink and plant both feet on the floor, tugging my tight skirt down the inch it will move. Running my fingers through my long hair, tossing it over to one side, I steal my spine.

The liquid courage warms my stomach and a thin layer of sweat forms over my skin as I sway to the back booth. I stop in front of his table, plastering a smile across my face before I set his drink on the table. "I couldn't help but notice you were staring."

"Yes." He wraps his arm around my waist, spinning me, pulling me into his lap, holding me tightly against his hard chest.

A rush of fear sweeps through me at the uncertainty of being in his grasp, but the thrill is like no other drug.

"I can still taste you." His hand snakes up to my throat, forcing my head to the side. A breathy moan coming from my lips as he whispers down my neck.

"How's your head?" I ask, teasing as I stare back at the bar, Bryce's gaze flicking back and forth to me nervously.

"How's your pussy? Still wet for me?"

I shut my eyes, letting those darker parts of myself come to the surface.

"You want more?" I ask. His other hand finds my left thigh and I part my legs slightly. He hums, brushing his thumb against my jawline. "We made a deal. A life for a life."

"We did," he confirms, and a weight lifts off my chest. Stupid or intuition, I'm not sure, but there's something in the way he says it that makes me believe he'll honor it.

"I want to make another deal," I say, hoping we're on the same page and he doesn't plan on slitting my throat in the middle of the bar.

"And what would that be, pretty girl?"

"Honesty," I say, my voice hitching nervously.

He inhales, shoving his nose into my hair and I stiffen.

Is he... *sniffing* me?

His hold around my throat tightens and his hand slips further up my thigh. I suck in a breath, feeling like this should be happening behind closed doors.

"You smell so good," he praises, raising my desires higher. His fingers on my thigh slip through the holes in my fishnets, teasing circles on my skin. "Tell me, Peach. Does danger excite you?"

My hands fist and as a few heads turn our way, my cheeks warm. "Yes," I answer in a hushed tone with the small amount of air he allows. I take note of my current state. Erratic heart, sweat on my lower back. Wetness between my legs.

Fear is rooted in people that are scared for their life to end. I've always chased that feeling. Death will come for everyone, one day or another, so why not chase it down and dance with the Reaper?

"Excellent," he praises, and I swear I can hear him groan. He runs his hands down my thighs, and I commit the feeling to memory, loving the high. "I'll be honest where I am allowed. You were honest. Now ask your question."

"What do you really want from me?" I ask, needing to know.

"Everything, all in the right time," he says, and I swallow nervously. What kind of cryptic bullshit is that? "Does that include killing me?" I ask, managing to keep my irritation hidden.

He's silent for a moment, his entire body still. The tension in the air thickens as an uncomfortable silence lingers.

"I don't know yet."

The answer sends a chill down my spine. I suppose that was expected. He's uncertain, which is a window for me. I can sway him, be worth more alive than dead. But what would that look like?

"I have an ultimatum," I say, chancing my fate, dancing on the edge of finality. "I give you want you want from me, whatever that looks like, as long as you keep me alive... as one of you."

His hands stop and it makes me second guess my delivery, though not my words.

"You just made a deal with death, darling."

To my surprise but utter excitement, he accepts. As my eyes find the bar again, I spot Celeste with her back to me. Her long red hair and glitter top are a dead giveaway.

"I have a friend waiting for me, but I'm sure you know that," I say, carefully sliding off his lap, surprised at how easily he releases me, all his coarse energy melting away.

He nods once. "You can talk to her about this but keep it basic." He pulls out his phone, effectively dismissing me. "Oh, and Peach. The next time you want me near you, just ask."

I smile, frail and unsure, but accepting. Turning on my heel, I leave him, sneaking up behind Celeste to press a kiss to her cheek. "You're late," I say, taking the stool beside her.

She narrows her eyes.

I check my phone, showing her the time. "Fifteen past. You're late."

"When were you going to tell me you left this cutie on the market?" she asks, winking to Bryce, as if she isn't rooting for me and her brother.

"By all means, take him for a spin," I tease, trying to play her game, though my mind is swarming with a list of things far higher on my agenda of things I need to talk to her about.

Bryce presses his hand to his chest. "Ouch, babe. Twist the knife."

Celeste juts her bottom lip out, reaching for his hand braced on the bar. "Laurel, you shot a puppy."

I narrow my eyes at her, hating the way she likes to play mind games just as much as her brother. "We're good, right Bryce?" I say, turning my head to him for his confirmation with a convincing smile that could persuade the Devil.

His eyes soften, the games and sarcasm disappearing. "Right."

"So when were you gonna tell me about that?" Her head nods toward the back corner and I sigh, utterly exhausted.

"Sometime between sessions of trying to convince myself I'm not insane and him doing what he does best," I say, defending myself before her motherly lecture can come out of her brown-painted lips.

"What the fuck are you doing with him?" She keeps her voice low, eyes flicking to the back booth, now realizing how sexual my comment sounds. "You are going to cause a dog fight."

I exhale, preparing myself for whatever reaction she may have to my cliff notes version. "The other night, before I came over and Daith showed up, he was following me."

Tossing her glass of whiskey back she waves her hand in a rolling motion. "Okay, hit me with all of it."

"That night, he cornered me when I was going home, and it may have been against a wall... with his hand up my skirt," I say, cringing, though saying it out loud now doesn't sting as much as I expected. "And he may have broken into my apartment, left me a slightly romantic note, then sexted me."

She stares at me blankly, blinking once.

"Then fucked me."

She doesn't move.

"Okay, is this the part where I need to explain that I'm not totally insane?" I ask nervously.

Silence.

Her mouth opens slightly as she processes. Fuck. I am totally insane.

She raises her hand, snapping at Bryce. "I'm gonna need a double shot."

Bryce obeys, obviously having heard what I said, because he too is looking at me like I have lost my fucking mind.

"Come on. It's not that bad," I defend to them both. "It's just work. He likes when I... dance for him." The words make me cringe as they come out.

She tosses the shots back and glances at the back booth where the Reaper sits back, idly watching the dancers.

She sucks her teeth and runs her fingers through her hair, fluffing the roots. "I'm gonna talk to him," she says, and I pull her back into her seat before she stands completely.

"No," I bark in a hushed tone. "You can't do that. I'm-"

"So, it's not that other guy." Bryce asks, his tone a bit more accusing than I care for, and a few heads at the bar turn my way. "You won't date me, but you'll date a murderer?"

Just as I'm about to deny the dating allegations, I decide to leave it be, giving him another reason to hate me, and Celeste gets up from her chair, practically sprinting to the back booth.

"Fuck!"

I race after her and slide into the seat next to Celeste who has her finger pointed in his face.

Reaper's back straightens and my heart begins pounding, though this time, it's sickening and not at all arousing.

I wrap my hand around her mouth, dragging her back out of the booth. "Nope. Nope. Nope."

I drag her out through the front doors, tossing a wave over my shoulder at Bryce who yells for us to be careful. As I shove her into the passenger seat, she squeals, crossing her legs to keep from peeing her pants. Her words are mixed with her hysterical laughs and hidden below the wheezing.

"How many did you drink?" I ask her, sliding into the driver's seat.

"Not enough," she says, finally catching her breath. "The look on your face was priceless. Like he was gonna kill me on the spot."

I narrow my eyes. "He could have."

"No," she says dismissively, just as my phone rings and Daith's name shines across my screen. She eyes it and her laughter kicks up again. "Speaking of trouble."

"I called him earlier," I mutter, answering it. "I need that knife. Do you still have the knife?"

"Knife? Are you flirting with me?" he teases, and I roll my eyes, waiting for him to answer. "I cleaned it, but yes," he says, his tone shifting to lazy and unfocused.

I groan. Of course he did, because he had his own plans for it. "Meet me at your sisters house."

"I have plans tonight, babe."

I grit my teeth. "I'm not asking," I bite back before ending the call and pressing my palms to my eyes.

"Should I light some candles?" she asks, wagging her eyebrows.

"It's not like that. Well, it is, but." I try to explain, nothing coming out right. I stiffen. "I made a deal with a Reaper."

Her smile slips from her face. "What kind of deal?"

"The one that likes me. He said if I don't stay away from Daith, he'll kill him." Cee's hand flies to her mouth. "I made a deal that I would be whatever he wanted if he promised he wouldn't kill Daith."

Her silence is damning. She presses her lips together, teeth clenching as she holds something back.

"He's in danger because of me. My how the tables have turned, huh?" I look down at my fingers, picking at the skin. "I didn't know how else to keep him safe."

"You're out of your mind."

"Maybe. But it worked. I just have to get Daith to listen." Make him drop the idea of something he wants. Have him be okay with being under someone else's thumb? I doubt that this is going to go over smoothly.

Three knocks tells me he's here, late, as always. I open it before Celeste can, heart thudding in my chest for reasons I hate and reasons I love. Daith stands in the doorway, dressed in denim jeans and a black T-shirt, his helmet tucked under his arm. As he steps inside, he drops his backpack to the ground and retrieves a pink shirt that is bundled around what I know is the knife.

He holds it out like it's no more important than the shit he took this morning. "You dropped this," he says, teasing casually. Our fingers brush for a second longer than necessary and my stomach warms.

"Thanks," I murmur.

His gaze flicks over me, pausing curiously. "What is it?" he asks, notably sensing my tension.

"If you two are going to start whispering sweet nothings, use the patio. I just cleaned in here," Celeste says from the kitchen, making another margarita.

Daith follows me through the house without comment. We step outside into the cold night air, where the porch light hums quietly and the pool glistens.

I unwrap the cloth and hold the blade in my hands, seeing it differently now that it's clean. Then I wrap it back up and clutch it against my chest like a secret I'm meant to bare. Daisy died because of me. The tears I shed that night were owed.

"I can't let anyone else die because of me." I say, keeping my eyes on the water. "So I made a deal with a Reaper."

His expression doesn't change.

"I told him I would accept being his if he leaves you alone. He wanted to kill you. He still might, but I had to do something."

That gets a reaction, barely. A subtle tilt of his head, the faintest twitch at the corner of his mouth. But he says nothing. I wait.

"You could say something," I mutter. "Anything."

His voice, when it comes, is quiet. Controlled. "That was pointless."

"It was the only leverage I had. He wants me."

He meets my eyes. "And if he breaks the deal after I give you up?"

"Then I burn everything down."

I would. Losing Daith. It might quite literally kill me.

He pushes off the railing and steps closer. His face is unreadable, but his voice is sharp now, low and cutting.

"You don't get to make choices like that for me, Laurel. If you think for even a second I'd walk away because some masked psychopath tells me to, you don't know me at all. Not even Death himself could keep me from you, sweet girl."

I swallow hard. Yeah, that's about how I expected that to go. The words feel strange coming from him. Like a dream, something I never expected for him to say willingly.

"Sociopath, I think," I say, chewing on my cheek, still replaying his refusal in my mind.

"What?"

"Nothing," I murmur, and he cups my face in his hands. "I can't blame him for wanting you, but I've killed men for less. You just do what he asks to keep yourself safe, and I will handle the rest."

I flinch at that. I had always suspected Daith killed more than his parents with the kind of trouble he's been in with drugs and fights, but hearing it come from his lips was different. I never wanted to believe Daith was a bad person, but the rose-colored glasses he gave me were thick, permanent, and custom made. He could commit genocide and I think I would still have my fingers interlocked with his and a smile on my face.

123

"I'll be back later. You did your part, now let me." Something in the way he says it makes the air shift, suffocating me with finality.

"You're not going to tell me?"

He steps toward the back door, hand pausing on the handle. "You wouldn't hold up well under torture."

I quirk a brow, but I bite my tongue before I ask the question. He has been tortured, worse than most. Instead, I inhale deep and release a breath with all of my worries attached to it as I step closer to him. "Just be careful."

He reaches out, brushing a strand of hair behind my ear, fingers grazing my cheek. "Always," he murmurs. "I'll be back soon. Try not to get into any trouble while I'm gone, yeah?"

"I'll do my best," I whisper.

And just like that, he's gone, the door clicking shut behind him. The silence he leaves in his wake is thick. Only a moment later, Celeste steps outside, letting the screen door creak behind her, scaring away the voices of doubt that begin to whisper to me. She holds her keys in one hand and her purse in the other, eyes soft and full of understanding.

"You gonna be okay for a bit?" she asks, glancing toward the street where Daith's car has already disappeared. "I need to run to the store before it closes."

I nod, but I must not be very convincing, because she steps closer and wraps her arms around me.

"You know how he is. There wasn't a chance in hell that he was going to go along with that and you know it. He loves you too much to let you go, especially to someone more insane than he is."

"It's not that that bothers me," I say, tucking my chin into her neck.

"I know. It's the uncertainty."

I sniff without answering. I don't have to. She squeezes my arm gently. "I'll be back soon. There's wine inside if you want to mope in style."

That earns a weak laugh from me. "I might."

She starts back toward the door, then pauses to glance over her shoulder. "But he meant it, you know. What he said."

"What part?"

Her smile is soft, almost sad. "That not even death could keep him from you."

Then she disappears inside, leaving me with the cold night air and an ache in my chest.

Chapter 18

"Have you lost your fucking mind?" Skid asks, her voice higher than my temper cares for. "You can't make her a Reaper."

I stand there, blank expression, letting her ramble her usual bullshit.

"Even if you somehow got her approved through CHAOS with her having no record whatsoever, Ezra wouldn't allow it. He would... He'd..." She runs her hands through her hair, frantically.

"It's just a game, Skid."

Her gritted teeth make it seem like I might as well had said I was going to dump our entire life database on the FBI's doorstep.

"Ezra doesn't like women in the ranks. If he even gets a whiff of the idea, you know what he will do to you." She talks low, steady, and I can feel the heartfelt caution in her tone.

"She is going to be by my side for the rest of my life, only time will determine what that looks like," I say flatly and full of certainty. Rather the tide changes and I mark her, or she ends up dead and just a bottle of ashes in my pocket. She will never know another day without me. "I feel it. Taste it in the air. She's holding back."

Skid rolls her eyes. "Not everyone is out to scorn you, Daith. Laurel isn't capable of the kind of things you want her to be. She is breaking herself to keep you alive and you are sitting back laughing."

"You're wrong," I tell her, my mind floating back to over a decade ago as if it is the present. "She stole a pair of panties when she was thirteen. Pink and lace, with little black hearts."

She crosses her arms. "So that means she is capable of killing? She won't survive it."

Still dazed, I remember the smile on her face the night she showed me. The first time she broke a rule, and all for me. That was the night I took her virginity and rewarded her good behavior.

"I think if she thought she was doing it for me, she would, and more." I focus my eyes back on Skid who is chewing nervously on the inside of her cheek. The tension in the room shifts. Brittle and harsh.

"Why did she come back?" I ask, making a point. "She knew my release date, and we made sure she thought I was behind bars."

"She crashed and burned."

I smirk. "Come on. You're smarter than that." I poke my index finger in the middle of her forehead. "You talked to her all the time. She missed the way this place made her burn. She self-sabotaged her life there so she would be here, months in advance, waiting for me like the desperate little girl she is."

Skid's face contorts slightly. "You think she has an entire side of her that she hides from us? You think that she is slipping away for hours at a time to kill these people, the same way you would, without leaving a trace of evidence, just for you?"

I roll that over in my mind. I had a flick of curiosity the night she followed me, she had a smudge of dirt just above her left eyebrow. Barely noticeable. And the way she reacted to Daisy being killed, it was almost rehearsed, like she isn't really bothered by the sight of death. Yes, it's entirely possible that with her obsession and the push and pull I gave her for years, something sinister forced its way to the light far before I ever planned to pull it out of her. Toxic love in the right people can create beautiful ruin.

If it is her, she has no clue how deep the organization runs and she is going to get all of us killed. But I want to know for sure. I can't have Skid spilling the beans and ruining a potential game that was made just for me. So I retract.

"No you're right. It's too much. She couldn't pull that off. Not without slipping up somewhere."

The heavy doors creak as Ezra pushes through them. "Fucking shit, I have been looking for your stupid ass everywhere," he bitches, storming down the aisle. "What is this? Family meeting without daddy?"

Skid shifts on her feet. "I was just talking to him about being at The Peach. Laurel is wound tighter than a nun's cooch so I think if he's going to take her, he should do it soon."

Ezra stiffens, making his dislike clear. "You better do this right. I won't watch everything I've created burn because you have a favorite fuck toy you couldn't throw away."

I smile sweetly, though I feel the sickening effect it has. "You'll die one day, old man. Keep working my nerves with the same tired shit, and I'll help you into an early grave."

Again and again. *Be smart. Be careful. Reapers only protect themselves. No feelings. No mistakes. No liabilities.*

I know. I know. I know. I know. I know. I know.

FUCK!

"Laurel will be here soon enough. Why don't you find a pet of your own. See how fun it is to have a woman desperate for any scraps you give her." My eyes gleam with a challenge. "I'm sure Skid would be more than happy to help you with that." I flick my eyes to her, enjoying the way she tries to keep herself collected. "With her connections and all."

Ezra refuses to look at her, which in part pisses me off. "I wouldn't do something so careless. I leave that to you."

Skid bows her head, and I don't miss the pooling in her eyes. "I'm going to head out. I'll keep an eye on Laurel. Let me know what you decide."

"Were making our first move on the club, so eyes open," Ezra calls after her, reminding her to have our backs, as if she needed it.

Our shadows cast on the front door of The Fuzzy Peach, well past closing time, our masks hiding our faces from the security cameras. Just as Ezra reaches for his keys, darkness overtakes us and the surrounding area for miles. Ezra and I look between us at Felix who chuckles.

"Come on, that is so much more fun than using a key, and you know it," he says, quickly typing on his phone and disarming the locks. They slide open with a loud clank and Ezra rolls his eyes, barely visible with the help of the glowing screen. "And you don't want to have to explain why your keycard was used to gain access in the middle of the night." Felix pulls the door up, mumbling over his shoulder. "Dumbass."

We head straight to the storage room behind the stage, taking the hallway under the stairs. I run my hand down the wall, feeling for the false wall. My finger hits a crevice, and I stop, rapping my knuckles against the wall, finding the hollow spot. Pressing firmly, a soft click allows the door to open and I pull it open, allowing Ezra in to clear the room while Felix checks that no alarm was triggered.

Thanks to one of our girls slipping me a note earlier tonight, we knew that Vic would have all cameras on a dead loop due to a customer wanting complete privacy when he came to pick up his order. We just manipulated that loop and used it to our advantage.

"All good," Felix says, confirming our plan worked. "Were ghosts."

My burner vibrates in my pocket and I pull it out quickly, only to find Laurel's ass filling my screen as her incoming call continues to ring. Clicking on my voice modifier, I answer the call.

"What's wrong, Peach?" I ask, a sickening feeling in my stomach that something is wrong if she's calling me now when she's supposed to be safe with my sister.

What sounds like a giggle comes distantly through the speaker before she speaks. "I just, maybe, thought you'd hear me and want to see me, like how I kind of want to see you. So big and scary, but maybe you can be nice to me. Right?" she rambles, slurring her words too close to the speaker.

"Laurel, I'm working. Are you in danger?"

She sniffles and her voice turns pained and broken. "I knew you only wanted to toy with me. You, Mr. Danger and Doom, don't have a fun bone. You should get that checked out." She giggles again. "You want me to check you out for you?"

I pull the phone away from my ear, putting her on speaker and quickly pull up her location. A breath of relief comes as her dot blinks at my sister's house.

"I'll add that to my list to do, right under purchasing patience for clingy women," I retort.

She's silent for a moment before a distant scream comes ripping through the speaker. "Laurel?!" I ask, pulling up the live feed within the house. I watch her superman dive back onto the couch where her phone is lying.

"I'm in danger," she says, holding her own throat to sound like she's choking. "I need-" she sputters and gags and I roll my eyes. Felix's chest shakes softly, seeming more amused than me, though I give her points for theatrics. "I'm in danger of my vagina shriveling up and dying." She then uses a deeper and professional tone. "The only cure is to be tied up and fucked, good and rough, with a screaming orgasm. Twice a week for the foreseeable future."

Oh, dear God, help me.

"Can you do that Reaper? Can you fuck me so good I scream?"

In the same moment, Ezra's head pops back through the open door and I groan.

"You know I can," I say, giving in to her. Ezra tilts his head, judging me. "Enjoy what's left of your night Peach. Soon enough you won't be leaving my sight." I swiftly end the call, giving her something to chew on.

"Are you done phone fucking or would you like some privacy?" Felix asks, thoroughly amused by the glint in his eye that tell me he hasn't outgrown that voyeurism kink I discovered a year and seven months ago.

I shove him aside and through the door first. We move down the stairs cautiously, our footfalls echoing off the smooth, untouched walls. The stairwell twists downward, and the farther we go, the more the air seems to become colder and lighter.

I pause at the bottom, the guys crowding behind me. Shining my flashlight around the room, I light every inch of the fresh white walls, finding a blank, unused room. No crates or storage — just bare, lifeless concrete. I glance around, disbelief creeping in. *This was supposed to be it.* The whole reason we came down here was for what was *supposed* to be here. What else would a hidden room be kept hidden for?

"There's nothing here," Felix says, the disappointment clear in his voice.

"Seriously?" I mutter, my voice echoing in the empty room. We spread out, inspecting the walls closer for hidden compartments, but it's clear. There's no hidden stash. No contraband. This room looks like it hasn't been used since the day it was made. There's nothing that Skid said was down here.

We stand there, the energy from moments ago leaving our bodies, leaving us with nothing but the quiet hum of our let down.

"Where the fuck is it?" I ask, irritation quickly flooding my senses.

Felix taps on his phone and looks around the room. "You have to be shitting me! What the fuck does he plan to use this big ass fucking room for if it's not this?"

A chill runs up my spine and that voice in my head whispers to me. What if he knows we are on to him... I didn't paint him to be a wise man, but perhaps he had a contingency plan—a red herring.

I chuckle to myself. "Seems Vic's might be smarter than we gave him credit for."

Ezra turns to me, and I can almost see the disagreement on his bored face. "No. There is a difference between smart and cautious. This was meant to clear his name if he ever went down. Not a single trace of DNA or paraphernalia in here. There is another room. We just need to find it."

Felix scratches the top of his head, ruffling his dirty blonde hair. "What now, then?" he asks, his voice tense. His hands flex at his sides, clearly itching for some kind of action.

"We get closer," I say, an idea coming in a rush of adrenaline.

"And how do you propose that?" Ezra asks, leaning against the cement wall. "If we get any closer, he'll figure you out."

I point a finger at him. "Vic's craves power – being the biggest man in the room. We let him think we are just like everyone else, looking for a little fun. Make him feel good by knocking us down a peg. We get him talking – showing off."

Ezra pushes off the wall, his interest peaking. "And he'll give it right to us."

"And what if he doesn't?" Felix asks. "What if he is too guarded?"

I take less than a second to ponder his question before I shrug. "Then I kill him and rip this place apart."

But I won't have to. The VIP rooms and his private areas where the real deals happen are going to be my ticket in. Use his products. Want more. He will gladly let me stroke his ego. "He trusts people around him, but he doesn't trust *everyone*. He'll want to keep his distance until he feels like we are eating out of his hand. Laurel is going to help with that."

Felix nods slowly, voicing the thoughts in my head. "We take our time, use his products. He'll trust us eventually."

I grin, a sense of purpose settling over me. "Let's get back upstairs. We've got work to do."

Chapter 19

She called my personal phone again and I watched it go to voicemail. A minute later, she called my burner, desperate for one of us to validate the choice she made to give into a life of being a pet to a criminal to protect the one thing she loves most in this world.

As much as she may hate to admit it, a part of her is more than excited to see what comes next. Reaper encourages that little part that's been banging on a locked door, waiting for permission. I can see that clearer than she can.

I'm going to play with her head, twist her and break her until she can't deny herself. Until she's perfect for me.

The front door opens, letting me know they are back from their midnight munchy run. I pull the dresser drawer reserved for Laurel's clothes open, fishing through her bras and panties until I find a pair of lacey panties that will do perfectly. After inhaling her sweet smell with a groan I shove them into my pocket.

I slip into the bathroom at the end of the hall, glancing around at her hygiene products, waiting for just the right moment. I hear them laughing, stumbling their way through the house, and I step out, tossing my backpack over my shoulder. I pat the top of my sister's head on my way to the front door, shoving my left hand into my pocket and tucking Laurel's panties into my fist.

"Whatcha still doing here?" Celeste asks, grabbing a spoon to go with her gallon of ice cream.

"Just looking for something I thought I might have left."

I don't miss the way Laurel shifts. A hint of guilt lurks behind those beautiful eyes, and I challenge her with a piercing stare, wanting to pluck the globes from her skull and suck on them.

"I'll let you know if I find anything," Celeste says, and she slaps the back of my head without stopping on her path to her room. "I've had a long day, but you can crash here if you want."

"You don't mind?" I ask. As kids, we were never lucky enough to land in the same foster home, but I always had a key to her place. Most nights, she was calling me over just to make sure I had a warm meal and a shower, so it shouldn't surprise me that has carried into adulthood.

"Of course not," Celeste answers, before looking at Laurel. "You don't need to be driving either and y'all could use the time together."

Laurel nods and I smile, dropping my bag on the couch, the truth of who I am hiding just inches from Laurel's dainty feet. I came straight here after the club, my need to touch her playing perfectly into our next moves.

For a little sister, Celeste has always attempted to be as much of a mom as she could be. Not just to me, but to everyone she loves. I knew she would force Laurel to stay the night after drinking, and without a doubt would invite me to stay. Despite her distaste or my actions, she can't deny how much she would love for Laurel to be her sister.

I nearly killed myself trying to get here after the first night I saw her at The Fuzzy Peach. I needed to be near her, each second burning with more urgency than the last, and knew she would come straight here. It wasn't my goal to rough myself up and fuck up my perfect paint job, but it did give me a better excuse and a reason for my sister to let me stay, with the very possible chance that she would say no after pushing Laurel away for so many years. I hurt her, I know that, but all for good reason. All leading up to this.

"It's late," Laurel says, grabbing her discarded shoes and bags that she just dropped. "I'm gonna turn in too."

I don't call her out on her excuse to put distance between us, only because I want her to dwell on it, thinking of Reaper while I'm only one room over.

"Laurel," I call after her, and she spins on her heel to turn and look at me.

"Look, I just don't think we should sleep in the same room right now, I just-"

"New shampoo?" I ask, recognizing she doesn't smell like she usually does.

"Uh, no. Just used a different one until I could get more today." She narrows her eyes at me, clearly confused at my lack of objection. "Stop doing that. It's creepy."

I give her a dramatic wink as I prop my arms behind my head. "Good. I like the coconut. Goodnight Laurel."

She hesitates for only a moment before disappearing into the guest room. Celeste comes out with a banket and pillow, setting them on the couch beside me. "No extra room, and I doubt Laurel will be willing to share while you have a target on your big ass forehead." She scrunches her nose playfully before turning back toward her room.

"Are you seeing someone?" I ask her as I get comfortable.

"Uhm. No. I'm not."

I hum, enjoying the bitter taste of her lie on my tongue. "You should. You deserve to have someone make you smile."

Giving a gentle nod, she turns, shutting the door behind her.

I'm lying silently with my eyes closed, plans so close playing like a movie in the darkness of my mind when the shower shuts off and the bathroom door opens. Steam rolls out and the smell of coco butter and jasmine surrounds me, enveloping me fully, making my senses more demanding and harder to restrain. I crack my eye open, watching as Laurel tiptoes to her room, a towel wrapped around her. My cock strains against my jeans. I could have her tonight if I wanted. She's feet away from me, practically begging me to take her.

Wait. You have to wait.

I ration with the darker voice in my head demanding her blood on my hands and her face between my legs.

My phone vibrates with a message.

SKID: we need to talk

I wait patiently for her to fall asleep before I creep down to her door and slowly turn the knob. I inch it open, peering in to make sure she hasn't woken. She's always been a heavy sleeper, not an earthquake able to wake her without a whiff of coffee first. Some of my favorite nights were nothing but a dream to her as a kid. Things she wrote in her diary, thinking they were wet dreams. Though sometimes I... helped her stay asleep.

I stand over her, admiring her porcelain skin. My eyes drift down her leg that's hiked up, bare and so smooth. Her arms tucked under her, one down between her legs. Oh, this is too good, so much better than what any camera can capture. I reach out, brushing her hair from her face and her eyes flutter softly at my touch.

"You are mine, pretty girl," I whisper, leaning down into her ear. I reach down, slowly pulling the sheet back a little further, revealing her ass. I unzip my pants and free my cock, fisting it with a low moan. Laurel's mouth parts softly and her steady breath resumes. Stroking myself, I focus on staying silent as I linger on her body and lips. I exhale roughly, her face inches below my cock, her soft breath teasing my skin, beckoning me in. Years of using only my memories and imagination make it unbelievably easy to lose myself, and I spill into my hand with hushed grunts.

Fuck, it's like I'm seventeen again. How exhilarating and utterly fascinating. I haven't cum that fast since I killed a guy in Georgia. I chased that clever bastard for a week before I could get my hands on him. A week of foreplay had me coming in my pants before I pulled the trigger.

I take one last look at her before tucking myself back into my jeans.

I lean onto the bed and climb behind her. She mumbles as I slide in close, pressing my body against hers. I reach over her, sliding my hand under her shirt, soaking in the feeling of her soft skin. She groans and I dive deeper, down and under the edge of her panties, careful not to wake her. With every inch, my cock grows harder, begging to be inside her, despite the release I just had.

I focus on her, and push my hand further, running a finger through her lips, teasing her entrance before coming back up to her clit, rubbing slow soft circles. She groans again, her body opening perfectly for me. She stirs awake, panicking as she tries to sit up, but I wrap my arm around her, soothing her softly. "It's okay."

"No, we can't." Her objection is cut off with a moan as I slam my fingers into her, pumping them fast, the way she loves. "You don't-," she says, though her eyes fall closed, and she does nothing to stop me.

I move to hover over her, leaning down to press soft kisses to her neck stretching for me, giving me better access. "What I know, is that we have waited long enough to be together. What else is there?"

Her chest heaves and her walls tighten around me. Her brows pinch, and I feed off the war I know is raging in her mind.

"He'll kill us both," she says, a tear slipping down her cheek and I dart my tongue out, plucking it from her soft skin.

"Let him try."

Her pussy clenches and I smile, loving the way it excites her.

"He's watching me. All the time." Her eyes open, holding mine with caution and lust.

I sit back, pulling my fingers from her to shimmy my pants down enough to free myself. "I hope he enjoys the show."

I pull her to her knees and guide her head down to my cock. She greedily opens her mouth, taking me in, diving deeper until she chokes herself. She gags, sputtering and drooling, but holds herself down.

"Fuck," I whisper into the darkness between us.

Wrapping both of her hands around my length she works me to the edge, the urgency she has nearly causing me to spill into her mouth before I've had any fun. I pull her hands away, gathering them in one hand behind her back, using my other to push two fingers back inside her. She spreads her legs wider and rocks back and forth, using the motion to take me deeper and fuck herself.

Right on cue, her phone chimes with an unfamiliar tone, a message sent from my phone at Felix's hand. How cute, she gave me my own ringtone.

Her body tenses but I hold her in place.

"It's just you and me right now, baby," I say, releasing her hands to run my fingers through her long hair. I pull her head back, then up to mine, taking her mouth and tasting myself on her. I kiss her deep, frantically, full of hungry desperation. Pulling her to me, lifting her, I fall back onto the bed before breaking our kiss. I push her knees up to her chest and plunge into her with a slow groan as I fuck her hard.

"Give it me to baby. Come for me. Let him watch how bad you need me," I say, taunting her with my own game. No one is watching. Felix had very clear instructions to send a message when the camera sensed motion and not to take a fucking peak at the feed. It was a risk of timing, but I couldn't let him see her like this. Only I get that privilege, now until the end of her life.

She reaches up, wrapping her hands around my neck, pulling me into her. Her breasts rub against my chest, and I sink my teeth into her neck playfully. "Tell me how good it feels," she begs and my balls tighten at the sound of her needy words.

"You feel so fucking good. Come on, cum all over my cock like a good little slut. Just for me."

She closes her eyes tight, digging her long nails into my neck as she rocks her body, fucking me back, taking me as deep as she can. "Only for you."

"Don't stop," she repeats, over and over until she is pulsing around me, taking me with her as we fall over the edge. I obey her wish, pumping into her, fighting against the sensitivity to draw her orgasm out until she is a shaking, breathless mess.

I let her legs fall to the sides, enjoying the way they shake softly. Sitting back on my heels, I enjoy the view of my cum dripping from her. I reach down scooping the excess, pushing it back inside her while softly brushing my thumb over her clit and she jolts with a giggle. "Stop. That's sensitive," she gasps in protest, reaching down to cover herself.

I swat her hand. "I'm not done looking."

She sucks her lips between her teeth and her hands fall away. I reach for her camera on her nightstand, and hold it to my eye, getting the perfect angle. It flashes with a click, snapping a moment I want her to have forever. Hell, I might ask for a copy to frame on my bedroom wall.

"I'm not on birth control," she says, chewing her lip.

I smirk. "I know."

For a moment, something surrounds us. Something warm and welcoming, safe and complete. Then it bursts and her eyes dart to the nightstand where her phone sits, and she slowly reaches for it, needing to assess the damage. Her eyes widen before the adrenaline dump takes a toll on her body and she turns to tears, handing me the phone.

I look over my own words as though it was the first time.

Restricted: Deals only stand if you hold up your end.

She scoots up on her bed, pulling the blanket over her waist and I pull my pants back up, reading the room. Our play time is over for now.

I furrow my brows moving to sit beside her. "Laurel, I can handle my own."

She tilts her head, resting it on my shoulder. "I just wanted to do what I could to keep you safe. Someone ought to."

I peer down at her, caught off guard, but I say nothing to admit to the odd feeling in my chest.

"You need to pay attention. I don't know how they work or all the connections they have, but he's everywhere. I don't know how he got in here but apparently, he got in easy enough."

It's right there in front of her face and I wait for any indication that she thinks I could be in on this, but as her body relaxes against mine and her breathing slows to a steady pace, I relax and let that worry slip from my mind.

"They have so much power. He's gonna come for me. He'll... fuck me again." A tear falls down her cheek. "Will you forgive me for everything he'll do to me when he takes me? I promise I'll come back to you. We just have to stay alive."

"Whatever you need baby," I say softly, pulling her to my chest and I slide down onto the pillow. She mumbles something incoherent, wrapping her arm around me, clinging to me the way she did when we were kids, soothing each other's nightmares.

Now, I'm her nightmare and the only thing she needs to fear.

The floor creaks, giving me away as I try to make my exit before the sun comes up, freshly showered and onto the next part of my plan.

"Where are you sneaking off to?" Laurel asks from the couch, catching me off guard. My hand pauses on the front door's handle, and the hopeful look in her eyes that she's trying to hide nearly brings me to my knees.

"I have some things to do," I say, unable to keep my mind from replaying last night.

She props her chin on the back of the couch in the sweetest way. "Which are?" I smirk at her attempt to peer inside my mind but give her nothing that she doesn't already know. She gives up with a small knowing sigh. "Keep your secrets."

"The less you know, the better," I say, trying to reassure her that I'm making moves to protect us both, she has to stay in the dark. Largely because she would want to help and logistically, that can't happen. "You have work of your own to do. Better go smooth things over with your Reaper." I wag my eyebrows at my own name.

"You look at me differently now, knowing I fucked him," she says, a hint of disappointment in her tone.

"I'm not one to judge on survival tactics," I say, moving closer to her. "And my love isn't jealous. Maybe because I'm not capable." I lean down, breathing right next to her ear. "But if you need to fuck him until I can get a bullet in his head, then so be it. I'll see you soon." I press my lips to her cheek before giving her my back and shutting the door behind me.

Chapter 20

LAUREL

The dressing room feels cold as I sit in front of the mirror, staring at my reflection. The usual hum of the club seeps through the walls, but all I can hear is the pounding of my heart. I can feel the weight of the deal I broke and the suffocating consequences coming to fruition. It's like a time bomb shoved down my throat, waiting to destroy my entire life.

The deal was simple. I belong to him. He gets me, no questions asked, and in return, he promised he wouldn't touch Daith. He wouldn't hurt him. Why couldn't I do my part? Why did I have to be so fucking stupid? Daith is careful and street-smart, but he won't escape The Reapers. There is a reason no one ever has. They are too good. No one even knows how many of them are. He could be outnumbered 1000 to 1. My stomach churns, threatening to spill everything I had for breakfast along with the alcohol from last night.

I know this is all about to end, one way or the other. The message I got this morning confirmed it.

Reaper: Don't think this will go unpunished. I'm coming home tonight and taking what is mine.

I adjust the strap of my top, trying to focus on the task at hand. Get through work. But my mind keeps circling back to the same thing. *Does he know Daith is trying to get to him first? Is he one step ahead? Is he coming to kill me first?*

His grip on me is suffocating with no end in sight. But for some reason, there had been something in Daith's eyes that makes me feel like I could escape this.

I swallow hard, wiping away the smudge of makeup under my eye. My reflection stares back at me, the mask of calm I've learned to wear slipping slightly. I don't know how much longer I can keep pretending.

The door to the dressing room creaks, and I freeze. For a split second I wonder if it's him coming to collect. But it's just one of the other girls peeking her head in to remind me that it's almost time to start.

I nod, forcing a smile. "Thanks, I'll be out in a minute."

She leaves, but the unease stays with me. I take one last look at myself in the mirror, adjusting my breasts in the pushup bra. I'm not ready for what's coming, but I don't have a choice. The night is starting, and I'm walking right into the mess I've created.

I move to the edge of the curtain, peering through at the crowd. The girls glide across the floor, smiling and dancing, each one selling the perfect illusion of carefree women here to please whoever walks through the door. One of them — Carly, I think, one of the usuals' girlfriends — prances over to the front entrance and leans in toward the bouncer. I watch curiously as she murmurs something to him. He gives a small nod, and they both move on like nothing happened.

A moment later, he shifts positions, angling himself slightly closer to the bar. He's not looking at anyone in particular. But he's watching someone. Likely just a customer that is on the verge of getting kicked out for crossing a line. The lights go off and I take my place on the stage, resting my hand on the pole. My eyes fall shut and my spine straightens. I pull on the part of myself that I taught to shove the nerves down and become fearless.

The spotlight comes on and I plaster a smile on my face as I live out my burlesque fantasies to "Diamonds Are A Girls Best Friend." In my all-black lingerie with sheer cut outs, I prance around the pole in my 6-inch heels, swinging a strand of pearls in my hand.

I drop to my knees, throwing my head up, whipping my hair over my shoulder. I look straight out into the crowd, making eye contact with Daith. He smiles wide, his eyes darkening as he watches me intently. I put on a show for him, adoring how his only focus is me, and for a few minutes, nothing else matters.

Sweat drips down my back as I finish, tossing my hair over shoulder, letting the cool air brush over me. I blow kisses to the crowd before taking the stairs down to the dressing room to freshen up. Sweat wiped, perfume and lipstick touched up, I push through the curtains and aim for Daith. Before I can make it to the back level, someone reaches out, slipping a hundred-dollar bill in my panties. "Got time to cure a broken heart?"

With another glance to Daith whose hungry eyes are locked on me, I turn to the customer needing his ego stroked. I jut out my lip before straddling his lap. "Of course I do. Tell me all about it." I push my hands into his hair, moving my hips slowly as he begins his story, flicking my eyes to Daith, teasing him, fucking him with my eyes as the man below me speaks.

"My girlfriend of two years cheated on me with some guy she works with." His hands dangle at his sides, letting me do all the work. The smell of whiskey wafts off his breath, mixing with the grease of his week-old unwashed hair. I hum, letting him know I'm listening as I continue to grind on him, roaming my hands over my own body. His eyes follow them, tracking the frame of my body before landing where I'm grinding on his cock through his jeans.

I look up, finding Daith glaring with a darkness in his eyes, and I eat that shit up. It's fucking delicious seeing him unable to hide the desire he likes to hide. The years of sexual frustration simmer between us and I can feel myself growing slick as my mind wanders far away from the task at hand.

I push the man's head between my breasts, rubbing the back of his head. "Do you want my advice or just a dance?" I ask, focusing on his issues again, trying to distract myself from the budding orgasm threatening to build.

He inhales, keeping his forehead against my chest. "I'm all ears."

"I think you need a good man-scape, a rebound, and then you leave that scum in your past. You deserve more than a woman that thinks you'll do anything to have her back after she spits on your respect." He looks up and pinches his brows, taking that in before he nods, accepting my answer.

Grabbing his hands and moving them to my breasts, I lean in to whisper. "On the house," I say, squeezing his hands firmly before I stand and give him a wink and his hundred-dollar bill. My eyes scan the crowd, and my stomach sinks as they land on the back corner booth.

Reaper.

Daith sits only five tables away, his eyes still on me. I swallow nervously, knowing what I have to do.

"Hi," I say, stopping in front of Reaper's table, smiling and tossing my hair behind my shoulder. He stares at me through his mask, unmoving, to the point I shift my weight uncomfortably. "I just, uh, wanted to see if we could talk."

"When I have a need for you, you will know. Where is Jewel?" His voice is lighter than before, though still disguised.

"Right," I forcibly laugh trying to ease the hint of nervousness threatening to turn my cheeks pink. "She didn't show up today."

"I just wanted to discuss our arrangement." I reach out to touch his shoulder and he pushes my hand away, looking past me, scanning the room as if he couldn't be bothered with having a conversation with me, and jealousy roars inside me at his need to see another woman. "Are you kidding?" I ask, letting my annoyance seep into my tone. I step in front of him, forcing him to look at me. "I know I fucked up. The least you can do is have a conversation with me."

He reaches up, grabbing a handful of my hair and yanking me into him. "Right now, you are lucky to still be breathing considering you brought him right to me. I suggest you remedy that before I finish with my current business." He releases me, shoving me back.

I stumble, my ego torn to shreds, fear rising to the surface. I plaster a fake smile into place and quickly run my fingers through my tousled hair. A small part of me is relieved that, despite the humiliation that comes with it, me and my antics aren't as high of a priority as he made it seem.

I glance around, looking for Daith, needing to get him the hell out of here. But I find his previous table occupied with one of the dancers and her boyfriend. "You told me I would be safe! I'm not just a pawn for you-"

"That is exactly what you are. Act like it, or get replaced," the man barks before sliding out of the table and leaving her with her mouth slack and her makeup smeared.

"Hey," I say, stepping up to the table. "Did you see where the guy with one eye covered went?" I ask, trying not to burst into tears along with her.

"Uh, he left just a minute ago."

I frown, giving her a nod. I guess it's a good thing. Maybe he saw Reaper and dipped before things got out of hand here.

"Want a cigarette?" she asks, pulling one from her bra with a sympathetic look. Without hesitating, I take it from her. I've never smoked a day in my life but with the week I'm having, I think I might pick it up.

"Thanks. I have some makeup wipes on my table if you need it," I say, nodding toward the dressing room before grabbing my purse and heading to the back. Taking the side door, I slip into the alley and hold the cigarette between my left two fingers. I reach in my purse, fishing for a lighter I know I won't have, as if it would magically appear because of my desperate plea to ease the feeling in my chest.

I sling the cigarette into the gravel, shouting as I kick the rocks. My tears fall freely. Hanging my head low and exhaling a deep breath, I press my hands to the brick wall.

What the fuck am I doing?

Moments pass before fingers grip my shoulder firmly. A gasp rips from my throat, and I spin, pulling the gun from my purse, pressing it to my target's chest.

"You intend to use that?" Daith's voice rumbles.

I move my finger from the trigger, keeping the gun firmly in place and my eyes narrow on him. "It *is* loaded this time," I quirk, wiping my tears with my free hand. "You need to leave."

"If you're going to shoot someone, you don't *pause*." He leans into the gun, pressing a hand against the brick, caging me in, completely ignoring my warning.

My breathing hitches as the jolt of fear I felt melts into thrill, and I consume the very thing I'm craving like a drug. The way he looks at me, the way he smells, it all adds to the addiction.

The beautiful color of his eye holds mine, and the contact is suffocating and so fucking delicious as it wraps around us, tethering us to the world and this moment in time. My eyes drift to his lips and the way his tongue darts out to wet them, wondering what his tongue would feel like trailing up my stomach. I'm lost in him when his arm shoots up, swiping the gun from me and turning it on me, holding it to my head. I don't flinch, knowing he would never pull the trigger with me on the other end. We've played this game as kids, seeing who got nervous first with a weapon pressed to their body. I always lost. He pulls the slide back, emptying the chamber, before dropping the clip into his other hand. He extends both to me with a grin that makes my knees weak.

"Are those tears for me?" he asks, swiping my cheek.

145

I stand silent for a minute, dumbfounded. Then I swipe my cheek and narrow my eyes with ridicule. Daith stares at me for a long minute, saying nothing, as if looking straight into my brain and pulling out the real answer he wanted.

"I just had to make a phone call baby," he says, seeing through the strong exterior I try to compose. He glances down at the broken cigarette in the rocks. "What did he say?" he asks, confirming that he saw him.

I adjust my purse. "He's going to kill you. You need to leave."

Daith reaches in his pocket, pulling out a pack of cigarettes. "You are attracted to darkness. What makes you think his abyss is any deeper than my own?"

He lights one and blows smoke with a grin as I take in his question. I suppose there is a depth to him that he has always kept guarded from me, and the things he did as a child is a clear indication of just how dark his future could look. What connections had he formed in prison? What things has he done and kept hidden?

He steps into my space placing a finger under my chin, holding my eyes on his. He holds the cigarette out to me and I take it, still feeling intoxicated on his presence alone. That's something he has that Reaper doesn't. No one else ever could. I inhale, sucking it deep in my lungs and holding it until my head spins. His open lips hover above mine and I blow the smoke into his mouth, our lips brushing, sending electricity through my body.

Daith blows it up before looking back at me. "You can't stop the inevitable. He wants what isn't his. Just stay out of the way."

He drops his hand from my waist and the sound of the gravel crunching under his boots is all I can focus on. I stare at his back as he walks away, swinging his backpack over his shoulder, breaking whatever little bubble we were in. "I enjoyed the show by the way."

Such a simple statement of appreciation but every ounce of air leaves my lungs at hearing it for the first time.

The night drags on, the usual rhythm of the club filling the air, but my mind is a constant whirl. Reaper was gone when I came in and now my mind continues to wander to Daith.

Is he okay? Did Reaper track him down? Is he still alive?

The questions gnaw at me, but I do my best to trust that Daith was right about being able to hold his own. I have to trust that if I want to stay sane throughout the night. I do my best, but every smile, every drink I serve, feels clouded by a fog—serve the drinks, smile when needed, give a personal dance, and keep moving.

By the time my shift finally ends, it feels like the night has passed in a blur, like I've been on autopilot the whole time. I grab my coat from the dressing room, trying to shake off the lingering unease. My body aches, utterly exhausted from such a long shift, my mind on the same level, threatening to shut down soon if I don't get some sleep. I glance at my gun inside my purse, still disarmed, and groan. I set my purse down on a table and work inside it, reassembling my only means of self-defense. I push the bullets back into the magazine before clicking it back into place. Tossing my bag over my shoulder, I step out of the dressing room and head to the exit, the dim lights of the club casting long shadows on the floor. The place is quieter now, most of the patrons gone. A strange emptiness wraps around me, and I try to shake off the tightness in my chest. I slip into the night air, the cool breeze doing little to ease the weight of everything on my shoulders, and let out a slow breath.

"Hey," a man says, and I nearly jump out of my skin.

"Jesus, you scared me," I say through heavy breaths.

The man I danced for earlier chuckles nervously. "Sorry, I didn't mean to... I just didn't know..." He struggles to find his words and I smile softly. "Can I walk you to your car?" He holds my eyes firmly and something in the air between us shifts. I glance around, finding us alone and the streets quiet. My grip on my purse tightens and I swallow. I nod slowly, forcing a relaxed smile to hide my growing nerves and the sickness swirling in my stomach. Strangely enough, Reaper comes to mind, and I hope he's watching as ineptly as he's promised.

His threat is suddenly a prayer, repeating in my mind and chest as I walk slowly with the man from earlier, out of the light from the club and into the darkness of the parking lot.

Chapter 21

I hover eagerly over my phone as silence comes from the call on speaker. "She's not here," Ezra says, and my stomach aches.

"I'm looking at her phone location. You're right on top of her," I say, furious and desperate. Tonight was the night I was going to take her home and move her in with me. I was there hours ago, utterly fucking annoyed that Jewel wasn't there as scheduled. She was on Vic's list and I wanted to get to her first. I needed someone that knew Laurel and could give me some insight on the part of her I don't get to see. Laurel doesn't particularly care for Jewel, but Jewel looks at her like an idol, despite her too-good attitude she does her best to use as a disguise.

I might have even released her back into the living population if she cooperated. By the time they tried to warn Laurel, I would have already had her locked in my basement. Laurel has already taken on extra work with the growing list of missing dancers resulting in new hires, and I wouldn't want to make her workload any heavier. But with Jewel gone tonight and my inability to wait any longer, I was going to move forward, leaving my questions unanswered and taking them as they come.

So, where the hell is she?

"I'm at her car. The club is empty and she's not here, Daith."

"Fuck!" I scream through my room, swiping all the welcoming gifts I got for her to the floor with a loud clatter. I knew I should have put that fucking tracker in her the other night when I had the chance. My gut never steers me wrong, so why didn't I listen when it comes to her?

I use my burner to call her, and it goes straight to voicemail. The voice in my head comes forward, screaming doubt and fear. My hands tremble as I twist my head back and forth, attempting to push him back and think clearly. I begin to mumble to myself, grinding my teeth as I fight my internal war. She needs me, I can't break down right now.

Please God, don't let me do this right now. I have to figure this out. I have to get to her. I just need to think. Think. Think.

"Stop talking!" I scream out loud, my anger targeted at the irritation in my own mind.

I replay tonight in slow motion, paying attention to every detail, searching for one that could indicate something wrong. Third table from the stage ordered the same drink three nights in a row, bourbon, neat. The stage lights were blue, trending on nights that the girls got bigger tips. One of the picture frames on the wall was newly cracked and tilting about 15 degrees off center. Laurel had no indication that she was uncomfortable. She was focused, but not off guard. Alert.

No. I need deeper.

One of our girls mentioned that there was a new man exploring the VIP room, but I watched him. He wasn't interested in Laurel. There was a group of men that came in for a party, but she only served them drinks. They requested a dance, but she was unavailable. He didn't take the rejection badly.

Fuck! What is it?

"Have Felix replay the feed from the front door," Ezra suggests after a moment of silence.

"Already on it," Felix says clacking on his computer, pulling up the feed from the cameras we hacked and the ones we placed. Dozens of screens appear, and I watch anxiously as he continues typing. I focus on each clack of the keys, and the voice quiets, moving to the back of my mind where he usually sits and spectates.

"Found her," he says, stopping the feed with her standing next to a man and walking out of frame toward her car, and I exhale a heavy breath of relief. It's only their side profile, enough to identify her but not the man that had the audacity to talk to her. Felix selects another frame from one of our cameras placed close to the stage, giving me a full-frontal image of the man's face as my woman sits on his lap. I hadn't seen that.

"I'm going to fucking kill him," I grind out, nearly cracking a tooth. "How did you not catch her leaving with him? Did any of our girls see anything?" I ask, voice thundering accusations through the phone to Ezra who starts his bike.

"I can only do so much, you fucking prick. Vic had a staff meeting to brief us on a big buyer coming in next week. We were all in there."

I clench my jaw, unable to deny that he did what was more important for the time being. My wide and burning eyes bore a hole into Felix's head waiting for a solution. His computer chimes and he exhales.

"Got him. Let's go," he says, letting me look at the blinking location of his phone before slamming the laptop shut and shoving it in his backpack that he slings over his shoulder.

We race through the empty night, zipping past the few cars that are on the 15 minute drive. My personal phone rings in my helmet and I hit answer, staying tucked low as I top 120.

"Daith?" a shaky voice whimpers through the phone.

"Baby?! What happened?" I ask, using every ounce of strength to stay focused on the drive to her.

"There's so much blood," she cries, her voice raspy and desperate. The sentence echoes in my head as a memory flashes in my mind. The same sentence, same tone, at the age of thirteen when she sliced her leg trying to jump fences with me. So much blood. It was art, utterly entrancing, but the fear in her eyes scared me for life. The tears and panic in her eyes as her trust in me waivered.

"Don't move! I'm on the way!" I scream, glancing over at Felix who nods and lets me take the lead.

"My phone died and I didn't know how to get out. He was here and then..." she sniffles, and the terror in her voice makes me murderous.

"I'm so close baby. Hang on!" I top 140, flying down the road faster than ever before, knowing if I wreck now, I'll be dead before I blink and I'll let her down... again.

I slide into the driveway of an abandoned house and let my bike fall to the ground. Slamming my foot into the door, it cracks and splinters, giving under the pressure. Laurel is curled in the corner of the disgusting living room, her face buried in her knees, her bloody hands braced on her head.

Quickly assessing the dead man from the club sprawled on the floor, I step over him and kneel before her. "I'm here. I'm here." I pull her into my arms, her body shaking as she sobs into my shoulder. "I need you to look at me. Look at me baby," I plea, prying her dirty, stained face up to look at me.

Her eyes are wild, and I can see the chaos swimming in them, her mind grasping onto reality with desperation.

"Who did this?" I ask, slow and deliberate to pull an answer from her fragile state.

She shakes her head in my hands. "I didn't see him. He was wearing a- a faceless mask. He said..." she pauses, calming her trembling lips. "He said he's coming for The Reapers and I'm next." Her face falls back into my shoulder, and I cuss under my breath. My eyes bounce around the room taking everything in. Her cuts, the fight that likely happened, the blood pooling on the floor. "How did we get so mixed up in this?" she asks, I grow numb, blocking out her fear.

I have to protect her, and if CHAOS wants to come for me, playing stupid fucking games, they can give it their best fucking shot, but I'll be damned if they fuck with her. I hold her tight, typing a quick message to Felix for our next move.

I pull Laurel to her feet, pulling her arm around my neck for support.

"Come on. Let's get you home."

She tries to protest, too worried about the dead man and her involvement here, but I keep moving toward the door. As I pull it open and we step into the cool night air, I let her get ripped from my arms to be met with a skeleton mask, inches from her face.

"Hi'ya Peach," he says and a scream rips from her chest, guttural and pained beyond anything I've ever heard come from her before. "Daith!"

Felix pulls a cloth bag over her face and I yell for her, selling the scene as he plunges a needle into her neck, her body going limp in his arms.

I lift my bike and Felix places her in front of me, straddling my lap. I pull my backpack on her and push my arms through, securing her to me.

"Burn it to the ground and meet me back at the house."

He nods, saying nothing as I pull out, clinging to Laurel tightly.

CHAPTER 22

LAUREL

The light is blinding, and it takes a second for my eyes to adjust as I come to, running my tongue along the swollen and tender skin of my busted lip. My skull pounds as I look around, trying to figure out where I am while attempting to wiggle free from the chains holding my arms above me. My heart rate spikes as I begin to panic, finding no give in my restraints.

The room is empty and barely looks like a room at all. The walls are cracked and crumbling, chunks of it missing completely in some places. A hanging lightbulb dangles above my head, illuminating only part of the room while the rest is cast in shadows. Dust and dirt fall on me as the ceiling above me creaks with the weight of someone walking.

I'm underground. I contemplate yelling, but obviously, no one here gives a shit that I want the hell out. How is my luck so bad, that I get kidnapped twice in one night.

"Fucking fuck" I growl, looking around me for anything I can use to my advantage.

"Tsk, tsk," a voice taunts as a tall frame steps from the shadows, the distorted voice familiar. The dim light reveals his skeleton mask and my chest caves, excitement and fear turning my skin clammy. Though an ease calms my erratic heart, I've been abducted by the psycho I know and not some stranger.

"Such a filthy mouth on such a pretty girl," he says, stepping closer. He watches me for a long moment, seeming to trail over every inch of my skin before I frustrated grunt comes from him and his hand whips up, holding a gun to my head. I squeeze my eyes shut, ragged breaths leaving my open lips. "Do you know how much is pisses me off to want you so bad?"

I slowly open my eyes, staring into the dark holes of his mask. Slowly he lowers the gun, mumbling to himself so low that I can't hear it. I watch him carefully as he moves away to the wall, grabbing the chain tethered to me. He yanks on it, stretching my arms, sending pain shooting through my body. My breathing hitches but I hold back my cries, only letting him get a gasp. He's pissed. I know he is. I fucked up and now, he's come to punish me for not following his rules.

"Where is Daith?" I ask, my throat tightening with the very real possibility that they killed him. "Let me down."

"I told you," he grinds out, stepping into my space, causing the chain to pull tighter and tighter. He grips my cheeks, digging his fingers into my skin. His grip turns soft before he trails the back of his fingers along my cheek, caressing me.

I swallow the small amount of affection whole, lapping it up like a starving dog. I stare into the black holes of the mask, steeling my strength with curiosity.

"You are mine." He crosses his arms, and even through his hoodie, I can see the taught muscles. "You are very bad at holding up your end of deals."

Even with my life on the line and my heart screaming for another man, there is something about this one that awakens something inside me every time he touches me.

He uses a single gloved finger to tilt my eyes back up at him. "The problem is," he says, full of disappointment. "You need to learn a lesson before you get anything from me." Turning from me, he walks back to the hook on the wall and pulls the chain tight.

I whimper as he secures the chain back on the wall, my toes barely touching the floor now. My heart rate climbs as he pulls a knife out of a sheath and flips it in his hand with skill.

"Shh. Shh," he soothes, dragging the blunt side of the blade down my lips.

I pinch my brows, holding my breath.

"We're just gonna play a couple games." He begins slowly cutting my shirt down the center. "You're gonna be my good little girl, and everything will be fine."

My shirt falls to the floor and the cold air does nothing to cool the sweat dripping down my back. The stale air is suffocating, mixing with his presence, there is no room to breathe. He leans down, and I stiffen as he runs the blade down my stomach to the button of my shorts, flicking them open. He nicks me and I grimace, watching carefully as he wipes the blood with a finger and brings it to his mouth under his mask.

He hums a low sound of satisfaction. "First game." He pulls my shorts down and they fall next to the scraps of fabric that were my shirt.

My thighs squeeze together, my eyes shutting, preparing for the worst. If he says I'm his, there is no stopping that. And as fucked as it is at this point, it excites me. Yes, I called Daith, but Reaper found me too. He came for me, just as ruthless and protective as Daith had, only he didn't need me to call.

He has kept me alive, letting me push the boundaries. He wants me here. Alive.

His voice, lower now, forces my thighs back open. "You'll dangle like fresh game until you are ready to apologize."

He walks back into the shadows as my eyes widen, panic surging through me again. He can't leave me in this hell hole!

"Wait!" I call after him, unsure of what to say, so I beg. "Please! Please don't leave me here! I'll do whatever you want! I'm sorry! I'm so sorry!"

He doesn't listen. He doesn't even stop. A heavy door slams shut with the sound of a lock clicking into place, my desperation echoing in the quiet room.

I quickly dry my tears, letting my exhausted head fall back. "Well, fuck."

CHAPTER 23

LAUREL

My stomach growls furiously as the only indication of time, letting me know days have passed, given the way my hunger has passed the nausea phase, turning into sickening numbness. The stench of my urine permeates the room and the embarrassment of that is worse than the smell. My eyes burn with exhaustion. I refuse to sleep, too paranoid that he'll come back in here. Hoping he'll come back. This is not what I had in mind when I fantasized about their power. I have stared at the concrete below me long enough to start using the cracks and stains to create distorted images.

I have searched every corner of my mind, trying to find the answer he wants. *Sorry* wasn't good enough. He wants a real apology, but the *what* has me worried. Sorry for fucking Daith? Sorry for plotting his murder? Sorry for...

I could get myself into more trouble if I spill something he didn't know about yet.

My exhausted mind is on the verge of snapping. I need out of here. I need to see sunlight. I need to call Cee. She's got to be so worried. I need to know if Daith is alive.

I can't breathe. I can't think. I just-

The lock outside clicks and I keep my eyes low, head hanging, though I don't think I could lift it on my own at this point.

"Peach," he calls, singing his nickname for me, and I part my lips, ready to play the part he needs to get me out of these chains. I'll have to gamble. His black boots come into view, and I lift my eyes, my body screaming in pain. My eyes meet the black mask, large flecks of chrome reflecting my ragged state back at me.

"Hi baby," I rasp, my eyes soft and forgiving. "I'm so sorry." Tears rolling down my cheeks, though my tears are for me and my every nerve that screams in agony.

He lifts a glass of water to my lips, and I drink it greedily, letting the excess drip down my neck to my bare stomach, cooling my skin. The feeling of contact, anything touching me, is enough to keep the tears rolling. The isolation has picked at my mind, eating away at my sanity, even more than the fractured walls that were there before, creating whispers and shadows.

I lick my lips, wetting them, soothing the dry cracked skin. "I know what was expected of me and I failed you."

His head tilts curiously. "Only three days. That's all you needed?" There's a touch of sarcasm hiding in those words but I don't let it provoke me.

I nod softly, "You chose me."

He nods, waiting for me to continue, giving me nothing to go off of.

"You needed me to be..." I pause. "Obedient."

He slides a knife from his pocket, flipping the blade open. "And what is it that you think you did to disobey, Peach?"

I stay silent, looking him over, his jeans and hoodie revealing nothing about him. My head turns as I look at the dungeon he's held me in. This is his home, his empire. Everything in it belongs to him. Including me. And Reapers don't tolerate someone trying to take what is theirs. That is public knowledge, of course.

Daith never stood a chance at keeping me to himself once Reaper decided I was worth *something* to him.

"You claimed me, and I let someone touch what was yours. I was giving someone else attention that was yours. Showing my body without any respect for your claim to me. And I called Daith to come save me when I should have called you."

His hand comes up to my face, slowly and gently, caressing my cheek with kindness. "Was that so hard?" he says, his voice barely a whisper, slipping below the voice modifier, something about it calming and reassuring. Safe.

"I'm yours."

He wipes a tear with his thumb, sweeping it into my mouth. "I love it when you cry for me."

His hands grip my hips and he pulls my body into him. Instinctively, I wrap my legs around him, my thighs feeling his hard frame.

"Can you do what it takes to be mine, no matter what I ask of you?"

I say nothing, my arms scream, begging for me to succeed in whatever it is he wants from me. I keep my chin high, defying the excruciating pain in my neck, not giving him the satisfaction of seeing my strength waiver. I can do what he wants. I can make it to the other side of this. I can be his.

I can protect Daith. I have to. He has to be alive.

"You think I can't break you?" he asks, seeing through my wavering mask. "You are already broken and mine to mold into something... exciting. You're options are submit to the happening or... die." He brushes a finger across my chest, swiping the sweat dripping down my skin, sticking his tongue out, licking it clean. I watch intently and unashamed. I nod slowly, submitting to his needs, though I can't deny the ache that is something far more shameful.

"I know everything about you. There is nothing you can hide from me and not a lie you can tell that I won't see through. I own every. Single. Part. Of you."

It takes everything inside me not to smile at that. Not even a twitch of my lips. He would notice. I brace myself, preparing for him to take what he wants from me, but as his hungry gaze travels over my body, he slowly drops to his knees, surprising me. He peers up at me and his hands run down my thighs, sending chills over my skin, before he hooks them over his shoulder.

"Close your eyes," he says firmly, and I don't dare disobey.

Tilting my head to the ceiling, I shut my eyes, and a moment later he grips my ass, shoving his face between my legs, devouring me. I gasp, trying to hold on to my sanity as electricity shoots through me. The thought of his identity revealed between my legs as he pleasures me adds to the ecstasy of the way his tongue slowly drags up and down. Damning proof that I could use to save myself and the man I love, yet I can't bring myself to disobey him again.

No. I can't bring myself to ruin the fun before it's even started.

My head clouds with lust and I wrap my legs tighter around his head, leaving all my embarrassment and shame on the disgusting floor beneath me. He groans into me, and I fuck him back, using the chains as leverage to rock my hips back and forth, slipping across his face perfectly. His stubble scratches my clit, and my breathing grows heavier, my pussy clenching, begging for something more.

I fight to keep my eyes closed, too scared to find out what he would do to me if I were to look down. I create an image in my head, needing something to focus on. Daith's face appears on the man I create, his tattoos following, and in my head, it's him between my legs, worshipping me perfectly.

"Fuck me," I whimper, desperate for him to fill me and fuck me into oblivion, though I know part of me will feel guilty in the morning.

He pulls back, running a finger across my clit, making me shake. Chains rattle as his answer comes. "No," he says, his voice still distorted

I wrap my legs around him tighter, squeezing my eyes shut, needing more. Begging for it.

"Cum on my face, saying that man's name with that pretty mouth."

My blood runs cold, wondering if he can hear my thoughts. The moment I say another man's name, he's going to slit my throat. He pushes a finger in me and I gasp. Then two, his thumb rolling over my clit before his tongue replaces it. His fingers curl inside me and I tremble, digging my heels into his back.

This is his game? He wants to make me cum with another man's name on my lips?

"I'm going to make you so dependent on me that you won't be able to breathe. You'll suffocate without me. You will crave even the worst things that I do to you. Go on Peach. Say his name. I won't mind." He thrusts his fingers in me roughly, hitting that perfect spot that makes my skin catch fire. I feel my orgasm building as I squeeze around his fingers desperately.

"Come on, cum for him," he says low, causing my stomach to flip, sending me over the edge as I stare at his mask, picturing the face of the man I've always loved.

I cum hard, seeing stars, thrashing with overstimulation as he jerks his fingers from me and covers me with his mouth, licking and sucking as I cum on his tongue. "Fuck, Daith. Yes. Yes!"

He sets my feet on the floor, and I feel his heavy breathing across my skin a moment later. Keeping my eyes shut, I fight for my own breath, sucking in air greedily. The cold air washes over me as the adrenaline leaves my body and he steps away from me.

"Open your eyes," he says, brushing his finger across my eyes. I obey, trying to focus in the dim room. "That's *my* good girl."

He moves to the wall, loosening the chain, his mask back in place. My body collapses with its own weight, and I fall to the floor, unable to lift any part of my body, my orgasm having taken every ounce of energy I had left. He scoops me up gently, and we move down a dark hall in silence. Though it's not entirely uncomfortable.

"Why?" I ask into the dark, needing to know why out of a building full of half-naked woman, he chose me.

He knocks on the door twice and light floods his mask as it opens from the outside, cool air rushing my skin and lulling my eyes closed.

"I've been watching you for a very long time. *You* were *always* going to be *mine*, and we're going to have so much fun."

CHAPTER 24

"**F**elix!" I shout, slamming the bedroom door behind me, leaving Laurel passed out and bound to her bed. A moment passes without an answer, and I grab a beer bottle from the coffee table, tossing it through an already cracked window. I'll make him fix that later. The sound of glass shattering and my voice booming echoes off the nearly empty walls. "Felix, I swear to -"

"Jesus, man," he groans sleepily, stumbling out of one of the bedrooms, likely hungover or still drunk. "Who pissed in your Cheerios?"

I throw his jacket at him as I pull the last location of his keys from my subconscious memory. "Wipe your cum off your face and let's go. We have to get his data today." I snatch the keys from the couch, and we grab our masks. He snorts a laugh following quickly on my heels. As much as he tries to stay out of it, he's enjoyed watching me toy with Laurel, feeding off the thrill.

Felix was a stray Ezra acquired, same as me. We're all brothers in every way that matters, Ezra just eludes father-figure vibes. We have each other's backs, but Felix annoys the piss out of me. We aren't far in age, but he tends to underestimate my difficulty of caring if he's breathing or splattered on the wall. Some days Ezra is the only thing standing between him and an unfortunate accident that results in the reapers being a two-man show and me keeping his toes for a necklace.

We park our bikes outside The Fuzzy Peach and slide our masks into place, turning our voice modifiers on. "It's not like CHAOS to play games. Why are they toying with us?" Felix asks.

He's right. Clean kills, waste removal, quick and efficient. They never play cat and mouse, so why did they mess with Laurel first, and why did they leave her alive?

The churning in my gut that makes me feel like I need to shit tells me that she won't leave this alive now that they have associated her with me. I had done well to keep Celeste as the only living connection to me to their knowledge up until now, but I half expected for them to want an explanation. What I didn't prepare for, is for CHAOS to show their corrupt government so openly.

Keep going. Stick to the plan. Take his empire. Bathe in the blood. Just keep your eyes open.

I soothe myself by going over the plan and thinking about the sweet sound of cartilage crunching. As we step to the door, bypassing the line, Ezra fakes a nervous gulp, bowing his head low letting us pass. I grin at the thought of the big bastard being genuinely afraid of anything.

"Up." I say, standing in front of the well-dressed man sitting in my favorite corner booth. He looks up in confusion, but the second his eyes meet mask, his stink face drops and he moves like a fire was lit under his ass.

"Order nothing. I'll be back in five," I say, leaving Felix at the table.

Moving down to the bottom level, I weave in and out of the tables, scanning the room intricately. Every flicker of light, every movement, every laugh, gets stored in my mind. The neon signs glow in patterns I know are there before I look. The bartender's movements are already logged permanently in my mind. Bryce's left hand always grabs the shaker first, then the bottle. I could draw this entire club in perfect detail, down to the frayed edges of the velvet seats and scuff marks on the stage.

"Welcome, Mr. Reaper." Bryce greets me with a careful smile, not holding my eyes for long, completely unaware that he knows the man behind the mask.

"Have we met?" I ask, propping my elbow on the polished wood bar and peering over at the schedule behind his back, noting Laurel's schedule in addition to the other dancers we planted and Vic himself.

He refills a drink, sliding it down to the other end of the bar. "No. We have a mutual friend and it's my job to remember our most important customers." His attempt to flatter me falls flat at the mention of my girl and he clears his throat. "Scarlette?"

"Yes. I'm aware of the name my property uses to hide herself from the scum that thrives here." I lean onto the bar, and he drops his gaze. It's cute how he pretends to still have any relation to her. He is nothing. He is the dirt she walks on. The leach that refuses to stop sucking her fucking blood, begging for the attention that I have already claimed in entirety.

"You can tell me where I need to go to have a little extra fun."

He wipes his hands on the towel tucked in his pocket before checking the watch on his wrist. "Lisa will be your girl to talk to. She'll be over there in about ten minutes." He motions toward the stairs on her right, wisely forgoing saying anything else about Laurel. That's the smartest thing he's done since I've had this displeasure of discovering his adoration for her.

I smack the bar in thanks and head back to my table. The stage lights up and the next dancer comes out, her track playing a slow, seductive harmony. Sliding into our booth, I ignore Felix and his uncomfortable posture. He's a more "behind the scenes" guy and hasn't had much time in the public. How Laurel was blind enough to believe he was me a few nights ago, I have no idea. It suited my plan, but she'll learn to read people like we do. She has to.

I put my earbuds in, taking in where our people are throughout the club, and out of the corner of my eyes, I see Felix looking around nervously, his gaze flicking back and forth. Focusing on the stage, I watch the current dancer finish and exit, dipping into the dressing room. I take a deep inhale, committing the oaky smell of the cigar a few tables down to memory, eyes closed and mind plotting, my mind's eye conjures the blueprint of the entire club.

Felix taps my shoulder, and a burst of anger comes to the surface, begging to spill blood. Opening my eyes, I pull one of my earbuds from my ear and glare at him.

"Don't you think you should be a little more alert?" he whispers but I can hear a touch of nervousness underlining the big boy tone he's trying to portray. Felix is smart and quick on his feet, but he's squirrely. He needs to actively be in the moment, anticipating every possible move. Years of working in the shadows doing clean-up and kill shots does that.

My eyes trail over his skinny frame and overall pathetic stature. "What gives you the impression that I'm not aware?" I take my gun from my pants and press it to the underside of his chin, forcing his head up an inch. "For instance, you forgot to put on deodorant before we left and the stench of your sweat tells me despite your steel expression you've been coached well to have, I still scare you."

"Intimidate is a better word," he says, a glint of fear flashing in his eyes as he struggles to keep them locked on mine, before tilting his head to Ezra for help. We both know I won't kill him—at least not for something as trivial as this. "You just looked distracted, and we have a lot at risk here."

"And you look like a waste of blood." I drop my gun to the table and his shoulders sink as he relaxes. "We have just about seven minutes before Big Bad John guarding the stairs takes his smoke break, trading with Lisa who manages the VIP and poker room schedule and wears too much Prada perfume. " I nod toward the subject, inching to sit up straighter. "I intend to take the available slot at eleven and you will need to play your fucking part of distracting everyone else long enough for me to get what I need upstairs. Can you do that, or would you like to keep questioning my competence? Or maybe you'd like to go cry to daddy Ez?"

He straightens his spine.

"Good. Now be a good bitch and go fetch." I hand him my card and he rolls his eyes, sliding out of the booth and heading to the bar.

Jane, one of ours, moves to one of her tables on the lower deck and her eyes meet mine. Her flirty smile she was wearing for the 50-year-old man with a foot fetish drops and I raise my hand, wiggling my fingers in a flirty wave. She gives me a forced smile that wavers as she turns her attention back to the man tucking a 20 into her neon panties.

Just as she turns my way, I hold my finger up in the air, motioning for her to come closer. "Hi, Sir," she says, doing her best to keep her character in place with a sweet smile.

"Have you heard anything about... *drink* changes?" I ask, toying with her.

She subtly looks over her shoulder and then back at me, wondering if she missed a code word meeting. "Um, no changes but the main one never sells out before midnight," she says slowly, a poor effort to code her words on the spot.

"What?" I ask flatly.

She swallows, leaning in close, trying to appear as if she's flirting. "Vic's doesn't come in until midnight to manage the VIP rooms. Please don't kill me." She stands up, her brows pinched nervously as she attempts to smile again.

Well, that was amusing.

"Very good. Scurry along little mouse," I snort. I spot Lisa trading shifts and I stand from my table. I pass Felix at the bar, taking a left straight to the stairs where Lisa stands with her clipboard.

"Lisa, is it?" I ask, drawing her attention to me. Her perfume assaults my nose, and I cringe.

"It is. Are you looking for something specific? We would be happy to have you join us in anything that might entice you." Her pitch is clear, unwavering, and I give her credit for not being shaken even the slightest about who we are. That tells me she's seen what lurks in the shadows.

"I'd be happy to learn about how your VIP rooms work as well as getting on the schedule for the next poker night."

She perks up, seeming to be pleased with my answer. "Of course. Mr. Vic loves having new interest in those."

Of course he does. Hustling in poker and over-priced sex. What's not to love when you are at the receiving end of the money?

"The VIP room is on a schedule each night that we are open. Your choice of any of our girls that are assigned to work the rooms. There is an annual membership fee and extra fees if you want to participate in activities beyond a private dance, basic intercourse, or request a girl that is not typically available." I nod, just as Felix moves next to me, handing me a drink and my card before sauntering back down the stairs.

Lisa continues, glancing nervously at Felix who pulls his gun, letting it hang at his side, though I have a suspicion that it's not for fear of her life at our hands. "We do run a clean and respectable establishment so a background check and a STD screening must be completed weekly for all VIP members." Her mouth parts, though she hesitates to speak as commotion breaks out, Felix at the center. "Though, given your... status, we can wave the background check. I'm sorry, please excuse me for a moment." She smiles kindly and rushes down the stairs, her heels clicking rapidly.

I take my opening, checking over shoulder before slipping up the stairs and down the hall toward Vic's office that is currently empty due to his current poker game I saw on the schedule. I pick the lock and round the desk, his musty cologne permeating the room is almost suffocating. *He even smells disgusting.*

My head flashes with a memory, latching onto the small hint of perfume that lingers, wondering if it's Laurel's. Has she been here? Has he touched her? Oh, the ways I would enjoy splitting him open nine different ways for putting his hands on her.

Stay on task. Fucking focus.

Quickly, I push my flash drive into his computer that effectively bypasses all the firewalls he has in place, downloading all files without a trail. Casually, I flip through the papers on his desk, invoices and more upcoming schedules, retaining every line.

A woman's scream rips through the air and shattering glass follows.

I make quick use of the time I have left, pulling his drawers open, grabbing a leger with random letters and markings. I sigh. I'll give that to him. The slimy fuck was smart enough to code it. I pull the drive free and replace everything back to its spot, down to the angle of his pen that laid across the stack of papers. Closing the door behind me, I lock it, moving quickly as the commotion downstairs settles. I lean against the wall, just around the stairs as Lisa's panicked pace comes clicking up the stairs.

"Mr. Reaper?" she says, gasping as she rounds the corner and nearly runs into me.

"Just appreciating the dated wallpaper and curious stenches coming from each room," I say, enjoying the concerned look she gives me.

"Uh, yes, well you aren't supposed to be-" she stammers.

"Wonderful," I say, cutting off her objection to my intrusiveness and hand her my card. "Go ahead and fill out my membership for me doll. I'll be using it soon. I'll have my screening sent over in the morning."

She nods, regaining her professional mannerisms, deciding not to object. "Poker nights are invitation only. I'll see to it that Vic takes your application into account, though I'm sure there will be no issues given your known worth." She scurries back down the stairs, as if agitated and flustered, and I follow casually. This lady seriously needs to remove the stick from her ass. I bet her and Ezra would make the best of friends. Maybe even braid each others hair. "I'll bring this to your table as soon as I have your receipt." She smiles curtly and motions for one of the girls to come hold her place at the stair entrance.

I stop at the bar on the way back to my booth, taking a seat at the end. Bryce spots me out of the corner of his eye and I notice the way his body tenses. Given the beer he almost drops, I would guess his issue with me is a little less to do with fear for himself and a little more to do with his concern with Laurel. Something I can easily fix. *She doesn't need your concern, you little prick.*

"What can I get you?" he asks, eyes flicking from me to the computer as he works on something that I would bet is less than urgent.

I slap the bar, making him jump slightly. "You can show me the respect of your attention while I'm speaking."

He nods, doing his best to keep his eyes on mine. "You like my girl?" I ask and he stares at me blankly, unsure if this is a trick question.

"Uh, I do, but we recently... broke things off," he says, hesitantly.

I nod, running my fingertip in a circle on the bar top. "Ask her out." I don't pose it as a question, and you'd think I just asked him to build a bomb from the utterly confused expression plastered to his face. "Relax junior. If you can make it happen, I'll let her go. Wish upon a star or find some magic fairy dust and ask her out on a date." The look of constipation doesn't leave. In fact, it gets worse, if that is possible. "And you will under no circumstance, tell her about this conversation or my inquiry on the VIP rooms." He stands frozen and my irritation peaks. What she ever saw in this meek little dipshit is beyond me. "Speak!" I yell, grabbing the attention of the few men around us.

"Y-yes. I understand."

"Excellent. See you around Bruce. Oh, she likes lilies, by the way." I pat the table, leaving him to chew on that. His idiocy is contagious, and I can't risk losing any more brain-cells than what I've already fried trying to quiet the voice that likes to torment me.

I slide my phone to Felix, noting the woman next to the stage holding her bleeding arm bandaged and Vic sternly talking under his breath, his eyes flashing to us briefly. "Can you break this?"

He looks over the encrypted leger, mumbling to himself as I crumble the receipt Lisa left me, taking the pen in my hand and twirling it between my fingers, my patience growing thin.

"Simple enough. But I'll need more. There should be an index," Felix says.

Annoyance grows at my simple error. I knew better, but she's in my fucking head, all the time. I thought having her with me would give me everything I've been missing, but she's making me lose my edge.

Felix's leg shakes idly under the table, working on my nerves as he thinks of another diversion to get me back upstairs. Harassing a dancer isn't going to work twice. I fix my stare on him, and it only takes a moment for him to realize I'm about to cut his foot off and shove it up his ass.

"Ah, your annoying behaviors. That reminds me," I say, and his brows furrow. "You put your hands on Laurel." I *"tsk"* him like disobedient a child.

The relief of his bouncing leg is short-lived as the rhythmic sound of something tapping against a metal table has my chest tightening and my head snapping to the side where someone a few tables down is idly bouncing their pen.

The same asshole from the first night I was here. It echoes like the familiar sound of water drops hitting a pipe in an empty basement. My teeth clench and before I can take another breath, I flip the pen in my fingers and drive it into the center of Felix's palm with my left hand. My right hand raising my gun, my finger squeezing the trigger. The asshole's body falls from his booth and the room fills with screams and the smell of gunpowder.

"There. Problem solved."

The club will be shut down at least for a few days, giving us some time to get the index to decipher his book of secret connections, and I get time with Laurel.

Felix groans, pulling the pen from his hand, then quickly relaxes, falling into motion at my side as I stand, accepting his punishment. I raise my palms facing the rest of the room staring at me, though no one dares speak. The DJ stops the music, giving me the floor. "Sorry, everyone! So sorry!"

Vic comes rushing down the stairs he just ascended, stalking toward us a moment later. His eyes meet mine and his intimidating posture shifts, ever so slightly before he puts it back in place. "Ah, Vic. Just the man I wanted to see about my membership."

"Did you also want to make a mess of my establishment while causing me to lose a well-paying customer? Mr. *Reaper*?"

I shove my hands into my pockets. "You should mind your mouth, Vic. An unhappy Reaper makes for very..." I step into him, my fingers twitching at my side. "Bad business."

"Hm." He smiles, doing his best to hide his disdain. "Of course. My apologies. However, now this is a crime scene and I'm about to lose quite a bit of money."

"Right you are." I pat him on the shoulder. "And I apologize for the mess. I assure you my contributions upon approval of my membership will be more than substantial."

He nods, clearing his throat. "Well, then. I hope you enjoy everything we have to offer. I look forward to seeing you more often once this trouble has been cleared with the police department." With that, he turns, brushing Felix's shoulder as he steps over the body sprawled out on the floor, a perfect shot between his eyes, draining blood all over the floor. His rush to dismiss us is likely because this place is about to be swarming with law enforcement and he has a lot to hide.

I turn to Felix who already has his phone out and we're out the door, mounting our bikes before they show up.

Chapter 25

With CHAOS on my ass and a recently unapproved house fire, I really should be limiting the lengths I go for Laurel, yet I still find myself sitting outside of her favorite Italian restaurant, watching all the happy couples having dinner and polite conversation. I watch through the glass window, watching this one particular man and the growing adoration in the eyes of the woman sitting across from him. From the ring on her finger and the way they sit comfortably in conversation, subtly touching each other beneath the table, I would guess they've been married for at least 5 years, though I would guess 10 to be more accurate.

I have my woman in my bed, waiting for me, and instead of preparing for her first impression of the hive, I'm here, waiting to use this man to give me some sound advice on how to achieve what he has. I've never been the type that saw a white picket fence future, but with her I can see it so clearly. Except instead of working a 9 to 5, we kill people, and instead of romantic candle lit dinners, it's takeout on the run.

Those don't exactly match up to the dreams she has and I need some compromising ideas.

He stands from the table and excitement shoots through my veins.

Yes. Yes. Yes. I need to kill something else so bad, I can feel a rash forming on my ass. I'll add cream for that to the shopping list along with flowers she's not allergic to and some girly smelling soaps. The dick at the club was not at all satisfying.

I stick to the shadows, keeping the distance as he walks her to their car, kissing her softly before she slides into the passenger seat. She's smiling wide, like her life is perfect. That's all I want. I want Laurel to always look at me like that.

As he rounds the back of the car, I step out of the shadows and jam a sedative into his neck, his body hitting the ground with a thud. He's heavier than I expected, and it takes all my effort to pull his limp body into the bushes and shadows. I inhale, walking back to their car and tap on the glass softly. The woman's eyes go wide, and I motion for her to roll the window down. She cracks it, just enough to hear me speak, her face now pale, her hand gripping the door firmly as she stares at my mask and not the gun in my hand.

"Your husband won't be coming home. I'm gonna need you to leave, and by all means, feel free to call the cops, but I'm gonna have to insist that you wait at least an hour before doing that or I'll kill everyone you love, okay?"

The woman starts hyperventilating, calling out for her husband whose name I just discovered is Thomas. I roll my eyes. My God, it's like a bad horror movie. He's not going to answer, dumbass.

She rolls the window up and slides over to the driver seat, scrambling for her phone, but before she can pull it out, I'm gone, slipping into the shadows, taking her husband with me, slowly but surely.

The sound of banging and tools clattering comes from the floor above me as Felix works to fix the window I broke.

"Where have you been?" Skid asks from the other end of the phone, sounding panicked. I can hear her clicking on her keyboard and papers rustling.

"Things got messy for a moment. Some pisshead took Laurel and then CHAOS attacked her with a message that they're coming," I say, using my knife to clean under my nails.

"I know. Felix reported the clean-up to me. But..."

Silence fills the air for a moment and I wonder if the call dropped. "Hello?"

"I'm here. I'm just confused because...." Her fingers click on the keys rapidly. "Yeah, there is no report of CHAOS being in town. That's what I wanted to talk to you about." I cross my boots, changing positions in the rickety chair for the hundredth time. "I'm not so sure this is them. We would know if they were planning a sweep right?"

I exhale, quietly, exhausted with everything trying to ruin half a decade of dreaming. "I'm not sure. If it's not them, we can request outside surveillance in compliance to see if they can see something we can't. This guy is not invisible."

"On it," she says, submitting the request to have CHAOS surveillance dispatched. Maybe they will see something we can't.

"Can I ask you something?" I ask, looking over at the unconscious man I kidnapped dangling from chains.

She's quick to respond, her tone completely different- softer and cautious. "Of course. That's why I'm here."

"Do you think I'm capable of having... normal things? Like Marriage. Dinner nights and kids."

She inhales slowly and I wait anxiously for her answer. "No. Not in the normal sense of those words at least."

"What do you mean?" Something in my chest stings but I quickly brush it off, more annoyed that there is something I now want but can't physically take by force.

"Your version of those things look very different than the rest of society."

"You seem happy with this new guy," I say flatly. She's never very open about her love life, but she seems happier lately.

"I am, but me and you are different."

"How so?"

"If having those things you want meant it didn't involve Laurel, could you let her go?"

I stay silent, letting that disappointment sink in. Something vile and putrid swirls in my stomach at that thought. "No."

"You aren't capable of feeling empathy. You're selfish, obsessive to an unhealthy level, and true love, a happy marriage, those things in the traditional sense, don't contain... you. But maybe, she is the one person that can survive your version of those things."

I end the call just in time for my new friend to start wiggling his fingers. He comes to, bound to the chains Laurel was in hours ago. He blinks

171

slowly before focusing on me. I pace slowly, circling him like a predator, studying him. He's different from the others. His fear is clear, but he's not begging. Not crying. His mind is still sharp, calculating. It's almost... irritating.

I stop in front of him, standing just a few inches away. "You've got a good life, haven't you?" I say, letting the words hang in the air. "A wife who loves you. Kids. A *real* family. How does it feel? To have everything. To have something *real*?"

He doesn't answer, just glares at me with defiance in his eyes.

I lean in, my voice soft, teasing, almost like I'm trying to provoke him. "Tell me, how do you achieve something like that? Did she ever doubt the bond between you?"

He flinches, just a little, but then he speaks, his voice rough and strained. "You brought me here for relationship advice? Where is my wife?" He looks around the room, both relief and fear in his expression.

"I'm not going to hurt her. Your wife is safe. And your kids are too. You on the other hand, well." I shrug, caring less if he gets to make it home for dinner. The heart ache won't kill them. Maybe this will be the beginning of their villain story. How exciting.

His breath hitches, and for a moment, I can see the confusion flicker in his eyes. He's trying to process this, trying to figure out what I want.

"I have this woman, and she's great, but you could see how all of this could be a lot to adjust to."

"You're asking me how to make her feel *comfortable* with you being a murderer?" He's almost choking on the words, still trying to hold it together. "How could she ever feel safe with you?"

His jaw tightens and I commend his efforts to remain stoic in the face of death. I take a step closer, not minding the anger in his voice. It's something I can use.

"There is no one she could trust more than a man willing to kill for her. You're not getting it," I say, my voice steady, but something darker in my chest. "I've never had anything like what you have. I've never been *wanted*. Everything I've gotten, I've had to take. But with her, it's different. She's... different." I let the words sit for a moment, almost tasting the frustration rising in me. "I'm asking you for answers. How do I keep her? How do I make her stay through the adjustment period?"

He stares at me for a long time, then forces a dry chuckle. "You can't control someone's love or comfort," he says, his voice hoarse but unwavering. "That's not how it works. It's a gift formed out of genuine trust. It's about choice. She won't stay if she's just another one of your prisoners."

He's trying to get under my skin, risking it all with nothing left to bargain, but as I roll his words over, they make sense. I suppose I knew that, but there's something in me that fears her choice to run.

"She is one of the only people in my life that know the real me and the only one that doesn't know this—" I motion to myself "—is the other side to the same coin. I can't let her leave if she decides she can't accept it. If I have to make her stay, I will, because the alternative..." I stop talking, keeping those words in my head, hating how bitter they would taste now.

He's still staring at me, his eyes more focused now, like he's sizing me up. "You can't keep her by making her fear for her life," he says. "You're not just looking for her love. You're looking to control her. And she'll never love you that way."

His words sting more than they should. I stare back at him, my heart pounding, because there's something *real* in what he's saying — something I don't want to acknowledge.

I don't know how to love her. Not without fear, not without control. That is who I am.

"You don't understand," I mutter, pacing again, turning my back on him. "You don't understand what it feels like to need someone that badly. To want to keep them so much, you can't breathe without them."

There's silence for a long time, just the quiet hum of the fluorescent light above, the tension thick in the room.

"Yes. I do."

Then, almost to myself, I add, "If she doesn't stay, it will kill me."

I wait for him to say something, but he stays silent, hanging from the chains, defeated and broken.

Taking my chair, I sit in front of him, watching my clock near the hour mark. *Time's up.* As I stand, grabbing my gun from my waist band, he speaks, keeping his eyes on the ground below him.

"If she knows the other side of you and loves you, just remind her what made her feel that. Chances are, parts of this side of you have leaked into the other and she is well aware of your capabilities, loving you thorns and all."

I nod, pulling the slide back on my gun. I hear him exhale a defeated breath of air and he looks up at me, staring my gun in the face. "I will love my wife to the end of this life and into the next. I have loved her with every fiber of my body, so much it's crippling. If she loves you like that, she will do anything for you if you are willing to love her the same way."

"Thanks Thomas."

I pull the trigger and his body goes limp, the single wound in his head leaking blood into a pool on the floor, waiting for me to harvest my favorite part. The windows to the soul.

Darkness feeds off darkness, twisted souls damn everything they touch, and I'll drown in the abyss to have her wreak havoc at my side.

Slipping into Laurel's room, I find her still out cold. I dosed her again, needing more time. It's eating at me—the possibility that she bolts the first chance she gets.

I strip my clothes off and climb on the bed behind her, slipping under the sheets against her naked body. I run my hands over the rolling curves of her body, loving the feel of her soft skin against mine, no border between us.

There will be time for me to have her rough and breathless, begging and drooling. Right now, I need her softly, our skin igniting with the fire that burns in my chest for her. I want to soak in every second that I have her wrapped around me, focusing on every inch I push into her.

Carefully and gently, I pull her leg up, giving me more access to swipe my lubed hand over her entrance before slipping inside her. I groan, pushing deep inside her as she sleeps, completely unaware. Nights of being teenagers, sleeping like this, buried in her on the couch come flooding into my memory.

For the first time in a long time, I just let myself breathe. I feel her, letting the moments stretch on, the sensation of her body against mine, connected settles the raging storm inside me. For this moment, it's just me and her. Nothing outside of this room matters. I savor her vulnerability that is just for me. Finally, I have what I have been craving for so long—not just control over her, her, in every sense of the word.

I keep holding onto her. Holding onto this fragile, beautiful thing between us that I don't know how to let go of—refuse to let go of. I inhale her scent, something uniquely hers, faded and mixed with the death still staining her skin. I push my face further into her matted hair, so every inch of her is touching me. I feel the rhythm of her steady breathing, my own syncing up, like our bodies were meant to move together—a perfect match. My fingertips trail over her spine and into the dimples of her back. I trace back up to her rib cage, dragging my finger over the tiny scar where I hurt her years ago, though she doesn't know that I know.

"You're so perfect for me," I whisper, close to her ear, and though she can't hear me, I say it again, brushing my lips across the soft skin of her shoulder as I sit inside her, unmoving.

I reach behind me, grabbing the injector I set on the bed, moving to her arm that is bound to the headboard. The device clicks, inserting the tracker under the skin, only leaving a small and easily overlooked dot of blood. I unbind her wrists and move them to her sides.

"Don't leave me. Okay?"

I sit in front of my monitor, watching footage of Laurel from the cameras I installed in her room, staring at the empty spot I was an hour ago. My chest rises and falls easier now. Her phone chimes and I grab it from the corner of my desk.

Bryce: Can we talk? I wanna see you. Dinner?

I grin to myself. The kid has no fucking game, but he doesn't waste time. Where's the spice? A woman wants to be told what she's doing for a date. Dinner. Be ready at seven. Here's a necklace I bought for that pretty neck I want to wrap my hands around later. Wanna see the knife I'll use to cut your tongue out if you say no?

I type in her password and begin typing her response. Seems she wasn't smart enough to change her password when she changed her security system.

Laurel: My house this weekend. 8 o'clock

I wait, seeing if he will fight back with his own plans or question her eagerness. To my annoyance but thrill, his response is less than.

Bryce: It's a date

It most certainly is fucking not, buddy.

His desperation makes this all too easy, and the increased urge to have his limbs as my new wall decoration is less than subtle.

I turn back to my monitor. The live feed of Laurel sleeping in her room next door to mine plays next to it. I dosed her again, deciding I needed more time to decide what I'm going to say to her.

I'm anxious. Giddy but worried she won't be everything I expect. Everything I need. I shake the thought. No, she just needs time to warm up to me. Our souls are bound, no matter what form they appear as, forever intertwined in the threads of fate. Her and I—we are cosmic, in any life.

"New fixation?" Ezra asks, slurping his drink. Gin with an orange peel, never anything different.

"Same fixation. New toy," I answer, my eyes glazing over as I fantasize about the pink panties I stole, her ass facing the camera and in perfect view. I lock the screen and spin my chair, annoyance bubbling under my skin. "Did you need something?"

His eyes linger on my monitor for a moment before he moves through the threshold, perching on the side of my king bed.

"You need to call a meeting and update everyone."

I groan, my temper now threatening to overflow. "Plans haven't changed."

Ezra raises a brow. "The fact that your body count has increased past what we expected and your... toy is going to cause a conflict of interest. You at least need to set the boundaries to our employees." He stands, and shoves his hands into his pockets, treading carefully but taking his stance as my brother. "We wouldn't want the body count to include our own assets. We need everyone we have, and you are a loose cannon with very thin boundaries. Felix's hand is a clear example."

I snort a laugh, though the big brute doesn't share the humor. He makes a good point, but I really need to take some time to try to lighten him up.

Standing from my desk, I move toe-to-toe with him. He's much broader than I am, but only about 3 inches taller. I hold a stoned expression, challenging him the way I always have. Then I soften my expression, patting his face playfully. "Always so serious."

He growls and I relent, only ever to him. "Fine." Then I turn back to my desk before pushing a paper into the center of his chest. "Here. Your boss needs to know my dick is clean. Pass this along, would ya?" I wink, moving past him, laughing to myself.

I send a text and wait in the chapel, sitting on my throne with a glass of whiskey in hand.

"Alright, you sacks of miserable shit." I lean forward, bracing on my knees. "The Fuzzy Peach is closed for the rest of the week, as you may have noticed. Sometimes we have to improvise."

I turn over my shoulder to the projector behind me and click the remote, throwing up the live stream of my girl. "This here..." I turn back to my boys. "Is *my* property." I click the remote again, spitting the screen with a picture from her social media. "You don't speak to her. You don't touch her. You don't fucking look at her." Territorial urges rush through me, and I twist my jaw to keep from breaking my own teeth.

Heads drop respectfully, their eyes dodging the screen.

"Look at her!" I scream, echoing through the room. I search the men sitting before me.

A pair of eyes shoot up, trying to obey orders, and I put a bullet between his eyes. He falls forward, head cracking on the pew in front of him before falling to the ground. Silence fills the room, not a breath being expelled as time stands still for me. Their fear fuels me like a fucking fire and I eat that shit up, daring another one of them to even think about what is mine.

"Fucking hell." Ezra sighs.

A manic giggle escapes, and I shake it off, getting back to business. "The part she plays in this will be vital and when I'm done…" I flick the screen off, tossing the remote on the chair behind me then tossing back the rest of my drink. "Well I don't know yet, but she will forever be off limits to you."

Murmurs sound off from my small crowd and before I can say anything, my hand is wrapping around a knife laying on the podium and it's being flung into the crowd aimlessly.

A few gasps silence the room, blade sticking out of the cloth pew in the second row, between Jacob and Terrance.

"I'm sorry, were there any questions?"

The crowd turns into statues, scared to even shake their head to appease me. Laurel will be the first female Reaper. I'll put my life on it.

I smack Ezra on the back, standing there slightly stunned, though I can see that part of him expected this. He may advise me, but I have the final say. I answer to no one, I just play nice when I want to.

"There. Meeting adjourned."

I bow before flipping him the bird and leaving him and Felix, who groans, to clean my mess.

"At least he didn't break any more fucking windows."

CHAPTER 26

LAUREL

The smell of coffee floods my senses, attempting to pull me from my deep sleep. My eyes open, revealing a room that isn't mine. Still in a fog, I roll, shoving my face into the pillow, smelling clean linen and cologne. A second later I'm sitting up right, my mind clear, my senses on high alert.

"Reaper?"

I look around the unfamiliar room, large enough to be my living room. Swinging my legs over the side of the bed, I push my toes into the fuzzy black rug and grab my head as it pounds.

Sighing, I take in the room, loving the deep tones and gothic decorations and furniture. It's my dream room, as if it was plucked straight from them.

I replay everything in my head, piecing the puzzle together and filling in the gaps. I expect fear to come rushing in as I remember the days I spent filthy and malnourished in a room that smelled like blood and decay, but it doesn't come. Instead, it's curiosity.

Looking down, I take inventory of my naked body, only aches and small cuts mar my skin. A man's shirt is laid on the edge of the bed for me and I can't help but shove my nose in it, before pulling it over my head.

I stand slowly, forcing my weak knees to hold my sore body as I rush to the door. Placing my ear to the wood, I listen for any indication that he's standing outside, waiting to lock me back up for disobeying.

I don't remember any orders to stay here. Hell, I don't even know where *here* is. He said he wouldn't hurt me. But then, how far can you take the words of a killer?

Despite every rational thought my brain screams at me, something alluring pulls me toward him. I slowly twist the knob, making no sound as I pull the door open one inch at a time. I peer through the crack, seeing an empty hallway full of rooms with closed doors. Stained concrete, cracked and worn, give me no indication of where I am. I step out into the hall, pulling his shirt over my ass. Following the hall, I walk cautiously, having nothing to defend myself, but unable to fight the need to find him again.

Stupid. Stupid. Stupid.

What the fuck am I going to do when I find him? Ask to leave? Run away? Stay for breakfast?

The hall turns, opening into a large common area with stained-glass windows. I stand still, admiring their beauty as the sun shines through them, painting the floors with distorted rainbows of color. The room is bare, only hosting a couch and TV, but littered clothes and dishes.

My eyes land at the far right where large double doors secured shut from the inside. My foot twitches to step to the right, the smarter part of myself screaming to run and try my hand at breaking out of here.

Turning left instead, I ignore rationality. Finding the kitchen, I note the location of the half-empty coffee pot, but not a single knife in sight.

Clattering comes from a distance, and I jump, sucking in air and fisting my hand. I wait, anticipating him coming around the corner or the other Reapers attacking me, mistaking me for an intruder.

There are others, aren't there? I haven't seen any, though I know I heard other people in the house days ago. My hands grow clammy.

My ears perk up, hearing something from deeper in the house. I follow the sound of the faint voice... no... music. I turn down another hall, and then another, beginning to worry that I'm going to get lost in this maze. Looking back, I try to remember my path in case I need to run.

I get to another large door, this one with an open lock hanging from the handle, and my stomach churns. Knowing what this is, I open it. The music pours through the crack, hiding the creak as I slip inside.

I need to see him. Need to talk to him.

I creep slowly down the cement stairs, the loud music growing closer with every step. Reaching the end, the hall takes a sharp right and I peer around the corner, keeping myself concealed as I try to see into the room.

My eyes scan the room I was held in. The same chains, the same single light hanging from the ceiling that looks as if it's seen better days. My eyes land on the dark puddle on the floor. Blood. I take inventory of my body again, though I know it's not mine. I move further into the room, needing to see more. As I stand in the middle of the room, looking up at the chains that held me, I spin back toward the door and my breath catches.

A mangled man lays dead on the floor against the wall I was just hiding behind. I shake my head, my hand covering my mouth to hold back screams.

A low growl comes from deeper in the room and I turn abruptly. A very large Doberman steps out of the shadows, bloody teeth bared, pink tinted slobber dripping from his mouth as he steps closer, closing the distance between us.

"Easy boy." I hold my palms out toward him. "Good psycho doggy," I tell him, my voice shaking and nervous as I take a slow step backward toward the way I came in. He lets out a resounding bark that causes me to lurch backward, slipping in the blood coating the floor. I scramble to my feet and back into a hard body that softly wraps his arms around me.

I quickly turn, gripping the man's shirt and I throw myself behind his tall frame. "Get your fucking dog!"

I push against his back, shoving him closer to the canine. He chuckles as the dog looks past him, walking in a wide circle to get to me. I move at the same speed, using the man as a human shield.

"Him? Dom's a sweet boy. Does anything I ask," Reaper says, his voice distorted and all too familiar.

"Ask him to stop looking at me like I'm his next meal!" I beg, not caring that I am holding onto his shirt with a death grip.

Dom snarls again and snaps in warning.

"Please!" I yell, and the dog lunges for me. I'm picked up and swung out of the way, Dom's teeth barely missing the hem of my shirt.

"Heel!" Reaper bellows and Dom stills, looking at his owner attentively, planting his ass on the floor. "Leave it," he orders again, showing the dog the palm of his hand. With a nod of his head, Dom leaves with his little nubby tail wagging. The fucker almost ripped my face off, and he prances away like he's the goodest boy.

"You are such a dick," I mumble, hopping down from the small table I was thrown on.

"Oh, come on. That was hilarious," Reaper counters, though as I right myself, I notice the blood coating my hands and reality comes crashing back in.

"You killed him," I say, voice cracking, heart aching for the man lying feet from me, his blood staining my skin.

"That's what we do," he says casually, grabbing my shoulders. "This is the world you wanted to be a part of."

I shake my head. Seeing it now, the amount of blood on the floor, the stillness of his body, his eyes missing. It's brutal. The reality of a life lost. It's chilling in a way nothing else can compare to. How could I want to be someone like him? This wasn't the thrill I felt in my dreams.

"What did he do?" I ask, my voice quiet. How awful could he have been to deserve such a fate?

"Nothing," Reaper says as if it's nothing to concern myself with, and a chill rushes down my spine.

With the swipe of this thumb, he smears the man's blood across my lips and down the side of my face. "Red looks good on you."

I stand still, unmoving, afraid to make one wrong move.

He steps toward the door reaching for my hand. I look down at his stained palm, my own matching, and I slowly place mine in his and he tugs lightly, pulling me toward him, guiding me out of the room of nightmares.

Chapter 27

He chains my wrists together. I let him, taking in his cave-like room instead of fighting back.

"Do you like it?" he asks, tucking the key into his pocket. It's a deep red, bright, but with something sinister tainting it, though maybe it's just the room. "You should," he says, pushing me to sit on the edge of the bed before looking at his work. "It's yours."

My brows pinch together.

"I did it the night I took you," he says, waving a strip of paper at me with a red swatch on the end of it.

This room is painted with my blood, or at least the color of it. My stomach swirls, though it's not disgust blooming in my stomach. The corner of my mouth tilts with a faint smile. That's oddly, romantic.

He stares intently, appreciating my adoration. "I hoped you would like it. You've invaded my mind, stealing my time and energy like a leach." He pushes a finger down the side of my face and taps my temple. "Now, I can feel like I'm living inside you every night when I lay my head down." He inhales the aroma of the acrylic, exhaling long and dramatic. "A second best to skinning you and decorating my walls with the real thing."

I swallow. Holy shit, he's a lunatic. There's something more wild about him now that I'm on his home turf.

He watches my throat with a hunger that now seems much more than lust, though still wild and unpredictable. He hands me a plate of food I hadn't noticed sitting on his desk and nods to further up the bed where a single Lillie lays.

I cut my eyes at him. "Again with the lilies?" I ask, annoyed and utterly baffled. Out of all the ways to kill me or torture me, he goes with anaphylactic shock?

I sit on his bed, as far away from the flower as possible, picking at the grilled cheese and flicking it onto his bluish-black comforter as I stare at his back. He types idly on his computer, the privacy screen blocking me from seeing anything. I look around his room, the deep red walls contrasting the black tones of everything else.

"You're not eating," he says, continuing whatever the fuck he's been working on for the past hour.

I rattle the chain connected to my ankle, making a stink face at his back. "It's hard to have an appetite when I feel like a prisoner."

He sighs spinning to face me, and though his entire head is covered by the mask and hoodie, I swear I can see the look of annoyance and a hint of discomfort.

"Doesn't that thing get itchy?" I ask, flicking a piece of bread at him.

"You're not a prisoner. You are restrained to keep you from doing anything stupid and pissing me off."

Does he think I'll run? Try to kill him? At the moment it is tempting to wrap this chain around his throat. I scoff and he grunts, snatching the sandwich from my plate and holding it in front of my face.

"Eat," he barks.

"Unchain me," I challenge, my stomach begging for me to stop being a stubborn bitch. But the way I see it, he won't let me die unless it's on his terms. My life is my bargaining chip.

He grabs my jaw with his other hand and pries my mouth open before shoving the food into my mouth, forcing me to bite it or choke. The second he lets go I spit the food onto the floor at his feet.

"You haven't eaten anything in days. Stop being stubborn."

"Unchain me," I state again, slower this time in case he didn't understand me the first time. "I'm not going anywhere. Get this bullshit off me."

His fists ball, knuckles cracking, but he caves, reaching in his pocket and pulling out the key to the shackle. A sense of accomplishment washes over me, and I smile, letting him see my contentment.

He sits back in his chair, slamming the key on the desk and crossing his arms, watching me expectantly. I restrain myself from shoving the rest of the sandwich down my throat, only taking a small bite and swallowing. The deliciousness dances over my tastebuds, my stomach clenching around the first ounce of substance since the morning he took me.

"I don't even like grilled cheese," I say, dusting my hands off over the plate. He chuckles, turning back to his computer.

"It's your favorite, paired with tomato soup," he says dismissively.

I pause mid-bite. "How do you know that?" I ask, chewing slowly, my eyes drilling a hole into the back of his head.

He clicks a few times before turning the screen to face me, now crystal clear as I stare at my bedroom. "I know everything about you, Laurel. When will you get that?"

I swallow, my throat now dry, my heart lurching at the creepy sentiment.

"Right," I say, thinking how stupid I was for asking. "But I know nothing about you," I say, finishing the last bite. Silence meets my ears and minutes pass. I shift uncomfortably and I ache between my legs. As the thought blooms, my eyes find him again and my lips part before I can stop them. "Did you... touch me? While I was asleep?" I swallow the lump that forms in my throat, watching as he continues to work at his computer.

Finally, he pauses, only for a moment to turn toward me. "Yes. I love how it feels to be inside you when you are... limp and unresponsive. Like a sex doll, made just for me."

My eyes widen. "That's... kinda fucked up," I say, my voice getting quieter.

For a moment, I'm worried he's going to stand up and strangle me to death, but to my surprise, he shrugs. "You're not wrong. But I still like it."

I sit in that silence, picturing myself dead to the world, completely at his mercy, wondering about all the ways he used me and for how long he enjoyed me.

"Yes," he says, with no context, and I raise a brow.

"Yes, what?"

"It gets itchy." I stifle a laugh, laying back on his pillow, staring at the black ceiling. I'll take it.

I wake to the bed shifting, Reaper perched on the side, reaching for my wrist. "It's time for you to meet the others," he says, and before I can pull my wrist away, a locks snap into place.

"God dammit! Enough with the chains!" I yell, trying to scramble further away from him. He slaps me across the face, shocking the hell out of me and a tear rolls down my cheek. I still, letting him bind my feet as I raise my palm to my cheek, staring at him, utterly hurt, my anger simmering low and unnoticed.

"You can obey me willingly, or you can fight tooth and nail, but don't forget you are living in my world now Peach." He reaches for me, and I pull the scalpel I snuck from the dungeon, lunging and stabbing him in the thigh. I run for the door, struggling to pull it open with my bound hands. I make it one step out the door before he shoves me, pinning me to the railing with one hand. I watch his other as he grunts, slowly pulling the scalpel from his thigh.

My eyes widen and he snatches me around the throat, a squeak leaving me as all the air leaves my lungs. He brushes my tangled hair from my face softly, taking a deep breath.

"And how far did you think you would get?" he asks, and I clamp my teeth down in anger. "You weren't trying to run, were you Peach?" He flips the instrument, holding it to the base of my throat, pressing hard enough to draw blood.

I whimper, shaking my head.

"No. No. Of course not. You didn't mean to stab me, huh?"

I shake my head again.

"No. That's right. My good girl wouldn't do that because she's not that stupid," he growls, encouraging my answer with the blade digging into my skin.

I nod as much as I can without pushing it in further.

Seeming satisfied, he drops the scalpel, and wraps both hands around my head, firmly squeezing my cheeks. "Your freedom is an illusion built solely on my self-control. You would be wise not to push my buttons Peach." He digs his nails further into the back of my head and I harden my stare.

A laugh bubbles to the surface and his arms fall slack at his sides as I burst into laughter. "Gotcha," I say, grabbing my ribs. "Oh, that was a good one. You're fast. I'll keep that in mind for next time."

He takes a step back, his head tilting curiously and as my laughter dies down, we are left in silence, awkwardly staring at one another.

"Okay, so that was only funny to me. Understood," I say, trying to make him believe me.

Shaking his head, he tosses me over his shoulder, and I say nothing as he carries me down the stairs and into the living room.

"You didn't have to chain me up like a dog," I say, trying my best to sit comfortably on the couch, but the chains dig in uncomfortably. I thought we were headed in the right direction after we fucked and made a deal. Now, I'm not even sure we are on the same fucking planet.

"Watch your mouth, Laurel," the taller masked man says, dismissal in his robotic tone as he stands before me next to my Reaper perched on the coffee table.

I raise a brow, watching him curiously. "And your name is?" I ask, though I don't expect an answer.

"This is Ezra," Reaper says and the man in question snaps his head to the side, tension spiking in the room.

"Uh oh, I don't think you were supposed to tell me that," I retort, bringing my bound hands to my mouth to cover a grin playfully.

"Enough!" Ezra shouts, pulling his gun and slamming it on the table. I stop moving. I stop breathing. "Let's get something clear. I don't like you or this situation. The moment you become a liability, I will kill you. You are nothing but a fuck toy and a convivence to what we want."

Silence fills the room, uncomfortable and equally chilling. Watching him take a breath, and despite my better judgement, I speak again.

"So... this is a first for me. Can someone tell me what y'all plan to do with me? I've never done a train before and honestly, it's against my personal morals."

Ezra groans. "Adorable. Isn't she?"

Reaper chuckles low, the sound dark and oddly delicious. Though he says nothing, pulling out his phone and typing something more important than acknowledging my discomfort as I wiggle and try to situate.

Ezra sighs, moving closer and unclasps my shackles binding my hands together, the chain still attached but dangling to where I have mobility. I wiggle my feet, raising an expecting brow at him.

"Don't be absurd," Ezra dismisses, checking his watch. He's taller than the Reaper I've come to know. Broader at the shoulders but less of an uncomfortable vibe about him. More... predictable, maybe?

Ezra moves back, checking his watch again. "He's late," he says, glancing to his side.

I silently watch them, attempting to stay small as I decipher who they are talking about.

"He's finishing a job," Reaper replies, continuing to type on his phone.

"Pardon?" Ezra asks, standing straighter now.

"Did I studder?" A message is sent with a swoop before he finally looks up, turning to his right and facing Ezra who stands perfectly still, an uncomfortable battle of power happening in front of me.

"There was nothing on the books for today."

"This one was... personal, for our new company."

They continue staring at each other and I take the opportunity to lean my head and arms back against the couch, stretching the sore muscles. I groan, rubbing my left upper arm that is more tender than the other.

A door slams from somewhere upstairs, the echo sounding through the large church, drawing the men's attention with the turn of their heads.

"I'm here," the third man says, taking the final spot beside Reaper, completing the trio of skeleton masks staring back at me. His voice distorted too, but lighter, though still familiar.

Before Ezra can bitch about whatever he clearly has an issue with, I beat him to it.

"Excellent. Now, can someone please tell me what the fuck is happening right now?" I ask, plastering a weak smile across my face and Ezra leans forward in warning. "Right, right. Sorry, *language*."

"Didn't he explain last night?" the third man asks, filling his plate before sitting back.

My eyes fall to the man in question.

"She slept for two days after her stay in the dungeon," Reaper says, hooking an earbud into his ear. I eye him curiously. "She was a little... spent, after our encounter." He tilts his head to the side curiously, waiting for me to continue.

That night flashes in my mind. Every touch, every feeling of fear I had drowning in pleasure.

"No. There wasn't much... explaining," I answer, doing my best to conceal everything I let him do to me after two days of dangling naked in a disgusting murder chamber, hoping the other two men don't already know.

The third man conceals his laugh, his shoulders shaking with amusement. "I see... or rather... heard as much." He clears his throat. "It seems you've been chosen as a new... recruit." He says it almost as a question.

"Recruit?" I mimic, it coming out as a question.

"Yes, that is what the deal involves," Ezra says, less than amused.

"What he means, is you clearly know who we are. You've met Ezra, and I'm Felix." He sets his hands flat on the table. "*He—.*" nodding toward Reaper. "Has allowed you to become an asset of ours, given you can follow orders. Congratulations." His tone is polite, but I don't miss the hidden snark behind it.

"And if I don't obey like a good bitch?" I ask, playing with my fingers nervously. "I leave and Daith dies?"

"You die." Reaper nods.

I pause, eyes flicking between the three of them for a hint of that previous amusement. Their stares fix on me sending unease swirling in my stomach. I swallow my fear, not letting it seep through my stoned expression.

"Women are not allowed in the ranks. You are a tool. Nothing more," Ezra barks and I narrow my eyes at him.

"Though," Reaper continues, "Considering the wound in my leg and how well you held up against an attack from CHAOS, I would say you show promise."

Right. CHAOS attacked me at the house. Right. Right.

Felix laughs. "I like her."

I look between Ezra and Felix, ultimately landing on the one who has laid claim to me. "Why can't I know *your* name?" I ask, unwavering.

The others fall silent, clearly letting this question rest in his hands alone.

"There will be a time. You're not ready."

What kind of bullshit answer is that?

"I'm not ready to know your name. What, are you someone important?" I gasp, feigning shock. "I bet you're the mayor. Is that it? Boy that would be a shock to the town."

"Enough," he says, growing irritated with my games, but I continue pushing.

"No, you know what, I bet its something ridiculous and you're embarrassed. Lenny. Is your name Lenny?"

With a flick of his hand, a knife flies and sticks into the couch, flying inches from my eye. "I said enough, Laurel!"

I swallow hard and I shut my mouth, not another word leaving my lips.

"Do not mistake my generosity for weakness. Your place is at my feet. You open that mouth again and you will find yourself back in that dungeon with my cock so far down your throat, you'll taste blood."

I blink and just like that, my fear returns, and no progress has been made. How stupid was I to think I was anything more than something to play with. I am a bargaining chip, nothing more.

I silently go over everything I know in my head, betting on my chances of survival.

If I run, I'm dead. If I fail at whatever they ask me to do, I'm dead. If I piss him off or bite his dick off, I'm tortured, then probably dead.

The Reapers know my name and that alone is enough for me to know I will never know another day of peace. He has made that clear. Making a deal and believing he would be honest was a joke.

Reaper inhales a deep breath and removes his earbud. "I'll bring your dinner to your room. For now, we need to go over the baseline." He kneels at my feet, unclasping my ankles. He hesitates, I'm sure waiting to see if I'll run for the door, but I stay seated.

"While you are working for us, you'll be under our protection as long as it keeps our plans secure. That extends only as long as you are obedient to whatever I ask of you. You belong to me personally. Disobey, and your death is your own fault."

I nod.

He stands, holding out his hand for me to take. I ignore it stubbornly, standing and wobbling slightly. Tucking his hand in his pocket he nods toward the stairs. "Your room is to the left of mine. I'll meet you in there in fifteen to go over the rest of my rules and plans."

I'm halfway up the stairs when he calls after me again. "Oh and take a shower. You stink. End of the hall."

I roll my eyes, flipping him the bird, then walk to my room and slam the door shut for extra measure. As if my current state is not due to whoever the fuck CHAOS is and whatever they want with him.

I lean against the closed door, eyeing the bed that is made with a freshly folded towel, beautiful flowers, and a pair of his clothes.

Thank God they aren't lilies this time.

CHAPTER 28

I sit patiently on her bed, waiting for her as I stew on how this is going to unfold. I stand as she comes in wrapped in a towel, hair piled on top of her head in a bun, and the smell of the shea butter crap Felix bought wafts in with her, making my toes curl.

"The fact that you even knew what body soap I use is disturbing." She motions for me to turn around as she grips the tucked corner of the towel.

I don't.

"That's what disturbs you about all of this?" I ask, moving and making myself comfortable in the corner chair instead.

Her eyes narrow before she turns, giving me her back, dropping her towel. My eyes slowly trail down the length of her bare body, enjoying every moment it takes her to get her clothes back on. They linger on the bruises around her wrist, the purple and red marks looking so beautiful on her like this. Naked, whole again and submissive to please only me.

Her face is bare, unmatching the clothes she wears to demand attention every night, reminding me of a time before, so unlike the woman that stands before me now.

My phone chimes and I barely notice, my single thought focused on her.

"Speaking of. Where is my phone? Purse?" she asks, and my eyes fall to the way she picks at her nails nervously. "My friend," she starts, trailing off. "And I have a shift tonight. My boss..." She pauses, trying to find the right words for "filthy pig."

I pull her phone from my other pocket. Her eyes soften, relief flooding them. "We have your cover for Celeste. The bar is closed for a couple days for... cleaning. You need to know my rules before I give you your next game."

Curiosity blooms in her eyes as she leans forward on her knees, giving me her full attention.

"The first rules are simple. You are mine. You disobey, you are punished. Understood? You have been given a lot of slack. No more."

She nods slowly. "I have a short leash. Got it."

I smile at that thought. "You will learn our faces when we learn if you are worth the time. Your first trial is at The Peach. I have a certain interest in your boss, and I need to get into the poker games. Gain access to his ledgers. See who his cash flow is coming from." Her brows pinch but she says nothing. "You are allowed to ask questions, Laurel."

"Oh, uh- I'm not understanding what you mean by cash flow."

"Dorian Vic is using The Fuzzy Peach as a cover for something much bigger. Drugs, sex trafficking, something."

She scoffs, nodding slowly, as if that doesn't surprise her at all. "You're going to want on the VIP list."

I nod. "Exactly."

"Okay, so where is my hot wire?" she asks, now seemingly more invested. Almost... excited. I can imagine she doesn't exactly have a soft spot for the bastard.

"Hot wire?"

"You know, I go too far and I get zapped. I do the wrong thing... zap!" She wiggles her head, miming electrocution.

"Ah." I stand, walking closer to her, taking her chin in my fingers. "You are free to do whatever you want outside of these walls, given it doesn't compromise your cover or ours. You come straight home to me every night, and you damn sure do not fuck anyone else. Be a good girl and no zapping."

Her pupils dilate slightly, telling me she likes that idea.

"And my cover?"

"I will be there to lay claim to you publicly when it's time. Where I go, you will go. No one will question it. As far as Celeste goes for now, you met someone. Get creative and I'll assist. For now, you stay here. I'll let you know when you have been good enough to be let out."

She juts out her lip. "I'll be such a good girl, I promise," she whines, peering up at me through her long lashes. "Do I get a reward?" My cock instantly gets hard. Fuck. How does she do that?

I clear my throat. "Second thing I need you to do." I say, and she exhales a deep breath when she doesn't get the rise out of me that she wanted. "I need you to get closer with Bryce. My intel says he has something on Vic." I hand her phone over. "I've taken the liberty of agreeing to a date on your behalf. Your house, tomorrow. It will be supervised."

Her eyes snap up at me and then to her phone, skimming over the text messages before she glares. "You want me to entertain him with the idea of sleeping with me to get information? But if I sleep with him, you'll kill him and me," she states, knowing the answer but seeking verification as if she must have heard me wrong.

I sit back in my chair, crossing my legs. "That's correct."

She lays her face in her hands, doing her best to grasp everything she's gotten herself into. I admire the strength she is determined to keep in place.

"Damn it. I literally just cut him off. Do you understand how clingy he is?"

Yes. I am aware of his fascination with you. "Then it should go rather well. No?"

She rolls her eyes. So far, I would say her first day and transition into our world is going as good as can be expected. Only one of us with a minor wound and she's cracking a joke. That's a good sign, right?

Chapter 29

I make my second cup of coffee, making a mental note to ask for any flavor or creamer and a can of cold foam. I walk slowly into the room where the three Reapers are passing papers around, talking in their modified voices that are getting more than old. It's grating on my nerves.

I wonder after I help them get what they want from Vic if they plan on killing me or... maybe selling me?

I lean against the door frame, looking down into my coffee swirling slowly, not really listening to anything they are saying. Not that I would fully grasp it if I did. But the room falls silent, all heads turning to face me.

"What?" I ask, taking a slow sip.

"This isn't for your ears, Peach," Reaper says, softer and with more kindness than I have heard from him since the night he snuck into my apartment.

I groan. "I'm not even listening. I'm bored out of my fucking mind. I thought you were supposed to be exciting and thrilling beyond my wildest imagination. So far, I'm not impressed."

His head tilts to the side. "Don't be mean to me. I'll cum."

I take another sip of coffee to hide my amusement.

"Go up to my room. Find some toys to play with."

"Fine." I head toward the stairs and he calls after me. "Enough of the coffee, Laurel. You're going to kill yourself."

It's only my third cup. "I just might!" I yell over my shoulder as I take the stairs two at a time and dip into his room shutting the door behind me.

I set my cup down next to his computer and flop down on his bed, staring up at the painted black ceiling. My eyes fall to the walls and curiosity takes over. Scooting to the top of his bed, I grab the scalpel I stabbed him with earlier. I wipe it on my jeans before pressing it into the tip of my finger, drawing a drop of blood. I reach out, smearing it on the wall, and it disappears into the sea of red.

I smile. I half thought he was fucking with me, but honestly it's kind of cute, in a weird, sadistic way.

Rolling to my side, I collapse on his pillow with a long exhale as my boredom slowly kills me. His cologne wafts around me and I inhale deeper, wanting to take it in again, deeper, to the point I can never forget it. I want to bathe in it—make it my oxygen. The smell of his cologne mixed with the sweat and grime of what he does has my arousal growing, demanding to be satiated. Fuck, he smells so good. Almost, familiar, which is so strange I can't begin to comprehend that.

I uncross my legs and firmly run my hand between my legs with a low groan. Then I sit still for a moment, listening for nearby voices as the need grows stronger, an idea sparking my excitement. When nothing meets my ears but low chatter from downstairs, I shuffle to my knees and rearrange his pillows.

I grab one, propping it at an angle on the headboard. I grab another that looks lumpy and tousled, and I lift it to my face, shoving my nose into the fabric. My chest heaves as the smell of his hair comforts me. I set it just below the other, forming a semblance of a body.

I train my ears one more time, tossing panties somewhere behind me. I straddle the pillow that smells like his face and imagine his mouth wide open, waiting to taste me. The cold fabric feels like ecstasy against my warm skin, and I fall onto the pillow that's wrapped in him.

My hips move slowly at first, grinding back and forth on the cotton as I mentally picture him between my legs and breathe him in. Then faster, my mind wandering deeper into my illusion. He grabs my thigh with one hand, pulling me down onto him harder, like he can't get enough of me. Gripping my breast with the other.

My small moans are muffled but still feel all too loud knowing they are downstairs. The thought of being caught only adds to my arousal. I fist the pillow harder, picturing myself bound and at his mercy. A loud whimper comes and just as I turn my head to breathe the floor creaks right outside the door. It sends me over the edge, ending the chase, my breathy cries spilling into the pillow again as I use it to mute myself while my hips erratically ride out the orgasm I was feigning for.

The door opens and Reaper stops, both of us frozen.

"What were you doing?" he asks, and I roll to the edge of the bed with a grin.

"I was trying to give you pink eye." I stand from the bed, righting his pillows, making a dramatic move to smooth the one I was riding, patting the small wet spot as I cast him a wink.

His shoulders shake slightly, and I think the sound coming through his mask is supposed to be a laugh, but with the modified tone, it is utterly terrifying.

Holy shit. He laughed. And I kind of loved it.

"You are welcome to hangout in here, but Ezra and I have to head out for a few hours to grab the cipher we need to break a code. Felix will keep you company and I'm sure Dom will find you soon enough.

"Can we play a game when you get back?" I ask, the word home almost slipping off my tongue.

"I love games," he says, tucking his hands in his pockets.

I grin. "I don't play fair."

"No one around here does," he says, and suddenly I'm more exited for him to return than I am for him to leave.

I creep down the stairs after an hour of sifting through his many sex toys and objects that didn't look like they belong in the same drawer. I walk softly, hoping Dom is in a cage somewhere or busy in the dungeon chewing on someone's femur.

"Felix?" I whisper yell and after a long silence, I try again. "Felix!" This time, a little louder.

I hit the bottom stair, holding onto the railing trying not to peer into the rest of the house.

"What are you doing?" he asks, a hint of amusement in his tone, and I jump, spinning around, looking back up the stairs to where he stands.

"Fuck, you scared me." I quickly walk back up the stairs, getting my workout for the day. He gives me his back, walking back into his room two down from mine, and I follow him, despite the lack of a verbal invite.

I take in his well-cleaned room and the computers lining the wall before flopping on his freshly made bed.

"Yeah, this is pretty much what I expected for you," I say, looking over the framed band posters and alternative rock vibes. "You just look like you have impeccable hygiene."

He spins in his computer chair. "Uh, thanks?"

"You seem nicer than the other two," I say, plopping onto his bed.

His head snaps around and though I can't see his face, I jump back up to my feet. "Off the bed," he says before turning back to his computer. "Don't judge a book you haven't read, or whatever that saying is."

I snort a laugh, not believing that this dude made it into The Reapers. Maybe he's got a Mr. Hyde in there somewhere. "No pictures or mood lighting?"

"Would you feel safer if I had a lava lamp?" he asks, still focused on his computer.

I sigh. "Honestly, yeah," I say, still looking around at the bare minimum décor.

"You ever had a girlfriend?" I ask and he nearly chokes.

"What?"

"Sorry, just trying to break the awkward tension if we are going to be forced to live together for a bit. Does it have to be just a work relationship?"

His body language doesn't change and silence settles for a moment. "Yes. I've had a girlfriend."

"What happened?" I ask, needing to know.

He shrugs. "This isn't really the lifestyle that is nurturing for relationships. Distractions are dangerous."

I scoff. "Is Ezra your dad or cult leader?" I ask, knowing that had to come straight from his mouth.

That earns a small twitch of a smile from him. "It's complicated. More like a big brother I guess. Much older big brother."

"Ah, brother grandad," I retort, and Felix's shoulders shake slightly. "Wow, that was almost human." He says nothing, shutting down what small progress we made in conversation. "So what, are you hacking or something?" I ask, trying to peer over his shoulder but he has a privacy screen just as Reapers does.

"No. Solitaire."

I giggle. "That's so lame." I quirk a brow.

"You have any better ideas while I'm on babysitting duty?"

"How long do we have?" I ask, wiggling where I sit crisscross.

He groans. "I really didn't like the sound of that question."

I wag my brows. "Wanna let me do some shopping?"

"Shopping." His tone sounds like he can't believe something so trivial and basic woman just came out of my mouth.

"Yes. Shopping. Your home looks like a bunch of frat boys live here. Let me freshen it up."

He sways back and forth in his chair and just as I'm about to give up, he speaks. "Fine. I'll have one of our boys pick up whatever you need to decorate and bring it over." He hands me a card and one of his laptops. "Stay under 150 grand."

My eyes nearly bulge out of my head, but as he turns back to his computer, I realize he is completely fucking serious.

Oh, hell yes.

Hours later, I sit on the bottom stair, drunk, waiting any minute for them to come back. Felix comes through the house, grabbing the last of the trash, shoving it into the largest trash bag I've ever seen. Though, I don't think they use them for purposes like this.

"Ezra is going to shit his pants," he says, over the loud music I have playing, tying the bag in a knot.

I look around, content with my work. Confident that I styled in a way that would fit their vibe. I kept the dark and alternative vibes, with a touch of classy wealth here and there, not unlike the white rug that looks like something Celeste would buy for herself.

"Because of the money?" I ask, kind of nervous now, hoping I didn't just dig my hole deeper. There is nothing I could do to pay off that kind of money in my lifetime.

He laughs, propping his hands on his hips. "No, darlin. That wasn't even our card. I lifted that. He's just not a very... homey guy."

I breathe easier hearing that, surprisingly not bothered by the fact that I just spent almost 120 thousand of someone else's money.

I scoff. "Well, he could use some help then. It looks great, right?"

"I think so, but he won't be thrilled that you went through the rest of his gin," he says, nodding toward my refilled glass.

I scrunch my nose, taking another sip. "That is such an old man alcohol. We need more of a selection around here."

"Oh, we do. It's just hidden," he says over his shoulder before dragging the bag out, and I can hear the humor in his voice.

Checking the time again, I grow irritated and increasingly horny. Drinking tends to do that me, but I have kept my clothes on, so that's at least something new to commend myself on.

I move across the room, loving the way the new rug feels under my bare feet, and turn the music up a few more notches. Sway my hips, nodding my head, bouncing to the beat of the music, having nothing better to do with my time.

As I spin around Felix comes back into the living room.

"Dance with me!" I yell, letting the beat flow through me, letting loose and dancing wild. Unpracticed and free, unlike my routines that are performed over and over again.

"Uh, I don't dance."

I move to him, grabbing his gloved hands. "Come on! Everyone dances."

He's slow at first, nodding his head as I hold his hands, jerking his body side to side in motion with my own. Letting go, I spin, flipping my hair, and he joins in, moving his legs and arms in time to "Can't Get You out of My Head" by Kylie Minogue plays.

I laugh at his dance moves that died ages ago, wondering who the hell he learned that from if he grew up without parents, though I guess I don't know enough about any of them for that to be fact. I just assume anyone that ends up in this line of work couldn't have had a healthy upbringing.

The front door swings open and he freezes, my hysterical laughing dying down as I spin around to find Ezra and Reaper standing in front of the closed door. The music turns off abruptly and uncomfortable silence fills the room.

"Surprise!" I sing, holding my glass of liquor in the air. "Welcome home!"

Reaper takes a few steps closer taking in the house. The new TV, the chandelier light fixtures, the large framed abstract paintings, tables and vases filled with flowers that appear to be dead.

"You did all this in the 5 hours we were gone?" Reaper asks, and I try to gauge his tone, the modifier making it infuriatingly difficult.

"Yeah," I say proudly, not giving a single fuck if they like it.

Well, no, I do care if they like it, but I won't apologize for my efforts.

I flinch as he rushes to me, picking me up and I instinctively wrap my legs around his waist. "I love it."

I lean back in his hold, wishing I could see his face. "You do? Really?"

"I do. We needed a woman's touch, I think." He spins, still holding me as he waits for Ezra's response.

Ezra moves closer, snatching the glass from my hand. "It was fine the way it was."

Feliz scratches the back of his hooded head and Reaper sets me down. I stagger slightly, trying to bite my tongue, holding back the venomous words lingering on the tip.

"Come on, man. She put a lot of work into this. It gave her something productive to do," Felix says, and I appreciate the defense.

"You were told to watch her. Not let her turn our home into her personal Barbie Dream Whore House."

My mouth parts as Reaper slaps a gloved hand over my mouth. "Go upstairs." His eyes stay locked on Ezra. Something prideful blooms in my chest, and I obey.

I'm halfway up the stairs when a startling thud has me jumping to look behind, finding Ezra falling to his ass. Reaper shakes his fist out, walking to hover over him.

Getting to his feet, Ezra rips his mask off throwing it across the room, revealing his busted lip. I inhale sharply, immediately recognizing him. The bouncer from The Fuzzy Peach. Jeff?

What the actual fuck?

Ezra throws a swing, missing Reaper as he ducks low, coming back up, planting his hands, shoving Ezra back by his chest. I continue walking, stopping just shy of the bedroom's door.

"You deserved that, and you know it."

Ezra snarls, his breath heaving. "That's how this is going to be?"

"Speak about her like that again, and I swear to God, it will be with the last breath you draw."

It's the last thing I hear before I shut the bedroom door and stand behind it, processing and quickly sobering.

The door creaks open, and I snap my head up, heart pounding in my chest. Reaper stands there, filling the doorway like a shadow come to life. His presence alone is enough to make the air in the room feel heavier-suffocating.

"I'm sorry," he says, stepping in, and the relief in my eyes fades as Dom follows him in. He tracks me with his eyes before laying down at the foot of the bed.

I take a deep breath, trying to push down the knot in my stomach, the one that's been there ever since I met him. There's something unnerving about the way he controls everything, including me.

But his apology surprises me. It's a side of him I've never seen, and as he moves to the bed, sitting next to me, there's something in the way he holds himself that's different. His posture isn't as rigid, his voice is softer.

"Listen," he says, his voice rough but still steady. "Ezra..." He pauses, like the words are harder for him to say than usual. "I need you to know that I won't let anyone disrespect you like that." His voice is quieter now, almost as if he's measuring every syllable with caution.

I blink. The sincerity in his tone, sounding true but dishonest all the same. I can't trust him. I barely know him, and I still have no idea what he's done with Daith.

I try to push the thought out of my head, focusing on what's in front of me. I should be angry, should be pushing him away like I've always done. But something inside me stirs, something I don't want to acknowledge. There's a kindness in his voice that disorients me. A softness I can't ignore.

My head tells me he's still dangerous, still the man who's held me captive, still the one I can't trust. But my body reacts to him in a way I can't deny. He's closer than I thought, this side of him, and it makes my chest tighten in a way that feels wrong but... tempting.

"Are you alright?" he asks, and I'm not sure if he's asking because he actually cares or if it's just another part of the act. But I can't stop myself from nodding. I don't want to show him how much it's affecting me.

"I'm fine," I mutter, my voice sounding smaller than intended.

For a moment, there's silence between us. And I can't stop myself from wondering why he's so comfortable with me.

Finally, he breaks the tension, his voice quiet again. "I just... want you to be comfortable here... with me."

I don't know what to say to that. I wasn't sure he was capable of such a human emotion, part of me is convinced this is all an act, but still, I find myself empathizing for him.

I swallow hard, unable to stop the faint flutter in my chest. I'm not supposed to be feeling this. But the way he's looking at me, the way he's acting—*caring*, even in the smallest way—it's... it's making me question everything.

"I am," I finally whisper, my voice barely audible. But the words feel real. I don't want to admit it, but I like it here. I like the rush he gives me and his protectiveness has only amplified that.

Reaper gives me a slight nod, and for a moment, he's still, as if he's trying to figure me out. But whatever he's thinking, whatever's going through his head, never makes it past his lips. He just stands moving before me, his tall form towering.

"Is there anything I can do?" he asks, and though I'm not as upset as he believes, I play along.

I nod slowly. "Turn off the lights."

Without hesitation, he for the remote that controls the lights and clicks it, surrounding us in darkness. My other senses peak, my ears focusing on his breaths as I reach out and fist his jacket with both hands. I tug firmly and he lets me guide him down to his knees before me. Carefully, with slow movements, I move my hands blindly to his face.

Pausing for only a moment to be sure he doesn't object, I pull his hood back and slide his mask from his face, discarding it on the floor. I run my hands through his long hair and around the edges of his face, drawing the image in my head. My fingers move up to his lips, and as my fingers tease the edges, his hands wrap around my wrists, pushing a finger in his mouth. My pussy throbs as he sucks it, drawing it out slowly before he places kisses to my flat fingers.

I twist my hands, grabbing his hand and guiding it to my hip. "Here," I whisper into the silence, the muffled sounds of the music from downstairs filtering in through the cracks of the door.

Gently, he pushes me back onto the bed, pushing my baggy shirt up. I brace myself as he leans in, pressing his lips, swiping his tongue over the sensitive skin of my hip. Again on the other. Then again, dipping lower to the edge of my soaked panties. I let out of a soft gasp for air, trying to take back my ability to breathe.

"Is this what you need?" he asks, low, barely audible. The raspy, bare voice is his own, and my God, it's criminal. Mixing with the lust-filled haze clouding my senses, I swear it sounds just like Daith's, and my heart aches with the need for him.

"Yes," I say, needing him to say more. I need to hear him. I want to know what he sounds like without something hiding him. Pulling my panties off and pushing my legs up, he dives into me like a starving man and every coherent thought leaves my mind as he eats me, passionately and full of the same desperation I feel crawling over every inch of my skin. I reach down, fisting his hair to pull him in closer, demanding he take everything I have to offer.

He reaches up, fisting my breasts, kneading them as he pays careful attention to his efforts. I squirm in his grasp, the sensation almost unbearable.

"Relax. Give it to me, baby," he says, taking a moment to kiss my inner thighs, calming my shaking legs.

Inhaling deeply, I relax my mind, letting my body give in as I give everything over to him. My body warms with the tensions release, and I reach above my head, arching my back as he resumes, pushing two fingers in. He pumps slowly, feeling every inch, savoring every drawn-out moment like it's the last.

My orgasm builds quick and I focus on the feeling, attempting to hold it back—draw it out for as long as I can, not wanting this to end so soon. But as he moves to hover over me, he pumps his fingers faster, fucking me with them hard and fast as he nips at my skin, trailing from my stomach to my neck, and I fall apart. My orgasm crashes through me, and he doesn't stop or slow down. I cry out, and Daith's name leaves my lips in a whimper of desperation.

"Good fucking girl. Say his name," he growls low, darker, full of venom, unlike the soft, careful tone he had before.

Fear washes over me, dragging my orgasm on until I'm shaking and breathless.

"Why do you like that?" I ask in the safety of the darkness that for some reason feels as if it holds more truth than the light of day.

He pulls his fingers from me. "Because you cum on my fingers, you live in my world, and soon, his name on your lips will taste like a sour plea for forgiveness as I overtake every corner of your mind."

I swallow, cold air washing over me, chilling my skin as he pulls away. A moment later, light floods the room, and he is standing before me, mask and hood in place. The only proof of what we just did, my naked body sprawled on his bed and my pussy on his lips.

"Come on, Peach. We have a meeting to attend," he says, tossing me my panties.

Without waiting for me to follow, Reaper turns and walks down the hallway, his steps steady and confident. I hesitate for a moment, my heart racing, before I slip my panties on, head reeling, and follow him into the next room. Ezra and Felix are gathered around a small book lying open on the table. Its pages are filled with random numbers and letters.

I watch Reaper, my body tense and exhausted, still not understanding my place here. He didn't want me to hear their discussions, but now I am being pulled into whatever this is.

I sit, trying to appear smaller, invisible, as they begin discussing the notes in the book, their voices low, each word filled with purpose as they uncover the names of the buyers, suppliers, and movers for both drugs and humans. But my attention keeps drifting back to Reaper, to the way he moves, the way he stands there, ever so controlled, ever so cold, not a hint of where we were moments ago. He looks so much like Daith, I can see why some part of my brain latched onto him. It was like I already knew him. Something about him whispered to my soul, begging to be let in.

I can't shake the thought that maybe, just maybe, there's something more to him—something under the mask. Something he's trying desperately to keep hidden. And that... that scares me more than the murderer.

CHAPTER 30

"I don't want to stay in this fucking room," she says, pouting as I secure her cuffs to the bed.

"We've been over this, Peach," I say, leaning down to kiss the angry lines of her forehead. "We have to show them that we are following approved orders and this gives me a chance to sniff out the rat with their approved surveillance. But you are not supposed to be here."

Her eyes leave my face, darting to the side in a sign of dishonesty. "I know, I understand. I just want to help."

"You will be plenty of help later," I say, kind of hating how pervy that sounded, though honest none the less. "I just need you to go to sleep for me. My perfect little toy."

She tucks her bottom lip between her teeth with a smile as she holds her arm out for me, welcoming large needle that doses her.

She grimaces as it goes in but she watches with a gleam in her eyes as the clear liquid drains from the syringe, into her body. Her eyes flutter softly as it begins working and her head falls back onto the pillow. I watch as the bliss takes over her body and she signs it over to me for at least the next few hours.

Once her eyes falls shut and sleep takes over, I lean forward, pressing a soft kiss to her parted lips. I groan, already hard at the idea of my fantasy that will get played out only hours from now. There has always been something so fucking hot about picturing her limp and cognitively unaware as I fuck her. Basically dead, but still warm.

Ah, fuck.

I leave the room before I come in my pants like a kid seeing his first pair of tits. The house smells like bleach—sharp, industrial. Like blood and grime was scrubbed out of the cracks in the tile only an hour ago, and the walls still remember the screaming.

"Fucking hell, dude," I say to Felix who stands like Superman in the corner.

"This house needed that. I'm so sick of month old blood covering up the beauty this place holds. You two are disgusting."

I stand in the middle of the old church's main floor and take in clean surfaces everywhere I look. Even the floors have been mopped. Twice.

I pull my phone from my pocket, calling in the last unofficial member of The Reapers. The wizard behind the curtain. "She's out. You can come in."

Skid steps into the room, her red hair pinned up, white silk blouse, heels clicking against holy stone. "I hate that we have to do this to her," she says, tucking her folder beneath her arm.

"You were the one that pointed out she would be in more danger if they figure out she is more than a fuck toy to me."

Skid's brown pinch. "Can you not talk like that, please. Have some decency."

I roll my eyes. For her being younger than me, she has a certain passion for trying to serve as my mother.

"Knowing we are keeping her safe from them is the only reason I agreed to this. We need to sniff them out, see if they are working an angle. If you sense it, keep it masked until after they leave. Keep them happy."

We all nod in unison.

"The rug looks good in the meeting room by the way," she says, smirking at Ezra who seems to have no brain behind his eyes for a solid ten seconds. He's dressed for the part. Black button-down, sleeves rolled, clean hands and rings. The breathing image of cool control.

I look them over and as she looks down at her folder, smiling like an idiot, an alarm goes off in my brain. Oh, these mother fuckers better not be up to what my dick-radar is telling me.

Before I can ask, Ezra steps up to the heavy front door. He nods. "They're here."

Outside, I hear multiple vehicles. CHAOS never rolls light, three black SUVS park outside as the men barrel out before pulling off. The doors open in sequence. One after another, the suits step out. Six men, one woman, all of them stiff-backed and soulless.

Agent Varner leads. Controlled, cold, and the leader of CHAOS. They approach the front doors like they own the place and push through the doors without knocking. Ezra holds the door for them with a perfectly flat face, and Skid greets them like this is a casual meeting between friends. "Agents," she says, sweet and measured. "Welcome back. We're so glad you decided to stop by."

Varner steps inside first, eyes scanning everything. He doesn't shake hands. Doesn't greet me. Just nods once. "You've been busy."

I give him the thinnest smile I can manage. "Clean house, clean conscience."

He doesn't laugh. Tough crowd.

The group begins its slow circle around the space. Ezra trails a step behind them, silent, deadly, calm. Skid walks them through the upgrades: Security measures. Lockable storage for weapons. Medical bay reorganization. File organization.

She explains everything as if this is a usual inspection, but we know otherwise. This isn't just about compliance. The illusion of order. Their control. This is about keeping the little man small.

Varner pauses near the hallway that leads to the basement. "This is your business room, correct?"

"That's correct," Skid says. "Soundproof. Cleaned daily."

He lingers too long. Ezra subtly shifts, just a degree forward. I feel the tension coil behind his stillness.

"Our files of every approved and confirmed kill are also down there."

He looks at me like he knows that was a jab at my disobedience to them, but they move on. They ask about numbers. We give them spreadsheets. They ask about weapon caches. We point to inventory logs. They ask about community presence, and Celeste smiles and hands them press clippings about allegations that were never proven and murders left unsolved.

It's all a dance. And we've practiced the steps.

The inspection wraps within the hour. Agent Varner shakes Celeste's hand with words like *commendable work* and *maintaining a stable system*. He calls us an asset. Like we're a spreadsheet, not a pack of wolves in clean clothes.

"You are wanting surveillance in order to help find the person responsible for unauthorized kills in this area? This is highly offensive and is punishable by death and dissolving of your organization if convicted of knowingly harboring the culprit."

We all nod, well aware of the rules.

"Very well. Approved."

Outside, the SUVs load again. Black tires roll across broken pavement. The doors shut. No one looks back.

Inside the church, Ezra finally exhales. Celeste loosens her shoulders. The masks fall, though not entirely, just enough to breathe.

But I stay standing. Stiff. Tightly wound at the truth I know. Someone is killing too close to my home, and it's putting a bomb below everything I have worked 5 years to create.

I look toward the room they didn't feel the need to check. They won't take her from me. Leaving the others, I rush up the stairs to see her. She lies on the mattress like my perfect girl, waiting for me like she promised.
I sit on the edge of the mattress and brush her hair off her face. Her skin is warm. Her lashes flutter, not awake, but not far.

"I didn't hurt anyone," I murmur. "Even when I know how good it would feel."

Her lips part, but no words come. Just the smallest sound, like she's dreaming of me. I lie down behind her, pressing my chest to her back, fitting my palm over the curve of her hip. She doesn't pull away. Her body knows me. Responds without question. This is the only place I feel comfort like this. In the dark, with her beneath my hand, just existing.

She breathes in, slow, shaky — like she hears me. "I need this," I say. "I need you to be still for me. Just like we used to play."

She doesn't protest. No fear. Just surrender.

I press my mouth to her shoulder, let the weight of her anchor me back into something solid as I pull my cock free and sink myself into her. I groan as I slide in and out of her slick hole that was waiting for me. She's so warm- relaxed.

I grip her hip, using it as leverage to sink further into her with a drawn-out moan. "Oh, fuck, baby. You are such a good fucking girl for me. Giving me what I need." I pump into her faster, her limp body rocking against mine, begging for more with each colliding movement.

As I get closer, I flip her to her back, spreading her legs wide for me, bending her at the knee. Her head falls to the side, her face relaxed as her body jolts with each of my thrusts. Her arms lay at her side, jostling slightly, pushing me closer to the edge as she doesn't hold my punishing thrusts back like she usually would when I go this deep.

"Look at you. So beautiful. Taking it so good." I tell her, hoping she can hear me on the other side of wherever she is. I go harder, faster, giving her everything I have, knowing that she will feel it tomorrow. She will wear the marks of my love, proudly.

Harder. Faster. Give it all to her. Everything. For her.

I come hard, groaning dramatically as I spill into her. I pull out, giving just a few drops to the soft skin of her stomach. Using my finger, I swipe a drop and bring it to her lips, making her taste what she does for me.

Such a good girl.

CHAPTER 31

LAUREL

He let me go home.

But of course, I have to come back. He's watching, I know that, and still, the excitement I thought I would have, isn't there. Part of me was disappointed that he wanted me to leave and pretend nothing has happened. I wanted to stay, wanted to get to know him more. He opens up to me, in the small moments, when it's just me and him. Then, in the blink of an eye, he's throwing me out, telling me to swim with an anchor tied to my feet.

My hand brushes the inside of my sore thighs and part of my chest aches that I don't get to spend more time with him, show him his marks, let him kiss them. But maybe this is him rewarding me for giving him what he needed. Or maybe they have more to talk about, things going on with CHAOS, that they don't want me to know.

I get to know that they are sanctioned and monitored, governed by rules and paperwork, but I don't get to hear about their plans. About these murders that are happening that aren't theirs.

It's humiliating that they think I couldn't help with that. But ill keep my mouth shut, do what they ask, and one day, likely in the near future, that will bite them in the ass.

A cab picks me up a few blocks from their house and drops me off at an unfamiliar alley where my car was moved and stashed. Standing next to my car, I stare back at the front door. It's quiet before business hours, almost as eerie as an abandoned church—holding secrets and bridges to worlds you can't fully imagine until you're immersed in them.

Like his secrets. They excite me, almost as much as his lingering stares and firm touches. It's thrilling trying to decipher the puzzle of why he is who he is and who he is beneath the exterior he shows the world.

My phone buzzes.

Restricted: Behave. I'm watching.

I smile to myself, changing the contact to "Death" then slide into my car. Using my small amount of slack my new owner has given, I decide to test my limits and yank on the chain, despite is warning.

I drive straight to Celeste's, needing her company before my brain explodes. I step out of my car and walk to her front door in nothing but a T-shirt, looking like a hooker that just got off shift. I stick my key in the door, but it's yanked open before I can twist.

"Where the fuck have you been?" Celeste demands, pulling me inside, slamming the door shut. "Hello, 21st century. You could have at least texted me to let me know you weren't dead on the side of the road."

I stay silent, my head reeling. What the hell am I going to tell her? The words are on the tip of my tongue, stinging with urgency. It would be so easy to tell her everything, to make her promise not to say a word. I trust her, but he would kill her. He would kill me. I know that with absolute certainty.

Celeste snaps in my face. "Earth to Laurel. Are you high?!" She grips my shoulders, staring into my eyes with concern before looking over my whole body.

My eyes snap to hers and I smile softly. "Hi, Cee." I catch the breath lodged in my throat. "I'm so sorry. I started seeing this guy. He took me back to his place, and I just... let myself get lost in him for a few days."

She pauses and I wait for her to call bullshit, leaving me trapped, but then she turns her nose up. "What a douche. He couldn't afford to buy a charger?" she asks sarcastically, and the weight on my chest lifts.

"We were too busy fucking," I say, lying, though wishing it was the truth. Reaper hasn't fucked me since he took me, and had plenty of opportunities, and something about that really chaps my ass. Why hasn't he?

"I seriously thought The Reapers had done killed you. I was one glass of wine away from calling the cops." She says with her finger pointed at me. Honestly, that's a reasonable thought and course of action. She relaxes, accepting that I'm safe. "I bet the dick game was awful," Celeste says, releasing me, and the tension leaves her body as she relaxes and we walk inside.

"Jealousy is a horrendous look on you," I tease, tossing my purse on the couch as my phone vibrates in my hand. I flip it, seeing the message I

213

expected minutes ago, demanding to know why I broke orders and didn't go home. I grin, looking back at Celeste.

"Hey, you wanna take a shopping day today?"

She looks at me like a mom who just doesn't know what to do with her naughty teenager. "You're going to give me a stroke." She snatches her keys from the counter. "Get some pants on and let's go. You're going to tell me all about this magical dick."

"So who is he?" Celeste asks, pulling me into a novelty store.

"Just a guy I met at the club," I say, rounding a rack of lingerie as I read Reaper's text.

> Death: You are pushing it, Peach. Don't think I can't see where you are.

I bet you can, and I intend to push all the limits until he can't resist but to spank me... with his dick buried in me.

Celeste grabs a 9-inch dildo from the wall behind us and wiggles it in the air. "He a big baller?"

I move down the wall and grab one that is so large, I'm not sure it's humanly possible to fit it fully inside a woman. "Bigger."

She whistles a tone, fanning herself. "You found him at the club? Are y'all hiring?"

I snort, knowing she's joking. She is one hell of a dancer, having taught me many of my moves herself, but she would never strip on a pole.

"Do we think he would like something like this?" Celeste asks, pulling a pink lacey corset off the rack, with two rhinestone bows over the nipples.

"Cute, but I think he's more, chains and whips." I keep digging through the racks, searching for something black, grinning at my own sick joke.

"Whips and chains. That's hot." She pauses mid-search, "Did he tie you up on this little vacation? Give you a punishment for being a bad girl?" She bends over, pointing her ass me, spanking herself.

I grin, holding my wrists up for her to see my faint bruises.

"You nasty bitch."

She holds up a black pair of lace panties with the crotch cut out, paired with a black sheer bra, fabric only covering the nipples. "Is this nasty enough?"

"Slutty, yes. But more bedroom style," I say. "I need something I can dance in, but he'll know it's for him."

She turns to another rack and gasps. "Oh, what about this?" she says, grabbing a strappy one-piece leather outfit with a collar attached and a silver chain that looks like an accessory but could be pulled and used as a leash.

"Oh my God, it's perfect." I flip the tag over, looking for the price. "$134.99"

Celeste swats my hand. "My treat. Stop looking at prices."

I don't argue with my wad of cash, knowing it isn't going to go anywhere.

"Are you gonna tell me what you're hiding yet?" I ask.

She groans, grabbing a few pairs of different color nipple tassels and walking to the other side of the store. I always could read her better than she could herself.

"Cee!"

"Okay, fine!" She stomps her foot and scrunches her nose, sucking her lips between her teeth. "It's just... Daith is in love with you, okay. He's been talking to me about you since he left. He's got it bad."

I stiffen, hope swirling in my stomach, mixing into something that makes me want to puke on my own shoes. "Oh, that's..." I falter and my smile fades, trying to find words to form. "When is the last time you talked to him?" I ask, holding back the tears threatening to spill with the words. I haven't had any calls to texts from him and I haven't done anything to be owed an answer.

"Um, like 4 or 5 days ago? I dunno. I've been so busy, it's insane," she says, dismissively, not knowing how much weight her answer holds. Right in the gap of either possibility, and it does nothing to soothe my worry. "But seriously, you need to throw him a bone or something. I think he really has changed... in the ways that matter."

"Daith and I aren't going to work out. But we all knew that." I let her see part of my heart shattering behind a fake smile. Everything has changed, though it doesn't stop my mind from wandering to what could have been years ago if he had just let me in back then.

My stomach sinks and I choke back the vomit threatening to spill all over the hundreds of dollars worth of merchandise in front of me. I can't tell my best friend the truth... I'm madly in love with her brother but I couldn't do the one thing I needed to keep him safe and now he very well might be dead.

"Did something happen?" she asks. "Between y'all?"

I let her believe something did. It's easier than telling her the possible truth. I can't plant that in her head before I know for sure. She'll hate me forever. A lifetime of friendship, gone in the blink of an eye. Anger burns in my chest, resentment forming not only for Reaper but for myself for letting him touch me the way he does. I should have killed him when I had the chance. Even if I had died in the process, at least Daith would have his revenge.

"I'm okay. I'll work it out," I say, grabbing a pair of platforms with a spike as the heel. "But I will not be okay if I don't get these."

She laughs, taking them from me and putting them in the shopping basket along with the lubes and oils she snuck in there. "Those might scare the shit out of some men."

"Speaking of shit... how is your new boyfriend coming along, Skid?" I ask, teasing her with the nickname Daith gave her as kids.

She scrunches her nose. "He *ran* me over and I get the nickname for shitting myself involuntarily." She shakes her head laughing lightly. "We're good, it's just... casual. Not something I see lasting." She shrugs.

"Does he have any dark secrets?" I ask while idly flipping through more clothes, not really paying attention.

"Hmm," she hums before gasping. "He sleeps with his mouth wide open. Every time. We take naps together and I'm tempted to drop something in there." She says, giggling. It's good to see her happy. She does so much for everyone else and rarely takes care of herself in the way she should.

After a pause, I shift the conversation. "Hey so, I actually agreed to have this new guy over tonight and I can't exactly bail so soon," I say, keeping my eyes low as I lie out of my ass. "And I was wondering if I could use your house for a couple of hours."

She shrugs, adding deep-throat mints to the pile. "That works. I have some errands to run, so just make sure you sanitize the pool after you get done fucking in it."

That's not really what I had in mind, but I don't correct her, not wanting to come up with a better reason for not wanting to bring Bryce to my apartment. "Just better hope Daith doesn't swing by," she adds playfully.

"What errands?" I ask, changing the subject, wondering what could be occupying her at 8pm.

She smirks as she thumbs through the clothes racks. "You have your dirty deeds, and I have mine."

I giggle, knowing she is probably going to see her guy. "Touché."

Pulling my phone out again, I send a message to Reaper, hoping he doesn't shit his pants that I changed his plans again. Though the place shouldn't matter. Right? As long as I get the job done.

My phone vibrates with his reply, and to my surprise, he is fine with it. Holding my breath, I tuck my phone back in my pocket, suspicion rising.

CHAPTER 32

S he thinks she's cute, like I don't know exactly what she's doing. I expected this before the front door hit her ass.

I type her another message, calm and collected watching her walking through my sister's front door, shopping bags in hand and a smile across her face.

> Restricted: Strike 2. You are in so much trouble when you get home.

Fuck, she's got me going soft. I had told her there wouldn't be any more slack, and here I am, giving her a mile.

I watch her read the message, and the smile on her face grows. Oh, I'm in so deep.

> Peach: Are you going to spank me?

Promptly after I kill someone to lessen this feeling of self-deprivation.

The three margaritas she had at lunch may be causing her to go against her better judgement when talking to me, but it would only be the healthy dose of fear blocking the loose lips she is known to have.

> Restricted: I'll do worse than that. Stick to the plan.

She strips down in the living room, trying on her new outfit for Celeste who cheers wildly. My camera on the TV, gives me the perfect view. She struts, wobbling in her new six-inch heels as she checks her phone. I don't let her know I can see her. I let her have her confidence. It's strangely provocative, this power struggle we have. But we both know she has no leverage. I hold all the cards.

She props herself on the arm of the couch to answer my text, her ass in the air, swaying back and forth. I can admit, she picked good with that outfit.

Peach: I'll believe it when I see it. I see the real you, Mr. Bossy.

She drops her phone and strips again, but my eyes gloss over as her words ring in my head. Something about it rubs my nerves, settling low in my stomach, making my hair stand on end.

Maybe it's a coincidence. Maybe is my oversuspicious conscious, always looking for the crack in the foundation. Though, maybe she's just intoxicated enough that she let a vital piece of information slip while too caught up in the banter.

I stare at the message, forcing my mind back years. Back two days before I left her.

She was standing before me, just below my chest, barely 15 years old. Tears filled her eyes as she peered up at me, fighting to keep them from falling. I had just told her I was in trouble, convicted, was leaving. Our whole lives, we were best friends. Sure there was something more under the surface, but at the roots, I was her anchor and she was mine.

And I was leaving her.

Her hands fisted at her sides. Even back then, so pure with her misguided adoration, she had so much fight in her. I knew one day I would come back for her and she would be ready.

"I'll come back for you. I promise," I said, reaching for the side of her face.

She pushed my hand away. "I'll believe it when I see it." Her tear fell and she turned from me, leaving me standing in the front yard alone.

That was the last time I saw her face-to-face.

No, that's no coincidence.

I stand, slinging my backpack over my shoulder, rushing through the house, passing Felix slumped on the couch beer in hand, watching some kind of cooking show.

"Hey!" he yells, slightly slurring as he attempts to sit up and I stop in my tracks with an annoyed growl raising a brow.

"You need me?" he asks, hopeful and already reaching for his bike keys.

"No, Felix. I don't need you. You need a shower, and a girlfriend," I say, pulling my boots, glaring at him.

"I need that steak," he mumbles, turning back to the TV, rubbing his stomach. "And we're not supposed to have girlfriends," he adds, huffing dramatically. "But *you* have a girlfriend. Naughty, naughty." He shakes his head, waving his finger in the air.

Annoyed out of my fucking mind, I take the time to round the couch, crouching down to his level. His eyes widen slightly as he backs his head further into the couch. "Laurel is not a girlfriend. She is my fucking wife. I don't need a piece of paper or a white dress to make that true and I am capable having a normal life. I make the rules, and I say, you need to stop rotting on my couch and stop treating your cock like a New York subway."

He swallows, nodding slowly. "Congratulations."

I take his beer, pouring it in his lap before throwing the bottle over my shoulder at the wall, shattering it. "Shower!" I scream, taking my growing frustration out on him, then I'm out the door.

I mount my phone to my bike, keeping my eye on her location as I tuck low, flying toward my sister's house. She left Laurel unguarded and alone hours ago but given her location reading, she was likely sleeping her hangover off in my sister's bed. One of the rooms I don't have a camera in, because... ew.

The roads are almost bare, leaving it wide open for me. There's no better feeling than the rush you get when taunting death. I skid to a stop in front of her door and tuck my keys in my pocket. She lives in a great neighborhood, but I don't trust anyone farther than I can throw them.

I knock on the door before running out of patience then use the spare key that Celeste made sure I had the day she bought this house.

The faint smell of chlorine in the house pulls me to the back door she left open. I pass through the kitchen, grabbing a beef taco on my way out.

I find Laurel swimming a lap in the wide pool, the faint neon green bikini glowing under the surface, contrasting her perfect tan skin. With my lips turned up in a smile, I perch at the end, waiting for her as I swallow another bite. As the water breaks and she comes up for air, I lean in, inches from her face.

"Hi'ya, cutie," I say as she opens her eyes, grinning at her shocked gasp.

"Oh my God." She chokes, sputtering on the water. "I thought you were dead!" Her wide eyes scream of the fear and relief coursing through her, but after a moment, she backs further away from the edge, trying to put some distance between us. I sit, putting my legs in the pool, soaking my jeans up to the knee, and finishing the last bite of my taco.

"Oh God, those were good." The side of her lips twitch but it's gone just as fast, that cute little scrunch between her brows returning. "He let me go with the promise I left town. I'm supposed to be long gone by now." I shrug.

Her eyes snap up to mine and she pushes water at me, fury clear in her beautiful golden eyes. "Are you insane! You're going to kill us both!"

"He let me live to make you happy. You think I'm just going to let him have you? That's the dumbest thing he could have done."

She runs her hands over the top of her wet hair, pushing back the strands clinging to her wet skin. Her eyes dart around frantically. "He's watching, Daith. You haven't seen what he's capable of. He'll come as soon—"

"Why are you choosing him now? I thought we were in this together?" I lean forward, and she holds my stare.

"We were, I just... He took us both with no effort. We don't stand a chance. If I got you killed..." She treads water, not very well, to keep from hanging onto the edge. My eyes fall to her breasts bouncing in and out of the water.

"No. Somethings changed. What is it?" I ask, tilting my head curiously, waiting to see how she plays this.

She pauses, only for a second but it's one that gives me a little tick by my alter ego's name. "Nothing. I just... never pegged you for the type to kill easily and I don't care to see how possible that is."

Liar.

"You've never pegged me at all. Wanna give it a try?"

She sinks lower in the water, hiding her smirk at our usual banter, letting me lighten the angst between us.

"Getting tired of trying to stay so far away from me?" I tease, leaning back on my hands. She narrows her eyes and defiantly swims closer, pushing herself up onto the edge between my open legs with that bratty look in her eyes that I love so much.

221

"You're the one that left."

Not taken. Is that a hint to what she knows? This won't be where I let us crack. No, I want to drag this out until she can't hold it in any longer.

Our faces inches apart, I let my gaze fall to her mouth with purpose then back to her eyes. "I promised I would come back for you. Why won't you let me keep my promise?" Her throat moves as she swallows, keeping her face void of any emotions. She holds my stare, her eyes falling to my jaw as I clench my teeth at the thought of slitting her throat right here. The blood mixing with the water in beautiful pink swirls. "Just trust me."

Her phone chimes from under the patio, effectively breaking the spell between us.

She pushes off the wall of the pool, swimming to the stairs, and all thoughts leave my head as I watch her step out of the pool. The water trailing down her back and over her ass has me thinking of everything I want to do to her for years to come. Walking to the patio table, she leans over, seeing the text from my burner. She scoffs, and shakes her head, grabbing the bottle of Vodka sitting next to her towel.

Taking a seat next to me, she drops her feet in the pool, taking a long drink from the bottle. "Well. We're both dead now, so what the fuck does it matter."

I pinch my brows, feigning ignorance.

"Enjoy your last moments with him Peach. My gift to you." She recites my message word for word, having no idea Felix sent it, yet again.

The mood between us shifts, trading for something nostalgic and full of sorrow.

"Aren't you underage?" I mock playfully, trying to get a rise out of her.

She rolls her eyes, giving me nothing. So, we sit in the feeling, letting it wash over us. All the years I missed and let her fall apart. All the secrets I kept from her. All the times I needed her but didn't let myself admit it. Something in me knew if I let her back in, I would never let her go.

There was never a part of me that could stop myself.

There was never a part of her that wouldn't sink into me the moment I let her back in. I own her in every way I person can be owned.

I just didn't realize how deep I was until the word *wife* poured from my lips tasting like honey.

"You have to leave. I'm serious," she says, keeping her eyes on the water's reflection glimmering on the bottom of the pool. She pauses, toying with the bottle label. "I'm happy with him. It's a fresh start." She lifts her chin, but I don't miss the way her shoulders sag.

Is she really doing it?

I reach out, using a finger to turn her chin to me. "Over two decades, and you choose the moment I can't live without you to cut me loose?"

Water pools in her eyes but her words are sharp, cutting me. "Hurts, doesn't it?"

She is. And part of me is so fucking proud of her.

I drop my hand, "Well, then we have tonight."

"No," she says. "I have a date tonight."

I scoff. "With who?" The humor and disbelief ringing loud.

"Bryce."

"You gotta be shitting me," I bark. "What fucked up shit is this? He's gonna claim you and then share you? He's as sharp as a fucking gumball."

My head whips to the side and my cheek smarts with a flash of pain. And why did it turn me on?

"It's not like that and you need to show me some damn respect. I'm not a classless whore."

"I heard all about how classy you've become. Fucking me on the edge of a cliff the first time you see me after 5 years was a clear indication of that."

Her brows furrow but she can't fight the playful smirk peaking at the edge of her lips.

"Why did you leave New York anyways?" I ask, already knowing the answer but needing to hear it from her. I had eyes on her, constantly while she was gone. There wasn't a dick she sucked or a step she took without me knowing about it. I only lacked information when she was right under my nose again.

Her eyes stay on the water, and she picks at the label nervously. "There was nothing out there for me."

I nudge her. "Oh, what is that? You know you can talk to me."

She exhales a breath. "You tell me your story and I'll tell you mine." She nods toward me, motioning to my eye.

My hand raises to the cloth wrapped around my head. "Nothing exciting there. I made a dumbass mistake of getting caught, though it was worth it to get a little revenge on the sick fuck."

"You're foster dad," she confirms, already knowing that part of the story. Laurel never had the displeasure of knowing the prick, thank God. I may have killed him a lot sooner if he touched someone I cared about. It's odd not feeling basic morals but feeling protective over certain people.

I nod. "I was young and the only thing that mattered was that he didn't see another day." She holds my eyes, as if there is nothing that could drag her attention away from my words. "I did five years and obviously, in a place like that, I had to do what I needed to avoid certain unpleasant circumstances. One particularly nasty fight, a rival that thought he would try and piss on my territory got a good hit in."

"Toothbrush?" she asks, with a playful grin.

I chuckle, "Yeah. I lost an eye. He lost his ability to walk. A fate worse than death, I think." To be robbed of your ability to defend yourself is almost as bad as learning everything you've known has been a lie. "Your turn."

She chews on the side of her lip. "I left to get away from... things that haunted me in this city."

Me. She would never say it outright but we both know the truth. No matter if I was in the city or not, she couldn't escape me, and the further she ran, the less she could deny the place she always belonged was in my arms.

"I tried to see where my photography would take me, hoping I would have creative liberties and freedom, room to grow and make something of myself," she says, taking another swig from the bottle before passing it to me. "After years and some self-growth, I got a little too creative for my boss's liking and bored with the box he put me in. I wasn't taking pictures of things I wanted." She pauses, and I stay silent, not giving her any indication of my thoughts.

What did she want to see through her lens? What inspired her?

"He really didn't like me fucking his intern on his desk either."

I choke on my drink, my jaw falling slack.

"So, you know. Got fired. Came home. Now I'm a stripper."

And threw a chair through his glass office before you stormed out.

I smile to myself, enjoying that her dreams falling apart led her back to me. "Is it rude for me to be happy about your failure?" I drop into the pool in front of her, fully clothed, dragging my eyes up her body, letting her soak in the long seconds of me appreciating every inch of her.

"Probably," she says. "But I'm sure you'll find a way to spin it and make it sound deliberately filthy."

"Filthy?" I ask teasingly, running my hands up her thighs and interlocking them behind her, pulling her toward the edge of the pool. I look up. "Because it means now I could have you all to myself?" I pull her into the pool, and she lets me. Bracing my arms under her ass, I pull us deeper. My chin rests against the soft skin of her stomach and her long hair falls around her face as she looks down at me. "I could have you wherever I want." I let her slide down and wrap her legs around my waist, squeezing her ass firmly, her pupils dilating as she fixates on me.

Backing her up against the brick, her back to the camera I placed. "He said to enjoy your time with me, yes?" I ask, low and sultry, gliding my hands to her bottoms, snaking my fingers under the edge to feel her. "He can only see me, and I have an excellent poker face." I push two fingers in her and she inhales, eyelids fluttering. "You'll still be his good little girl when you go back to him," I say, leaning in closer. "Just stay very, very still."

Digging my fingers into her waist, I work her with my other hand, watching the way she struggles to keep her composure. Her eyes flutter closed, and I allow it, letting her fantasize over either version of me that she prefers. "Nod your head. Make him think were just talking," I order, and she follows suit, nodding her head slowly, in a way that I know is meant for me and the pleasure flooding her. She softly moves her hips, trying to fuck my fingers and I tighten my grip on her.

"Mm, mm," I tsk. "You're going to give yourself away."

Her lips part and I mirror her, enjoying the way she melts under my touch. I've watched her with other men, and none of them elicit a response the way I do. She doesn't just give herself to me, she becomes pliable, fearless, letting her desire catch the wind, taking her wherever I lead.

"I need more," she whispers like a plea for mercy, but there is no mercy here.

225

I give her nothing more, pushing her to the edge, consuming every struggled breath she passes to my lips. She tightens around my fingers, and I give her what she needs, rather than what she's begging for. I sink lower into the water, peering up at her in pure ecstasy. "I need you to cum for me. Please, baby. Come for me." I beg, desperate to take another piece of her.

Her brows pinch and she clamps her lips together, doing her best to muffle her moans. I keep working her, letting her drown in every last second of her orgasm. My name rips from her lips and then her eyes open and she's staring at me. There's pain taking over her soft features, a tear falling down her cheek.

She pushes me away and I hate the way my body aches the moment I'm not touching her. A hand covers her mouth.

"You need to go, now," she says, pulling herself back up to the edge, scrambling out of the pool and I follow.

"Laurel." I grab her hand, pulling her back to face me.

She pulls out of my hold, grabbing a towel, wrapping it around her waist. "Leave," she says, peering up at me the same way she did the day I left, with agony.

"You're choosing him?" I ask, hating the way it feels to have to pretend she's choosing someone other than me, But I'm so fucking proud of her. Rather it's the lust for Reaper or the fear of Daith dying, she is doing her best to stop herself from stepping through the door she's been waiting her whole life to open.

Another tear falls as she answers firmly. "Yes."

She doesn't avoid my eye contact, or shift her weight. She's confident in her answer, resolute and unforgiving. I'm proud of her performance, remembering vividly how blatant her true emotions were before I left.

I stare at the little girl I once knew, fawning over the man that carried that stench of darkness, too scared to dance beyond the shadows, now obeying death. And I give her something I never thought I would.

Mercy.

Tracing the frame of her face, I smile softly. "Don't let this eat you alive, baby. Give him hell." I press a kiss to her cheek. "I'll be just fine without you. You know that."

I mean for it to sting, hitting it right where I need, giving her an edge to stand firmly on as I leave her without so much as a glance back.

She had one thing right. Tonight will be the last time she sees the man she's known her entire life.

My instincts chew me up and spit me out, leaving me aching to know. Her emotions were raw, executed perfectly, as if completely natural, but there's something in the pit of my stomach that just doesn't believe it.

I dismount my bike and wave at the old woman who looks at me like I'm a thug here to take her purse and shove her down.

"Excuse me, ma'am. Can you tell me where apartment 308 is?" I ask, hooking my helmet on the handlebar. I know where it is, but what I don't know is the likelihood that this old hag will report me for snooping around.

"I'm visiting my girlfriend for the first time. Got a special date planned," I say, softening my face, tucking my hands into my packets like a nervous 15-year-old boy.

The convicting expression on her face eases and she smiles, bracing herself on her cane. She points toward Laurels apartment.

"Down that way, hun," she says, her voice raspy and shaky. I give her nod and continue on my way. I'm nearly to the door when she calls out, coughing at the effort. "Bring her chocolate next time. Every girl loves chocolate."

I smile at her, dropping it the second I turn my head. Don't tell me what my girl likes. I'll break that cane off in your wrinkly ass.

I use my phone to disarm her system and begin picking the lock. Pushing through the door, I lock it behind me. I look around her small apartment, taking in the decor that isn't much different than the room I put together for her at my place.

If I was a girl who had a secret, where would I hide it?

She's a smart girl; she wouldn't leave her secrets so vulnerable. My eyes shift to her computer. Bingo. Moving to it, I wiggle the mouse and a locked screen stares back at me. I type in her usual password.

WRONG.

I narrow my brows. *Excuse me?*

I try again.

WRONG.

The fuck?

Her birthday.

Reaper.

The Fuzzy Peach.

My birthday.

The year we met.

All wrong.

Would you like to reset your password?

No! She would know someone is trying to hack her.

I know everything about her. I know what kind of toilet paper she uses. I know when she's fucking ovulating. How does she have a single thought I don't know about?

My phone rings and I jolt. What the fuck is that about? Am I scared she's going to catch me and beat me up? No. I don't flinch.

Shaking my head, I pull my phone out, rolling my eyes at the picture of Laurel's ass staring back at me.

"What Laurel?" I ask, clearly annoyed and occupied with something more important than whatever she feels the need to whine about. I have eyes on her. She's secure and waiting for her date.

"What are you doing?" she asks, slurring her words as she attempts to be seductive but I catch the sniffle at the end of her sentence.

"I'm working Peach. What do you need?"

She giggles, slurping a drink before she replies. "Your dick buried in me."

My fingers stop on the keyboard, wondering if I heard that correctly or if that irritating voice in my head is playing games with my psyche. That shit can be seriously distracting and result in some less than productive accidents.

She giggles again, low and sultry, and the sound sends my eyes rolling in the back of my head. "I don't think I've ever known you to be speechless."

"You've known me for two weeks Peach." I say, switching my phone to my other ear and looking around her room, my senses tingling.

"Right," she says. "But will you?" She curses under her breath as she stumbles over something.

"Will I what?" My eyes connect with the camera I placed above her door.

"Will you fuck me? Hard and deep, like you need it to breathe. Like you could never let me leave."

Suddenly, it feels like the oxygen is sucked from my lungs and the vision of her spread out on my bed, panting and needy, is painted vividly in my mind. "Show me you can follow orders and I'll make you feel so fucking good."

I end the call as I open the security feed and slide it back in time. I watch her shift the computer, blocking my view of her screen.

Oh, you little minx.

I sit for a moment, racking my brain, thinking like her. I take a seat in her chair, seeing what she would see.

I see you too.

Her words come back to me. She would see me looking back at her.

I see you, you see me.

I type it in, in every variation I can think of before it finally lets me in.

I'm a fucking genius. Yes, such a genius that I couldn't see it staring right at me. She was always a sucker for poetic songs and play on words.

Files pop up, filling the screen, and my stomach drops.

Fuck.

Fuck, fuck, fuck.

I'm going to kill her.

No.

Not really... I think.

I'll play your game. Let's see how far we can take this before I want to rip her spine out of her mouth.

I look around her room for more, and my eyes land on her closet, something about it pulling me closer. Sliding out of the chair, I pad across the room and turn the knob, finding it locked.

Why the hell is her closet locked when she's the only one that lives here?

It takes seconds to pick the lock and the anticipation nearly kills me as I slide my hand into the cracked door, slowly pulling it wider.

As my eyes fall on the collage of hundreds of the same photos pinned to the back wall, my stomach drops and something sour forms in my mouth, mixing with a certain blood lust that feels a lot like a boner.

I don't like liars, and I don't like people in my business. But what I really don't like, is a woman that plays dumb. Though, if I'm being honest with myself, she's played this very smart. And that is pretty hot, and likely the only reason I'm not headed to kill her.

She wiggled her way in with a plan. Let's see if she deserves to live.

Chapter 33

I sit on my back porch, tapping my phone on my thigh, the wind blowing gently through the windchimes, dancing through my hair. My fresh clothes feeling stiff and uncomfortable. The faint rustle of leaves in the wind fills my ears beside the hum of distant traffic, but all of it feels so far away.

I press my palms against the arms of the chair, willing myself to breathe, to steady the whirlwind in my chest. I keep telling myself I did the right thing. I *had* to protect him. *Reaper won't give him another chance.* Not that it stops the absolute torment swirling in my chest.

After everything, I forced him out. I can still see his face. The way he accepted it. Knowing it was the last time he would touch me, the last time I'll have him like that... I feel as if all the air has been sucked from my lungs. I want to scream at the unfairness of it all.

Rubbing my eyes, I clear the tears from my blurry vision. There's no going back now. I have to see this through, and I *will* give him hell. For Daith. I glance at my phone again, the screen still silent, nothing from Reaper.

The truth is, I'm not even sure how I'm supposed to handle Bryce once he shows up. Am I supposed to flirt? Act interested? Just get the information I need and get out? The thought of pretending to be interested in him again makes my stomach churn. There is nothing wrong with Bryce. He's a perfectly great guy, but stepping back in feels like a slap in the face.

The back gate creaks and I look up instinctively. There he is with that grin that always feels like he is trying to undress you.

"Sorry I'm late," he says, dropping into the chair across from me without waiting for an invitation, though he shifts nervously in his chair.

"Mm." I offer him a tight smile, trying to focus. Trying to think about Reaper's orders.

"You're looking... different," Bryce says, glancing over my jeans and low-cut shirt, my half-dried hair in a bun on top of my head, my bare face, likely red and puffy.

Different. I hate that word. It's like he can't decide if it's a compliment or an insult. "Thank you. I feel different. Good."

He nods, and suddenly I can see what Daith saw. Aside from his charm to get you naked, there really isn't much between us. Though, that could be entirely on me and what I was looking for going into whatever we had.

I let the small talk continue, giving easy responses as my mind wanders on to the possible ways tonight will end once I report back to Reaper.

Across from me, Bryce sits a little too eager, his bright eyes catching the fading light, unaware of the weight of the situation. The more I talk to him, the more I realize he's just... innocent. He's not involved in anything deeper, nothing to do with Vic or the shady business he has going on behind the scenes.

Bryce shifts uncomfortably, looking down at his hands, the nervous energy in his posture making him seem more naïve than I've known him to be. He has no idea what I'm really after or any indication of who I'm working for.

"So," I start, trying to keep my voice casual as I shift the conversation. "Have you heard anything from Vic's about the missing dancers?"

Bryce looks up, blinking a little in confusion, clearly not expecting the question. "Uh, not really. He doesn't really share stuff like that, you know?" He shrugs, rubbing the back of his neck, his smile a little sheepish. "I think he'll be hiring again soon."

I nod, pressing my lips together, trying to hide the disappointment creeping in. This isn't going anywhere. Everything he says is just... nothing. I try to keep my face neutral to hide my frustration. Reaper's orders were clear. *Get him to open up... Figure out what he knows...* But if Bryce is involved in anything shady, he's doing a damn good job of hiding it.

Bryce leans back in his chair looking around the yard, clearly trying to steer the conversation into safer territory. "It's nice out here. She's got a great place."

"She does. I love it here." I force a smile. *Why did Reaper think Bryce could help?*

Bryce continues to ramble on about the weather, something about the stars, and I barely hear him. My mind too busy trying to piece things together. Reaper wouldn't have had me follow this lead if he didn't suspect something. Right? What am I missing?

"He seems to favor you," I say, hoping I can squeeze a little more out of him, but it's more of a formality at this point.

"Really?" Bryce says surprised. "I don't think he even knows my name."

I snort a laugh. That doesn't surprise me. Lisa handles all of his hiring and important paperwork.

"Well, he doesn't force you to do things that weren't on your terms of employment," I joke, but we both know the severity behind the statement. "With the shit he makes us do, I wouldn't be surprised if he was into more shit than what we see."

I glance at Bryce, his face open, eyes wide with the innocence of someone who's never even thought about the darker side of the world we live in. *This is a waste of time.*

"I've had... a great time tonight," I say, and he beams, clearly not noticing the change in my tone, and I force a smile back, masking my real thoughts. Losing my desire to keep this going.

I cross my legs and his knee brushes mine. "Can we get to the point here?" he asks and I inwardly groan.

"What point is that?" I ask, batting my eyes playfully.

Bryce raises an eyebrow, leaning forward a little, his expression turning serious, the playful mask slipping away. "You agreed to see me. So what does this mean for us?"

I drop my gaze to the ground, hating that I have to do this again.

He stands, moving in front of me, pulling me to my feet. He leans in and I turn my face, pulling back before he can kiss me.

You'll kill us both idiot.

Bryce sighs. "I get it, you've got a lot going on, and being around a Reaper has to be intense but... you don't have to do this alone. I'm here, if you want someone who actually cares about you."

His words hit too close to home, and for a brief moment, the walls I've spent so much time building feel like they're crumbling. I bite back the frustration rising in my chest. I've already pushed him away once, and it felt horrible. Doing it again is torture to us both.

But before I can answer, he sighs. "Are you still sleeping with Reaper then?"

I shake my head, trying to push the heaviness of it all down into something I can manage, and a laugh comes out, hiding the rage blooming in my chest. "No, I'm not sleeping with Reaper. He just prefers me at the club."

The silence between us feels heavy, like the air is thick with the weight of his thoughts. He's processing what I've said, but I can't read him. I don't want to.

"I get it," he says after a long pause, but his voice is distant, guarded. Eyes flickering with something I can't quite place—maybe disappointment, maybe something deeper.

I swallow, suddenly feeling the weight of the conversation pressing down on me. *This is it. This is where I have to let him go again.* The illusion of what could've been is fading. Bryce will never understand the web I'm tangled in, and if I'm honest, I don't want him to.

"I'm sorry, Bryce," I say quietly, my voice low. "I thought I could, but I can't—"

He holds up a hand, giving me a small, sad smile. "It's fine," he says softly. "Just... don't shut me out completely, okay?"

I nod, my throat tight.

But for a brief second, as I watch him turn away, something inside me aches. Something small, something fragile, that I quickly bury. I can't let myself care this much anymore.

Why did Reaper think Bryce knew anything? I question it over and over, the doubts creeping in.

Either way, I've got nothing to report back except that Bryce knows nothing. And that feels like a failure. But I've learned one thing tonight—*I don't trust Reaper's orders without question anymore.* I have to keep my eyes open, and my mind sharp. Because if there's one thing I'm sure of now, it's that I'm being led down a path that doesn't quite make sense.

I glance back at the pool, then take one last look at the empty patio. Time to report. Time to lie, just a little. Always just a little.

CHAPTER 34

I stand in front of the double doors to the church, duffle bag over my shoulder, only now realizing he didn't give me a key. Raising my hand to knock, rocking slightly on my heels as my head spins and my stomach churns, I pause.

I pull my phone out, checking the time.

Midnight on the dot.

I sent a quick message to Cee, letting her know all went well and I locked up her house before I left. Looking around at the empty street, I question everything I've done up to this point.

God, Laurel. What the fuck are you doing?

I take a step back, ready to turn around, ready to run to Daith and tell him everything. Tell him I'm sorry. But I freeze as the front door opens, Felix stands to the side clearing a path for me in his stupid mask. "Are you going to stand out there all night?"

"No. I was just—" I stop, having nothing worth explaining to say, and step inside as he locks it back.

I look around, standing awkwardly in place. The church feels oddly comforting, like a warm embrace I didn't realize I needed. The stone walls, the familiar scent of incense and wood, the new décor. It all wraps around me, grounding me in a way I wasn't expecting. It welcomes me home.

"He's not here yet," he says, confirming what I already felt in my gut. I'm just a good little dog, obeying orders. I nod, still unmoving.

"You can come sit, or go to your room or whatever. You don't breathe by his command," he says amused, walking toward the living room and I cautiously trail behind.

"You sure?" I mumble, unsure if he heard me. I sit on the couch as he disappears into the kitchen, leaving me in utter silence.

Felix isn't like the others. He doesn't carry the same dangerous air. He's calm, gentle in his own way. There's a softness to him, even if it's hidden under a tough exterior.

I kick off my shoes searching through my duffle bag for something more comfortable. "I didn't find much on Vic," I say, my voice still light as I strip my clothes off, trading my jeans and tight top for an oversized T-shirt, both which I stole from Cee's closet. "Bryce doesn't know anything. It was a bust."

Felix comes back in with a water bottle, cautiously eyeing me as he sets it on the table in front of me. "Figured you could use some of this to sober you up."

"What fun is that?" I eye the stairs, tempted to fall into bed and forget today ever happened, but my eyes trail around the house, lingering down the hall.

Felix nods. "Figured. Vic keeps things close." He sounds almost amused, as if he finds it all a bit of a game and hairs on the back of my neck stand on end.

"I guess so," I answer carefully. "What are you doing up so late?" I ask, hoping he will be the one to open up, even the slightest bit.

"Just finished up some work. About to turn in, you should do the same," he says, nodding up the stairs.

He turns, giving me his back and I follow him into the kitchen, snatching the bottle of water on my way. "Go to bed Laurel. You don't want to piss him off more than what is already done."

I swallow at that, half terrified of what that means for me.

"You know?"

He rounds the other side of the kitchen bar, fixing himself a glass of rum. The smell has my jaws tightening, vomit threatening to spill if it comes any closer to me and I scrunch my nose. "Reapers don't keep secrets from each other."

I nod. Right.

"I'm not tired."

He ignores me, placing the bottle up one shelf higher than it was, just out of my reach.

"Please. I'm so bored and I'll bet he has no intention of rushing home to me," I beg, batting my eyes, leaning over the table so my shirt hikes up on my ass, but the truth in my words sting.

Felix looks up to the ceiling. "Dear God, you don't have to do that to get what you want. He will cut my eyes out and make you eat them."

Something about that makes me smile, soothing the sting. What is his fascination with eyes?

He groans. "Fine, come on. I can teach you to play cards."

I smile wide, knowing I have a fair chance to hustle him. I follow him into another room of the old church, taking in the space as he sets the cards.

"You know," he says, breaking the silence. "he can be a lot, but I know he cares about you." I smile softly, unsure what to say to that. His eyes flash up at me then back down to the table. "It's easy to see why."

I take my seat in front of him, tucking my shirt under my ass. "Is it normal for him to..." I struggle to choose my words carefully. "lash out?"

Felix face twists in discomfort. "He has been through things that most people can't even fathom. He struggles with certain things that go on in his head and sometimes that can... distort things." I nod slowly, understanding a lot easier than he likely thinks. How did I manage to be involved with two men with these issues within a single lifetime?

"I can give you my number... you know, if things ever go sideways and you need a lifeline."

My brows pinch.

"Not that I think he would ever intentionally hurt you, given you didn't try to get him locked up or killed or anything," Felix says, laughing half-heartedly. "But he can slip into a world that isn't here and it takes a while for it to clear sometimes."

My forced smile turns genuine as I find something in Felix I wasn't sure lived in this house. Genuine empathy for me.

"I would like that," I say, sliding my phone over to him.

"What the fuck is going on in here?" Reaper's voice booms from the doorway.

I look over my shoulder, finding a very irritated Reaper standing with his arms crossed.

"Hey!" I cheer, now completely sober. "He's teaching me to play cards."

"You know how to play," he says, unmoving and unamused.

I wince. "Yeah, but he didn't know that."

He stalks toward me, snatching me from the chair I was kneeling in.

Felix gathers the cards into a stack, getting the hint that the game is over. "Come on man, she was bored out of her mind. We were just having some fun."

Reaper nods, before swiftly planting a foot in his friend's chest, sending him flying backward, the chair banging against the floor, cards flying everywhere.

I give Felix an apologetic look over my shoulder as Reaper drags me out of the room and to the bedroom, leaving Felix to gather himself.

"It was harmless!" I protest, tugging at his grip. "Stop being such a cave man!"

Reaper picks me up, tossing me over his shoulder, my ass in the air for God and everyone to see.

"Harmless fun, that required you to be without pants?" he asks, tossing me onto the bed, my body bouncing roughly.

"I wear less than this every night at work!"

He ignores me, taking the rope from a drawer, restraining me. He refuses to look at me, focusing on binding my hands to the bed. "Let's get something clear. You do not belong to *us*. You belong to *me*." He moves to my feet. "I am a very selfish man," he says, firmly slapping my cheek before soothing the stinging skin with a firm rub.

I scowl, giving him nothing else.

"What has gotten into you?" he asks, leaning over me with a heavy presence. He stinks of sweat and something rotten. *Death*.

"Don't you mean *who*?" I smart, smirking, only to receive another slap across the face. I dart my tongue out, tasting blood. Then laugh, wild and angry, letting my broken heart pour out of me.

"Now, be a good little whore and smile again, like when you were having your innocent fun."

I grit my teeth, holding my scowl as tears sting my eyes. I came back, for *this*? I left Daith for this?

Reaper pushes my shirt up over my breasts and straddles me, his weight crushing. "I said." He hooks his gloved fingers inside my cheeks, pulling painfully into a forced smile. "Smile."

I squirm, fighting him, jerking my head side to side. The taste of dirt and grime fill my mouth. I spit and he laughs manically. "What you don't like the taste of your consequences?" He releases my mouth, holding his gloves up for me to see the filth coating them.

"I talked to Bryce like you asked! He didn't know anything!" I shout, confused and desperate. "If he does, he isn't telling me," I pant desperately.

Reaper reaches behind him, pulling out a blade stained with dried blood. "I don't give a fuck about Bryce right now. I gave you simple rules Peach. You may not have fucked Daith, but you got a little too close for my comfort. I hope you said your goodbyes."

Horror flashes in my eyes and my stomach sinks, my heart shattering into a million pieces.

He lifts his head to the side, lifts the lower half of his mask, and licks the blade. "You knew what I would do... yet you let him touch you anyway." His hands slide down the length of my legs, taking my panties with them. "Hm?" he hums, what's left of my heart beats painfully in my chest.

"Did you want me to kill him? Make it easier on you?" He flips the knife, trailing the handle up the inside of my thigh.

"Answer me!" he shouts, digging the tip of the knife into my leg.

"No!"

But my mind goes to war. Do I? Do I need Reaper to make the heartbreak easier? I can't chase after a man who's dead.

I shake my head, tears streaming down my face. "Please, tell me you didn't!"

He hovers above me, his mask inches from my face. "Tell me you love him." He moves the handle to my clit, pressing firmly before rubbing circles. My body betrays me, warmth blooming where he touches me.

"I love him," I say, my voice cracking with the truth.

He growls low, almost inaudible, but I catch it. He moves the handle lower, wetting the tip in my arousal, teasing my entrance. "Now tell me you want *me*."

I open my mouth to speak, eyes still holding where his should be.

"Aht." He stops me. "Don't lie to me now."

I hesitate, rolling over what he wants me to admit. Is it true? Do I want him? How fucked up is it if I say yes?

He pushes the tip of the handle inside, teasing me, and my head goes back, eyes shutting with the truth we both know.

"I want you."

He grabs my face, forcing me to look at him, shoving the handle inside me, only stopping once his fist touches me.

I whimper hating myself but loving the feel of everything he is making my body do for him.

"That's my good girl," he praises, and I let out a moan, unashamed and untamed.

He groans, head tilting down to watch where he's fucking me. Unexpectedly, tears roll down my cheeks, the emotions of everything too much to contain any longer.

He repositions his thumb, every time he thrusts in his leather glove rakes across my clit perfectly.

"Does that feel good?" he asks, and I arch my back, letting him see my response.

"I need more," I beg, trying to grind against him the same way I had on Daith.

I watch him frantically as he moves to my bag, pulling out one of my shirts before coming back to me. He wraps it around my head, blinding me.

My chest heaves with anticipation and fear, blind and at his mercy. The ropes on my legs are given more slack, and he grips me under my thighs, shoving my knees to my chest before the ropes tighten again. My body jolts with electricity as he dives in, his mouth consuming my pussy.

I groan in ecstasy, Reaper wasting no time, licking me up and down, slowing but with purpose. He eats me like a starving man, his own breathes ragged and frantic.

"Oh, God," I praise. His hand comes up to grab my breast, firmly squeezing until I cry out in pain, though it feels like praise. He pushes his tongue inside me, tasting me from the inside before he replaces it with his fingers. They're bare now, his skin on mine. I see stars as he hits the perfect spot, combined with his tongue on my clit. His hands move to mine, spreading my fingers, holding them firmly.

My toes curl under as I chase my building orgasm, needing to go over the edge like I need to breathe. My entire body shakes as I fight to hold on to it, willing it to come closer with the thought of seeing his face between my legs. He adds another finger, or maybe uses a toy, filling me up more, stretching me wider. I grit my teeth, my orgasm right on the edge but before I can come, he moves quick, straddling my neck, holding my mouth open as I fight to catch my breath. His hard length jams down my throat punishingly and he groans, sliding in and out of my mouth, gliding along my tongue that I stick out for him. The sound of his whispered praises has me begging for more, needing it more than I need to breathe.

The headboard creaks as he uses it for leverage, fucking my mouth, fast and without mercy. I gag, uselessly fighting for air, drool spilling over and down my cheeks. His hand wraps in my hair and he sinks to the hilt, taking every drop of oxygen and my pussy clenches, aching to be touching again. He spills down my throat, pulls out, and holds my mouth shut, pinching my nose. I swallow, but he doesn't release me. I jerk my head, frantically fighting for air. Just as I think I'm about to die, he lets go and I choke on the oxygen I greedily suck into my lungs.

The blindfold is jerked off my head and I blink against the sting of light, fighting to see him clearly. When my vision clears, I wish it hadn't. Standing in front of me is Reaper, his mask and gloves back in place, and in his right hand, he holds a severed arm, limp and dripping blood from the veins exposed like torn wires. He dangles it casually like it's nothing more than a piece of rope or a tool. He tilts his head to the side, watching me, and I realize with a hollow drop in my stomach that he just fucked me with a severed limb.

Oh, my God. I fight to curl into a ball. To vomit the entire contents of my stomach. I yank on my binds, tears streaking my face and I cry out.

"Let this be a lesson. Next time, I'll kill you too," he says, calmly and stern.

I swallow hard, the sex fog clearing. He turns, giving me his back as he walks to the door.

"Wait!" I yell after him, yanking on my binds, confused, disgusted, and still desperate to come.

"Dom will keep you company," he says, and my eyes widen. His sharp whistle sounds through the house and a moment later, Dom comes prancing in, taking the arm from Reaper's hand, and lies on the bed, keeping space between us.

"You can't keep locking me away! I'm a fucking person!" I yell as the lights flick off and the door shuts, locking behind him. "Fucking asshole!"

CHAPTER 35

I eye the dog sleeping peacefully at the end of the bed now that he finished his snack. I haven't moved an inch in an hour, but as he snores softly, I begin to wiggle my hands, working the knots the way Daith taught me all those years ago. Keeping my movements small and as gentle as possible, it takes longer than I'd like, but my binds eventually give, and my hands slip free.

Keeping my eyes on the murderer next to me, I unbind my feet and slowly inch me leg off the bed. My foot touches the floor and I carefully shift my weight off the bed. Dom's snoring stops and I freeze, though his eyes stay closed, still deep in his slumber. I let out a quite shaky breath before holding it again and taking my first step toward the door. I glance back checking that I didn't wake him before I take another, my eyes on the door. So close, yet so far.

The floor creaks and I cringe, sinking lower, fearful this fucking dog is going to eat me. After a moment of silence, I start again, taking each step slowly. I wrap my hand around the knob, planning to jerk it open and jump on the other side before trapping devil dog by himself. I test it, attempting to turn it carefully. It doesn't budge and I grit my teeth.

Planning to find something to pick or break the lock, I slowly turn around only to be met with a snarling canine baring his teeth at me, a growl of warning ripping through the air, making my blood run cold.

My eyes widen as I slowly hold my hands up in front of me. "Okay, Okay. I'm just looking for—" I take a step toward the nightstand and he steps to the side cutting me off. I quickly step back, my back hitting the door. "Shit," I mumble under my breath. "He's going to fucking eat me. This is it." I look up at the ceiling, saying one last prayer before I lunge right, and he pounces, mirroring me.

I shoot left, taking one large step before leaping through the air and landing on the bed. Rolling to the furthest side, I pull my knees in, covering my face as he spins and jumps, mouth wide open, foam dripping out the sides. I scream, bracing myself, his weight causing the bed to dip on either side of me.

After a couple seconds, I realize I'm still alive and there is no pain shooting through my body. Slowly, I lower my hands and open my eyes, finding Dom looking down at me, panting, tongue hanging out of his mouth. His tail wags with excitement, only stopping as I shift my weight to try to get out from under him. He bares his teeth in warning and I still, his wagging resuming.

Oh my God, I'm his fucking chew toy.

Deciding there is no chance in hell I'm moving, I rest my hands on my chest and close my eyes, getting comfortable for a nap.

Minutes later, I open my eyes, watching as Dom gets comfortable at my side, keeping his head pointed at the door, getting his body as close as possible to me. I wait a moment before I slowly move my arm and set my hand on his side. His ears perk up but he doesn't move, allowing me to stay there. After another moment, I slowly stroke down the length of his back. After another moment, he relaxes, sinking into me again.

"Good boy," I whisper and he turns his head, licking my arm.

I wake up from my nap suddenly, jerking spastically. I exhale slowly, finding Reaper laying next to me and Dom on the floor in front of the door. I stare at Reaper for a long minute, confirming he's asleep and wondering what the chances are of me getting a peak under his mask without waking him up.

Deciding there isn't a chance in hell, I let my eyes wander down the length of his body, settling on the outline of his dick through his sweatpants. I tuck my bottom lip between my teeth and slip my hand between my legs, lightly brushing over my clit, testing the waters. My entire body groans, desperate for the release he deprived me of hours ago.

I debate for a long minute before deciding, *why the fuck not.*

I carefully shift my weight on the bed, crawling to my knees and pausing, making sure he isn't awake. Though, I guess, with his mask, I couldn't truly know for sure. Grabbing onto the headboard, I lift up and carefully step out of my panties. Straddling his body, hovering above his face, I slowly squat, facing his dick and letting my mind wander, using my darkest imagination to work myself up.

Images of me tied up in the basement, at his mercy while he ruthlessly fucks me until I am a whimpering mess, shaking and writhing, begging for him to stop. Lowering myself even more, I let my clit brush the sharp peaks of his mask, slowly grinding my hips back and forth, trying to keep my breaths quiet.

I clamp my lips together, imagining his big hands around my neck as he uses me like a fuck toy, telling me how good I feel and how much he needs my body. As my head falls back and my orgasm is nearly ready to come cascading down, my body jolts as his hands fly up, gripping my waist.

"What the fuck are you doing Peach?"

I suck in a sharp breath and my heart lurches, nearly giving me a heart attack. I bare my teeth, trying to find a good explanation, but nothing comes, so I try honesty for the first time in a while. "Getting that orgasm I'm owed." I look up at his raging hard-on now standing at full attention.

"Is that right?"

My pussy clenches and every bit of self-control or respect leaves my body as I drop down on his mask. "Yeah, that's right. Now shut up and be still."

His grip on me tightens for a moment, then he moves with me, encouraging my movements as I ride his face. I fist my breasts, squeezing my eyes shut as I let my mind continue its journey, fantasizing about all the filthy ways I would let him have me.

My orgasm peaks and I lean forward, gripping his stomach, riding it out as I cum hard enough to see stars. Taking this one for myself, not following his rules or limitations. I collapse onto his firm body, loving the way he smells, the way his hands lay idly on my ass.

Rolling off him, I flip back around, taking my place on the bed.

"Feel better?" he asks as the bed tilts and he stands, using his sleeve to wipe my cum from his mask.

I roll over, giving him my back. "Shut up."

He chuckles before the sound of the door shutting follows, and I can't help the smirk forming on my face.

I feel much better.

Chapter 36

"**I**'m not a fucking pack mule," Ezra groans, dropping my surprise for Laurel into the basement chair before he steps back, to the side, feet shoulder width and arms braced on his hips, as usual.

"Sure look like an ass to me," I say, getting my tools ready.

He looks over our handiwork. "I don't know, man," he says, running a hand through his hair. "You're putting a lot on her. Laurel's proven to follow orders well, but this—" He gestures toward the chair, his face a mix of concern and doubt. "What if it pushes her away instead of pulling her in?"

I can't suppress the smile tugging at my lips. It's not humor, it's certainty. "It's just a push. A little shock to the system. She needs to understand what it really means to be a part of this. To be *mine*."

"I'm not saying you're wrong," Ezra continues, his voice soft, full of hesitation. "But pushing her too hard could backfire."

I let out a short laugh, because the idea of Laurel backing out now... it's almost laughable. He sees her as a liability. But she is my personal prayer answered in physical form. "Why do you care? I thought you wanted her gone?"

Ezra's quiet for a second, his eyes on me, his mind clearly somewhere else. I know he's worried. But that's what Ezra does. It's why he's not the one making the hard calls. I am. He exhales slowly, still standing there with that damn concerned look on his face. He's not fully convinced. But he never is.

"Fine," he says, shoving his hands in his pockets. "Keep an eye on her. We don't know where this will lead."

"I always do," I say, and we part ways, leaving me to it.

"I have something for you," I tell her, taking her hand, pulling her up from the bed. Dom whimpers, wagging his tail eagerly. I hold my palm out to him, instructing him to stay but leave the door open for him.

I drag her behind me down to the basement and she digs her heels in at the door, eyes wide as she looks at me nervously. "I don't like it in there. Please."

Fuck, I love the way she looks at me when she's begging. "Easy Peach. This room is already reserved tonight."

The doors creak as I pull them open, guiding her down the curved stairs with a hand on her back. As we round the corner she stops in her tracks, frozen taking in the man tied to a chair, slouched, head hanging.

He groans, lifting his head, and Laurel gasps. "Bryce?" She turns to me accusingly, eyes wide and pleading. "Why is he here?"

Rushing to him, she cups his face in her hands. His right eye is swollen shut and his mouth is beat to shit, leaking blood down his chest, meeting with the blood flowing from his broken leg like a stream into a river. He offered to come without a fight, like the titty sucking sack of shit he is, but what satisfaction is there to get out of that?

She looks him over, mumbling as she squats and inspects the bone sticking out of his calf.

"I told you, he didn't know anything! Your intel was wrong," she scolds me, storming toward me with her finger in my face. I move around her to my table full of tools.

"There never was any intel baby." I spill the beans, enjoying the horror on her face, as if I'm the monster that haunts her dreams. "He likes you. He wants what he can't have."

She grits her teeth, taking another look at the broken man. "He was never a threat to you."

I run my finger over my tools, trying to decide which would be the most fun to use if I were making the choices tonight. Taking my time could be fun, but I am sick of this motherfucker and the soft spot she has. His new purpose is to harden that spot in her.

"You think he's cute? You think he cares about you?" I move closer to her, grabbing my gun tilting her chin up with the barrel. "You think he saw you as anything more than an easy piece of ass?" Her eyes glisten as tears threaten to pool, and fuck, I love it so much. " You think he can protect you? No one will ever love you like I do."

"Please, let him go," she begs, and the look on her face would be enough to convince me... if I had remorse or empathy.

I guide my hand down her arm to her hand and flip it over in my palm, my eyes never leaving hers. I place my gun in her hand and wrap her fingers around it.

"Kill him."

Her eyes widen just the slightest bit and her shoulders tense.

"What?" she squeaks, choking on the word. She knows there is no room for debate and not a chance I'll change my mind, yet, she asks anyway.

"He's seen my face, heard my voice. Knows where I live. You think he won't turn me in the second you let him go?" Bryce gurgles through the blood pouring from his mouth no tongue to stop it, and my temper boils, lashing out like a whip. "No one asked you to speak!"

I grab Laurels shoulder, squaring her in front of me, facing Bryce head on. He wiggles in a sad attempt to do anything about his current predicament, and I help Laurel aim the gun. One quick shot in the chest, that's all I need from her. I'll deliver the headshot, for good measure. Bryce's eyes soften at my girl before they flick to me, pleading. "You don't know what she's capable of!" I snap, cutting off what I know he's thinking, the grip on my anger and patience wearing thin. I brush her hair from her sweaty neck, planting a kiss on the salty damp skin. I inhale, wondering if I can smell her fear mixing, turning into arousal. "It's him or me. Choose." For emphasis, I move in front of her, standing next to Bryce, hunching over on my knees so that we're level. I narrow my eyes, challenging her.

Her lip quivers as her head, no doubt, spins with a choice she will live with for the rest of her life.

"Ten seconds or he dies anyway, and you die with him."

"Please," she whines, holding the gun at Bryce. Her eyes move to me, a plea for the right answer screaming at me through her beautiful eyes.

"Five."

She swallows.

"Four,"

She shifts uncomfortably.

"Three." My excitement begins to peek. Not that I want to kill her, but my God the anticipation is like Viagra.

BANG.

The gun goes off and screams of cheer and excitement explode from my chest as Bryce's body sags, blood pouring from his chest. I kneel in front of him, pulling his head back by the scalp, forcing his eyes open. I love to see the void within them as what tethers us to this world, what makes us who we are, disappears, leaving only a rotting sack of flesh behind.

His empty vessel stares blankly back at me, but it does nothing to take away from his handsome features. It pisses me off honestly.

"Fucking asshole, thinking his pretty face will get him whatever he wants," I mumble, not caring if Laurel hears me.

I'm not jealous of his looks, nor insecure of my own. It's the fact that he got even an ounce of her attention. That she adored him, let him touch her. She gave him what was mine because of his stupid fucking face.

A fabulously horrific idea comes to mind, not exactly marking me boyfriend of the year, but I don't let that stop me. I stand and move swiftly to the back wall, fishing through my drawer of toys.

Laurel shoves the gun into my chest as I turn to her, tears streaming down her face that is full of anger. "Here," she says, pain lacing her venom as her hands shake, outstretched and holding my gun. "Don't you dare say I never put The Reapers first."

She tries to move past me as I take my gun, but I whip my arm out, stopping her, pushing her back against the cement wall.

"No. No. No. No. You stay here. Wait."

Finding what I need, I turn my radio on and rush back to Bryce, starting at his chin. Doing my best to keep clean lines, I slice his face clean off, tossing the tool to the ground and holding up the flap of skin to inspect it.

Excellent work, If I do say so myself. I look down at the red flesh and muscles aggressively staring back at me. *Not so handsome now, are you Brycey-Poo?*

"Laurel," I say, turning to find she has obeyed and has sunk down on the wall, knees to her chest, face in her hands. Her body shakes softly as she sobs. Laurel feels everything deeply, and it's natural for those who have that connection I lack to need an adjustment period after taking a life.

She's clearly not having a good time, but I'm having a fucking blast, enjoying the fact there is one less man who thinks he has a chance with her. I hold Bryce's face up, placing it on top of my mask. Holding it into place, I walk closer to Laurel.

"You wanna kiss me now, baby?" I ask, smacking my lips at her as I sway my hips. She stares back at me.

"Stop," she says, voice cracking as she pleads, doing her best to hold her composure.

I persist, leaning closer. "Come on baby. I want you so bad," I say, grabbing my cock.

"Stop!" she screams. "That's enough!"

Holding his face with one hand, I shimmy my sweatpants down over my ass, wiggling my hips in rhythm to the music. "Oh, Laurel. Fuck me. I'm so handsome," I say, raising my voice an octave to mock the faceless man behind me.

Laurel's face turns cold as she stands, crossing her arms. And I stop dancing, letting his face fall to the ground with a smack.

"No? How about this?" I ask, moving toward her and she flinches. I grab her by the arm, dragging her toward the chair. Planting the heel of my boot in his shoulder, I kick what's left of Bryce onto the floor and shove her in his spot.

"Best seat in the house. Do. Not. Move."

She keep her eyes low and her mouth shut. She's still, obeying perfectly as I bring in our next guest that Ezra had already bound to a rolling chair, drugged, and gagged for me. Such a sweetie.

"You want to disobey, and I for some ungodly reason cant stomach the idea of hurting you in the way I need to. So," I say, pulling ole Patrick, another crew member, into the light for her to see more clearly. "Every time you want to be a brat, someone else will take your punishment." I pat him on the shoulder and her brows crease, tears rolling down her face.

"I'm sorry," she squeaks, and I'm not sure if it's meant for me or him, either way, neither one of us give a damn. Her apology fixes nothing. Sorry is just a word that people use to cover up the wound of their own selfish actions, hoping that it makes you forget. If you want to be cold, you can't be sorry. Sorry is bullshit. I want to see you write sorry in your blood. I want to see you rip your heart out and hand it to me. Maybe then you'll feel the way I felt when you took me for a joke.

"You think I like doing this? I'm wasting perfectly good men here." I pull my cart of toys closer, and Laurel begins to fidget with her fingertips. "This right here, is me. This is all I am," I tell her, taking the biggest blade I have and swinging it into his chest. Blood spurts from his mouth and his half-conscious head falls forward. I didn't want to deal with all the screaming and begging today. No, this is about me and her. About respect and obedience. Consequences.

She cringes, looking away and I slam my hand down on the metal cart, causing the smaller tools to clatter on the concrete floor. "You will watch!" I scream and her head snaps up. "I do this, so I can keep you. I am cutting myself off at the legs because I would rather destroy everything I am than lose you."

She begins sobbing, but obeys, keeping her eyes on the man slowly fading away. I shove my spreader into his check cracking his ribs open with a grumbled grunt to hold his chest open. I shove my hand into the red sea using my other to cut his lungs from his body. I hold them out in front her. "You want to steal the breath out of the life I made for myself? Here!" I throw them in her lap, and her head tilts up to avoid them, but she doesn't move and after a moment, her eyes are back on me.

I reach in again, wrapping my hand around his heart and ripping it out, his blood splattering on my mask. "How about my heart? Will that make you behave? Make you happy?" I ask, throwing it at her feet. "I will give you whatever you want, until you are satisfied, here with me. Until there is nothing left of me but a shell. I will gladly be whatever you want if you will just *stay*!"

I spin, grabbing my machete, angrier by the minute as I let myself rage. I chop both of his arms off in single swift motions, blood gushing to the floor, and fuck I love the way it looks. The way it smells. The way it feels between my fingers. The crunch of his bones and the squelch of his organs.

I snap out of it, not believing the words that just came out of me, and return my focus back to Laurel who is still sitting where I put her. Splattered with blood, her hands limp at her side, and her eyes on me—red and puffy, glazed over, but on me. For a moment, looking at her like this, I think I would give it all up for her, just as I said.

Then it's gone. No, she will live in my world under my terms. I will not change who I am for her or anyone else. I will not leave behind everything I have created. I will not bow to anyone.

"Is that good enough? Do I need to get another or have you learned a lesson here?" I ask, heaving as I drop my weapon at her feet.

She nods. "Can we go up now?" Laurel asks, looking up at me with something earth-shattering in her eyes. Submission.

Reaching out, I take her hand in mine and she leans into me, holding on to me.

I whistle for Dom.

Dinner!

CHAPTER 37

LAUREL

I curl on the bed, tears streaking my face, finally letting them fall. I just killed someone. I took their life. Someone's son is gone, no remains to be found and buried. Because of me. He liked me. That was his crime, punishable by torture, a bullet to the head, and corpse mutilation.

I sob quietly while Reaper finishes cleaning, letting my heart ache for the part of myself that died with Bryce. No matter how much he wants me to be cold and callous, mirroring the creature he is, that's not me.

Will I still do anything he asks of me? Yes. And maybe given an adjustment period, I could do it without hesitation. But for now, I have to shove that part of me down and be what he needs me to be until it becomes as natural as breathing.

I can do that for him.

I hear his steps coming and sit up, quickly wiping my tears. The door opens and Reaper moves to the bed, standing before me, mask smeared with Bryce's blood. I hate the stupid mask, always blocking me from seeing his face. I can't see his expression, read how he's feeling.

"Did I do good?" I ask, seeking his approval.

"You did perfectly," he says, cupping my head in his hands.

A relieved breath leaves my lips, his thumbs brushing beneath my puffy eyes. "There's no room for tears Peach."

I nod, hating that I couldn't hide it better. I'm not weak, and he needs to see that.

"Do I get to know why?" I ask before clenching my jaw, holding back the aggression forming.

"You killed for us. You can ask whatever you want," he says sitting next to me and I cringe at the blood that will be left on my clean blanket when he leaves.

"Why have me interrogate him if you didn't have a real suspicion?" I ask, needing to understand the game. "Why have me kill him when the reason you wanted him dead was because of your own insecurities?" I push my boundaries, owning the place I have here.

He grabs my hand rolling it over in his. "Bryce was so interested in you that he was concerned with where I was involved. A liability," he says, his voice softer than he's ever spoken to be before. "But in all honestly, because I wanted to." His grip tightens and his tone hardens. "I don't have insecurities. I protect the life I created. I protect you. Whether you like this or not, you are part of my life until I decide it's your turn to sit in that chair." His grip is punishing, and I grimace, not letting the groan slip free.

I nod, and he releases, rubbing his thumb over my sore knuckles. "Don't forget where you stand pet."

I clench my jaw, hating that word. It's belittling and humiliating to be called less than I deserve.

"Why protect me?" I ask, pulling my hand from his and soothing it. "I break your rules. I push my limits. Why?"

He exhales, taking a pen out of his pocket, writing something on the palm of my hand as he talks. "Because when it mattered most, when I was breaking the rules that were set, trying to survive in a place that seem inhabitable, no one protected me."

I look down at the finished drawing, the sketch of an hourglass. He pulls his sleeve up, revealing a tattoo on his bicep, identical, beautiful and intricately done. I feel like I've seen it before, like the ghost of a memory, haunting me but unable to place it.

"This symbol marks you mine forever. You live up to what I know you can be, and you'll be more than a pet Peach."

I grin, unable to hide my excitement shining in my eyes, but that word still grates at my nerves. He stands, moving toward the door.

"No!" I shout, standing from the bed and he pauses with his hand on the door.

"No?"

"I left Daith for you... I killed for you! And I will again," I say, pointing my finger at him. "I am not a pet. I have earned a little more respect than that. A lot more!"

He tucks his hands in his pockets, adjusting his posture, but says nothing. The silence between us grows.

"I am not your fucking pet! I would do anything for you. I deserve more than that, damn it!"

He slowly pushes my finger down from where it's jammed in his chest. Stepping into me, he brushes my messy hair from my face.

"There she is." I can hear the smile in his voice and something between us shifts.

"Go home and get ready. The club is open and we have work to do."

CHAPTER 38

LAUREL

T he pulsing beat of the music vibrates through my chest. The lights are dim, the air thick with the scent of sweat, perfume, and alcohol—a far cry from the stillness of the old church, but it feels good to be back in action.

A new girl was hired to replace Daisy. She looks similar to what Daisy looked like, but she struggles to walk properly in her 8-inch heels and chews gum like it's her profession.

"Name's Darian," she says, smacking her gum aggressively. "But I'm going by Annie on stage. Like the orphan, but hotter." She pulls the gum from between her teeth, twirling it around her finger and I cringe. No one laughs, not even Dolly, and she laughs at everything.

By hour two, Annie has every girl in the dressing room ready to pull their hair out with her less than constructive criticism and her self-proclaimed genius tips. "She called my outfit "tired," advised Christa to "hold her gum in her cooch if it was tight enough" so you "don't have to waste, and it leaves your puss smelling minty." Then, hand to God, she told the stage guy that "her mother was an escort and she doesn't mind showing him what momma taught her to get extra stage time."

I about choked on my drink watching some of the girls literally sprint away from her. Grabbing my tray, I begin making my round, when I see her head straight for Reaper's table.

Oh, this is going to be good.

I smile, keeping my eyes on his table, watching her put her tits inches from his face as she flirts for a tip, though he's looking at me. I wonder if she knows the last girl that was in her position is dead.

If Annie doesn't move along, Annie is going to die.

I snort a laugh as Reaper pulls his gun without taking his eyes off me and points it directly between her eyes that widen before her mouth promptly shuts and she moves faster than I thought possible, though she wobbles like a baby giraffe as expected.

A gentleman gets my attention, and I round him, dawning my new outfit, dragging my hand around his shoulders. I sway my hips, dragging my hands down my body, flashing a glance to Reaper watching intently, as I hoped. I slide onto the customer's lap, grinding my hips, tilting my head back, putting my tits inches from his face.

The man hardens beneath me and an ache forms between my spread legs conjuring a masked face under me. Time escapes me as I grind to the music, letting my orgasm build. A hand taps me on the shoulder, and I jerk my head up, opening my eyes to find a skeleton face tilted at me behind my customer and a gun held to his head.

"Times up," his modified voice growls.

The man below me is stiff as a board, except for his penis, now flaccid. I fake a look of fear, scrambling to my feet, waiting for my next order.

"Follow me." He holsters his gun, nodding toward his corner table.

He tucks a hundred-dollar bill in my thong as he sits and I grin, straddling his cock.

"Jealous?" I ask, whispering below the music for only him to hear, already knowing the answer.

He says nothing, and the silence is suffocating as he holds my stare as I begin grinding on him. Once his ego is intact, and I feel better, he grips my jaw tight. "Now, go work without trying to make me murderous, and wait for me to call you."

I take a deep breath walking back across the club. Guilt nestles somewhere deep in my stomach when I get to the bar and see Dolly standing behind it, filling in for Bryce. She's wearing her usual confident smile, effortlessly mixing drinks with the smoothness that comes with experience. She looks up, catching my eye with that knowing look she always has, like she can read me in an instant. Her smile widens just a fraction as I approach.

"Busy night!" she says over the loud crowd. It's expected after a week of being shut down.

I force a smile, pushing aside the discomfort. "Yeah, had to make up for lost time, huh?"

Brittany Spears' Slave begins playing and green lights cast over the club as Annie struts on stage, overconfident and under skilled. She blows kisses at guys who are clearly just here to forget their wives exist and I lean on the bar next to Christa and sip a whiskey that Dolly hands me without asking for it, watching this disaster unfold.

"She told one of the new girls that she was "God's gift to men," Christ says, raising her brows dramatically.

"God should ask for a refund," Dolly says and I my smile hits heavy as her words sound so much like something Bryce would have said.

"The only thing she is giving is a yeast infection at the minimum," I say, watching as she grabs the pole like it owes her money and begins climbing it like a rope in a fitness test. She's fighting gravity and losing, her body sliding back down the pole inch by inch.

"Don't do it. Just grind and smile," I mumble under my breath.

She crosses her ankles and leans back, throwing herself upside down, and as expected, her grip slips and for a moment, she's airborne. Arms flailing and an awkward squawk comes from her and she slams into the stage, head bouncing off the polished wood.

"Oooh," the crowd says in unison, but she gets up, sweeping her hair back with a bright smile.

"There it is," Dolly says, grinning as she pours another drink.

The music continues to play and she begins to wiggle her body awkwardly, jerking and writhing off rhythm. She grimaces, holding her head as she side-steps. Her ankle bends, she stumbles, trying to catch herself, but her next step is off the stage.

She lands in the front row and a few men grunt, cussing and cleaning their drinks from their clothes. One of Vic's beefy guys is already moving, calm, unhurried, as if babysitting mischievous toddlers. He kneels beside her and she blinks up at him, dazed, mouth open like she wants to say something. He lifts her like she weighs nothing, cradling her limp body in his arms like a child. She groans again, barely conscious, mumbling nonsense about him being her hero. He doesn't speak as he walks past me and out the front door, the bouncer shutting it behind him with a soft click.

The music shifts and the chatter resumes as if nothing happened. Moments after the big buy comes back empty-handed and resumes his post, Reaper is standing, hands in his pockets, leisurely strolling toward the side door.

He brushes my hand, leaning in for only a moment as he passes me. "I hate her too," he says and I grin as he continues walking, pulling his cigarettes from his pocket.

"What was that?" Dolly asks as I grab my tray.

"Just requesting time with me when he comes back from his smoke break."

She nods, cleaning a glass. "Got that dangerous dick."

My mouth drops in hearing her be so crass, unlike her usual self. "Hey, no judgement." She says with her palms up and I shake my head.

"Filthy," I say, leaving her to make my rounds, keeping busy until he calls for me.

It's only 45 minutes later when my heart leaps nervously.

"Scarlette."

My name is yelled from the stairs and my heart stalls in my chest as I turn to Vic storming toward me. I slide my empty tray to Dolly and Vic meets me at the end of the bar. "Mr. Reaper has requested you join him tonight in the poker room."

Game on.

I still for performance, gaze flicking to Dolly who says nothing, though her face speaks volumes. "Uh- Yes sir," I say, wearily, letting nervousness coat my shaky voice.

Vic grabs my arm firmly and Dolly casts me a worried look. He pulls me up the stairs faster than my stiletto heels can keep up, causing me to stumble. The lighting dims as I reach the top of the stairs, the stench of overwhelming cologne of douche bags that can't get laid without a credit card seeps from under the closed doors. "You will not speak unless spoken to and you will do as asked without question. Understood?"

I nod, staying silent, keeping a look of nervousness plastered in place.

"For God's sake, stop looking like a deer in headlights and at least act like you know what you're doing if you prefer to leave the room breathing. Fuck knows we are losing too many staff as it is." He steps back, looking me up and down before grabbing my breasts, wiggling them up so that they hang out a bit more. I fight the urge to slap him, keeping my wits knowing he will be dead soon enough. "Now, go be a good little whore and stand in the corner until you're relevant."

I nod again, keeping my head low, watching my feet as I take a right into the open room, cigar smoke rolling out and take my spot as a wallflower.

Lisa finishes setting the table, five drinks, only leaving one spot empty. The high dollar players start rolling in, taking their seats as they continue their talk of financial winnings and their large estates. A moment later, the air shifts, and a heavy presence looms, revealing my Reaper without my eyes needing to leave the old red carpet.

He takes his seat in the empty chair to the left, angled just enough that he can see me.

"You're dry," says nodding toward the empty glass in his hand, his face twisting as he glares at Lisa who says nothing to defend herself. Though I know Reaper wouldn't trust a drink being made where he can't see it being poured. His reputation proves he's smarter than that.

"No fault to Lisa. I like to keep a clear head when my money is at stake," he assures, his true voice hidden behind his modifier, as always.

Vic nods, clearing his throat as the dealer takes his position standing in the hold of the table, facing me head on. "You know, Reaper. We're all friends here, and what happens in my club, stays in my club. You should know that you are free to take off that silly mask. Your identity is safe with us."

The man across from snickers with a vile grin flashing across his face before it's gone. And I grit my teeth, nervous that the night will end before it's started.

His distorted laugh fills the room that has fallen utterly silent. "The silly mask is who I am. Let's not show our hand so clearly, hmm?"

I bite my lip to hide the smirk. Reaper pats his leg like he's calling a dog. "Sit Scarlette."

My eyes snap up, then quickly avoid the eyes of all the men in the room that fall on me. I obey, sitting politely on his thigh, legs crossed, holding most of my own weight. He lets out a frustrated sigh, pushing my legs apart, forcing me to lean into him. He rests his hand on the inside of my thigh, inches from my crotch.

"Are we going to play or waste my time?" He looks around the table, stopping on Reaper who grabs a chip from his highest stack, throwing a thousand dollars into the pot and starting the game.

Reaper plays, taking two of the same chips, creating the buy-in amount and tossing two chips into the pot. "That right? I'm a little rusty," he asks, toying with a chip and flipping it between his fingers.

The buy-in rounds the table until it gets back to Vic, and he places the other half of the buy-in.

"Texas hold-em boys," the dealer says, passing two cards to each player before dealing the flop, placing three cards face up in the center of the table. Everyone peeks at their cards, folding just the tips, and Reaper nudges me to make sure I'm paying attention. Eight and Seven of spades.

He places his cards back on the table, tapping them once with his finger. I look at the flop. Eight of hearts, six of spades, and ten of spades. He's going for a straight flush.

Vic looks down at his cards and bets another thousand confidently, though his face remains neutral. Reaper matches him, sliding a chip to the center with one finger. The man to our left is staring at where his hand rests, toying with my skin under the fishnets.

"Are you going to play, Barley, or are you going to continue to stare at what's mine?" Reaper asks, drawing his attention back above the table.

Barley's eyes round at the use of his name that hasn't been offered, and he readjusts in his seat. "S-sorry. I didn't—"

"Then don't." Reaper's voice holds both warning and promise in his possessiveness.

Barley takes another look at his cards before matching the bet, and the next three men follow.

Vic runs his tongue over his yellowing teeth. "You see, the problem I have with that mask is that I can't see your poker face. Your tells are fair game, and I might just declare you a cheat for hiding under who you are."

"If you aren't confident in your skills, just say that," Reaper says, flipping the chip through his fingers intricately. "I don't have any tells, because I don't have any emotions. Pesky little perk of being a psychopath and all."

I giggle and Vic narrows his eyes on me, promising me a punishment for that. "Watch yourself, girl."

"Though, you should have no problem beating me considering I haven't played in over five years."

Liar, Liar.

Vic sucks his tongue, deciding to hold back his annoyance. The dealer lays down the fourth card for the turn, revealing a nine of clubs and I keep my face neutral.

Holding Reaper's stare, he bets two thousand-dollar chips, letting his arrogance show with a smirk. "Tell me, do you have any experience reading people? Am I bluffing?"

Reaper matches him, moving his hand to my side, teasing the spot that makes me squirm. "Experience seeing under the facade that people put in place to cover their insecurities. Can't say I do. I'm more... active than passive."

Vic hums in response, as Barley and the guy next to him fold, pushing his cards back with his fingers. The next guy matches, passing to the last who avoids looking up from the table as he does the same.

The dealer lays down the last card for the river, revealing a nine of spades and Vic bets five thousand, clearly confident in his hand.

"Scarlette, do you think we should fold?" Reaper asks, tapping my side in question.

Vic snorts. "Asking a woman to play for you is a sure way to lose. Not to mention, it's cheating."

"If it's ignorant to ask her, why would you be concerned with her input?"

Vic stays silent.

"Oh, uh-" I fumble. "I've never even been in this room before today, much less actually played such a man's game," I say timidly, not a hint of my lie showing though my nervous expression.

"Give it your best shot," Reaper says, enjoying our game.

I pick up five thousand and hand it to him in answer. He drops the chips into the pot. "The lady has spoken. Boy I hope she's not wrong," Reaper says, dangling bait for Vic who is all but foaming at the mouth.

"Your loss, son."

The last two men fold, not willing to go any further, and Vic chuckles a sickening sound I have only ever heard in my nightmares. He flips his cards face up, revealing nine of hearts and diamonds. "Four of a kind."

"Shit," Reaper breathes, sliding his cards off the table and shaking his head. "That's a good hand." He fans his two cards out between his thumb and index finger. "But I think this one's better." He drops his eight and seven of spades on the table. "Looks like a... straight flush?" he asks, knowing there isn't a question there.

Vic face turns stone cold, annoyance clear in his body language. "Well then, Reaper, by the looks of it, you're welcome to come back any time. Good play."

Reaper nods, checking his watch. "I appreciate such good sportsmanship, and I look forward to the next game boys. But if you don't mind wrapping my winnings up, I have other plans starting soon that I must admit, are bit more important than this."

Reaper tucks a large tip from his winnings into my hand, successful in gaining the true intel he wanted on the hidden room inside that one but leaving without me. I know it's the appearance we have to keep, me not being of importance and just a favored whore, but it stings just the same.

"Scarlette, Vic wants you. Says it's urgent," one of the girls says on passing.

I head up the stairs where Vic is waiting for me, less than enthused. He holds his hand out and passes me two small tablets, nodding to one of the five black doors.

"In case you need to relax," he says with a hard glare.

"Oh, uh. I don't work the VIP room unless it's Reaper." I put my hand out again, offering the muscle relaxer back to him. Like hell, I will be going in there. One of our girls works the weekends in there and she always comes out in worse shape—high, beaten, bloody, crying, or crawling.

Yeah, I'll fucking pass. No amount of money is worth that to me. That was my agreement with Vic and it isn't about to change.

"Seriously, I don't care how much he paid. Ask someone else."

He sneers grabbing a fist full of hair and my necklace, yanking me into him. His breath stinks of stale cigarettes and as I look up at him with watery eyes, I notice the remnants of white powder under his nose.

"You work VIP today."

He releases me and I turn, picking up my necklace that he ripped from my neck and carefully pulling my phone from my bra, quickly dialing Felix before tucking it back in my bra, praying he picks up.

"You were specifically ordered, and we don't turn away business. Especially the ones that pay two thousand for a Reaper's bitch," he says, spitting his venom and rage at me, Vic says, giving no room for rejection.

My heart falls from my ass, knowing Reaper is well gone by now and I'm on my own if I went to voicemail. As I step back, Vic's henchman wraps his hand around my arm, hard enough to bruise, stopping me from moving another inch.

"Get ready to spread that pretty pink pussy princess," he spits in my ear, and I jerk my head to the side. "I might be next."

My stomach curdles and my knees buckle, but it does nothing to hinder their plans. Vic pulls the door open, and I'm thrown into the dimly lit room, nearly face-planting on the old orange carpet. I stumble in my heels, using the wall to help me regain my ground. The door shuts, then locks, and Vic props himself in the corner like an old dusty lamp.

He gives me a nod with his dead eyes giving me a clear command. *Do as you are told.* A lump forms in my throat.

I turn to face the man who requested me. He sits slouched on the torn red couch stretching along the length of the back wall. His potbelly is nearly level with his chin, his leather belt already hanging down, his jeans unbuttoned, his bulge straining against the denim. Bile rises to my throat as I take a step toward him. I couldn't make myself fuck him if I tried. His body odor alone is enough to put me off. Fuck, I can only imagine what his dick smells like.

"Would you like a dance?" I ask with the sweetest tone I can muster, hoping we can settle on me getting him off by dry humping.

His voice is low and grimy. "What I would like is for you to use that cute mouth for more useful things than asking bullshit like that." He pushes off the couch with one hand to sit up and the other reaches out for me. I hesitantly place my hand in his, hating the way his sweaty palms clamp around my fingers. "On your knees, girl," he spits.

I hear the floor creak behind me, and I hope that Vic is about to demand more respect towards me as *one of his valued girls*. Praying that for once, he shows a sense of dignity and compassion for his employees.

But I'm wrong.

Just as I peer over my shoulder, a hard hand meets my cheek, and I gasp as I'm shoved onto my knees. "He paid for the hour. Behave or you'll be forced."

Tears sting my eyes, and I sink into myself, realizing there is no way out of here. I open my palm, realizing I still hold the small pills in my hand.

I take my phone from my bra, sparing a quick glance, finding my home screen staring back at me. All hope leaves me, and I accept my temporary fate. His will come soon enough.

I lift my eyes to the pig in front of me, hardening them with every ounce of defiance I have, and place the pill on my tongue.

Chapter 39

The last gurgle trails off like a broken instrument. Felix pulls his blade from the man's gut, the blood dripping onto the floor with a satisfying *boing*.

I light a cigarette while he works, finalizing the sanctioned hit that crossed into our territory, doing CHAOS a favor. They usually tend to the more overhead kills, rogues, rebels, newbies... but at the moment, they needed proof that we were still on their side.

Nolan Cortland. A CHAOS adjacent operative who's been skimming funds and leaking information to government law enforcement.

Naughty double-dipper.

"You want the eyes?" Felix asks without looking at me.

I raise a brow. "You know I do."

He hums a little tune, something classical and annoying, as he moves to the clean-up kit to grab the pliers. We're in and out of this rat motel in under ten minutes. The kind of precision Ezra would jerk off over if he weren't so busy playing babysitter at the club.

I'm about to ask Felix if he wiped the hallway cams when his phone buzzes on the blood-stained sink. He glances at the screen, then tosses it my way. "CHAOS broadcast. Internal feed only. You're going to want to see this."

I flick ash on the corpse and move closer to see. It's a blurry screenshot of some woman walking out of an alley where a body was found two nights ago. Black coat. Face turned, just enough that you can't make out any identifying features.

Below it, a few lines of intel:

Signature inconsistencies. Appears to mimic internal contractor styles.

Suspect is female. Operates close to known Reaper territory.

No ID yet. Unregistered.

My jaw tightens. I read it again.

"A woman? About time. I'm tired of the sausage fest," Felix comments, attempting to be funny.

"She's close, stupid fucker," I murmur.

He raises an eyebrow. "To us?"

"To me."

Felix pauses in his packing. "You think she's one of ours from CHAOS? Planted?"

"No," I say, but the word is too sharp. Too fast. "CHAOS doesn't hire women for field work like this."

"You got someone in mind?"

I take another drag, burning the cigarette down to the filter. "A freelancer maybe."

Felix snorts. "Freelancers don't stage scenes like this. You saw that last job. That wasn't just a hit. It was like someone was—" he pauses, turning toward me.

"Showing off." I fill in the rest of his sentence as my suspicions rise. I look back at the screen. At the curve of a black coat and a too-casual stride.

This hasn't been someone trying to frame me. This is someone trying to get my attention. There's only one woman I can think of.

But she wouldn't do this. Could she?

It's 2am when a knock comes from the front door, and I stop my mental spiral of determining if I have been oblivious to the woman living in my house.

Thrill shoots through me as I rush to let Laurel in, half excited that she is home, and the other half is excited to hold her under my knife until I get the truth.

Ezra stands, Laurel slung over his shoulder. Her purse hangs in one hand, her shoes in the other crossing Ezra's chest. My smile quickly fades as she lifts her chin, her matted hair falling from her face, revealing a bruised face and busted lip. I reach out, turning her face to the side to get a better look, and something deep in my chest cracks as her lip quivers and a tear rolls down her cheek.

"Who did this?" I ask, barely able to get the words out, pulling her inside the house, slamming the doors shut and sinking to my knees in front of her. Her tears fall fast, and she sinks to my level, burying her face in my chest.

"I needed you," she says, voice cracking, full of desperation.

Ezra stands beside me, horror and guilt painting his face.

"Where were you?" I bark, not understanding how he could let this happen.

"From what I could gather, Vic only wanted to meet with her. I planned to-"

I stop him, holding my hand up in his face. Nothing he could say would make this acceptable. She clings to me, digging her fingers into my jacket and it takes every ounce of strength I have to make myself pull her back. My eyes trail down her legs covered by sweatpants, not in the clothes she wore to work.

"Did he touch you?" I ask Laurel, though I already know the answer. She can hold her own. She wouldn't break like this from something insignificant. No, he took a part of her without her permission. Something that belonged to me.

Her broken eyes turn murderous as she tilts her face up to me. "I want him dead," she seethes, sure and unforgiving.

Be still my cold fucking heart.

"I want him dead tonight."

"Done."

I stand outside my bedroom, unable to look at her current state and control myself enough to get a plan. Felix steps out, shutting the door behind him.

"She's okay, but that motherfucker drugged her enough to kill her," he says, slinging his bag over his shoulder.

Ezra turns his phone toward me, showing me the hallway feed of the club. "He's a regular, but first-time flyer in the VIP room."

Snatching the phone from his hand, I go back into my room and brush Laurel's hair from her face, rousing her from her sleep. I turn the phone toward her. "Is this him?"

She nods, barely conscious.

I pull her blankets up and as she dives back into her sleep, I pull my mask back, pressing my lips to her head. "Don't worry Peach. I got him."

Shutting the door softly, I sneer at Ezra. "You will stay here and make sure she doesn't overdose. You better hope to fucking God she's okay, or I swear, I'll rip the heart from your fucking chest, eat it, and shit it out on your shallow grave."

He nods, accepting his duty after his actions. I owe him for getting her home when I was none the wiser, and that's on me, but never again.

This—her life in someone else's hands—will never fucking happen again, so long as there is air in my lungs.

"There's something else," Ezra says firmly, and my head nearly explodes. "We lost a girl today. She was chosen by Vic and she folded as soon as a gun was pointed at her. Luckily I took her out in the holding room before Vic heard anything detrimental."

I grit my teeth. "Were going lockdown. No more girls or CHAOS. This is Reapers only. Pull them out. Now!" Ezra nods and I glare at him, warning him to give me one more reason and I will end him today. "Someone call Skid. Keep her up to date."

Felix is quick, running his face through our recognition software and getting me and answer before I have to ask. "Eddie Fitley. He's at The Grandmont Casino. Has a room for the night."

I race there my vision growing darker, my head screaming, seeing nothing but a bloody head mounted on my basement wall. Felix slides into a parking spot next to me and pulls his skull mask into place to match mine.

"We get in and we get out. I need to get back to her." The chill running over my skin, knowing I'm about to spill blood is orgasmic. I grab my bag, careful not to damage the special cargo I packed just for Eddie.

I can feel the tension building in the pit of my stomach as we move through the hotel lobby, the low hum of music and chatter surrounding us. Felix is quiet beside me, but I know he's just as focused as I am. Eddie's here somewhere.

"You still think it could be her?" Felix asks and I hate that he was able to read me.

"I don't know," I answer honestly. Something in me is screaming, that's exactly who I want her to be, but the other part of me just worries that she's not capable.

The moment I spot Eddie sitting at the bar, those thoughts are pushed to the back of my mind and that familiar surge of anger rises again, but I don't let it show.

Not yet. I stay calm. Calculated.

Felix speaks low, barely a murmur. "That's him."

My eyes never leave Eddie as he sips from his glass, his posture relaxed, as if it's another normal day.

We move to the side, making sure I'm out of Eddie's line of sight but close enough to keep track of his every move. "From the looks of it, he's due for a piss any moment," I say, confident we won't be waiting long.

As if on queue, he stands, pushing his chair back with a scrape that makes me smile darkly, and I motion to Felix. He follows Eddie casually, keeping enough distance to not make things too obvious, but the tension mounts as we close in. Eddie pushes through the men's bathroom door and

Felix slips in behind him without a word. The door to the bathroom closes behind me and I lock it.

Felix corners Eddie against the sink and he freezes, his face draining of color. The fight, the bravado he thought he had, gone in an instant. Excellent.

"What the hell do you want?" he stammers, trying to recover, but it's too late.

I don't bother answering, letting the silence settle between us, thick and heavy. Wanting him to feel the weight of this moment.

Leaning against the doorframe, I cross my arms, my voice low and steady. "You hurt someone who belongs to me. You think that's something you just walk away from?"

His eyes dart between Felix and me, looking for any chance to escape, but there's no way out. Not for him. Not now.

"I-I..." he tries to speak, his words faltering as he stumbles backward. "I didn't mean any harm."

I push off the door, stepping closer to him with a slow, deliberate pace. Fear growing in his eyes. The realization setting in. It's too late for apologies, too late for explanations. I'm not interested in his excuses.

Felix grabs him by the arms as I throw my fist into the center of his face. His head jerks back and we drag him toward the door. Through the hallway and to his room, Felix having already swiped his key from his jacket pocket.

I tie him to the chair, securing each of his hands to the arms. The rope cuts into his fat belly and the wrinkly skin of his arms as he wiggles frantically. I've always enjoyed watching them squirm, like rodents. Insignificant and putrid.

Felix stands behind him and wraps a blindfold around his head, keeping him from seeing what I am about to do. Magnifying everything he feels with fear. Enhancing the experience for us all.

Felix distracts me, something not right about his posture and tense movements. It's unlike him.

"Please, I can pay you whatever you want!" Eddie begs as Felix flips his knife open in a swift motion jamming it into his shoulder.

"Really?" I ask over the sounds of Eddie's screams, before punching him in the face.

He looks up at me, shaking his head. "She called me. I didn't pick up. I gave her my number so she would always have a backup, and I didn't pick up," he says, and I can hear the pain in his voice, even hidden below the modifier.

"This is not your fault. You were with me. Neither of us saw it," I reassure him, surprising myself.

"I can hook you up with my dealer. Anything," Eddie begs.

I snort, flipping my knife in the air, catching its hilt, slamming it into the back of his right hand. He wails and Felix is there to shove a rag into his mouth, stifling the sound.

"This isn't about what you can give me, Eddie. This is about you already taking what is mine."

He grunts a panicked sound, a sweet melody to my ears.

"You see, I can respect a man that takes what he wants, as I do just that. However, I can't let that stand when it's my property that you help yourself to." I begin unzipping my bag, reaching for my first trick.

"One time," Felix says as he gets comfortable. "He sharpened this rib bone from this man we killed and then used it to kill his wife. We got paid for that one too." He whistles low. "Epic."

I grin. "I still have that bone, actually," I say before jerking my head back to level with Eddie. "Which fingers did you put inside her?" I ask, flipping my wire cutters.

He whimpers, still struggling against his restraints.

"Which fingers!?" I scream, inches from his face as I yank the blade from his hand, replanting it in his thigh.

He shakes and screams in agony, causing small amounts of satisfaction to flow through me. His fingers lift from the velvet upholstery as he pulls against the restraints and I quickly snap off his index finger with a satisfying crunch. Blood squirts from the severed appendage and he wails. Felix pulls him back against the chair and I cut another, enjoying the way the blood gushes, coating him and painting the floor.

His screams fade into whines, his torso slumping to the side.

Slapping his cheek repeatedly, I smirk. "Uh-uh, you can't miss my favorite part."

I rip his blindfold off, then remove my mask to meet his red, strained eyes as he fights to stay conscious. "I want my face to be the last thing you see before you're dragged to hell." I drop the wire cutters, reaching into my bag for my final act.

The rat squeals, fighting to get free as I place it on Eddie's lap, directly on his cock. I grin wide, placing a clear cylinder over the rat, holding him in place as I light the torch and hold it to the top.

Eddie's eyes widen as he frantically pulls on the ties binding him.

"What's wrong Eddie? You don't like your own kind?" I laugh loud and Felix chuckles from behind Eddie.

The heat has the rat begins eating his way through Eddie's clothes and flesh, giving us a show. Blood pours from his crotch, flowing between his legs to the floor. Felix scrunches his nose at the sound of flesh crunching as the rat fights for survival, but I lean in closer, wanting to hear every miniscule pitch.

Eddie's eyes glaze over as his soul is dragged from this earth, down to the gates of hell and his specially reserved spot. I remove the cylinder, clapping enthusiastically at the rodent's work as he scurries through Eddie's cock and up into his stomach, leaving his intestines mangled and hanging out of his body.

"Good job, buddy," I say, shoving my tools back in my bag before pulling my mask back into place. I grab his severed fingers from the floor and tuck them in my pocket as a gift for my girl, but I leave his eyes.

Chapter 40

LAUREL

I wake up slowly, the weight of sleep pulling at me, but it's the sharp sting of pain that brings me fully to consciousness. My body is sore, every inch of it aching, like I've been used as a punching bag. Bruises bloom on my skin, tender to the touch, reminders of last night—or rather what I can't remember. It's all a blur, but I can recall enough. I push myself up, my head heavy and thick, a dull throb pulsing in the background of my mind. The air is cool against my skin, but it does nothing to soothe the tension in my muscles.

"Reaper?" I call out on instinct, walking toward the bedroom door. I twist the handle, peeking outside into the hallway. Silence meets my ears, and I wander out and down the stairs into the living room, calling for him again.

I head for the kitchen, the coffee machine's aroma drawing me to it. I groan and my stomach growls. Taking another step, I lean against the wall for support, feeling the cold against my hand, my head still pounding from the drugs.

Just as I take the pot off the warmer, a low growl comes from behind me. I turn, finding Dom inching closer, nipping his teeth in warning.

Grabbing my empty cup, I hold it above my head in warning. "I don't put myself above killing feral animals. I killed a squirrel one time, you know." Granted that was on accident but he doesn't know that. "Aht!" I yell at him, and he bares his teeth in response.

"And you call me the psychopath," Reaper says from behind me, snatching the cup out of my hand.

Dom sits, licking his chops, his nubby tail wagging as Reaper steps between us.

"Where were you? You left me all alone." I don't mean for it to sound as pathetic as it does.

He sets the cup on the counter and steps into my space, cupping my face in his hands. "I'm never far Peach." He presses his mask against my forehead, and I ache to feel his lips on my skin.

He pours my cup, two sugars and a heaping dose of caramel creamer and cold foam before handing it back to me and pulling me after him to the couch.

"You did good last night Peach," he says, and I can't hide my appreciation. "I got you something." He pulls a small box with a white ribbon wrapped neatly around it in front of him. What looks like blood is smeared on one of the tails. He opens it for me, tilting it toward me to see inside.

"Are those... fingers?!"

"Yes!"

Some twisted part of me beams with appreciation for the gesture. "That's... sweet."

And not at all disgusting.

"Not a typical gift you would expect. Is this how you confess your love?"

Severed fingers were never on my list of things I would hope to get, but he did kill someone for me, and I know in my gut that he would have even without me asking.

"The need to put you above everything is driving me to the brink of insanity. I'll put these in a jar for you. That's how I preserve mine."

I swallow a laugh as I curl into him. "I think you're past the brink."

I inhale him deeply, not meaning to, but I can't help it. The smell is just... *so comforting.* It sinks into me, tugging at something deep inside, something I don't quite understand. It makes my heart beat a little faster, a strange attachment blooming in my chest.

I can feel the weight of his stare on me. The air between us feels charged, like something unsaid is hanging in the balance. It's strange and confusing. But I can feel the pull. And maybe, I don't want to fight it.

"This feels like a dream," I say, closing my eyes as he wraps his arms around me.

He brushes over my bruised wrists. "Being abducted and turned into a killer is what you dream about?"

I tilt my head to look at him, growing beyond annoyed of the mask hiding his eyes.

"Fever dream?" I try to remedy, and he chuckles.

A door shuts and someone clears their throat. "Sorry to interrupt."

"Are you?" Reaper asks, not taking his hand from my neck or his face from mine.

"No, not really," Ezra says, and Reaper finally releases me.

I suck in a breath and sit up. Ezra stands leaned against the wide door frame as Reaper yanks my T-shirt down over my ass possessively.

"Felix is set up. Are you bringing her?"

Reaper nods, grabbing my hand. Ezra moves further into the room, standing in front of me. "Ready or not. It's your turn."

My heart sinks, skipping a beat. Somehow, as unhinged as Reaper is and he has an attachment to me. Ezra hates me. Which scares me a little more.

Ezra scoffs, shaking his head and turning to Reaper. "If she gets us killed, that's on you."

Reaper turns his head to me, darkness peering at me. "If she gets us killed, I'll take her with me."

I follow him up the stairs into Felix's room. The smell of cleaners and air fresheners fill the tidy room just like the first time I was in here.

"Files are ready. Here's everything I have on the target," Felix says, turning to face us, all the screens showing something different, and I have no idea what I'm looking at.

"You never did say why you killed Daisy. Was she a target?" I whisper, trying not to interrupt.

We stand behind Felix, Reaper pulling me to his side. "No. She got in the way. This is the target." He points to the screen as the frame freezes on Crysta on her way out of the club. She's our youngest dancer. "Your target and the window is closing. We've left her for you."

My eyes go wide.

"We have a certain amount of time to get this done with a plan that gets us out clean. I decided to give this responsibility to you, to prove you can do our job."

I take a step back, about to vomit on Felix's freshly cleaned floor. "Isn't there a rule on things being personal? I- I trained her. I work with her. I can't... Kill her."

"You don't have an option," Reaper says, pushing me in front of him. "Make yourself comfortable Peach. Study up." He pushes me into the chair next to Felix and moves to the back of the room, taking a seat and pulling out his phone.

My eyes stay low, too scared to let any one of them see the fear and doubt in them.

"Okay. What's first?" I ask staring at the screens, readjusting my body.

Felix stares at me for a minute, something softer looming in his presence. "Right. Here is her schedule." He points at another screen. "You can do this any place, if it has cameras, we will get them down before it's time. Night time only. We will provide your mask, and you'll stay in the shadows until you're ready."

I nod, hearing every other word he says, eyes on the screen, my mind floating beyond that to the girl who has barely lived.

"You know her work schedule, that's where you benefit. We used poker night to get the interior cameras set up."

I nod, picking at my fingers before moving my hands below the table to hide my nerves.

"She goes to the gym every Tuesday and Thursday, even on her days off. Every Sunday night she goes to visit her mom on the East side. You're going to want to avoid those. You follow?"

I nod again.

"Do you know what weapon you want?" he asks, turning to face me and my stomach churns.

"What did she do?" I ask.

"You've been told," Ezra says. "It's just a job. The why's don't matter."

I take a breath, picturing someone else's face. A stranger. A horrible criminal. "Well, if she's a sick person, someone who is just vile to the core, a gun. If she's someone who deserves more of a punishment, someone who preys on the misfortune of others, reveling in their pain and terror, a knife, so she can choke on her own blood, feeling the life drain out of her until the very last moment before she is sent to hell."

The room falls silent for a long moment before Reaper manically laughs from behind me. "Fucking hell. I think I might believe in love after all."

Felix shakes his head, but it's Ezra I tilt my head up to look at and something between us shifts. "Her ex-husband hired the hit on her for abandoning their newborn child and emptying his savings, leaving them with nothing to start over on her own. Her real name is Mckenzie. She gambled half of it away in the first six months and blew the other half on drugs and parties."

I stay silent, rolling it over in my mind. I look back at the screen, now seeing someone completely different. I turn back to Felix, glancing at Ezra.

"Knife."

Ezra nods, and something in my chest soars with his approval, making me feel worthy, and one step closer to being accepted as one of them.

The question is. Can I take a life if mine depends on it?

CHAPTER 41

LAUREL

I stand in front of the mirror, appreciating the outfit Reaper sent me home to get.

I focus on the material, trying to push Daith from my thoughts. After that night, I know he's gone. I tell myself he's dead. That's the easiest to believe. A body that's buried somewhere far enough away that I never have to see it. A funeral I never have to attend. A grave with his name on it that I'll never visit. Easier to mourn a ghost than to admit I might still be haunted by the death I caused.

But sometimes, when I close my eyes, I see him standing there like he never left. Watching me. Not angry or hurt. Just... *there*. Like he always was.

I don't know if he's alive. I don't know if I want him to be. What kind of life could he live running every day, wondering if he's being followed.

No, that's not true. I want him to be breathing and angry and close enough to hurt me again, because at least that means he can still fight. He can still come for me. We can still be together.

The door opens and Reaper stands in the doorway. I meet his masked eyes in the mirror. "If you're going to continue to stare, I'm going to have to charge."

He moves behind me, towering over me as he looks down the length of my body in the mirror. "Have you forgotten who I am?"

I grin at his overused self-appreciation. I spin, placing my palm in his chest and he lets me guide him back onto a chair. I pull my leg up, placing my foot in his lap expectantly. He hesitates for a moment before his hands caress my calf and he zips my heel.

"Can I ask you a favor?" I say, giving him my other foot. He zips it and stands as I spin to check my outfit again.

He steps into to my back and I look back up at him through the mirror. "Anything Peach. You know that."

I release a long breath, steadying myself.

"Can you be honest with me?"

He nods.

"Did you hurt Daith?"

He brushes the hair off my neck, sweeping it around my shoulder. "I'd never lie to you if you ask me straight out." His gloved hand trails down the base of my neck, making my hair stand on end.

"Did you kill him?" I turn around, a blade meeting my throat, and I tilt my chin up.

He reaches into his pocket, his movements deliberate, slow. And I watch him closely, my stomach flipping at the sight of his hand slipping out a small folded picture. The corners worn, the paper creased.

He holds it up in front of me, his hand steady as he pulls the blade back, and I feel the blood drain from my face. It's a body, lying face down, blood pooled around him and matted in his long hair.

A sickening chill runs down my spine as the details start to fall into place. I recognize the clothes, the shape of the body, the familiar dark hair. The tattoos covering his forearm.

Daith...

My throat goes dry, the words trapped in my chest as I stare at the image in disbelief.

"You-" I manage to choke out, though I can't force the cold words to leave my lips. My head spins, the pain from my body suddenly feeling distant, like it's not the only thing I should be worried about anymore.

His voice is low and cold. "I did what I promised. You knew that." He pauses, letting the weight of those words sink in. "This was *your* fault."

The air around me seems to collapse and I struggle to get another breath. I swallow hard. "You killed him."

Reaper doesn't flinch. "Yes." He taps the photo lightly with his finger. "This is the last you'll ever see of the man you knew. Do you want to keep it?"

The ground beneath me is slipping away. Daith is dead. My best friend. My first love. The only man I've ever wanted... before now.

My mind jumbles the feelings that were blooming just hours ago... all torn away by the truth before me.

My mind struggles to comprehend how I'm still existing in a world where Daith doesn't. And yet, the reality of what Reaper is saying settles over me like a stone. The ache in my chest grows stronger with the realization that his blood is on my hands. I shouldn't have let him dig his claws into me the last time I saw him. I should have made him leave the moment I saw him.

I did this.

"I didn't... I didn't think you would actually do this," I whisper, my voice trembling.

Reaper watches me for a long moment, his body language unreadable. Then, without a word, he slips the picture back into his pocket, as if this cruel display wasn't even worth another second of his attention.

The silence is suffocating. I don't know what to say. I don't know what to feel.

"Yes, you did," Reaper mutters, his voice harder now, almost distant. "We've got work to do. Now it's your life that hangs in the balance."

He turns and walks away, leaving me standing there, the image of Daith's lifeless body burned into my mind.

Chapter 42

LAUREL

I sit on Reaper's leg during the game, using every ounce of strength to hold back the tears that have ruined my makeup twice earlier tonight. Vic eyes me with annoyance, though he quickly smooths it over as Reaper clears his throat. I swear the man hates women, no matter how well we perform for him. Though, I suspect his hatred goes a little deeper with me, considering Reaper threatens everything about him.

"Another win," Vic chirps, disdain clear in his voice. "If I wasn't a better man, I would kick you out for making me look bad."

Reaper pats my leg and I stand, moving to his back, resting a hand on his shoulder. "How lucky for me."

"No one likes a greedy man," Slader says, not trying to hide the way his eyes are focused on my breasts.

"I could say the same thing for you," Reaper says, breaking the man's wandering gaze. "I hear you have a wide selection of women and substances you keep all to yourself."

Slader's eyes flick to Vic whose jaw clenches, before a sickening smile forms.

"If you are interested branching into other services we offer, Scarlette will need to be excused so the gentleman can talk freely." Vic cuts his eyes my way with an order, but I stay planted behind Reaper like his guardian angel, waiting for his instruction.

Reaper chuckles in a disgusting way, that though for show, still fills my stomach with unease. "Of course," he says, avoiding unnecessary confrontation with Vic. He needs him to open up, give him the intel he needs to move forward. "Scarlette would you be a good girl and get my smokes and excuse us for a minute?"

I obey, knowing what comes next in our plan. "Of course."

Felix comes out of one of the VIP rooms, subtly passing Vic's office key he swiped off of him earlier tonight. Felix winks at me, pushing back into the room to keep Christa occupied and away from any eyes, just as I planned. Everything tonight is my order and their guidance.

Checking that Lisa is still guarding the bottom of the stairs, I quietly race to the office door, unlock it, and slip inside. Digging the flash drive out of my bra, I push it into Vic's computer. A firewall warning flashes, and I quickly type in the code Felix taught me to bypass the security system and prevent the detection of our device.

I glance at the door nervously and then at the computer as I watch the bar finish loading, giving Ezra's member ID access to the hidden room. I hear Lisa outside the door, likely guiding another customer to their room. Sinking low, I prepare to dive beneath the desk, as if that would save me if she came in.

The computer chimes and I suck in a breath. *Fuck!* I pull the drive and shove it back in my bra moving to the door, pressing myself against the wall.

My phone vibrates, and I glance down at it.

Death: DON'T MOVE.

The doorknob turns and I stop breathing as the door cracks open and I see Lisa's blonde hair out of the corner of my eye. A moment later, it shuts, and I blow out a long breath, clutching my chest with shaky hands.

I wait a moment for her to go down the stairs and I check my phone again.

Death: CLEAR.

Rushing out, I lock the door behind me, and head back to the poker room. Reaper opens the door just as I grab the handle, and I smile wide.

"Where is she?" he asks low, pulling me down the dark hallway.

"VIP room 3. Felix is in there with her," I whisper, my palms sweating profusely as adrenaline courses through me, slight panic at the next step.

He pins me against the wall just before the stairs holding his knife between us, pressing it flat against my cheek. "Felix will wipe the cameras."

I hold out my hand and he flips the blade, placing the handle in my palm.

"Don't hesitate, don't leave fingerprints. Meet me in the alley as soon as it's done." Reaper drops his backpack at my feet and I quickly pull sweats on over my lingerie.

I hand him the office key to slip back into Vic's pocket, who is unconscious with the rest of the men. Felix steps out and gives us a nod before he leaves down the stairs and through the front door, avoiding any of Vic's guards. With a steady inhale, I pass Reaper the flash drive and he turns, leaving me alone in the quiet hallway.

My phone chimes a moment later.

Death: 10 minutes before the drugs wear off and Vic finds you. Better hurry.

Shit. I have to move fast. I set my timer for nine minutes and rush down the hall to room three. I turn the knob, slipping the knife into the back of my waistband before pulling my mask over my face, absolutely loving the way it feels to be stepping into Reaper's shoes.

Unnamed, unseen. A whisper of death in the dark.

Christa looks up in a panic, heels in her hand and I raise a finger to my lips, motioning for her to be silent as I pull the knife from my waistband. She rears back, chucking a heel at my head, and I lurch at her, my hand covering her mouth before she can scream. I use my other hand to grab a hand full of hair, tangling in a section matted with cum. She screams under my hand, and I hold back my grimace at the thought of Felix's sperm.

"Shut up," I say, hearing my modified voice.

She fights me, reaching up for my face and in a quick motion I pin her down, slashing her arm as she thrashes below me.

Her eyes squeeze shut, tears rolling down her face as she screams. Holding the blade to her throat, I stare at her pleading expression, and for a moment too long, I let my emotions get the best of me.

I flash back to the other night, how I felt in her position, in these same rooms- terrified, helpless, and desperate to live another day. Under the weight of someone else, at their mercy, praying they have any.

I hold her for long minutes, contemplating my next move as incoherent pleas fall into the silence between us.

I drop my knife to the floor beside me and check the time. Five minutes. There's not enough time. I can't do this.

"Run," I say, before rearing back, I hit her across the head, knocking her out cold before I jump up and rush out the door and down the stairs to the alley door.

Reaper stands, stepping out of the shadows enveloping him. "Is it done?"

Silence fills the space between us, and I pull the mask off, my face saying the rest.

"No," he says, stepping toward me.

A tear falls down my cheek, "I wanted to. I'm sorry. I-"

He pulls the back door open, wrapping his gloved hand around my arm, yanking me back inside. His grip on my arm is unrelenting, dragging me through the halls with such force that every step feels like a punishment. The pain in my muscles burn with each stride, my body protesting, but I can't focus on that. I can only focus on the bitter taste of disappointment sitting heavy in my chest. I failed, and I can feel it in every breath I take.

His fingers dig into my skin, and the pressure only intensifies as we pass Vic's office. I try to suppress the scream wanting to claw its way up my throat, but I keep my lips sealed, careful not to draw attention.

Reaper pulls the VIP room door open and locks it behind him before fisting my hair, pulling my head back. "You finish this." He lets go of my arm and pulls his gun, placing it in my hand. "I don't care if I have to kill every person here to get us out. Kill her."

Tears stream down my cheeks as I stare at Christa's limp body, picturing my own. My pulse pounds in my ears and my knees give out. The gun falls from my hand, and I sob softly. "I can't," I whisper. "Please."

He moves in front of me, his voice barely a whisper. "We're done." Without looking, he moves to Christa and jams a knife down into the center of her throat, ripping it wide open with a grunt.

He moves to the door with ease, tucking his knife back in his pants.

Wait. *No, no, no.*

I scramble to my feet and reach for him, but he pulls away, cold and dismissive. "We're done! I had to clean your mess up, so we get paid," he says, seething. "You failed. We're done."

My throat aches with the need to burst into tears, the need to beg him for another chance, to make it right. He can't leave me. I just need another chance. A better plan. A target I don't know. He can't leave me. He needs me.

I need him.

He shakes his head, holding the phone to his ear. "Leave Laurel. I'm giving you a head start. If we find you, we kill you." He turns, gripping the doorknob. "Felix. Code Red. Get me out of here." The door shuts behind him and I call after him, knowing he can't hear me.

He doesn't stop. He doesn't come back, and a moment later, the club blacks out, giving him his exit strategy. I use the same cover to run for my life, only steps ahead of him, down the stairs and back out the door leading to the alley. I sprint, bumping into a man carelessly on the street. I look over my shoulder, seeing his concerned face, but I don't stop to worry about him seeing Reaper right behind me and screams following behind his rushed exit.

I keep moving, going a separate direction than Reaper.

I don't stop. I failed and now...

My days are numbered.

CHAPTER 43

LAUREL

We're done.

The air in my apartment is thick with tension, and the smell of hair dye. I can't shake the echo of his voice as it cuts through me, repeating over and over again. *I failed.* But that's not the part that eats at me the most. It's the way he left. Like it was nothing. Like I was nothing.

My chest tightens, a knot forming in my stomach as the anger begins to rise, slow at first, but then like wildfire. How dare he? How dare he walk out like that, as if I'm just some casualty of the game he's been playing? Like I can be discarded so easily?

The weight of his rejection presses down on me, but something inside me snaps.

I walk over to the bed slowly, almost mechanically, staring at my empty suitcase. I walk to the window, my hand gripping the edge of the sill with my green stained fingertips as I stare out into the night. The city lights flicker below, distant and cold. My heart just as distant, just as cold.

I don't have anything left. He's taken it all, shattered it, and still expects me to leave without a fight. He's ruined me. I can feel it in my bones. Every part of me is broken in some way because of him. And Daith...

But that doesn't mean I'll run. It doesn't mean I'll just let him decide my fate.

I'm meant to be one of them. I *belong* with them. I've bled for this life. I've sacrificed too much. I'm not going to throw it all away because Reaper thinks I've failed some bullshit test. I turn from the window, my chest heaving, eyes landing on the suitcase again. No. He doesn't get to take this from me. He may have turned me into someone I don't recognize, but he won't break me. I'll find a way to make this right, even if I have to burn everything to the ground. This is my life, and he may have forged it, but I own it.

I own him, whether he knows it or not.

He can't want me to leave. That's not what he wants. I felt the shift between us. He told me, he's never cared for anyone the way he does me. If he wants to kill me, so fucking be it, but I won't be going down without a fight.

I drag the crowbar, the metal scraping loudly against the concrete outside the old church I started calling home. Rounding his bike, I grin to myself, before screaming toward the crumbling church.

"Fuck you!" I swing the bat into the side of the bike, cracking the plastic. I swing again and again, letting the anger flow out of me. My hair swirls in the wind, sticking to my damp face.

"Fuck you!" I scream again followed by manic laughter.

Walking to the church, I bypass knocking and hook the crowbar behind the boards covering the front windows. Wood and nails clatter on the ground and I swing, shattering the stained-glass.

"What the fuck?!" I hear Felix yell from inside before he rounds the corner and comes to a stop, staring back at me. His brows pinch and I smile wide.

"Hi'ya. Is daddy home?" I run the crowbar against the broken glass, giving me a wide enough gap to step inside.

"Are you really this fucking stupid?" Felix asks, but I don't miss the hint of amusement in his masked voice, though it seems darker, matching my own.

"I'm this fucking devoted. You don't get to kick me out." I walk toward him as Ezra rounds the corner and stands next to him, fury bright on his gruff face, his pistol hanging in his hand. "None of you do!"

I swing again, clearing the living room table, shattering beer bottles along with the vases I bought. Ezra leans forward and Felix slams an arm over his chest, stopping him. I swing again, shattering another window, and they bark orders I don't hear. "Where is he!?"

I raise the crowbar again and it's snatched out of my hand and pinned around my throat, forcing my back into a tall frame.

I grin, staring at Ezra and Felix. "There you are baby. Where you been?" I ask, struggling to get the words out through my crushed windpipe.

"You come here and destroy my home, and you think that will make me take you back." He growls in my ear, his mask pressing to the side of my head. "I gave you a head start, and you come straight to the slaughterhouse." He pulls tighter and I cough, fighting for air as I laugh.

I grab his hands, pulling tighter. "If you aren't going to keep me. Kill me," I say through strained breath. "I have nothing else to live for."

"You have a death wish?" he asks, using one hand to fist my hair and pull my head back to look up at him.

"You are death," I wheeze. I release my weight, and he lets me fall to my knees. "I am a shadow."

I shut my eyes, accepting whatever fate he has for me. The crowbar clatters to the ground and I open my eyes to find him in front of me, Ezra and Felix now at his side, their masks in place. They step toward me in unison, and I raise the crowbar to defend myself. Reaper lunges snatching it from my hand, striking me across the cheek with his other hand, forcing my head to side. I cry out in pain and raise a hand to my busted lip, tasting copper filling my mouth.

He clutches my face with one hand, squeezing my cheeks painfully. "You are nothing to me," he snarls. Ezra rounds me and stands at my back, blocking me in.

"You don't belong here," Reaper says, shoving me to the ground. Planting a boot in my chest, he kicks me down. I groan as my head hits the concrete, and he presses down on my sternum. They loom over me and looking up at them, at their mercy, is utterly terrifying.

"Well?" Ezra asks, turning to look at Reaper.

Reaper squats down, taking his weight off my chest and fisting my hair. "He says..." he yanks me up by my hair and I cry out, struggling to find my feet. "She's gonna paint my fucking walls with her blood for real this time."

My eyes widen in fear, and I wrap my hands around his wrists, fighting against him as he drags me through the house. I trip, falling to my knees, twisting my back scraping against the hard floor. I kick and fight against him, tears welling in my eyes as the other two follow behind, a sickening aura around them.

I scream, knowing where he's taking me to die. "Not the basement!"

He needs me. He can't do this to me. This isn't how this was supposed to turn out.

We stop at the basement doors, and I spin in his hold, kicking at the back of his knees. Reaper grunts but my attempt to escape his hold fails, resulting in Ezra gripping me by the back of the neck, wrapping the other around the front and cutting off my air.

"Shut the fuck up," he spits, low and full of wrath that rattles my bones and curdles my stomach.

Reaper chuckles low and dismissively, not even turning to glance back at me before he pulls the door open.

"You had your chance to become one of us. More than most can say," Felix says, tucking his hands in his pockets. "You're the one that couldn't get it up."

I grit my teeth, wanting to sink them into his carotid. My body thumps down the stairs, bruising my legs and spine, tearing the skin on my back, distracting me for the slightest moment. I'm slammed into the wall, my head bouncing off the brick, pain splitting through my head. I make an attempt to lunge up, only to be met with another boot to the chest, knocking me back down.

"If you keep fighting, I'll peel your skin off and wear it like a fucking coat before your Reaper gets to have any fun."

I stop moving.

Reaper says nothing as he cuffs my hands and feet to the wall, tightening the chain until there is only a few inches for me to move, my arms are pinned above my head. They gather in front of me, standing silently, unmoving for what feels like an eternity.

"Do it! Fucking kill me!" I yell, spitting on Reaper's boot. "You're pathetic."

Reaper turns to Ezra, whispering something my ringing ears stop me from hearing, then he and Felix turn, leaving us alone for whatever depraved plans Reaper has to get his rocks off before he kills me. Maybe, while he kills me.

A tear rolls down my cheek as he squats, leveling his gaze with mine. "You were so close," he says, his finger tapping where it hangs over his knee. Something so simple, shows unease. Nervousness.

"I can still do it," I plead, and his hand reaches out to stroke my cheek as he always does.

"No Peach. You can't," he says, pulling his knife from his pocket and flipping it open. "Because the dead do nothing but sleep." He flips the knife in his hand over and over, playing with it. Taking his time, drawing it out to make me sweat.

"If you're gonna kill me anyway, can I at least finally see who you really are?" I ask, sinking back into the wall.

"This is who I really am. My face is only the painting that disguises the underlying. The skin is a barrier between the soul and the receptor's eyes, coercion into trusting the darkness."

I lower my eyes to where his mouth would be and bring them back up, parting my lips slightly. I squeeze my thighs, adjusting my position with the small amount of slack I have, forcing him to notice. "I just want to see your eyes, watch the way they light up when you discover how wet I am, simply because I want to please you. I'll die begging for another chance to make you happy."

He doesn't move, but I can feel the heat of his gaze shift down between my legs curiously. Reaper likes to pick apart his toys, see what makes them tick, determine which of his tactics work the best for the results he wants.

He pushes his thumb through my lips, gripping my bottom teeth. "I don't give second chances. You know that. You also know, I don't make mistakes." I suck his thumb as he pulls it out and gasp as he slaps my cheek softly.

He stands, taking another look at me. His gaze follows my chain, confirming I'm confined to his liking. He hums his approval and begins walking out, leaving alone in this God forsaken place once again. "Be a good girl until I get back. May be a couple hours, but we'll have some fun. Don't you worry."

I pull my knees under me, raising myself up just enough to get the few inches of slack the chains allow. I jerk my arms, slinging the chain toward the hook over and over until the end jumps up and over the hook it sits on, falling to the ground. I groan, pulling my arms in, rubbing my sore shoulders.

Pulling all the slack toward me, I pile it at my feet. With my eyes on the keys, I scoot backward on my ass, trusting this isn't all in my head. He wants me to get out of here. He wants me to fight. This is my chance. I get out, I kill a new mark, I make him happy.

The chains lock inches away from the table and frustration rips from my throat. "No! Fuck!" I yank on the chains, straining hard enough the metal cuts into my skin, making me bleed, but they don't give.

This whole fucking room looks like it could crumble at any moment, yet these fucking anchors are secured tighter than the stick that's up Ezra's asshole. I sit, catching my breath as I contemplate my slim options. The silence rings in my ears and that voice in my head screams in desperation for me to quit wasting time and do the only logical thing I have left.

I stare at the cuffs and glance over my shoulder one more time with a defeated sigh. This is going to hurt like a fucking bitch. I brace my left wrist with my right hand and shut my eyes tight as I push against the cuff with every ounce of strength I have, folding my thumb under. I whimper and as the bone in my thumb breaks, I scream, clutching my free hand to my chest. Wasting no time, I reach out, gripping the leg of the table, pulling it toward me. The cart rolls and I shove it over, the keys clattering among the tools. I scramble for them, unlocking all my bindings.

Exhilaration floods my body, drowning the pain, giving me the rush I need. I stare down at the previously sanitized tools laying in the filth and begin mindlessly picking them up, cleaning them off the best I can before I right them, just how he likes them.

I push through the unlocked doors of the basement and fly through the house to Reaper's bedroom to grab everything I need. Gloves, gun, mask, hoodie. I tuck them all in a backpack and sling it over my shoulder. Snatching keys from the hook, I head straight for the spare bike, secure the helmet, and tear out onto the road.

I race to The Fuzzy Peach, tucking low, weaving in and out of cars like lightening. Adrenaline courses through me the same way it did as a kid. There's nothing like the feeling of flying like a bullet, and once you feel it, nothing will ever compare. Riding on the edge of death, playing with fate.

It's not the fear of dying, it's the fear of not living.

The uncertainty of your future as you lay there, life slipping away, moment by moment. Balancing on the edge of finality.

The possibility of all the words you've spoken and the life you've built will turn to dust. There's a fear that you didn't do enough to matter. You didn't say your final words. People you are leaving won't know how you really felt.

I race through the back door, and up the stairs of the club, running straight into Vic. He catches me by the arm, and I gasp as he pulls me into him, snarling in my face. His breath reeks of tobacco and his skin seeps whiskey and cheeseburgers. "Where the fuck have you been?"

"I know, I know," I say, trying to pull out of his grip. Being close to him has always made my skin crawl. "Let me go get cleaned up and I'll-"

Pushing me against the wall, prying my mouth open, he shoves two pills in my mouth and slams my jaw shut, pinching my nose so I'll swallow.

No. No, no!

A man I don't recognize grabs my arm and Vic releases me, whipping his hand on his suit. "Strip her down and clean her up. She smells like shit." He scrunches his nose and waves his hand, dismissing me.

Chapter 44

I sit at my usual table, waiting until my timeslot in the VIP room. I couldn't kill her, not now. Not ever. I don't care what she did. I need to see how this plays out.

Ezra's voice takes over in my head and I dig my nails into my palms.

Stop it. Stop it. It's going to be fine. It *has* to be. If I lose her, or I lose my brothers...

"Mr. Reaper. She's waiting for you in room three," Lisa says, motioning to the stairs and I uncurl my fists. I nod, swallowing the lump in my throat, following her through the crowd and up the stairs. She smiles softly, resuming her post at the bottom of the stairs. Despite her smelling like a French whore, she isn't bad at what she does. I could use an addition like her when I take this place and turn it into its full potential.

Standing before the door, I take a minute to drop my hood and run my hands through my hair. My heart beats wildly and my stomach churns. Fuck, am I making the wrong decision?

Before I can talk myself out of it, I open the door and find Laurel waiting for me like a good girl. I walk slowly toward her, and she keeps her eyes low, focused on the floor as she's been conditioned to do, her newly green tips of hair draping over her shoulders. Submissive. I stand in front of her, tilting her chin with one finger, forcing her eyes to mine.

She swallows hard, a small amount of fear looking back at me. I wrap my hand around her throat and slam her into the wall, using my hand to protect the back of her head. Her wide eyes stay frozen where mine would be. Like a sweet fawn caught in headlights, ready for the slaughter.

She rasps, trying to catch her breath and my cock gets hard at just how close she is to being unconscious, completely at my mercy for me to use as I want. Her shoulders drop but her body doesn't completely relax.

Something dark and challenging shifts in her eyes as she pushes her hips into me. I glance down to see her hand open and two small pills fall to the ground.

You clever little minx.

I flick my knife open, press the blade against her neck in one swift motion. A cut-off squeak comes from her lips and her hands wrap around my wrists. I angle the blade further up, tilting her chin further to look up at me. "Aren't you scared Peach?" I ask, taunting her, but she doesn't waiver.

She shakes her head. "You're everything I've ever wanted."

I hover over her mouth, breathing in her breath. I inch lower to her neck, inhaling her scent. She groans, tilting her head to the side, allowing me in further, making the blade nick her.

She hisses, panting as she lets her arousal take over. There's no need for the drugs. Even sober, she's gone. Completely and utterly mine, and she's about to know who she truly belongs to. Who she has always belonged to.

"I know you let me escape," she says confidently. "You want me just as much as I want you," she rasps, her breasts brushing me with every desperate inhale.

Holding her head to the side, I lift my mask above my chin and flick my tongue over her lips. "Such a clever girl. I knew you would figure it out." I brush her broken thumb and she whimpers, but she wiggles, needing more than I'm giving her, her body betrays the sound. A grin spreads across my lips, and I pull my mask down to hide myself from her one last time. "Your language gave you away. I knew you were perfectly calm, trusting me entirely, even if you didn't quite figure it out until after I left."

She proudly bares herself to me, spreading her legs further, inviting me in without so many words. I lower the blade and motion for her to move to the S-shaped couch.

She obeys and I kneel between her open thighs.

A smirk teases her lips, and her eyes soften as she looks at me. Her hand slowly makes its way between her legs, she softly brushing the tips of her fingers over her clit.

"Touch yourself. Slowly," I say, sitting back on my heels, watching intently as she circles her clit, her eyes fall closed and I smack the side of her thigh, making her jump.

"Eyes on me."

She obeys, steeling herself despite how difficult eye contact has always been for her. She eye fucks me as she runs her fingers through her arousal, using it to help her fingers glide across the sensitive skin. She moves them lower, teasing her opening and my mouth falls open, watering at the thought of tasting her, nothing between us but weeks of pent-up frustration being released. She pushes two fingers inside, and as her mouth falls slack, my hand jolts out, snatching her wrist to stop her.

I flip my knife in my hand and place the handle in hers. Something wild and hungry blooms in her, understanding my intentions immediately. She carefully flips the knife away from her, grabbing the handle just before the blade and pushes it into her mouth. I groan as she slowly sucks it, dragging it down the length of her tongue. Then she slowly lowers it, dragging it between her breasts, down to her glistening pussy. She pushes the handle in, slowly, deeper until her fingers meet her skin. She inhales, soaking in the satisfaction of it filling her.

Seeing my knife deep her pussy, the sharp blade staring back at me, the same blade that has been buried deep in my victim's chests, has me barely hanging on to my sanity. She pumps it in and out slowly, and I can't take it. I rush forward, removing her grip on it, replacing it with my own, my gloved hand wrapped around the blade. I brace my left hand on her chest, pressing her back against the couch as I begin to fuck her, fast and hard. She moans, spreading her legs wider for me, taking all of it desperately. She palms her breasts, squeezing them hard, pinching her nipples. She moans, and my name comes out of her mouth, just as I have taught her.

Fuck, she was made for me. How did I not see it this clearly years ago?

You are just as mad darling. I made you that way, just for me. I am your madness. You will never rid yourself of me. I'm in your head, in your heart. In every breath you draw to stay alive, I am there. Twisting and feeding your soul until it matches my own. Black and fragmented, never to be tamed again. You and me baby, reapers of this world until you draw my last breath.

I pull back and get to my feet. She stills, dropping her hand and pushing herself to sit upright. Shock and embarrassment wash over her as she questions her action.

I step back, holding my soaked knife at my side. I can't take it anymore. I need her to call my name, knowing it's me between her legs. Knowing it's okay for her to know.

LAUREL

Reaper reaches up to his mask, slowly pulling it over his head. And I still, all the air leaving my lungs. My stomach flips then ties in knots, butterflies filling it and decaying just as fast, as the object of all my desires stands before me. A blush rushes across my cheeks, and I swiftly close my legs and cover my chest.

"You're dead," I croak.

Daith stands before me grinning, roughing up his sweaty hair. "Don't be modest now Peach. I was so enjoying this new side of you," he says, his voice now clear echoing in my head.

"I don't understand." My words catch in my throat.

"Manipulation. It's what we do Peach. Right?" he says, wiggling his mask in one hand and adjusting the strip of fabric that covers his eye.

"Why do all of this?" I ask. "Why all these games?" Hurt lingers, his harsh treatment in the passing weeks less than what our relationship calls for.

Why lie and taunt me? Tie me up and torture me? Spend time with me, pretending he was someone else. Threaten me and use my love for him against me in sick and twisted ways.

He smiles softer. "I wasn't sure you'd want to play along. I had to make sure you didn't have a choice. But now I know."

I narrow my eyes on his. Would he really kill me if I wasn't up for his lifestyle? The man that has been my comfort and the biggest piece of my heart for as long as I can remember.

A part of Daith has stayed hidden from the world, separated into a complete other entity. Reaper terrified me in the most exhilarating way, but there was always something about him that lured me in. He didn't scream unredeemable monster to me. And there were so many times our souls clicked on a deeper level, and I felt safe with him. Something unexplainable now explained.

Daith stands whole, baring himself to me, believing me to be capable of handling both sides of him. I swallow as all my fears and worries wash away. The two men that raged war in my soul are the one person I have loved more than anything in my entire life. Suddenly, nothing else matters. Not life, not death. Only him.

"All you had to do was ask," I say honestly, peering at him through my lashes as he steps closer, towering over me with his eerie presence sending a heat through my limbs. "I've always been yours. You know that."

I speak the truth that has always lingered between us, no longer dancing on the tight rope that separated us. Dropping my arms and spreading my legs for him again, I let him feast on me, tearing me apart with just his gaze that trails down my body, stopping where he can see just how much I want him. "I would do *anything* for you."

His gaze darkens and he reaches out, cupping my cheek. I lean into him, closing my eyes, letting my heart soar with the freedom bursting in my chest. My eyes flutter open, taking in his steady gaze as it roams my face. His finger brushes over my lips and my tongue darts out, wetting them. A desperation lights within me, pulsing between my legs.

Eyes on him in question, I reach for his belt buckle with one goal in mind. When he doesn't stop me, I pull it open and pop the button on his jeans before shimmying them down to his feet. My heart beats wildly as I tuck my fingers into the waistband of his black boxers. His erection stands for me as I pull them down to his knees and I wrap my hand around his length. His head falls back with a groan and the praise urges me forward. I lick up his length before taking him in my mouth, forcing him down the back of my throat. He fists my hair, moaning freely, cursing under his breath.

I gag, come up for air, and shove him down again, keeping him as deep as I can working him with my hand. He hums in pleasure, and as I come up for air, he forces me back down, choking me. I cough and sputter around him, my eyes watering as I fight to take him the way he needs. He fucks my mouth deep and I look up at him through my smeared mascara, desperate for his release.

My neck aches as he holds the back of my head at a sharp angle, thrusting his cock down my throat, unforgiving, urgent. He moans as I take him fully, and the sound sends a self-appreciating thrill through my body.

In coherent mumbles mix with the sweet sound of his pleasure as he frantically chases his orgasm, nearly ripping my hair out, using my mouth just the way he needs. His eyes glaze over as he holds me down, his release filling my mouth, his dick pulsing on my tongue. He pulls out and hooks a finger in my mouth pulling me up to stand.

"Let me see," he says, and I obey, opening wide for him to see. "Swallow." Keeping my eyes on him, I follow his order before licking my lips.

He pulls me forward and I fall to my knees at his feet. Gripping my face, he runs his thumbs through my smeared mascara, dragging them down my cheeks. "I love when you cry for me," he says. "My good girl. So fucking pretty."

My heart leaps out of my chest and into his hands. *His good girl.*

I sit back on my heels, and he sits on the couch in front of me, slouched with his thighs wide.

"I have something else for you," he says, reaching in his bag tucked on the side of the couch.

Eager, I smile wide, excited for what comes next. He leans forward, scattering pictures at my feet and my heart sinks.

My photography photos of a span of nearly 8 years. I glance over the collage of incriminating proof of his identity. Pictures of his day-to-day activities, deals and exchanges, murders and paid jobs.

I can see it in Daith's eyes — the realization. He's figured it out, I can't hide it anymore. The facade I've kept so carefully in place, the perfect little lie I've crafted falls away, leaving the two of us naked and honest, for the first time in our lives.

A truth is being dragged out into the light. And I don't deny it.

The lie is that I left Redwater to escape. That I didn't know what he really was. That he was gone. But I knew. I knew the night he "went to prison." I knew when Celeste sobbed on the porch, and I saw her look just a second too long at Ezra. I left anyway. Because staying meant staring that lie in the face every day. It meant waiting for a masked ghost to crawl back into my bed and ruin me. And I was afraid I'd let him. So I ran to New York. Told everyone it was about art. Told myself I would come back when I knew I could be his equal. When I could dish it right back. Distance doesn't kill obsession. It starves it until what is left is an unrelenting and selfish monster.

Now he knows. And I don't know what excited me more — that he's furious I lied and he didn't catch it sooner, or that he finally sees the version of me that always belonged to him.

He watches me closely, the smirk playing on his lips, but I can see it there — the flicker of understanding. "You've been pretending," he says, his voice low, but the amusement in it is unmistakable. "You're just like me. All this... this act, this mask you wear — it's all a lie."

I laugh, a sharp, bitter sound that cuts through the tension. It's wild, uncontrolled, and it makes the edges of my vision blur as the truth spills from me. The truth I've kept buried for so long. The truth I tried so hard to ignore before it consumed who I was.

"Is it really a lie?" I ask, my voice taking on a darker edge. "Maybe it's just survival. Maybe we're both just playing a game. And I've been pretending to be someone I'm not for so long, I almost believed it myself."

My breath catches as I push myself closer to him, the mask slipping away completely. I can feel the cold, sharp edges of myself cutting through the calm, the parts of me I've locked away for so long. I feel alive, untethered from everything I've been pretending to be, only letting myself free for short intervals in the dark of night.

Daith watches me carefully, his smile widening, as if he's finally seeing me. I throw my head back and laugh again, the sound raw and unsettling. My fingers curl into fists as I feel the anger, the desperation, the madness swirling inside me.

"The truth is, I'm just like you, Daith. Maybe even worse. I've been playing along, but that's over now. You wanna see the real me?" I crawl closer, my eyes darkening, the madness crawling to the surface. "Here it is."

I let the mask slip entirely, letting him see the twisted, broken part of me that he created. The part that knows no limits, no boundaries. The part that thrives in the chaos. The part that feeds off the darkness.

"I know you never went to prison, and when you left me, something inside me snapped. I followed you, found your secrets. Made secrets of my own." I smile, wild and unhinged. "I killed Jewel, for liking you. I killed a man just yesterday when you sent me home to get ready before your little test, just for funzies. And more than those. I played your game, let you think you were toying with my head, but I've been one step ahead for years baby. You've always been the Reaper of my soul."

I can see it in his eyes. He's shocked, but he understands. He *gets* it. Of course he does. He created this.

For the first time, I let myself *feel* it—the insanity that flows through me, the dark part of me that I've been ignoring, pretending isn't there. And as I let it take over, the laugh comes again, louder, wilder, a sound so sharp it feels like it could split the air itself.

For the first time, I stop pretending, and it feels so fucking good.

CHAPTER 45

I slip my mask back into place, reaching into my bag and handing Laurel's to her. Then motion for her to follow, and she falls into step behind me, her pulse quickening like mine. The night is alive with tension, and I can feel it crackling in the air between us, a cocktail of adrenaline and something darker. We move like shadows through the hall. Every step is calculated, synchronized, like we've done this a thousand times. The few stragglers left are too distracted by their own world to notice us slip past Lisa's unmanned post, and we glide down the stairs without a single glance in our direction.

We slip through the back door, leaving no trace behind. My hand brushes against her back, guiding her with purposeful steps, leaving no room for hesitation.

I guide her into the parking lots dark corner, and she stops when she spots another gift. It's parked right next to mine, sleek and deadly, gleaming in the dim light of the parking lot like some predator waiting to pounce. The pink paint stands out against the darkness, almost jarring, but perfect in its own way, complimenting the sleek black of my own.

Her steps quicken as she gets closer, and I smile wider than I have in ages. Her fingers brush the chrome, and I see her breath catch. I can feel it now, the excitement coursing through her, the thrill of the rides we've had in the past.

"Like it?" I ask, my grin spreading wider as I watch her reactions. My voice is teasing, but there's an edge to it that is full of lust. She played me, and I don't think I've experienced anything more erotic in my entire life. I want to see free edges of her soul, see how they mirror my own.

She doesn't answer immediately, but I don't need her to. The hunger for the open road, the need to escape, the desire to feel alive—it's already building in her. She swings her leg over the bike with a smooth motion, her fingers tightening on the handles, and I meet her gaze. I take the moment to quickly braid her hair and replace her mask with her black helmet.

"Race you?" I ask, my voice dropping, almost a challenge.

The laugh that escapes her lips is sharp, wild, and it sends a thrill down my spine. She nods. "You're on."

The engine of my own bike roars to life beneath me, and I feel the vibrations all the way down to my bones. The bike hums, ready to launch. My pulse racing in sync with the engine, and for a brief second, everything else falls away.

"You better run fast Peach." I twist the throttle, and we take off, side by side, tearing down the road. The bike responds to every turn, every shift of her body. The streets are empty, quiet at this hour. Only the sound of the engines and the rush of wind, pushing us faster, harder, like we're escaping everything we've done and caused.

We round a sharp corner, the tires screeching as we lean into the curve, and for a heartbeat, everything feels like it's teetering on the edge. One wrong move, and we could crash, could be ripped apart in a fiery mess of metal and bone. But that's the beauty of it — the danger. The thrill of pushing ourselves to the absolute limit, to see how far we can go before everything tumbles down.

I push harder, the wind smacking against me, and I can see her bike pulling closer, her presence a force I can feel at my side.

We fly down the road, pulling into her apartment complex. She takes my hand in hers, interlocking our fingers, nodding toward her place. Following her in, I send a quick text for the other bike to be picked up from The Fuzzy Peach. Tucking my phone away, I lock the door behind us, checking it twice, never letting go of her hand. She leads the way to her bedroom, pushing me gently back onto her bed. She releases my hand and for a moment, I fight the urge to snatch it back. Standing between my legs, she lifts my helmet off and sets it on the floor next to her own. Her soft eyes flutter with exhaustion, still shining with the adoration she had with my cock down her throat earlier.

I repress the urge as she straddles my lap, running her hands through my sweaty hair. "Could we just lay here?" she asks, her voice soft and trusting. For a moment, we're kids again, sneaking touches in the middle of the night, only to pretend they never happened when daylight came.

I wrap my arms around her, leaning back, pulling her into my body, intertwining our limbs. My cock strains against my jeans, pressing into her leg and she glances down, giggling. I missed this side of her. The one I held onto on the nights I had nothing of real substance to look forward to. Her smile fades as she looks back up at me. "What are we going to do?" she asks, grasping more on her own than I have yet to explain.

I sigh, running my fingers along her spine. "Well, we thought your kills were CHAOS. We need to see how many flags you have raised for them. If they weren't watching you, they very likely are now."

She scrunches her nose apologetically, though I give her grace, knowing there was no way for her to know about them. They are so far underground, you don't meet CHAOS until you have fucked up. "And you're going to have to make up for tonight." The boys have to witness her success, and I'll have to make more extreme measures to ensure her safety if they vote not to accept her late obedience and secret personality.

She hums, tracing the hourglass on my arm. "They aren't going to accept me back easily, are they?" she asks, already knowing the answer. If it were anyone else, her head would be on a stick. But she's not, and it's going to take more than a murder to keep them from killing us both when she walks at my side. "I have a plan," she says, easily and without doubt.

"Why didn't you just kill the target? Why pretend that you were less than you are?" I ask, racking my mind and for once, coming up blank for reasonings behind behavior.

She shrugs in my hold before looking up at me. "I guess I just wanted to show you just how easy it is for me to manipulate you the way you used to do me." She chews on her lip. "It feels really good to be the one on top when you spent years trying to make me feel small." She rolls her hips into my leg, showing me just how much she likes the idea of me on my knees before her. "Just being a brat, I guess. Once I realized CHAOS was an issue, I stopped killing. I'm not a total idiot."

"You are very lucky I like you, because that's a serious breach in our code. With any luck, we will both make it out of this alive. When they see I let you live, they're going to want my head too."

Her brows pinch in questions. "I thought you were their... leader?" she asks.

"It's more complicated than that. I have their respect and obedience for my success as a member, leading what we do and how we do it, but we are still a collective. I broke a rule letting you live. Blood in. Blood out."

Her jaw clenches but there is not an ounce of fear or regret in me. They want to take me down for keeping Laurel alive—I'd like to see them fucking try. I'll kill them both if it comes down to it. Nothing matters more than her.

Curiosity hits me. "What do you do with your bodies?"

She pushes up, removing herself from my arms and she smiles wide, excited to tell me. "Well, the man, I shot, I just left him there. He was way too big to move. I barely got him behind the dumpster in the alley." She bounces lightly on the bed like a child, excited for a surprise. "The girl you brought on our double date, Malia, she got dumped in the sewers where she belonged. And Jewel..." she wags her eyebrows and my curiosity peaks. "I fed her to you. Those tacos were good huh?"

She doesn't flinch. She just stares back at me, that same cool, detached look in her eyes, like she's in control of it all. My stomach turns.

I blink, trying to clear the fog in my brain, but it's there, sinking in like a bad taste in my mouth.

Jewel. She what? She fed her to me? Like its nothing. She's got to be fucking with me. I would have noticed. Right?

I have to stop myself from gagging right then and there. I can feel bile rising in my throat, fighting to get out. I can't even look at her for a moment, my eyes burning as I try to keep my composure. "You did *what*?" My voice cracks, unable to hide the disgust.

She just laughs. That sharp, cold laugh that cuts through the tension in the air, like she's enjoying watching me squirm.

"Yeah," she repeats, almost like she's amused by my reaction. "I got a little jealous the first night you came to the club and after that, she was asking all these questions about you and I just..." She motions across her throat with her index finger, sticking her tongue out. "Just a little taste of her, since you looked like you wanted it so bad. I seasoned her up so nice. You didn't even think twice." She scrunches her nose. "You ate her. How disgusting is that?"

"That's... Yeah that's disgusting, Laurel," I manage to say, my words coming out harsh and disbelieving.

"You're not mad are you?" she asks, jutting her lip out in a pout.

She watches me, that same sharp look in her eyes, waiting for me to react. There's this moment where I can feel her holding her breath, like she's afraid I might snap. She asks quietly, "Are you mad?"

I let out a long exhale, shaking my head. More than anything, I'm trying to process. I've never been one to cook someone but I guess it isn't that far of a cry from shoving someone's own cock down their throat. I've don't that once or twice just for shits and giggles.

"No, I'm not mad," I say, my voice a little softer. "I was just... surprised, I guess. Didn't expect you to be so... *blunt*." My lips curl into a half-smile, and I can't help the weird feeling that lingers there. "I mean, it's pretty fucked up. But it's kinda cute, the way you got so territorial."

There's a pause between us, and I can see the faintest flicker of something in her eyes. She's not sure if I'm messing with her or not.

"So what else were you doing in New York that Cee didn't know about?"

She looks up at me, a question lingering in her eyes, but I can see the amusement starting to surface too.

"I learned all about you, how to operate like you do. I watched you form the reapers. Watched the way you killed and had fun, like it was a Tuesday outing in the park. I learned to be your little shadow. Just like you. Perfect for you."

Holy shit. She's a lunatic... just like me.

Perfect for me. I knew it.

I just watch her, curious if she's going to throw something back at me. "And if you flirt with anyone again, it will be you that I feed to Dom."

Oh, this is going to be so much fun.

CHAPTER 46

LAUREL

My fingers glide with practiced ease as I apply my lipstick with precision. I tilt my head to the side, staring at the perfect appearance that mocks the girl on the inside. Bringing the lipstick to my eyes, smearing the deep color under my eyes. I bring my fingertips to my eyes and drag them down, smearing the color like black tar tears. Daith loves when I cry for him, now, I am forever weeping tears for the lost part of myself that died to be with him.

I sit back, taking myself in once again with a deep inhale and a too wide grin. I glance over at my bed to the black sweats that match theirs. I am one with them. My mask lies on top of the hoodie, staring back at me with wicked promises.

I slip it on and take one last look in the mirror, adjusting my outfit, making sure everything is in place. I hold the mask up to my face, appreciating the way I look just like them, smaller and more petite, but unidentifiable and carrying the same sickening vibes they do.

I run my fingers over the sharp edges of my mask before slipping it into my backpack. The cold, smooth surface promises anonymity, power and control. I'll be able to slip in and out without a trace, just like them. Just like Reaper.

My heart starts to race in anticipation. The thrill of stepping into this role, of playing the part, has my blood pumping faster than it ever has before. This is my chance to prove that I'm not just following behind them anymore. I'm capable. I'm ruthless. I'm here to stay. This is my chance for me to show them that I have their backs. This is not a mask. This is *me*.

The streets blur as I drive, my fingers gripping the wheel with a sense of calm.

DEMENTED

The city is alive with movement, but I'm focused only on the destination. I know where the man is, the one who too much at The Fuzzy Peach. I had seen him before. It took me a bit to place him, but it was the jacket logo that pushed me to the realization. He frequents the bar that Daith went to the night I followed him. A drunk nobody on the streets, trying to stumble his way home to his motel. It's very likely that he doesn't remember me passing him or know anything about what happened, but regardless, death is coming for him.

The adrenaline is already beginning to course through me, my pulse quickening as I pull up to the rundown bar. I park the car in the shadows, making sure it's far enough out of sight that no one can see me slip inside. My heart races as I kill the engine. The air is thick with the scent of rain, and I breathe it in deeply, letting the cool night air steady me. The darkened streets feel almost like they belong to me now, a world of shadows and danger where I can move unseen. I step out of the car and pull the collar of my jacket higher, tucking the mask into the back of my pants.

The door to the bar swings open and the dim lights inside cast long shadows across the sticky floor. I scan the room quickly, my eyes landing on him almost immediately. He's sitting at the bar, nursing a drink, looking completely unaware. Honestly, barely looking conscious.

The bar is crowded, but no one pays us any mind. I can hear the low hum of conversation, the clinking of bottles, but it's all background noise now.

"Excuse me sir," I say sweetly, lightly touching his shoulder. His glassy eyes attempt to focus on mine. "Can you help me with something?"

"Huh?" he murmurs, barely coherent.

I motion for him to follow me, and still confused but with no objections, he stands, wobbling slightly as he blindly follows me out the front door.

I look over my shoulder, leading him into the alley, heart pounding wildly in my chest with thrill.

"You needed help in the dark?" he asks, bracing himself against the wall.

"Mhm," I hum, smiling sweetly as I continue walking backward into the dark.

He pauses, still in the dim lights cast from the street lamps.

"I'm no gentleman miss." He slurs, raising his hand, waving it in the air dismissively.

I spin, giving him back and inhale through my nose, blowing it out as I slip the skeleton mask over my face and pull my hood up over my head.

"I need another drink," he groans low.

"I'm not a gentleman either," I say with the modified voice from my mask and I jam a sedative into his neck. His body falls limp, collapsing to the ground.

Curiously, I pull his eyelid open, and his eye rolls into the back of his head.

Okay, Let's fucking do this.

I grip his ankles and drag him further into the alley to my car.

I grunt under the weight, really wishing I had taken a workout class or something. I'm just a girl and this scrawny man is heavier than he looks.

With every ounce of strength I have, I shove him into my back seat and haul ass to the old church.

Throwing my car into park, I open the back door and his head flops out, hanging off the edge of the seat. Grabbing the machete laying on my floorboard and with my heart in my throat, I keep my eye on the goal.

Rearing up, I swing, but it doesn't go all the way through, leaving it dangling awkwardly. "Ugh," I groan, rearing back again. Thick skinned bastard.

Blood splatters my face and his head thumps to the ground at my feet. My shoulders fall with ease and a rush of accomplishment courses through my veins like fire. My head spins and my arms tingle, but I snatch him by the hair, head dangling in one hand, my machete in the other and I prance up to the church. Walking to the one window I didn't smash, I swing at the glass, knocking the excess off before stepping through it.

The doors of the meeting room creak as I pull them open, a wide smile across my face. The entire congregation turns to look at me, Ezra and Felix standing at the front on either side of Daith's chair he sits in like a throne.

I stand unmoving, hands dangling at my side as the blood drips on the white rug. The doors slam shut behind me, the echo like a drum in the utterly silent room. Daith's eyes fall to the severed head in my right hand.

Drip. Drip. Drip.

The sound of his blood falling is the only thing I can hear.

"You wanted me to kill the mark? Here's your fucking mark," I say, rolling the head down the aisle like a bowling ball, his nose making him roll off center, landing just to the right of Ezra's boots.

Daith's eye slowly rise down the aisle, a grin forming on his face before a manic laugh bursts from his chest. "Oh, he is going to kill you for staining his rug."

I level him with a challenging glare, playing my part.

Ezra snarls, stepping down and toward me and wrapping his hand around my neck, crushing my air way. "Why the fuck are you still breathing?"

I grin in return and he turns to Daith, piecing our fuckery together.

"Let her go Ezra," Daith says without moving a muscle.

Reluctantly, Ezra releases his grip and I clear my throat, rubbing my neck.

"You must have gotten a lot of last place ribbons with that brain you got there," I say, enjoying the way his vein protrudes on his forehead.

Daith chuckles, getting to his feet in preparation for his trial. He reaches his hand out and I walk forward, taking it as he leads me to his chair and stands behind me.

"Is she really worth your life? Are you this stupid?" Ezra asks with a hint of pain deep in his throat. He can't make an exception with no valid reason for not slitting my throat the day I failed to pull the trigger. No second chances. And only one loophole.

I spread my thighs and Daith slowly pulls my sweatpants down my legs, revealing the hourglass on the outside my thigh. I flip my palm, revealing the angry cut across it and Ezra's eyes widen. Felix cusses under his breath.

"You marked her?" Felix asks, looking at Daith with disbelief shining in his blue eyes, though I don't sense discontent.

Daith holds his palm out in front of him as he rounds the chair, standing behind me and bracing his other hand on my shoulder. "I did. Like it or not, she's not going anywhere."

Ezra snarls. "You had no right to do that. Not without our approval and damn sure not after her failure." His eyes fall to the mark on my thigh and I kick the pants from my ankles. "That mark doesn't mean shit," he spits, fury blazing in his eyes. "She failed!"

Daith's fingers curl into my skin and I place a calming hand on top of his. "That mark means everything."

"Do not forget your place," Ezra booms, stepping toward me.

"Do not forget yours!" Daith screams, murder in his tone. He takes a breath, slowly inhaling. "If you don't like it, call it."

I peer up, catching the wildfire in his eyes, daring for a challenge.

Ezra's eyes flick to Felix who glances down at the severed head. "Who is this?" Felix asks before Ezra can make a move.

"A man that saw us leave the night Daith killed my mark. Easily overlooked, but I saw him. A threat."

Daith nods, confirming.

"We don't overlook anything," Ezra challenges and I narrow my eyes before a wicked grin spreads across my face, baring all of my teeth.

A flicker of something familiar flashes in Ezras eyes.

"Actually, you missed quite a lot," I beam, squeezing Daith's hand, indicating for him to grab the images he confronted me with. He passes them to Ezra and Felix crowds closer, their eyes widening as they see their various crimes and truths in the light. "You missed me trailing you all for years. You mistook my murders for CHAOS, and you played right into my act for weeks." Lethal pride courses through my veins like fire, begging to explode. I played their game and I could have taken them for everything they had, if only my goals were to do so.

Ezra looks up at me, his face still stoic and void of the emotions that must be reeling inside of him.

"Where's the rest of him?" Felix follows up with another question, nodding toward the severed head, who has one eye open wide, staring at the four of us.

"In my car. In the ally. Waiting for our usual disposal," I say confident.

Felix's eyes hold mine as he thinks, rolling over every possible angle. "How have you been getting away with the kills? You're not trained. You should have slipped up by now."

I grin. Honestly, I was waiting for that because the truth is just so good. "You'd be surprised how easy it is when people come to their own conclusion about who I am." I cross my legs, getting comfortable. "A small, busy woman, now the victim of an obsessed gang member," I gasp for added drama. "There is no way she could have learned how to be a shadow, this insane killer when the lights go down. No." I smile wider, letting it reach my eyes. "That would be... improbable." I hear Daith snort a quiet laugh from behind me. "I studied The Reapers for years, and you never noticed. Not even Cee knew I was home during those weekend trips. I focused on learning everything about your process until I was confident I could do it myself, leaving it looking like you were just being lazy."

Felix sucks his teeth, his annoyance clear at my jab. I know he takes pride in his work, never leaving a single hair or shred of evidence.

I shrug. "I admit I didn't know about CHAOS and their rules but I wanted him to see the bodies. They were beautifully done."

A lie. I did know. I saw them checking in, heard the calls, watched Daith dig his hole deeper with his impulsive kills. But I didn't care if I got them in trouble. The only thing that mattered to me, was Daith being proud of the new shade of black painted on my heart. I learned how they made bodies disappear, quick and efficient. How they never returned to the same dump site, burned fingerprints, pulled teeth, and left nothing to chance.

The truth is, I haven't gotten caught because I'm better than the men who taught me without meaning to, but I don't say that, sparing their egos that barely fit in this room.

Felix nods slowly, it all coming together for him. Out of all of them, I trust Felix to be the most level-headed. He assesses all angles, with a touch of empathy but I won't out him on that either.

"If her mistake was righted, and she was able to hide all of this from even me, she has my approval. Seems we let her stay, or we kill them both. Logically, the answer here is clear. Approval or not, she's been marked and she has the skill."

The room is still for a long minute, our fates hanging in the balance as Ezra battles his internal righteousness and control issues. "You're not registered with CHAOS, and the trail of bodies you've left have been more than enough to attract them." He sighs, running his hand over his scruffy beard. "But dead or alive, they will figure out your connection to Daith, putting a target on all of our heads unless we convince them you were not aware of the implications of your actions."

There is another long moment of silence, and I wait for them to deliver my fate. Our fate.

Ezra groans, then growls in anger as he turns to Daith. "No. No women. You knew the rules. You knew *my* rules."

Daith doesn't flinch. "Your rule is bullshit with no reason behind it. You trained me to succeed you. To take what I want. Now, you are crying like bitch because I followed through?"

Ezra's fist flies without warning, connecting hard with Daith's jaw. A loud slap echoing through the chapel. Felix barely has time to object before Daith tackles Ezra to the floor, splintering the wood of a pew with Ezra's head as the two of them collide.

"You are going to ruin everything!" Ezra screams, rearing his fist back, and Daith dodges it with ease.

He grips Ezra's head slamming it into the ground. "This isn't about rules! This is about control! About your fear!"

Ezra grunts in pain before managing to flip him, elbowing him hard in the ribs. "What will you do when she leaves you? Huh? You think CHAOS will let her live?

Daith snarls, bloody teeth bared. "She won't leave me."

Daith throws another punch, grunting. Then only the sound of panting fills the large room. Ezra lies on the floor, chest heaving, Daiths arm pinning him to the ground. "It's not that I think she is weak, Daith."

"Then why?" Daith growls.

Ezra blinks up at him, finally letting something real show through. "Because love is damning. I taught you that. She is going to get you killed."

Daith leans in, nose to nose. "Then your objection is void. Every Reaper for themself. Right? You don't get to object based on your concern for my safety."

Then Daith lets go, standing and moving away from him with heaving breaths as he wipes his mouth.

"You love her?" Ezra asks, a defeated tone lacing his words.

"I don't know how to do anything else."

Ezra nods once. "Then so be it. But if you die for her, I will kill her myself."

It's me who speaks next. "I'll gladly accept that fate." I hold his eyes, firm and solidifying the words a promise.

He nods again, finally relenting. "Blood in. Blood out," he finally says and air fills my lungs once again, breathing easier.

Ezra takes a step back, turning to the crowd of men who sit silently. "Laurel," he nods. "The newest Reaper and the first woman to join the ranks."

I watch in awe as their backs straighten and they all nod in unison. My breath catches at the eerie sight.

"You will obey her, just as you would the three of us." Daith says.

"The crew will do anything for her, that includes giving their life to protect her. She is mine to protect, and they are an extension of me when in my house. She will be held on a pedestal, to a higher respect than they give us three."

His demands overwhelm me and feel like too much. I just wanted to be one of them. I wanted him. Not to be worshipped or held any higher than him. I look up at him nervously and he brushes my jaw softly.

I subtly glance at Felix who has moved to stand next to Ezra.

"A woman is a gift. More fragile, not weak, but different in her ways of thinking. She brings compliment to the works of men and will serve us, just as we will serve her," Ezra says, surprising me with the sentiment. I smile softly. "I think a woman's role in our organization is well overdue, and maybe we will have more to come as we grow and expand to something greater."

"We are honored to have Laurel join us. From this moment forward, she is family," Felix says, reaching to rest his hand on my arm. "Dismissed."

The room begins to clear, the men exiting in a single file line, not a single word coming from them.

Ezra is the last, stopping beside me. "The only reason both of you are not dead is because unlike Daith, I have genuine love for the boys I have raised, and if I were to deny you and report you, as I very well could, they would kill Daith and turn around and hunt the two of us for harboring you, even unknowingly."

I say nothing, accepting where I fucked up. But, creating the mess I did was just too fun, and I was too focused on one goal alone. And if the worst thing that happens is, I get killed, then I have nothing to fear. Because I'm in love with The Reaper and sleeping with Death.

The doors shut, leaving only Daith who kneels in front of me. I sit forward, furrowing my brow. "Are you sure about this?" I ask, worrying his taken this too far and I'll be the downfall of all of this.

He smiles, genuine and full of light, something I don't see often enough. "I've never been more sure of anything in my entire life. We will report this to CHAOS and we will clear everything up. You didn't know. This is when they register you, and from here out, you will be held accountable."

I take in the empty room, inhaling deeply, committing the smell to memory as my new favorite. "Right."

Chapter 47

The room clears and it's just her and I. She sits in my chair, crossing her legs, the air thickening in the room.

"You and I have some things to talk about," I say, standing in the middle of the cleared aisles.

She stands, grinning at me, dark and mischievous with her face painted, showing the crazy just beneath the surface. "Yes, we sure do." She tucks her thumbs into the waistband of her panties, pulling them down and tossing them to the side. My eyes widen as she strips off her shirt and sits back down, completely naked in my chair.

"Crawl," she says, daring me—ordering me. Ordering *me*.

"Excuse me?" I ask, chuckling slightly. She's kidding, right? I take a few steps toward her and she holds her hand up at me, stopping me.

She spreads her thighs wide and rests her arms on the sides of the chair. "I said... crawl."

Fuck.

I drop to my knees, obeying the woman that owns me completely. I plant my hands on the floor, keeping my eyes on her, and I crawl. I make it her feet and her dark gaze strips me bare. "You have a lot to apologize for, *Reaper*," she says, giving a whole new sound to the name on her lips.

I grip her knees, staying low at her mercy. She's right, I owe her a lot of explanations, though I'm not convinced that she doesn't already know most of it.

She runs her fingers through my hair, gripping it at the back. "You were never in prison. I want to know why you tried to lie." She pulls my head back, glaring at me with a fury that is rightfully placed and surprisingly erotic.

"I never got caught for the fire."

A crease forms between her perfectly arched brows. So, she did miss something. I grin and she yanks my head back further, bending it at a painful angle, clearly hating that.

"That's one thing I was never able to figure out. Give me an answer I'm satisfied with and you get a treat. Got it, *pet*?" She smiles and I growl, my temper flaring. I can see why it got under her skin so much. She pulls my head back up, waiting for her answer.

"Luther and his wife, Janine, were whoring me out to pay their bills, kept me locked in the basement until someone wanted to rent me for whatever sick agenda they had. The specifics varied, and some were far worse than others."

I never lied to her about that part, but pain still flashes across her delicate features as she hears it again with a truth she's trying to process.

"So when I got a chance, I ran. Another man found me slumming it, running from the system. He took me in, trained me, taught me everything he knew of almost 30 years. Then when I was ready, I found my fosters again." I run a hand through my hair, dragging it back, trying to steady myself. The memories are flooding in, and I can't escape them. "I cut their breaks and killed them in a car accident." She nods, her gaze steady and unwavering as I give her the truth I know she's been starving for. "After building a record of petty crimes as a troubled kid, I needed a cover to protect my connection to The Reapers. In order to form who we wanted to be, Daith had to be cleared, so we set the fire and used this man's connections to fake documentation and transportation to the prison." I let the words hang in the air for a moment before I finalize the truth of my past. "On paper, I couldn't have been connected to the Reaper's suspected crimes because I was behind bars and in solitary at the time."

I wait a moment before I deliver the best line yet.

"This man is the closest thing I have to a father, and it's Ezra." Her eyes widen in disbelief. "A retired special operations assassin and the first Reaper of Redwater." I grin as everything comes together in her mind, enjoying that there was still one thing I got to reveal. She took the fun out of everything else, so I am eating this shit up.

I watch her head reel, and her eyes bounce around my face as she processes. Something flashes in her eyes. Her tongue flicks across her lips before she shoves my face between her legs. I groan, opening my mouth wide as I lick her slowly, savoring every second I have to taste her.

"Consider me satisfied," she says, groaning and grinding against my face.

I grab her, flipping our position. She kneels between my legs and my head falls back as she shimmies my pants down and takes me in her hand. The doors creak open and her head jerks around, staring at Dalton who stands frozen with wide eyes.

"I just... forgot my phone," he croaks and Laurel groans exasperatedly, pulling my gun from my crumpled pants, turning in a quick motion and pulling the trigger.

"You're ruining sexy time!"

Dalton's body collapses to the floor and at the same moment, Felix passes the open door. His eyes flick from the fallen member of CHAOS to Laurel's bare ass before they land on the ceiling and he scrubs his face with both hands.

"My God, she's worse than he is," he says, pulling the doors shut again.

Laurel turns, grinning at me before she takes me in her mouth, bottoming out and taking me to the hilt, holding me there until she gags, my gun still in her right hand and rested on my thigh.

My God, she is...

Fantastic.

CHAPTER 48

LAUREL

We sit around in Felix's room, pictures, documents, and electronics scattered and being sifted through as I sit on the bed, now fully clothed.

"I found something we missed," Felix says, spinning in his chair to face the rest of us. "We have his drug connections, his bank accounts, and his buyers," he says as the bar loads across the screen and anticipation swirls in my stomach. "We knew that he was drugging and selling women, letting men test them out in the VIP rooms first." Daith's fingers wrap around my thigh, and I place my hand on his.

Daith straightens his spine. "Well spit it out. What did we not catch?"

Felix places a beer bottle next to the screen. "His drugs are being imported in beer bottles."

Confused, I speak up. "In the liquid?"

Felix shakes his head, pulling up a file with a complex chemical equation and blueprints. "No. It's in the glass."

Daith's head tilts to the side before his head snaps to me as he recalls something from his stone memory. "Tulip. She had scratches all over her body. I had thought nothing of it until now. In the creases of her arms, the palm of her hands."

"Daisy. What is your issue with her name?" I ask, rolling my eyes. He does it on purpose. There's no way he doesn't.

He disregards my question. "He's using the girls to test his drug before he distributes out right."

Felix snaps and points at Daith. "Exactly. There have been five cases at his previous bar where the women he was selling were dying in transport. They were perfecting his chemist's formula and found a way to bind it in the glass. One cut and these girls are tripping for six hours if they make it through without dying from cardiac arrest."

Felix clicks the screen, pressing play on a video of an unfamiliar woman, nearly unconscious, her body bloody and her clothes torn. Broken glass is shattered around her, and the man sitting on top of her holds a broken bottleneck at her throat.

He strokes her hair, "Sorry, darlin'. I do hope you'll forgive me, but you handle the drug so well. I think I'll keep you for myself."

Bile rises and I cover my mouth. "Oh my God."

Felix nods. "The ones that live are used and likely live the rest of their short life like this. It's expected that with the effects that have been reported, the brain activity would deteriorate in less than six months of constant use.

I can't imagine six months of living in a hell like that. Fury rises to the surface and I clench my jaw to fight back the tears that threaten to well in my eyes for the women that have died and survived at the hands of Dorian Vic.

I swallow it down, steeling my strength. "He's importing and distributing and paying for it with the girls. We'll take his drugs too," I say, rolling this over in my head. Vic has to die and for using those girls as his guinea pigs, he will die at my hand.

"I couldn't give a singular shit about those girls," Ezra says, pulling the drive from the computer, and the screen goes black.

"I want the club," I say firmly. "Keep it standing and as many of girls alive that you can."

Ezra crosses his arms, looking at me for a beat before he answers. "Fine. You heard her."

I can't help the small, almost unnoticeable smile that pulls at my lips. I've fought my way into this world, fought to earn my place, but tonight, it feels like the hard work is finally paying off. Ezra isn't just tolerating me anymore. He's respecting me. He's letting me take my own space, make my own decisions. That is more than I ever expected.

"We need to move soon. After Daith drugged him, he isn't going to let him back in it's only a matter of time before he figures it all out." Ezra says, making a great point. The question is, if I can pull off the act that I had no part of it and if Ezra's cover is still intact.

Daith stands and pulls me up with him as he speaks, though his eyes stay void and distant. "He won't see us coming. We take the drugs, the club, and the contacts. We have no use for sex trafficking and once under new management, we will inform those in that category that they no longer have our support."

I hear his words but my eyes stay locked on him for a moment, wondering where his mind is going. I squeeze his hand in confirmation, only to be met with a loose grasp.

"Understood," Felix says. "I'll send it into CHAOS."

The room falls silent as they wait for next orders. I take a chance, speaking up for Daith as he fights a war we can't see but one that I am all too familiar with.

"Vic stays late on Thursday nights. I work that night and can stay behind without him noticing. Let's go over how we are going to execute this."

Ezra steps forward, and in place of the correction I half expect, he grabs a piece of paper from the desk and hands it to me. "In his poker room, there is a hidden room that I can get into, with a tunnel leading to his stock and holding rooms." He passes me another paper and I'm still processing that so many of our girls were being held in the same building, enduring God knows what, and we were none the wiser. "You need to keep your eyes open and call for us if things get hairy. We will have you out in seconds."

I nod, holding the sentiment close but keeping my mind focused on the plans.

"This is our cover." The document appears as if Joshua Bowman, his bodyguard, has been double-crossing him with plans to take over everything. "We will plant this to look like Bowman wanted to kill him and take over a deal that was predated and signed over to us.

Impressed I nod, looking over everything. "Lisa is aware of everything Vic is tied into. We need her."

I see the disagreement on their face and I hold a hand up. "Here me out." I grip Daith's hand firmly, still giving him my touch as he sits silently. "Our name is powerful, and we can get pretty far on that alone, but Lisa manages everything for him. Calls, contacts, meetings. She fears you enough and has a strong sense of self-preservation. Pay her well and she will do whatever you ask, not caring who it's coming from."

Felix face shifts into an approving smirk. "Not bad."

I smile wide. "Thank you."

"Okay," Daith says, drawing himself back to the present. "It's final. We move tomorrow night. Laurel, go home and pack the rest of your things. Make it look like a forced entry and I'll meet you at Cee's."

I scrunch my brows.

"Tomorrow, you go to jail and Mrs. Reaper commits her first crime. You completely become one of us. A true shadow."

CHAPTER 49

I slam my fists into my head as the memories come flooding back. My ears ring and reality flashes in and out as I sink to the floor. I held it back as long as I could, barely making it the basement to keep myself separated from the rest of the people I care about while I wait for this to pass.

The world spins around me, warping into something unrecognizable. My breaths are shallow, my chest tight as the voices in my head begin to creep in. At first, it was just a whisper, a murmur I could almost ignore. Now, they're impossible to avoid. They're all I can hear. All I can feel.

"Shut up." My fingers dig into my skull, pressing hard against my temples as if I can crush the noise out, but it does nothing to stop the memories.

"I'll fucking kill you one day," I state to the man hovering above me. Not as a threat, but as a promise to us both.

He spits a laugh, leaning just close enough that I can headbutt him. Pain shoots through my skull but it's nothing compared to what he has inflicted before. "You wanna play? Let's play." Venom laces his words as he reaches for the electric paddles next to the piss and blood-stained mattress I'm bound to.

His yellow coated smile is all I remember before electricity courses through my skull, causing my body to convulse. Then it all goes black.

I slam my fist into my head again before grabbing the cement wall and throwing my head into it again and again. "Fuck you. Fuck you. Fuck you."

Another flashes in my mind.

"I'm sorry, honey," the woman who was playing mother says, brushing my wet hair from my clammy skin. "Daddy just needed some money. You understand right. You help us take care of you. You're such a strong boy. Such a good boy."

The smells that filled the air fill my nose again and I laugh, remembering how I watched the life drain from their eyes. I sang to the sweet sound of him begging me to let him live as he clung to every breath, sprawled out on the road next to his totaled car.

I can't breathe. My chest is too tight. My vision is narrowing, everything shifting in and out of focus. The walls feel like they're closing in on me. I stagger, reaching out to steady myself against the edge of a table, but my hands shake too much to grip it. I fall to the ground and my head crashes into the concrete floor. I sit up and throw my head into the floor again. My head drips blood and my skull aches, but the memories continue flashing, his voice in my head, overtaking the one that has become a welcomed friend.

"Daith?" Someone calls, and the voice morphs into his. He's everywhere, haunting me. I look up from the basement floor and he's standing before me with his hands reaching out toward me.

"Daith, it's okay. It's me."

No. No. Get the fuck away from me.

"Get the fuck away from me!" I scream, reaching for my knife and hurling it toward him. He dodges it, getting closer with every slow step he takes. Darkness swirls around him, his face distorted with black eyes and peeling decayed and burned skin.

"I'll fucking kill you!"

I stand, staggering with my head pounding and my vision swirling, unable to tell the difference between the horror of my mind and that of my life.

I pull the gun from the back of my pants and pull the slide back, holding it at his head that won't seem to stay in one spot. It sways and spins, doubles and flips.

"Get the fuck out of my head!" I scream until my voice cracks and I fire a round before falling to the ground, head in my hands.

Get out of my head. Get out of my head. Get out. Get out. Get the fuck out.

Heavy doors slam and I lift my head, prepared to defend myself again, prepared to defend the child that couldn't until his already broken soul was nothing but shards and bile.

But I don't see him. He's gone, but still in my head, whispering.

Give me him back. Give him back!

CHAPTER 50

LAUREL

Holding my backpack in my hand, I take one last look at my trashed apartment and admire my work. Glass shattered everywhere, clothes and valuables that I won't miss thrown sporadically, my security monitor smashed, and spray-painted words of a disgruntled tenant. Sorry Ms. Peterson—you're great!

I have to peel myself away from the door, leaving behind multiple pairs of my heels, outfits, and most of my makeup. With only the things I need to jump start my new life in my bag, I leave the door cracked, slip my mask over my head and quickly sling it on my back.

Everything here will be photographed and used as evidence that will fabricate a paper trail of me being booked and charged with criminal mischief and vandalism, resulting in 90 day jail time and a perfect sever of ties to the crimes the reapers will commit tonight.

Thank you Felix and whoever works their computer magic.

The engine roars to life beneath me as I kick the stand up and climb onto my motorcycle. I rev the engine and shoot out of the parking lot. The thrill of the ride is immediate with hope for my new life. The city's lights blur past me as I speed through the streets, the hum of the engine vibrating through my chest and into my bones.

Cee's house is just on the other side of town, tucked away in a quiet corner. I can already see it in the distance, the looming shape of it casting long shadows under the streetlights.

I push the bike harder, urging it to go faster. My heart is beating in time with the thrum of the engine, an urgency that makes everything around me feel distant.

When I pull up to Cee's house, the familiar tension in my shoulders loosens, but only slightly. I still feel the rush in my blood, the adrenaline keeping me sharp, focused, anxious for Daith to get here. I wonder if he will want to tell her everything. Part of me wonders if she is capable of handling my truth or if she would want to throw us both behind bars and throw away the key.

Quickly, I pull my mask off and slip it into my bag. Just as I swing my leg off the bike, Celeste comes barreling out of her front door. "He's not with you?!"

"Daith? No, he's coming later."

She shakes her head frantically and worry immediately blooms in my chest. "No, you need to get to him." She turns her phone toward me, showing me a message we used as kids.

Daith: HYDE

My chest caves. No. I knew I shouldn't have left him. I thought he was over it and was thinking clearly, but I saw the signs there.

"Go!" she pleads, voice breaking with a familiar gut-wrenching pain.

I rush to the old church and beat on the front door, still careful to park my bike down the road. I try my key and yank on the handle with no luck. I hit the door again and again until my knuckles are red and aching. "Felix! Ezra!" I shout, begging for any one of them to hear me. "You changed the locks, you fucking pussies!" I scream, trying to peer between the newly boarded windows.

The door is pulled open and Felix's grim face tells me something is wrong.
"Where is he?" I ask, panic lacing my voice, a hundred bad scenarios flashing through my head as I try to push by him. "Move!" My heart beats wild in my chest and I attempt to push the door open again.

"This isn't a good time. You should wait for him at Celeste's house like he said."

I narrow my eyes, anger boiling beneath my skin. "This is my fucking home! He is my home! You don't get to stop me from coming in! Let me help him!"

His eyes soften, pity looking back at me, but he doesn't relent. Dropping my chin, I take a breath. "Fine. Can you at least give him a message from me?" I ask, my voice calmer and much quieter. Felix nods and cracks the door a little more, leaning his head closer. I rear my fist back and deck him square in the nose before pulling my leg up and kicking the door with everything I have, sending him falling back on his ass and the door swinging open wide.

"Sorry, Felix!" I yell as I jump over him and rush through the house, his gurgled curses falling behind me as he chokes on his blood. Muffled screams come from far off and I dart to the basement, keeping an eye out for Ezra.

Racing down the stairs in the dark, relying on my memory of the turns, my heart beats painfully in my chest, not sure what I'm hoping or expecting to find. "He's unpredictable when he's like this! Laurel!" Felix calls after me again, but it doesn't stop me.

When I burst through the basement doors everything stops. Time stands still as I take in the crimson coated room. Blood is everywhere, dripping off the walls, flooding the floor, and coating a man who kneels on the floor, his head hanging low with defeat.

His soft whimpers echo through the room and crack something in my chest. "Daith?" I ask quietly, stepping closer, blood squelching beneath my feet. He mumbles something, too low for me to hear. I kneel in front of him, listening closer. Daith's hands tangle in his hair, covering his ears. "Tap, tap, tap, tap," he repeats over and over again, groaning in pain. I look around the room, hearing nothing.

Taking his face in my hands, I carefully tilt it up to look at me. His hands shoot out, gripping my wrists. I check him over, praying the blood coating his skin is not his own.

The basement door creaks and Felix steps in with Ezra one step behind, his face firm and emotionless. Daith's eyes flick to them, widening like a rabid animal about to bolt.

"Shh," I soothe, "I'm here. It's Laurel." His eyes bounce around my face and his hands grip my wrist harder. "I got you. I got you." I sit back on my feet, pulling him into me. He buries his face in my neck and I stroke his matted hair.

"Please don't leave me alone. He's here. He's in the dark. Don't turn the lights off."

My chest cracks open, my heart falling at his feet. A tear rolls down my cheek at the confirmation of his hallucination, his recession bringing him back to the mentality of a kid again. "I'm not going anywhere," I tell him, holding him tightly.

I glance back at Felix, nodding toward the back wall where a mangled body lays, and he nods, moving silently to inspect one of the crew men that had likely tried to come help.

"How do you help him through this?" Ezra asks in a low voice as he steps closer.

"Just be there for him. Ground him and let him come out of it on his own."

I look over Daith's shoulder at Felix who holds up three fingers and I swallow a lump in my throat, knowing that can't be good for anyone.

Ezra sets a hand on my shoulder. "He never let us close enough to help in this state. The best we can do is lock him up so he doesn't kill us."

I nod, expecting as much, but utterly hating that they cage him like a fucking animal. How many times has he had to go through it like this? Daith isn't lucid enough to allow anyone to help, but one day, I stepped in, and something in him let me. In any mental state, in any life, in any form... his soul welcomes mine home.

"You handle this. We'll take care of the rest," Ezra says, moving past me.

I nod and continue to hold him. I hold him until Felix is done wrapping what is left of the bodies and has taken them to dispose of. I'm sure Dom is part of that process but I try not to think about my cutie pie crunching on a stranger's femur. I sit with Daith in silence for what seems like hours, only his occasional whimpers and mumbling creating sound.

"Can we clean you up?" I ask, not sure if he'll let me move him. As kids, this didn't happen often, but when it did, it lasted for hours. Sometimes days.

I grab his face, leaning back for him to look at me. His tears have streaked through his dried blood and his blind fold has slid down and around his neck, his scarred skin where his eye used to be exposed and covered in filth. I brush my thumb over his cheek, just as he does for me, and I smile gently.

"Come on, handsome. Let's go get you in the shower." The hollowness in his gaze tells me the voices that haunt him have quieted for now, but he's still out of it. Pulling on his arms as I stand, I get him to his feet and walk him to the door. There is a water hose down here but fuck that. He needs a real shower, and light to fight off whatever he sees in the darkness.

I manage to get him to the bathroom, not bothering to worry about the trail he leaves. Stripping his close off, he stands there, numb and lost inside his own head. I open the shower door for him, but he grips my hand, refusing to let go. Readjusting my plan, I step under the warm water, and he follows, keeping his eyes on me as the water cascades down on us. I grab the rag and gently wash the filth and caked blood from his skin and hair, taking extra time on his face, gently cleaning his scars. I smile as the man I know becomes recognizable again. "There you are," I whisper with a smile.

The water shuts off and I drop the rag on top of the drain, muffling the sound of the water drops that will sound too much like that old basement. I strip off my wet clothes and wrap a towel around him before grabbing my own. He lets me lead him to his room and as he sits on the bed, he pulls me into him tightly as we fall onto the pillows. His fingers intertwine with mine and he holds me firmly, his breathing coming slowly as he relaxes. The light stays on, but as I pull a cover over us, I close my eyes and he sleeps, safe with me as I wait for him to come home to me.

CHAPTER 51

Tapping sounds softly on the bedroom door and I cringe, peering over my shoulder at Daith before carefully sliding out of his hold. I pull the door open, and Ezra stands, looking worse for wear.

"Is he?"

"He's still asleep. We won't know until he wakes up. We may have to do this ourselves if he isn't himself by tonight."

Ezra's jaw clenches and I step out, softly shutting the door behind me.

"Did he hurt you?" Ezra asks as he reaches for my arm that is coated in blood.

"No, that's from his head and hands. He cut himself pretty bad."

Something eases in Ezra's stance, though the permanent crease between his brows remains firmly in place.

I pull up my shirt, showing him an inch wide scar on my side, barely visible now. "He was 14 and cut me with a piece of glass in the middle of the night. He was like this, unaware of what he was doing." I pull my shirt back down and lean against the door. "I told him I had dropped a knife and nicked myself. He hid all the knives from me for two years." I smile softly, remembering that soft side of him.

Something resembling a smile twitches on Ezra's lips. "I'm glad he had you. What you just did was more than we were ever able to do for him."

Pride swells in my chest. "We still have time. Give him that. He'll be ready."

DAITH

I find her on the bed, her chocolate brown hair spread out around her, and Dom lying on top of her with their noses touching. She is idly scratching him behind his ears, half asleep, and the slow wagging of his tail tells me I may have been replaced.

"I take it y'all resolved your issues?"

She stops scratching him to look at me and he protests with a whine, nudging her hands with his long snout. Her eyes widen with surprise, laced with pure joy, but she lets it fade, choosing not to address it at the moment. "Oh, yeah. We are best friends now. He loves cuddles."

I snort. "Dom does not cuddle." Though, clearly, he does.

"You have work tonight. You need to get dressed," I tell her, moving to the closet and grabbing a change of clothes now that my current shirt is soiled with my own blood. She doesn't move, only her eyes tracking me as I move around the room. Reaching into my pocket, I flick my knife open, pointing it at her in warning. "I won't tell you again Peach."

She raises a brow, challenging me.

I step toward her and Dom's eyes pop open, his teeth bared as he snarls at me. My eyes widened and I step into him. "Who the fuck are you growling at Dahmer?" I snarl and Laurel chuckles. "I will put a bullet between your eyes, motherfucker."

His ears drop and his mouth snaps shut. Laurel wraps her arm around Dom's neck, hugging him closer. "You will not!"

Great, they've teamed up on me.

She snaps her head toward me with wide eyes. She scrunches her nose. "His name is Dahmer?" She looks down at him curiously before looking back at me, seeming to go over the significance. She nods, scrunching her nose, and I can almost see the images she conjures in her head. "Raw meat is a good diet, I guess."

She giggles at her own joke.

"So, how bad was it?" I ask, turning back to my closet and fish through her clothes that now overtake my own, and pick my favorite outfit for her that she happened to buy just for me.

"You don't need to worry about that. You didn't hurt anyone that matters, aside from yourself," she says, grabbing the black lingerie from me.

My fingertips brush over the bandage wrapped around my head, a slight ache coming from my scalp that is now stitched closed.

"Thanks for bringing me back," I say solemnly, hating that she had to see me like that again, even after all these years. It doesn't happen often, and for years, I have had to fight through it alone.

"Thanks for coming back," she counters, leaning off the edge of the bed to press her lips to mine, and they taste as sweet as the first time.

"So, what do we tell Celeste?" she asks.

"I let her know that you're okay, but she wants to see us both."

A pathetic whimper comes from Dom as she pets between his ears. I narrow my eyes at my dog as he relaxes into her, tilting his head further for her to reach the spot he wants. "Tell her whatever you want. You're in too deep for it to matter if she disapproves."

CHAPTER 52

For the first time in my career, I selfishly put my own interests before The Reapers. I can't let Laurel go into this, knowing her life would be in danger. My focus would be on her and her safety, not on the job. Really, it would be a hazard for everyone involved, because if she got hurt, I wouldn't care about ending up in prison for real this time. I would mangle every single body that stood against me until they were so unrecognizable, even their dental records wouldn't be enough to identify them.

Love is a weakness.

"I need you to do something for me," I say as I stand behind her as she curls her long hair with freshly dyed green tips and smeared back eye makeup. I like the new look and how she uses it to embrace who she is.

"Anything." A simple word that ignites my every cell. This was my dream- to have her, completely mine in every way. Desperate to please me, obsessed with my attention.

I can't risk losing her now.

"When we move in on him, I need you to leave."

Her face drops, and she spins, pointing the curling iron in my face. "You wanna run that by me again?" Pure anger rolls off her and fuck, I love seeing her mad almost as much as I like seeing her begging for release. There's something about a woman's rage that just gets me hard.

"This isn't up for discussion. It's not a risk I'm willing to take."

She disregards the finality in my tone and yanks the cord from the wall, chunking the hot metal at my head as I walk out of her room.

"Stop walking away from me! You don't get to say shit like that and walk out."

I continue walking down the stairs, eyes rolling in the back of my head as her relentless rampage continues.

"Uh oh. Mom and dad are fighting," Felix smarts off from where he lays slouched on the couch with a beer in hand.

"You don't get to decide I'm not part of this when you're scared!"

A hot spike of rage shoots down my spine and I spin, pinning her to the stair rail as she hits the bottom step. "I am not scared," I sneer, hating the way I feel exposed. She knows I care about her and I feel that fear down to my core. There is no need to figuratively pull my pants down in the middle of the house, making me feel like a premature little boy.

"You get in the way," I say, cutting her instead of owning up to my feelings.

Those are new to me, and I don't like them. They're messy and unpredictable. My hands run down her hips, her body perfect and made for me. She grabs my left hand, pure mischief looking back at me. Then she whips a knife out from behind her back and I tilt my head, wondering where the hell she was hiding that when she has barely any clothes on.

She pins the blade to the underside of my throat. "Say that again."

I push my chin down, the blade cutting into my skin and I use the railing to push further into her. "You're not staying. Keep pushing it and you'll find yourself chained to a bed and we will do this without you all together."

She grits her teeth and in a swift motion she retracts the knife and slams it down into my hand with an irritated scream.

I hunch over, grunting in pain. She wraps her fist in my jacket, putting her nose to mine. "You don't get to take my choices. Try again, and I'll remove your other eye, since you can't seem to see what is right in front of you anyway."

She moves around me and I watch over my shoulder as she passes the couch, snatching the beer from Felix's hand. "A bad bitch!" he says, throwing his hand in the air and she smacks it as she throws the bottle back, chugging the rest of his beer.

I pull the knife from my hand, slinging it across the room at her. I hold the wound shut and glare at her, hating her strong will just as much as I crave it. Beyond frustrated with the war raging inside me, I move to the kitchen and wrap a strip of cloth around my hand and the accomplished smirk on her face falls as I continue walking to the front door.

"Where the fuck are you going?" she demands, and I say nothing, slamming the door behind me.

LAUREL

I chase after him on our bikes and the cold wind burns my bare skin. He needs space to cope in his own way, I know that much, but I refuse to let him spiral in solitude. Not now that I'm here. We do this together.

I grimace, determined to cut him off as his bike roars ahead of me. I cut down a different road and pull the throttle back, racing down the shortcut and cutting back onto the main road in front of him. I look over my shoulder before I slam on my brakes and slide to a stop in front of him. I prop up the bike and stand in the middle of the road.

He breaks hard, skidding to a stop and kicking his stand down, barely missing me. Rage consumes me as I slam my fists into his chest.

"Stop!" I beg, pleading for him to give in.

His hands slip into his pockets, his face passive. "Stop what Peach? You are the one making a scene and acting out once again. You got what you wanted. I just needed a fucking minute, you impatient pain in my fucking ass!"

"Am I too much for you?" I ask, annoyance growing in me. "I kill someone without your permission. Bad girl. I want to be part of the plans. Bad girl. Everything I do is a problem for you, yet you marked me as your equal!" I pull my gun, pointing it at his chest. "Love me like your equal or let me go! I will not live the rest of my life fighting for your attention! I am not that little girl anymore!" I scream, begging for him to hear my heart begging for him.

"You got what you wanted. You can stay. You're equal." His eyes widen, a wildness that I crave spreading as he steps into the gun pointed at his heart. "Death is the only thing that will allow you to escape me. So, pull the trigger." He brushes my hair behind my ear, his thumb trailing down the frame of my face.

A tear slips down my cheek, and he lets it fall. "All I ever wanted was your heart Daith."

He pulls the slide back, the sound of a bullet loading into the chamber clicking between us. "Then take it. Stop the beating in my chest. Put me out of my misery and take what you really want."

My lip quivers as I hold back the pain in my chest. "Is a lifetime with me misery?"

I falter, and he whips the gun out of my hand, turning it on me, holding it against my temple as he pulls me into his chest.

"Misery is this feeling you give me. You call it love... but a weak spot, a target for my enemies, that is misery. To call it happiness... is demented."

I close my eyes, accepting my fate in his hands. The clatter of the gun hitting the asphalt pulls them open, Daith's hands cupping my face. His jaw twitches with the anger of his acceptance. His eyes are soft with truth.

Daith loves me.

He captures my lips, kissing me deep, pouring himself into me, all his unspoken words sinking deeper into my soul. Our lips part but neither of us pull back, breathing in each other's air as a life force. I reach up, gripping onto the front of his jacket in desperation.

"Hurt me as many times as you need, deny your love for me if it makes it easier for you to be with me, but please don't ever leave me behind. Don't push me out. I'm scared of the darkness that doesn't have you in it."

He spins us and pushes me back onto his bike. He leans in and his eyes focus on my parted lips that ache for his. Slowly he lifts my leg at the knee, and I wrap it around his waist. He reaches between my legs, ripping my fishnets wide. My pussy clenches and a wave of heat washes over me in a flash of unrestrained need.

"I am the only thing in this world you need to fear," he says before he frees his dick, letting his pants fall to his feet. He grips my waist and slides his hand between us, moving my panties to the side and feeling how soaked I am for him, despite how much he pissed me off. I'm still so mad I could slit his throat as he comes, but the desperate need to have him inside me overpowers any coherent thought I was able to form moments ago.

He groans, sliding two fingers in me and I let my head fall back.

"Fuck," I whisper, not caring that we are on the side of the road, only the slowly growing darkness of night covering us from cars passing by.

Daith wraps his hand around his dick, stroking once from base to tip before he lines himself up and thrusts into me. I let out a loud whimper, loving the sting of the pain as he pushes every inch of himself inside me. My head bobs with each thrust and I grip onto the bike as I let him have his way, slowly moving in and out with punishing thrusts. I keep my eyes open, needing to see the way he watches where our bodies connect. Seeing him whimpering with each thrust that is better than the last, his lips parted, and his brows scrunched is enough to have my orgasm building. He keeps his slow and desperate pace, fingers digging into my thighs. His head sags and he holds himself inside me, buried to the hilt as he spills in me with a shuttering grunt, and in this moment, not a single other thing in the world matters.

He slowly pulls out and watches as his cum leaks out of me, only for a moment before he pulls me up and flips me over, bending me over his bike. I separate my feet for him, and he pushes in again, pulling a gasp from me as the new angle hits the perfect spot.

"Oh," I moan, knowing I won't last two minutes.

He tangles his hand in my hair and pulls my head back with one hand, wrapping the other around my throat, using his hold on me as leverage to deliver quick thrusts. My body rocks back and forth with his frantic motions and I snake a hand between my legs, rubbing my clit furiously. The cold metal of the bike against my hard nipples adds to the pleasure and my knees grow weak and my eyes roll back.

I pant, needy and desperate as I chase my orgasm.

"Come for me baby. Say my name," he says, and I clench around him as my mind plays the thousands of fantasies I've had with his voice in my ear, saying that very thing.

My orgasm builds fast, and I relax into the rush. He holds me up as my knees give out and I scream in ecstasy as I let it consume me, setting every nerve on fire as I scream his name to the sky.

CHAPTER 53

LAUREL

I tuck myself in the hallway that goes behind the back of the stage, making sure I'm unnoticed as all the lights shut off and Lisa does the final walk through and locks the front doors before heading upstairs for their meeting.

I've always been curious about what they discuss on a weekly basis, because I know it's not about how he needs to increase the pay for his dancers and create stricter guidelines on who we allow in the club.

Lisa's heels click up the stairs, and I tuck my earpiece into my ear, whispering as I crack the door open. "Can you hear me?"

"Affirmative, Lillith. You are clear to move. Death out."

I put my finger to my ear with a grin at his random use of code names. "You are a child."

"Come on, role-playing is fun. Now move your ass before I bite it."

I look down at my body to make sure all skin is covered in black sweats and gloves, then I pull my mask down and my hood up, covering all of my hair. "Mmh, promise?" I ask teasingly. I tuck my hair in and glance up the stairs before stepping out of the hall. "Hey, the next time we role-play, I call Dom, but I promise to use lube."

"*Lillith,*" a different voice teases, and I pause in my tracks. "We need you to confirm how many people are there before we can move," Felix says with urgency in his voice.

I giggle. "Oops. I didn't know this was a three-way."

"Four," Ezra says, and I clap and hand to my mouth to retain the laugh that wants to burst from my chest. "You owe me Twenty, Felix. Knew you two were going to be insufferable."

Silence fills the line, and I struggle to breathe as I imagine the look Daith is giving the both of them. Cautiously, I move up the stairs, quickly pass Vic's office, and to the poker room where they usually meet.

Me: Okay, I'm upstairs. I can hear at least three people.

I text the chat, and Daith responds in my ear.

"Move to a VIP room. We will trip the alarm to get them out," he says, and I nod to myself, remembering the plan and hating that at any moment, this could go so wrong.

I slide into the first room and crack the door, just enough for me to see into the room once they open the door.

"Clear," I whisper, and a moment later the club alarm blares. I get a small amount of peace knowing they aren't here yet.

The poker room opens wide, and Vic storms out with a gun hanging at his side as he storms down the hall and into his office to check the report as planned. His bodyguard follows behind him and down the stairs.

Two more men I don't recognize follow and Lisa stands by the door, peering around nervously. I pull my face back inside the room.

"Five, including Lisa," I whisper. "I can see the door leading down into the warehouse."

"Stay put. Once the alarm clears and the door shuts, we will set a loop and disarm the alarm," Felix says, reassuring me.

A moment later, the alarm is cleared, and I inhale a calming breath. I press my ear to the crack, listening for them in the hall.

"Looks like motion tripped it from outside. Beer bottle hit the door," someone says, and I stifle a laugh. Fucking Felix.

Vic scoffs, followed by a door shutting, and a weight lifts off my shoulder as we check off another step of the plan. Fuck, I don't know how they do this for a living and still look as good as they do. I'm going to start sprouting grey hair before I'm thirty at this rate.

"Okay," Daith says. "We're on the way Peach. You're doing so good."

His praise soothes my heart and mind, and I nod to myself, bringing my blood pressure back down to normal levels.

A moment later, the door next to me opens, and I freeze as Dorian fucking Vic stands staring back at me with a sickening, too wide, smile.

"Death," I plead as Vic raises his gun, whips it across my head, and everything goes black.

CHAPTER 54

I don't see red as I race to her, ready to step in. I see the most perfect masterpiece I'll ever create. I will have his head mounted on my wall before tonight is over. Felix and Ezra follow behind me, zipping through traffic, all black and masks on, like death coming to claim its victims.

Jerking to a stop, we leave the bikes out front and break through the front door, nearly ripping it from the hinges. The alarms red light flashes but no sound emits, and Felix grins with accomplishment.

"I left that for the ambiance. Gotta set the mood," he says, wiggling his fingers.

We continue through the club, clearing the empty spaces with careful steps. "Something's not right," I say, feeling it in my bones. "They should have come out by now." My stomach ties in knots at the thought of them being too busy with Laurel to bother welcoming me in with guns blazing.

Ezra nods to the stairs and I take them two at a time, needing to get to her more urgently now. The poker room door is cracked, and I kick it open, finding it empty. Felix clears all corners as I continue to the open door leading to his secured room we found on the blueprints hidden behind a false wall.

A guttural scream rips from a woman's throat, and I recognize it immediately. I sprint down the stairs and around the corner, stopping dead in my tracks at the sight before me. Blood paints the walls, chunks of flesh and organs are scattered among the severed limbs laying about. Laurel stands in the middle of the hall, covered in blood that doesn't appear to be hers, and Dorian Vic's head in her hands with a wooden stake speared through the bottom.

My eyes widen, full of amazement and astounding arousal.

"Holy fuck," Felix breathes, moving to stand beside me.

"That's the hottest thing I've ever seen in my life," I admit, unable to take my eyes from her.

Ezra groans as he steps into a puddle of what appears to be someone's intestines.

"I'm serious. I have a raging hard-on right now."

Laurel wipes the blood from her mask with her arm, and knowing the feeds are now cut, she pulls her mask up. She's smiling, full of pride. I step toward her, and she holds Vic's head out to me like a bouquet.

"What happened to the plan, baby?"

She looks down and around the room with a shrug. "He threatened you with me, and I really just didn't like that. So, you know." She picks a chunk of someone off her bra and tosses it to the floor next to the bloody axe. "I handled it."

Ezra groans. "So much for the cover up plan. This looks a lot worse than a double cross gone wrong." I laugh at the thought of the vein on Ezra's forehead bulging.

"I left the rest of Vic's body intact in there and cut Bowman's hand off. I think it could pass easily with some planted records. I'm not stupid," she says, nodding toward one of his soundproof rooms that lock from the outside. "Lisa can take the fall for cutting off his head and get off on self-defense. We can break her out easy enough, right Daith?"

I chuckle. "Excellent work Peach." I grip her face, bringing her into me for a kiss, our lips and tongues colliding and mixing with blood.

I pull the fabricated document showing Bowman's plans from my pocket and move to the soundproof room. Carefully picking up Bowman's hand, I press his bloody fingers to the document and fold it nicely before tucking it into Vic's suit pocket.

They'll find him, think he went batshit nuts, killing everyone when he figured it out and Lisa stopped him with the axe before he could get to her. Yeah, that will buff nicely.

I step back out finding Lisa pressed against the far corner of the room, quivering in fear, her hands covering her head as she hugs her knees tightly. Laurel steps up, reaching for her hand that shakes vigorously.

"Shh, you're okay," she says, trying to soothe her. "We're not going to kill you. We need you."

Lisa's eyes open, but the glazed look in her eyes tells me that did very little to calm her nerves.

"We have a problem," Felix says and I grimace, hating when he fucking says that. "We're missing one."

I look around, not seeing enough body parts to equal four men. I turn back to Laurel. "You said four, plus her?"

She nods, confirming the shit storm. Knowing what we have to do, we all pull our guns, and I pass more ammo to Laurel who tells Lisa to stay put until we come back for her.

Ezra clears the poker room again, Felix takes the hall, and we go down the stairs. I stop as the lightning outside lights up the room and a body stands in front of the front doors.

I step closer, keeping Laurel behind me as I close the gap between us to get a better look. He stands with his gun at his side and a too wide grin on his face as he steps into the light that is cast from the bar.

"Hello, Reapers," he says, and the burned symbol on the back of his hand causes my defenses to rise even more.

"Who the fuck are you?" I ask as I realize we have made a serious mistake somewhere.

I reach for Laurel as she steps beside me. But I don't hold her back. Never again. Though that promise doesn't soothe the fear blooming in my chest.

"The Hollow," the man says and Laurel grips my hand tighter.

"What do you want?" she asks, but I answer for her.

"He works for CHAOS."

I can feel it, his lethal presence, similar to my own but more... structured. This is who they send to clean up the big messes. To make people disappear.

His grin confirms it. He's been here, and it's why we couldn't see him. It was like he didn't exist.

I didn't know for sure, but it's the only logical explanation.

"I'm not here for you, Reaper. You just happened to be a perk of the job, along with your sister." He winks suggestively and now I want to see what his heart feels like, mushed between my fingers. "No, fortunately enough, I'm here for her. You three are just... casualties." He nods to Laurel and my stomach falls out of my ass and my vision teeters on the edge of blacking out in rage.

The Hollow. The enforcement wing of CHAOS that erases people, leaving nothing behind. Of course we couldn't see him on the reports. Those things are sealed, so you never see them coming. That's their whole purpose.

"She's the one that's been dropping unapproved bodies left and right for months. But skills beyond some low-life. Her signatures changing to match yours is what sold her out. Now, she's coming with us."

I'd like to see him fucking try.

Feliz and Ezra move in behind us, guns aimed at him. He's out numbered, but he's trained by federal level military adjacent criminals.

How the fuck are we getting out of this one?

Just as I think the only way out of this is for one of us to take a bullet, Celeste comes in through the front door, her gun aimed at his head. She fires, but not fast enough. He spins, jumping out of the way. I wrap my arms around Laurel, taking us both to the ground.

"What the fuck is she doing here?" Laurel screams over the commotion of Ezra firing another shot, landing one in the man's leg before he can lunge for my sister.

"Ethan, you piece of shit!" Celeste screams, firing again.

"Honey, can't we talk about this?" Ethan says from somewhere behind an object to shield himself.

"Get the fuck out of there!" Celeste yells, glaring at me.

I grab Laurel by the hand and we break for it, sprinting through the unguarded door, followed by Felix and Ezra.

"Were down a bike!" Ezra yells as we hit the parking lot.

I sling Laurel on the back of my bike and Felix takes hers. Ezra throws Celeste on the back of his bike and in unison, our bikes roar to life and tear out of the gravel. We tuck low, racing from the club through the pouring rain that feels like bullets bouncing off of our skin. Laurel tucks herself behind me, shielding herself as much as possible.

Ethan is quick on our heels on his own bike, firing shots after us.

"Shoot him!" I scream, my head pounding and my vision blurring, the pain from my head wound mixing with the impairment from the rain.

Laurel pulls my gun from my waist band and turns her body, firing shots rapidly.

"He's too far!" she yells, cursing as she waits, counting the bullets out loud. Four left, and then we're fucked.

"Get ready!" I scream over the heavy rain. Laurel fires shots and I slam on my brakes, losing the gap between us and giving her a closer range.

The bike hydroplanes and jerks, sliding before it throws us off onto the road at 210mph. I spin my body to face her as we continue sliding over the layer of water and I open my arms, catching her body as it slams into me. I protect her head as we continue to slide and roll, only stopping when we collide with a tree.

The world feels like it's moving in slow motion as I glance over at Laurel, checking her over quickly. Her body is sprawled out, her eyes a little dazed, but she's alive. Her breath is shallow, but she's not seriously hurt. Not that I can see. I kneel beside her, carefully checking her body, my hands grazing over her skin, trying to make sure she's okay. The last thing I need is for her to fall apart now, after everything. As my hands graze her ribs, she groans and grimaces. Okay, we can live with broken ribs.

"I'm fine," she mutters, though her voice betrays her. I can hear the pain in it, and I can see it in the way she shifts, wincing in pain, unable to sit up. But I don't push it.

I don't have time to focus on her completely. Not now.

"Make sure that bastard is dead," she says, her eyes closed as the rain pelts her face. She coughs, choppy and struggled. "I hit him."

Hope blooms and my eyes snap up to the bike laid over in the rain half a mile from us. I hear one of our bikes coming back, getting closer, and I brush the tops of Laurel's head. "I'll be right back. The boys will be here any second."

She nods and I break into a sprint, ignoring the ache in my limbs and the pain in my stomach and head. I slow as I reach Ethan. My eyes flicker over to him and the blood pooling around him. I step toward him and lean down to check his pulse with my knife in hand, ready to defend. It's faint, slow, and then nothing.

Felix's bike comes to a stop beside Laurel and without another word, I jam my knife down into Ethan's chest, pull it out, and sprint back to Laurel with an urgency I've never felt in my life.

"Take Laurel home," Felix says, his voice clipped and firm. "I'll handle this."

Without debate, I leave him to clean-up. Wrapping her arm around my shoulders, I haul Laurel into my arms and set her on her bike facing me, giving her a place to rest her weight.

"I'm so sorry," she says, burring her face into my chest. "I didn't mean to cause all of this."

"It's okay, Peach."

I take another look over my shoulder at Felix who begins making calls before I shift the bike and slowly pull off, taking extra caution to get her home and prepare to run. CHAOS wants her, and if there is one thing you can't outrun, it's death.

Chapter 55

I wake up in my bed with bandages covering my torso, shoulder, and legs, the smell of antiseptic and old incense. My mouth is dry, my skin itches under the bandages, and my throat tastes like blood. Grimacing, I push myself up and find Daith missing. Panic surges through my body as I struggle to remember what happened after I hit the ground.

Did I kill Ethan? Did he kill Daith?

Oh, God.

I fight the pain that shoots through my skin as I stand and rush to my bedroom door, clutching my side in agony. I pull it open, hearing screaming coming from lower in the house.

"The first thing I taught you was that you never get close to someone you can't trust with your life!"

Oh my God, that sounds like Daith. Hope blooms in my chest as I make it down the stairs, finding him standing in the chapel with his back to me. Ezra and Felix's eyes shift to me, and I smile, so fucking thankful they are all safe.

He turns and my smile slowly fades as Celeste stands in front of him with tears running down her face.

"Cee?" I say, confused, glancing at the boys for an explanation of why she is here.

"You're hurt," she says, reaching for me as Daith steps out of the way.

"What did you think was going to happen? You're smarter than this!" Daith screams and slams his hand down on one of the pews, making her jump.

I cut my eyes at him. "Why the fuck are you yelling at her?"

His jaw clenches and he waves his hand, motioning for Celeste to talk to me. She swallows hard before her eyes find mine. "I haven't been totally honest with you."

My brows furrow. If either of us have more that we haven't been honest about, I promise it's me... but I let her talk, saving my truth for another moment.

"I've known Daith was a Reaper since he joined. I've known everything," her voice cracks, knowing the betrayal she's dishing out.

Weight crushes my chest, and I stay silent as she continues, letting the sting sink in.

"I've actually managed a lot for The Reapers over the years, training Felix and helping him with coding, passing them orders, helping them with intel, but I never got involved more than that." She reaches for my hand, and I pull away, holding my palm up, needing to process everything. She nods. "It was my job to screen everyone as a possible threat. I messed up. I didn't catch Ethan, and he-"

"You almost killed her! So you could get laid?" Daith screams, shoving his finger in her face, and this time, I don't stop him. "You let your guard down and he used you to get into our system and see inside."

"You were sleeping with him?" Ezra asks, angry and accusing. "For someone as smart as you, your taste in men is impressively stupid. And you are a fucking idiot?," he lashes at her and I can see her coil into herself.

"Watch it," I snarl, defending her, despite the knife in my back. It's not my life that concerns me the most, it's the fact that she has lied to me since we were kids. All the nights I spent confused and crying over Daith, all the times she kept his lie going, feeding them to me to keep me in the dark when the entire time, I thought he was lying to her too. I felt pity for her. But in the end, I was holding the same amount of truth behind lies.

"Oh, I'm sorry. Are we just supposed to ignore that she was sleeping with one of the only people that can make it look like we were never born?"

"If you're using that logic, none of y'all caught me, so can I cast a stone too?" I ask, holding my aching rib.

Felix leans against the edge of the pew, arms crossed. "How deep did he get, Cee?"

She blinks, refusing to let more tears fall. "Not very. He got into our backup feeds and basic file reports. Once he saw Laurel with us, his focus switched to her and that's when I'm guessing he dug into the past and formed the connection."

"It was never about us," Felix confirms, chewing on the inside of his cheek.

All of their eyes shift to me. "What?" My eyes widen. "What does that mean?"

"It means we need to confront them and smooth things over or they may not stop coming for you. Especially that you have now killed two of their own."

I show all my teeth in a grimace. "Yeah, that's my bad."

"You're making us look bad," Felix teases.

"Celeste really brought that one home," Ezra asks and a cut my eyes at him. If I could move faster, I might would take my chances and pop his old ass in his mouth.

"Celeste covered your tracks, stayed hidden, lied for you, and despite one mistake that any of us could have made, we are all alive." I turn back to Celeste and lift her hanging head. "That's a Reaper in my book by any measure."

Their accusing eyes turn softer as they let my words sink in and Celeste's pained expression turns confused.

"I have no right to throw stones when I have been keeping half of who I am from you."

She nods, attempting to smile through the tears. "I knew there was something insane in you if you could love him," She sniffs, wiping the running makeup from under her eyes. "I was sure that you two would kill each other and I would have to give the most uncomfortable eulogy to ever exist."

I snort a laugh, grabbing my ribs as my chest shakes softly.

"What do you say, boys? Shall we vote on marking her?" I ask and it's Celeste that cuts in.

"Oh, no," she says, shaking her head. "Absolutely not. I am perfectly okay with being behind the scenes. I have no desire to fake my jail time or death and become a murderer. No offense for your guy's hobby. It's just not for me."

I nod, taking her hand in mine. "Come on. Me and you have a lot to talk about."

She interlocks her fingers in mine, laying her head on my shoulder. "As long as it doesn't include my brother's cock, I'm all ears."

We are halfway out of the room when Daith calls after us. "Just like that? You are going to let it go? Reapers don't give second chances!"

I narrow my eyes at him. "Enough pet."

As if he could kill his sister. It's cute that they think they still run this show. His jaw falls slack and I blow him a kiss before giving him my back, flipping him the bird behind my back.

The CHAOS building is too clean. 25 stories of polished concrete and mirrored glass, sealed off, hiding the filth it governs. No name on the front, just a metal plaque near the front door that reads "Federal Department of Systems Integrity."

I don't miss the irony there.

Security meets us in the middle of the lobby's marble floor. Smiles that don't reach their eyes, perfectly tailored suits, and concealed weapons. Daith reaches for my hand, tight enough to remind me to stay on guard here and close to him.

"Were here to see Varnis," Daith says, and the big man nods, leading us to an elevator. I wiggle on my feet, my body still sore, and the 5 hour flight did nothing to help that. The doors close and the man taps something on his tablet before we start moving. I look at the wall curiously. No buttons. No option to leave or go somewhere unapproved.

The conference room is nearly empty, except for a long glass table, leather chairs, and matte black walls. I take a seat between Daith and Ezra, my eyes following the three men that enter, shutting and locking the door behind them. The guard stands at the exit, his expression blank and his stance like stone.

"Jesus, it's like a morgue in here." I whisper, and one of the men speak up as he takes his seat at the end of the table. "Laurel Sinclair." I jump lightly, sitting more upright. "You have made quite the mess."

"So have you," I bite back before my brain can stop the idiocy.

He raises a brow at me and I can't tell if it's because he's impressed or if that was my strike one before he throws me in a vat of acid.

"You killed two of our agents, and you are here requesting... what?" he asks, seemingly bored out of his mind.

I swallow, but it's Daith that speaks up. "As the speaker for The Reapers, I'm submitting her acknowledgment of becoming one of us. I would like it noted that she was marked before Ethan confronted us."

There's a flicker of something- maybe amusement. "You have rescinded your stipulation of rejecting women into your organization." He taps his chin. "Interesting," he says, looking at Ezra who stays unmoving.

"So, you are going to accept responsibility for her actions and therefore, bear the consequences as a whole?"

All three Reapers nod in unison. "Correct."

I speak up, holding my place among them. "We were hoping that, given my lack of knowledge of you, we could offer a substantial payment from our hit this week to help your funding, and as a result, you might forgive my transgressions?"

"We expect big growth soon as we take over Dorian Vic's roll in multiple undergrown rings," Ezra adds.

The man turns to the other two for the first time, but they say nothing before turning back to us. "We might, depending on the offer."

Ezra takes a pen, writing down a number and sliding it across the table. The men look it over before peering back up. "Accepted."

I internally relax, though on the outside, I don't dare let them see that.

"However," the man on the left adds, "there is an internal debate. Some of us feel your talents would be... better utilized elsewhere."

Laurel meets their gaze. "You want me to work here?"

"You've proven efficient. Precise. Timely. Unnoticed. All qualities we value in The Hollow."

The room chills.

Daith shifts beside me, eyes locked on the man, cold and warning. "She's not yours to take."

"She may be one day. Tables are always turning, Reaper."

Another silence. Heavy. Final.

"Very well," the left figure concludes, "All is forgiven, and she is recognized as a Reaper of Redwater. Use it wisely."

They rise in sync, chairs gliding silently. No handshakes. Just doors opening and a silent escort.

In the elevator again, I stare straight ahead. "They want to *own* me."

Daith's jaw flexes. "Not while I'm breathing."

Ezra watches the numbers descend. "Sleep with one eye open."

CHAPTER 56

I sit in the shadows, camera in hand, cross-legged on the club's upper floor. Below the stairs, Daith stands above a warm body, blood pooling at his feet, silence surrounding him- everyone too scared to make a mistake like the lifeless man lying on my new wood floors. His head shifts up, giving me just enough light from the hanging chandelier for a good picture.

Click.

The shutter hums as I capture the moment he smiles under his chrome skeleton mask. No one can see it, but I know it's there. It's relief. Pressure release. Ecstasy. It's my favorite. Not the charming one he uses to lure, or the crooked one he uses to charm. It's venomous, sharp- true.

Click.

This is where it started. Me in the shadows, him covered in blood. Always something I could never touch.

I never hid from the black inside his soul or tried to wash it away. I adored it, craved it, wanted some for myself. And when I looked inside, I saw a part of myself that would become anything he wanted. Darker. More twisted than the original.

My soul isn't pure darkness. It is... the possibility of endless destruction with only a single word from his lips.

He sees me before I stand, hunting me like a predator, his head tilting to look right at me.

"I feel you watching, Peach."

With my mask in place, I stand, pulling my shoulders back and prance down the stairs that are now splattered with blood and brain matter.

The club smells new. Glue, sawdust, and fresh paint permeating the air from the remodels. Most of the lights are still off and tarps hang over the stage. This place used to stink of foul play, and now all I can feel is legacy. The promise of a future.

"Why do you have to ruin my fun?" I ask, teasing as he meets me at the bottom step, and I wrap my arms around his neck.

He laughs, and God, that sound... it doesn't comfort, it devours.

Daith moves behind me, hand sliding up my spine and around the base of my neck, not tight, just as a reminder. "Do you love what I've built for us?"

I lean back against his chest, grinning dark and dangerously, though no one can see it through my matching mask. I look around the club, taking in the renovations, changes he's added to my request, down to the pink checkered floor. "You built it for you. But I'll gladly rule at your side."

He growls, turning me to face him. "At my feet."

"Only when you've been a good boy."

His hold tightens and my breath catches, sending a thrill through me. Oh, it's just too easy to get him riled up.

"I'm not asking you to stand behind me," he says, holding me firmly. "I have always wanted you beside me, but make no mistake- You will still kneel to me."

My hand snakes down to his dick, cupping him through the outside of his pants. I giggle softly, knowingly, though still enjoying our game. "Maybe."

"Careful, you challenge me too much and I'll kill you."

I lean into his mouth. "It's cute that you think you could."

In physical capabilities, absolutely. But I know without a doubt, he couldn't stomach losing me.

He pulls me into a booth, the tabletop scattered with papers. Blueprints, contracts, and plans. I set my camera down, giving him my attention.

A black envelope sits in front of him and he slides it to me with one finger. Cautiously, I watch him as I pull the document out before I begin reading. "What is this?" I ask, my eyes skimming words I can't process just yet.

"A crown," he says, and my eyes snap up to him.

"Pardon?"

"The club is yours now. The paperwork. The land. The false fronts. Your name is on everything."

I narrow my eyes and tilt my head. "Did you have a stroke?"

"This is all for The Reapers. Our Kingdom. But you are its head. Nothing shall pass without your hand."

I look at the papers again. "You're giving me everything," I say softly, the hint of a question in my tone.

"No, Peach. The Reapers have possibility. You choose if you want to make it everything."

There is a challenge to his tone. A game.

Flicking my knife open, I prick my finger, smearing it over the pad of my finger before pressing it to the paper, accepting his proposal.

Every deal. Every plan. Every move. It will all go through me.

Blood in, blood out.

In a rush, he stands, and pushes my mask up to match his own. His lips crash into mine like war, and I melt against him, giving myself to him, eating at his soul as he wraps his arms around me, pulling me closer until every inch of our bodies are touching. Submission is my weapon. He'll always want to win, and I'll let him, but I'll never forget... I won his game. I beat him.

I suck the tip of my finger, the taste of copper rushing over my tastebuds. Movement catches my eye near the bar, and I turn to Ezra and Felix, chrome masks glinting in the low light that hangs over the retired bar. Felix reached over the wood top and retrieves a bottle of whiskey, discarding the top over his shoulder before tossing the bottle back.

Celeste's heels click as she rushes down the stairs, a look of panic on her face as she types furiously on her phone, balancing the clipboard in her hand. Ezra seems to look frozen in place as she rushes to him, her mouth going a mile a minute about whatever has her worried. I pinch my brows, doing my best to intercept.

"CHAOS is having some kind of meeting. They want us all there," I say, still looking over my shoulder.

"I expected that. They are going to want to meet you and swear you in."

I hum a sound, excited for the chance to meet the people I royally pissed off. I feel the rush of adrenaline, the weight of what we're about to do sinking in deeper. This isn't just about owning the club. This is about owning everything. The businesses, the drugs, the money flow. Everything for this city's control will be in the palm of our hand.

An idea sparks and I brush Daith's hand before moving across the room. Felix nod's half slumped and hanging off the end of the bar. "Madam," he says, raising the bottle.

"Celebrating early, I see?" I ask playfully before I snatch the bottle from his hands. "Act like an adult or mommy will send you off to bed."

He mumbles something, bouncing his head back and forth mockingly before he drops himself in a booth. As I step next to Celeste, Ezra stops talking, and the energy around us shifts. "This is a safe space," I say dramatically. "Please continue."

Ezra inhales and sucks his teeth. "CHAOS wants to meet you. They decided to brush your body count under the rug, thanks to our generous donation to their funding, but they are less pleased with another loose cannon joining our ranks."

"Do they have an issue with women in the ranks, or is that just you?" I ask, and I don't miss the way Cee's shoulders stiffen.

"Just me." I say before letting that comment hang between us.

"Your skills are clearly up to par, it's just-"

"My vagina offends you," I say with a knowing tone, hoping to piss him off.

"Your vagina is... no one's *vagina* offends me," he begins to say, tripping over himself.

Cee's lips tilt up in amusement.

"Look, I'm just old fashion. Having emotions tangled into business just asks for mistakes."

Cee snorts a laugh that is tinged with something darker than humor. "Oh, yes. Clearly, any emotions surrounding you is huge mistake. I'll keep that noted in our business file for fuck ups," Cee says, tapping her clipboard.

Ezra's fists tighten and release at his sides before his eyes meet mine again. "This isn't about you being a woman. You need to understand what walking into CHAOS means. Whether you and him work out or not, you will forever be tied to us. There is no going back on that. They won't care that you broke up."

I reach out to touch his arm. "The only way Daith and I are ever ending things will be in the dirt, cold and dead, with worms eating our decaying flesh. If he ever tries to leave me, you won't have to worry about CHAOS, because I will kill us both."

Cee scrunches her nose. "How romantic. I pray a love like that finds me one day." She winks at me and I pull her close. "Ez thinks vaginas have teeth. You won't find it here." I gasp, gripping her shoulders. "Perhaps Felix likes vaginas. Let's go explore that."

I push her toward Felix who is nearly asleep in the booth and Daith who is hunched over the dead body in the middle of my club, plucking his eyeballs out of his head.

"I don't have a problem with you being here, Laurel," Ezra says, pulling my attention back to him. "I just... don't want everything I've built to be lost when you two destroy each other."

"That's not how this is going to turn out," I say, leaning into his side.

"How do you know?" he asks, seeming genuine, stiff, but he doesn't move away.

"You can't feel it?" I inhale deeply. "I've only ever been this sure of one other thing in my entire life." My eyes falling to Daith, who is now tucking body parts in his pockets.

Ezra chuckles softly. "He told me something like that years ago when The Reapers were just me and a kid running from who the world thought we should be.

He leans down, pressing his mask to the top of my head. "You belong here, babe. I believe that."

I spin toward him, a stark expression on my face as I rub my arms, mocking hell freezing over. Patting him on the chest, I grin wide before stepping back into the center of the club. Ezra can be a real hard ass with the biggest stick I've ever seen permanently fused in his asshole, but he's growing me.

I stand in the heart of the empire I know will soon come. I think I'll keep the club's name- tied to who I am to my Reaper. It's almost done, but what this town doesn't know is that this isn't just new ownership and a reopening. It's being reborn.

This is a kingdom. For the name that's whispered when it's too dark to say it loud.

Reaper.

I remain a shadow under a mask. My presence is felt but never truly seen. My identity in the power of a name you can't outrun.

I am a Reaper of Redwater.

THE END

BONUS SCENE

My sister's guest room sensor pings at 2:14 a.m.
I click my monitor on, pulling up the feed, expecting to see Laurel crashing after a night out drinking with my sister.

The feed loads with a flicker of static, then clarity, and my body tightens at the sight of what I've caught on camera.

It isn't her. Not even close.

It's Celeste. My sister. Legs wrapped around Ezra's hips, her head pressed back against the guest room wall, her shirt half-off and her mouth parted in a way I don't want to see.

Ezra's got one hand braced above her head, the other digging into her waist. Celeste's shirt is bunched around her ribs. Her head's thrown back. She's making sounds I can't un-hear.

His rings catch the light as he moves sensually around her body. His face is buried in her neck, tasting her. She moans. Loud.

I don't blink. I don't breathe, trying to process what it is I'm seeing. It's like a car pile-up. You don't want to see the damage but you can't help but keep staring until it repulses you and doesn't allow you to eat for hours.

I reach that point as he pushes a hand into her shorts.

I kill the screen and nearly puke my dinner all over my keyboard. Darkness washes over the monitors, but the image stays burned into the back of my mind. I sit there, hands flexing uselessly on the desk, throat dry, pulse punching the inside of my skull. I wanted to see my wife half-naked and stumbling in before she called me to come get her, like always. Instead, I got something new to unpack with my therapist. Or I would if I saw one.

My little sister is fucking my best friend. My brother. The man that is basically my dad. He's old enough to be her dad.

What the fuck is happening?!

Oh, I'm going to kill them.

I don't forget. Anything. Especially not betrayals caught in high-resolution at two in the goddamn morning.

TATUM DIRE

FIND ME:

Website: Tatum-Dire-Author.square.site

Facebook: Tatum Dire Author

Instagram: @Tatumdireauthor

Email: Tatumdireauthor@gmail.com

Thank you for reading!

All of my stories have mood boards and playlists if you'd like to dive deeper!

The links are also on my website.

https://pin.it/48h6pnxf1

https://open.spotify.com/user/31y22aa62yef6m7d3co2u5vasn5e?si=195733d11a0b43d1

ABOUT THE AUTHOR:

Tatum Dire writes dark romance—stories that dive into the messy, intense emotions people often keep hidden. She enjoys weaving raw, emotional journeys that push boundaries in the most twisted ways, though she may dabble in a little bit of everything as her career progresses.

What she's most proud of is her ability to create characters and worlds that feel real and flawed, where readers can see pieces of themselves in the struggles, heartbreaks, and hopes, all while still creating a fictional world that takes you away from this one.

What drives her isn't just storytelling, but the freedom in it—the chance to weave raw emotion, lived experiences, and even the wildest dreams into something that resonates. For Tatum, the greatest reward is knowing her words have touched, healed, or empowered the readers who give her stories a chance.

Tatum began writing as a way to understand herself, putting shape to feeling, then found, in the silence between the pages, others were listening. For her coming plans... she can only hope that continues.

COMING NEXT

IN THE SILENCE OF SHADOWS WORLD

Demented is the first book in a planned three-part interconnected standalone series. Be on the lookout for book two where we will see what comes next for The Reapers and their relationships.

MORE BOOKS BY THIS AUTHOR:

A standalone reverse harem.

To read more and review the content warnings, go to my website!

BOOKS | Tatum Dire Author

www.ingramcontent.com/pod-product-compliance
Lightning Source LLC
Chambersburg PA
CBHW020655110726
47901CB00001B/202